ZOIA'S GOLD

A NOVEL

Philip Sington

Scribner
NEW YORK   LONDON   TORONTO   SYDNEY

SCRIBNER
1230 Avenue of the Americas
New York, NY 10020

First Scribner edition 2006

Originally published in Great Britain in 2005 by Atlantic Books,
an imprint of Grove Atlantic Ltd

Published by arrangement with Atlantic Books

SCRIBNER and design are trademarks of Macmillan Library Reference USA, Inc.,
used under license by Simon & Schuster, the publisher of this work.

For information about special discounts for bulk purchases,
please contact Simon & Schuster Special Sales:
1-800-456-6798 or business@simonandschuster.com

Designed by Kyoko Watanabe
Set in Minion

Manufactured in the United States of America

1   3   5   7   9   10   8   6   4   2

Library of Congress Cataloging-in-Publication Data

Sington, Philip.
Zoia's gold : a novel / Philip Sington. —1st Scribner ed.
p.   cm.
1. Korvin-Krukovsky, Zoia, 1903–1999. 2. Women artists—Fiction. I. Title.

PR6119.I54Z42 2006
823'.92—dc22   2006045025

ISBN-13: 978-0-7432-9110-1
ISBN-10: 0-7432-9110-7

For my mother and father

The distinction between past, present and future has only the significance of a stubborn illusion.

ALBERT EINSTEIN
Letter on the death of Michele Besso

Prisoners

1

He sees her bathed in dawn light, face pressed against the claw-marked wall. He pictures her with her back turned, one arm covering her head like a beaten child. There in the cell she reaches for untainted beauty, for memories she can embrace without fear. They offer no protection, no pardon, only passage to a different place, a place transcending sin and retribution. Now it's all over, this is how he sees her: a prisoner, beyond the reach of a pardoning God, still craving redemption.

At 6 A.M. they start up the trucks in the yard. Heavy two-stroke engines pounding the air, fan belts screeching. The trucks aren't going anywhere. The first morning she wondered why they didn't move off. Then later someone told her: they start the engines to mask the sound of shooting.

Now it's the sound that wakes her every day. It steals into the vortex of her dreams, and then she's bolt awake, listening, waiting for the engines to cut out again. If the engines cut out, it means the danger's past. You're going to live at least another day.

Moscow, July 1921. The summer she should have died with all the others.

No one speaks when the engines are turning. Eight women, crammed onto lice-ridden bunks, they lie silent, staring, as the sulphur stink of diesel slowly creeps into their nostrils. Some of them know why they've been arrested. Others don't. One old woman has been here a year without even being questioned.

Over the throaty pulse, muffled explosions. Sometimes you can't be sure if you really heard them or not. Firing squads are officially decried nowadays, likewise the tradition of handing out a blank with the live rounds, so no one can be sure who the killers are. Now they make you kneel down, and shoot you in the back of the head. It's messier. Blood and brains blow backward no matter how you angle the revolver. They say the executioner needs a clean uniform every day. But it's a statement untainted with apology. Bloodshed is a touchstone of proletarian resolve, sanctioned and celebrated at the highest level.

One morning, a girl of Zoia's age had a breakdown, started screaming like someone was tearing her eyes out. Nobody tried to console her. They were afraid of drawing attention to themselves. There are spies among the prisoners. Any kind of fraternization is dangerous. So, as always, they just went on lying there, listening to the engines, trying not to think. A couple of the women muttered prayers, beseeching mouths twisted toward the blistered ceiling.

A few days later they took the girl away. Everyone knows what happened to her. If the guards tell you to leave your possessions behind, it means they only want to interrogate you. If you're told to bring them with you, it's the end.

A thing she noticed from the start: the voices of the guards are always bored, like this is a queue at the post office or the bank, like you're asking for something the system doesn't cater to, making a damned nuisance of yourself just being there. They sound bored whatever they say, even when what they say is a sentence of death. Most of them are Lithuanians or Asiatics, imported specially. Local men, even Russians generally, are eschewed. They're too prone to talk about their work, and the things they've seen.

The girl had been told to bring her things. They dragged her out by the arms.

That was yesterday. Now the guards are coming back again. She can hear their leaden footsteps in the passageway.

Always Zoia closes her eyes.

The first time she stepped into Shchukin's gallery was like stepping into a dream. The shapes and colors danced on the walls with a power and brilliance that was more than human. This was art as she had never seen it before, pictures she could not find words to describe, obscure yet compelling. A secret language she burned to know.

Zoia Korvin-Krukovsky, curious and defiantly pretty, with dark, heavy-lidded eyes, watchful and clear, three years before they arrested her.

Sergei Shchukin had been buying pictures since the 1890s, lining the walls of his mansion in Moscow. Two hundred and twenty-one canvases, bought or commissioned during his protracted sojourns in Western Europe, from artists no one in Russia had ever heard of. Zoia had been in Moscow a few months when Andrei Burov took her to see them. By this time both mansion and contents had been confiscated by the Reds and restyled as the Museum of Modern Western Art, complete with a pair of sentries at the door, bayonets fixed. Andrei was the son of a Moscow architect, and enthusiastically conversant with the French avant-garde. But that wasn't why Zoia went along. The truth was she had liked him from the moment they met in the experimental chaos of a state school classroom. It was nothing to do with his looks: he was tall and skinny, with a beaky nose and bad eyesight. But they shared a desk together, and though the lessons were sporadic and disorganized, it had soon become obvious he was the brightest boy in the room. He was only two years older than her, but those two years had brought him a confidence in the power of ideas, confidence which even an empty stomach could not extinguish. He used to escort her to and from school, always mindful to be off the streets by nightfall, but she liked the idea of stealing away with him, in secret, of discovering places for the first time. Besides, she was in no hurry to get back to the freezing apartment in Arbat, which she and her mother and grandmother were forced to share with strangers.

He took her to Shchukin's palace on her fifteenth birthday.

She tries to remember what she'd *expected* to see there, captures faint imaginary pictures: ladies in formal dress, posing with affected languor; rolling landscapes at twilight; still lifes with dead game and peeled fruit; nature mimicked in oil, stroked into immortality with faithful, practiced hands. Like the pictures that used to hang on her stepfather's walls.

Nothing had prepared her for what she saw.

She remembers Andrei's complicit smile as he pushed back the door of the great hall. She remembers the pearly sunshine streaming through the skylight, the echo of hushed voices like the rustle of wings. She was on the staircase when the figures jumped out at her. She remembers stopping dead, the pulse pounding at her throat.

The moment that changed everything.

Two huge panels: *The Dance* on one side, *Music* on the other. Towering figures, primal and prophetic. Swathes of fathomless blue and green.

The first thing she felt was panic. The idea leaped into her brain that the Revolution had been here all along, waiting its chance to sweep away the rotten old world, and her with it. Shchukin had been hatching the new order in secret. A new language for a new age.

But she couldn't take her eyes off them. They were essential, timeless. Beautiful, but about more than beauty. They beckoned her into a different world, like the hieroglyphs of an ancient tomb.

Andrei was watching her from a few steps down, trying to gauge her reaction. "Henri Matisse," he said finally, as if there were some insight to be found in the name. "There are thirty-five more upstairs."

Where did they come from, these strange visions? Where were they trying to take her?

Andrei dug his hands into his pockets, wanting some reaction. "So? What do you think? Was Comrade Shchukin wasting his money?"

She found herself blushing. The pictures made her blush. She picked up her skirts and carried on up the stairs.

Every day that spring she and Andrei went back there, or to Ivan Morozov's Babylonian palace half a mile away. Morozov was another industrialist, now fled to the West. He had a taste for ornament and scale that Andrei disdained. On the staircase a massive triptych by Bonnard depicted the Mediterranean in different seasons. The story of Psyche was played out over eight panels in the music room, the nymph herself ostentatiously nude.

Morozov was the younger man, the man of appetites. His motivation was pride of ownership. He devoured Gauguin, Matisse, Cézanne. But there was no place in his collection for the melancholy dissections of the little bug-eyed Spaniard, the fifty-one Picassos Shchukin had amassed with cathartic zeal.

The difference in acquisitions wasn't just about taste. Zoia could feel it. Picasso had entered Shchukin's life just as the millionaire's world fell apart. First disease took his wife. Then his brother and two of his sons killed themselves. It was in the aftermath of loss that Shchukin's buying began in earnest: Picasso and Matisse, Matisse and Picasso. Works envisioned with the inner eye, works most collectors openly ridiculed. But this was not collecting for collecting's sake. Shchukin was searching for something, and Death was his guide.

Sometimes Zoia would find herself shuddering in Shchukin's house. Picasso's twisted faces were like an icy draft at her back. It never happened at Morozov's. At Morozov's she even got a sense of connection, a delight in color and opulence that felt familiar. *Memory of the Garden at Etten* was her favorite picture, Van Gogh painting not from life, for once, but from his imagination. The two women in the foreground, huddled and shawled, were like characters from Russian folklore.

They kept their visits a secret. If Zoia's mother had found out they were dawdling in galleries, she would have put an end to it right away. The city was running out of food. The Revolution was not yet six months old. Deserters and thieves still roamed the streets. God help anyone who went out in a good overcoat or looked like they might have money on them. Her mother kept them alive shoveling snow in the street, doing needlework, selling the last of the lace and jewelry she'd managed to hide from the soldiers. There was no safety anywhere. Sometimes whole families disappeared in the night.

In the hours before dawn, Zoia would lie awake, listening to her mother crying. It was a frightening sound. As a child, she had never believed her mother capable of tears, had assumed that they were the preserve of children. But she cried a lot in Moscow. The idea had been to go somewhere they weren't known, where they wouldn't be prey to malicious whispers. In St. Petersburg even their old employees—even the ones they trusted like family—had stolen from them, threatening to denounce them if they protested. But in anonymity was loneliness. It closed around them like a shroud. They'd burned every memento of their old lives—scrapbooks, correspondence, everything that betrayed past connections to the court. They burned letters that were entrusted to them by the ballerina Kshesinskaya, love letters from the czar. They even burned the photographs of Zoia's stepfather. If only he hadn't insisted on posing in his officer's uniform. But they were to be nobodies now. They were to go unnoticed and unremarked upon, until the nightmare was over.

Sometimes Zoia's mother would come to her bedside and stroke her hair. Everything was going to be all right, she would say. They would get their lives back when the Reds gave up on their foolish experiments. Or when the Whites closed in from the South.

Zoia would shut her eyes, and picture herself in the garden at Etten, feel herself in the presence of the solitary artist. She would gaze at the winding, dappled road, and try as hard as she could to imagine where it led.

After three days and nights in the holding cell they'd stripped her, looking for valuables. Two Chekist women did the business, handling her body like a carcass on the turn. Their hands felt like claws on her tender skin.

Then the first questions. An interrogator with a black beard. He wanted to know about her family and what she was doing for work. When she said her mother had gone to Sevastopol, they took her away again.

Six days in solitary, a hole without windows or light, except what crept beneath the door. Day and night, a sewage stench and the coughing of consumptive men. She screamed when she felt the cockroaches dart across her skin.

The second interrogation was longer. A man with crooked teeth and brown gums barked questions that made her jump.

So her mother and grandmother had gone to Sevastopol. Why?

Of all things, they had fixed on that.

The interrogator's first hit the table. "Sevastopol: *Why?*"

There was one thing she knew they would believe: that they were trying to flee to the West. White armies had risen in the Ukraine and the Caucasus, the Crimea between them, low on Bolshevik support and ripe for the taking. Gleeful stories of counter-revolutionary daring were whispered among genteel refugees still hopeful of escape. How Krasnov's Don Cossacks carved their way through jargon-bawling Red militia, lopping heads off in mid-slogan.

But it was an explanation she couldn't use. Anymore than she could bring herself to tell the truth.

"My grandmother was sick. She needed to go somewhere warm."

"I want to know why *you* went."

"To help look after her."

"Really. But you came back two weeks later. Weren't you needed after all?"

He seemed to know she wasn't telling the truth, although she couldn't see how. The contempt in his voice made everything she said feel like a lie.

"I wanted to see Yuri. My husband."

The interrogator grunted and rubbed at his jaw. It came to her that he had a toothache, an abscess maybe. She saw his tongue working the gum behind his lower lip. It was said that the Cheka's torturers were all high on cocaine, supplied by their superiors to desensitize them and keep them in the job.

"Your husband, the traitor?"

She hung her head. That was what her mother called him, at least when she thought her daughter was out of earshot. She said other things too, like she should never have married him.

She felt the tears well in her eyes.

"And *have* you seen him?"

"No. He's . . ."

"Of course not. He's in prison. A prison for the criminally insane. But you knew that before you left, didn't you? So why *did* you leave?"

Her mother had held out great hopes for Sevastopol. Before the war, people of her class would holiday there. In the summer they would promenade along the front while bands and string orchestras played in the cafés and the casinos. It was a place where matches were made and liaisons of a less reputable kind conducted. Every impediment to pleasure could be excised for the right price, and every embarrassing consequence.

Her mother had said they would make a new start there. They would put the past behind them. But it turned out she had in mind more than escape.

The interrogator was shouting questions again, about Sevastopol, about St. Petersburg. He wanted to know how she'd landed the interpreting job at the Third International Congress. Through the fear, it came to Zoia that there was, after all, no pattern to these inquiries. She was supposed to let something slip, that was all, to incriminate herself, or somebody else.

Maybe incriminating herself was the only way to stay out of solitary. Maybe it was better to die now than go slowly mad.

"What's the matter with you?" the comrade interrogator demanded.

She realized she had been clutching her stomach. She forced herself to sit up straight.

"I'm bleeding," she said.

The interrogator sniffed. Nothing new there. He riffled through a notepad that was covered in awkward, schoolboy writing. They had gone south, all three of them, hoping to reach the Whites. That much made sense. But then the girl had come back to Moscow. That was the part that didn't fit.

Zoia thought he was all done when he leaned forward, fixing her with hard gray eyes.

"Your mother didn't put you on that cattle train, did she? Ten days across bandit country, a pretty thing like you?"

His voice was suddenly gentler now, almost sympathetic. Out of nowhere she found herself sobbing openly. The interrogator took out a pencil.

"Now tell me. What exactly were you running away from?"

Five weeks on she hears the footsteps stop outside her cell. With the hum of engines the Lubyanka is a factory now, processing its human load in thirty-minute batches. A woman in the bunk below is praying again, although Zoia can't make out the words. She's praying it isn't her turn. Or maybe she's praying that it is.

The locks and the bolts take a long time to turn. The noise brings a familiar scampering with it, as a rat disappears down its hole. The Lubyanka is full of rats. At night they try to get up into the bunks. Given a choice, even they prefer meat that's still fresh.

The guards bring distinctive smells with them: tobacco, gun-barrel grease, sometimes boot polish. All fresh new smells, smells of the outside. The stale sweat stink she used to notice on them is never there anymore.

Always the pause while they look for their quarry. She squeezes her eyes tight shut.

"Krukovsky."

Her eyes blink open. She rolls over, sits up.

One of the guards is new. A Tartar boy, hardly any older than she is. The boy looks away, avoiding her eye.

That's when she knows.

"Bring your possessions."

One of the women lets out a whimper. Another rolls over, hiding her face. What comes to Zoia is that these are her last moments in daylight. There are no windows in the cellars. They are taking her down into the darkness, and she will never return.

She feels her limbs tremble as she gathers her things. Suddenly it's the darkness she fears more than anything.

As they lead her away she casts a final glance through the small barred window high up in the wall. Above the dark roofs, the little square of sky is touched with gold.

THE INTERNATIONAL HERALD TRIBUNE.
DECEMBER 4, 1999. ARTS & LEISURE SECTION

Death of "painter on gold" marks end of era

Christiana Lorenz, *The New York Times*

STOCKHOLM. A little chapter of history drew to a close yesterday in a wind-swept city cemetery, where a small group of well-wishers, mostly elderly, gathered to pay their last respects to Zoia Korvin-Krukovsky, the famous Russian-born "painter on gold."

Korvin-Krukovsky, known to the art world simply as "Zoia," was the last known survivor of the Romanov court. Born in St. Petersburg in 1903 into a wealthy family, she played as a child with princes of the royal blood, and was befriended by the czar's mistress, the ballerina Matilda Kshesinskaya. At the age of ninety-six, she was thought to be the last person living to have met Czar Nicholas II. She died of multiple organ failure, following a battle with cancer.

Zoia studied under several teachers, including the abstract expressionist Vassily Kandinsky, and the Japanese master Tsuguharu Foujita. Foujita was one of a legion of painters—among them Modigliani, Picasso, and Chagall—who made up a notoriously Bohemian scene in the Parisian district of Montparnasse in the 1920s. It was Foujita who taught Zoia the art of painting on precious metals: the beginning of an extraordinary, if enigmatic, artistic journey, in which Zoia struggled to marry expressionist and colorist sensibilities with a deep and abiding passion for Russia's artistic traditions—traditions under threat of annihilation in her native land.

She was later lauded in post-Communist Russia, where, in 1993, Boris Yeltsin arranged a special exhibition of her works inside the Kremlin.

Ironically, it was the intervention of an enamored Swedish Communist, that saved the painter's life after the Bolshevik coup in 1917. Zoia had been imprisoned on suspicion of complicity in a counter-revolutionary plot. Her future husband, in Moscow for the third congress of the Communist International, pleaded for her release with the deputy head of the Cheka. Eventually she left Russia for Sweden with nothing but a small suitcase and a toy bear, inside which she had hidden a cache of religious icons.

Zoia's private life was as mysterious as her art. She survived three husbands, but left no children. Would-be biographers who requested her cooperation were repeatedly turned down.

Even those who gathered at her grave-side were mostly latter-day acquaintances who confess to knowing little of her early life. Whatever prompted this aloofness—an aristocratic upbringing, or something more troubling—it has not dampened interest in Zoia's work. There is talk of a major retrospective next year, and an accompanying sale. Russian collectors, including the Hermitage Museum in St. Petersburg, are reported to be interested.

Almost invariably, death increases the market value of an artist's work. But this is not simply a question of rarity. The work ceases to be of the present and becomes instead a tangible link to the past, to vanished perspectives and, in some cases, to lost worlds. Given Zoia's history, the interest promises to be all the more intense.

2

Swedish air space, February 2000.

The day he found the picture was the start of it. Looking back over the
wreckage of the last three years, it's clear to him: that was the moment she
found a way back into his life. As if he had woken a ghost.

Everything had been moving forward until then, safely, predictably,
shaping itself into something recognizably sound. The dealership was
turning a profit. He had a young and beautiful wife. He had friends. But
Zoia led him back into the shadows, one step at a time, needling him with
questions he couldn't answer and couldn't any longer ignore.

The *Chinese Princess in Paris,* a picture known latterly as the Paris self-
portrait. A work with an uncertain history. Oil on gilded oak, it was
painted in 1929, a year Zoia spent among the artists and pleasure-seekers
of Montparnasse, a year when the whole frenetic scene finally imploded,
madness and death descending like a biblical plague on the high priests
of excess. The subject was a young oriental woman in a gray silk dress,
seated in a lacquered armchair. That this might in fact be the artist was
only suggested years later, after Zoia reportedly hinted as much. In those
days she could not afford to pay a model, she had explained to a curious
visitor. So she had modeled for herself, experimenting with hair and
makeup, and presumably posing in a full-length mirror. There was no
known self-portrait from the Paris years. People started thinking the *Chinese Princess* must be exactly that.

Elliot had found it hidden away under the stairs in his father's house,
wedged between a pair of worm-eaten deck chairs. When he touched the
surface, the dust came off as thick as paint on his fingertips. He dragged
it out into the narrow hallway, saw the little arc of gold glimmering. It was
only then he realized, with a welling, unsteady feeling, what it was he was
looking at.

14

He wasn't surprised at the dust and the neglect. What surprised him was finding it in the house at all. He'd always thought his father had destroyed it twenty-five years ago, or sold it at the very least. It was disturbing to learn he had kept it, had in fact been *living* with it all that time. Every night as he had climbed the stairs to his lonely bed, he must have thought of it down there, looking up at him with its dark, disdainful eyes, a reminder of everything he had lost: his wife, his son, his mind. The harbinger of ruin.

It was the one thing of value Elliot took from the house that day—technically tax evasion, since he was still months away from getting probate. (Everything had to be valued for the purposes of estate duty, right down to the curtains and the kitchen furniture, before he could legally help himself.) He wrapped the picture in newspaper and put it in the back of his car. At the time he had no sensation of engaging in a criminal act, of taking his first step into darkness.

For a week or so the picture stayed in the garage. Then he moved it to his study, and after that to the storeroom at his gallery on Westbourne Grove. He wasn't thinking of selling it. He just didn't feel like showing it to his wife, Nadia, and having to explain the whole story. He had a feeling she wouldn't understand. She had never been one to dwell on the past in any case. "The dead cannot hurt us," she used to say, some old Czech aphorism she had brought with her from the old country.

He never told her she was wrong.

For the first few weeks he did nothing. He didn't know what *to* do. The picture wasn't logged into the gallery's books, so there was no point putting it on display. He didn't even insure it. As far as the business was concerned, it didn't exist.

Then one day, for no particular reason, he decided to get the picture cleaned. Suction did the job without recourse to water or solvents. The frame had taken a heavy knock somehow, and was split down one side. He had that seen to as well, but by a different repairer from the one he normally used. The day the picture came back he hung it up for the first time, over the fireplace in his office. It was the only available space, apart from in the storeroom. And he couldn't put it back there.

She looked pleased with him: the Chinese princess re-enthroned. There was something condescendingly magnanimous in her eyes. Francesca, an art history student who was working for him that summer, recognized the style and asked him about the subject. Who was this Chinese princess? What was her story? Elliot didn't know. He'd never handled Zoia's work. Living artists, even those of Zoia's age, were strictly not his field.

"Do you think it might be a self-portrait?" she said. "It's such a playful title. And do the Chinese even *have* princesses?"

He laughed at the idea. It made no sense to him. They were not looking at pen-and-ink, an exercise on paper. This was a solid oak panel, painstakingly prepared and covered with twenty-four karat gold. In any case, why would an artist paint a self-portrait of herself in disguise? And then compound the deception with a mendacious title? Painters sought to capture the truth, like all artists: the truth *within*. What else was a portrait for?

It was only later he learned that Francesca might actually be right. First in newspapers, then in academic articles, the existence of the one-and-only self-portrait was treated as an established fact. If it was true, one of Zoia's first forays into a medium that defined her, perhaps *the* first, was a kind of private joke.

He wonders if his mother had shared that joke when she bought the picture in the autumn of 1970, ten days before she died. He wonders if she knew it was Zoia she was taking home.

The Airbus banks, descending past towering cumuli. Then the coast is there beneath him, although not a coast in any recognizable form, a dividing line between land and sea. This is a splintered mass of rock and ice and gray-blue water stretching to the horizon, giving no clue as to which at last gives way to which. He catches the shadow of the plane skipping over snow and patches of dark forest, feels the speed of it.

Zoia's home. Zoia's place of rest. He pictures her body entombed in the frozen earth. Why didn't he come long ago? he asks himself. And then looks around, wondering if he hasn't said it out loud.

The blonde SAS stewardess is bending over him with a coffeepot, smiling with capped teeth.

"Mr. Elliot? Another cup?"

She must have read his name on the boarding pass. A touch of personal service.

"No, thank you."

With a muted ping, the FASTEN SEAT BELT sign comes on. Turbulence shakes the wings. He's never been a good flier. He finds it hard to trust, the way other people do, that all the endless checking and maintenance have been carried out with the necessary diligence.

He opens the cardboard file in his lap. It was sent to him by Cornelius Wallander, the art department director at Bukowskis auction house in Stockholm. Inside are press cuttings, obituaries, photocopied catalogs from past exhibitions, a syndicated essay by the Russian art critic Savva Leskov, first published in *Le Figaro* in 1989. It's just the starting point for the fat, glossy catalog the auction house has planned for the Korvin-Krukovsky sale, a catalog it will be his job to elaborate and embellish into publishable form. Cornelius has high hopes for a faux monograph. Nothing substantive has been written about Zoia's work in years, nothing on her life in living memory. With all the publicity the sale will generate, they might move a hundred thousand copies globally, maybe more. At forty dollars each, a useful source of extra revenue for all concerned. Cornelius thinks insights and details will be easier to come by now that the artist is dead and her effects are in the hands of lawyers and friends.

He runs his fingers over the type.

It was a surprise hearing from Cornelius after all that had happened. These days most of Elliot's old business contacts keep their distance, as if wary of contamination. Elliot still remembers the call: Cornelius full of seasonal bonhomie, like it was just another Christmas, bellyaching about Y2K costs and millennial hysteria, he himself feigning enthusiasm for the ten empty days ahead. Then they were talking about Zoia's death, the sale of her private collection, and the retrospective Bukowskis was planning. Somehow Cornelius had picked up on Elliot's interest, knew he had started dealing in Zoia's work in a small way. He was kind enough to say that he would consider it a personal favor if Elliot would write the catalog, as if there weren't junior staff at Bukowskis who were perfectly capable. It was the one welcome surprise of the festive season, a gesture of friendship from an unexpected quarter, maybe even a first step back to the life he once had.

Good old Cornelius.

Elliot flips through the cuttings. The Leskov essay is the most useful item, an attempt to place Zoia in a Russian art–historical context. Her foreign influences and studies have always made the nationalistic approach problematic, but Leskov has an understanding of Russian undercurrents that most Western critics can't match, and his analysis still holds sway.

Elliot rereads the essay, drawn in by its confident, proprietorial tone. Russians on Russians. There's always a suggestion in such pieces that it takes one to know one. That even a command of the Russian language, such as Elliot has, is not enough, especially when the subject has a spiritual dimension. And, as far as Leskov is concerned, this subject clearly does. Zoia's calling was not one that followed the Western tradition of individual expression, he says. Zoia was not exploring her inner landscape through a language of color and form, as Vassily Kandinsky, her one-time teacher, demanded. She was preserving a Slavic artistic tradition, one that her Westernized enemies were determined to erase, along with the last traces of despotism and fatalist religion. Hers was an art of contemplation, a shining mirror on a mystical universe, at the heart of which dwelt a single, unknowable God.

The plane swings out to the northeast, dipping beneath a cloud layer into the rays of a wintry sun. Somewhere, a few rows back, a child begins to cry. Elliot closes the folder and looks out of the window.

All he can see to the far horizon is ice.

3

There were four passengers aboard the airport bus. Elliot sat surrounded by empty seats, watching snowflakes materialize out of a black sky. Points of light marked the waterfronts and harbors, the promise of coziness radiating through the windows of solid, stately buildings. Scandinavia was the real home of Christmas. In England the festive season was self-consciously worn, like a fancy-dress costume for hire: Santa Claus in the rain, pounding the shopping center in a nylon beard. It was something he'd always planned with the family—a white Christmas with reindeer and sleigh rides, in the land where his mother was born.

The bus rumbled along spacious, snow-dappled streets. His daughter Teresa was almost old enough now. Next Christmas would be the perfect time, or maybe the Christmas after, when his finances would at last be back on an even keel. He would get some friends together and organize a group. They would go sledding in the hills and watch the northern lights in the evening. This would be Teresa's magic place, a place that would be with her forever afterward. And he would be there too, enfolded and pre-served in a bright, inviolable memory.

A bell was chiming when he arrived outside Bukowskis. The building was like a Victorian doll's house, immaculate period interiors visible from the park outside. The founder, Henryk Bukowski, had been a Polish nobleman, exiled by his country's Russian overlords. He'd been the first to introduce cataloged auctions to Sweden, cleaning up when King Charles XV's vast art collection went under the hammer in 1873. His company had been the top dog in Northern Europe ever since, its sea-sonal auctions the premier sales events in the buyer's calendar. In between times, the big-ticket items, from Empire furniture to Plexiglass sculpture, were displayed as if in a private house, in appropriately decorated rooms.

He stepped out of the taxi and stood looking up at the classical facade while the driver retrieved his bags. His last visit, three and a half years ago, had been prompted by very different motives: Marcus Elliot, the dealer, had come to buy. Art and artifacts entombed inside the Soviet bloc for sixty years were at last finding their way on to the market—icons hidden under floorboards or pillaged for state museums, artworks misattributed or mislaid, paintings and craft goods reclaimed by exiles and redeemed for cash. Meanwhile, new buyers were emerging from post-Communist rule: the nouveau superrich of privatized industry, media moguls, and oil magnates, men whose hunger for the trappings of old money was matched by the ferocity of their national pride. Good markets, if you knew how to tap them. Potential margins far greater than a middleman could expect recycling Dutch genre product or the work of third-rate Impressionists. Less risky too, or so he'd thought.

He paid the driver and headed for the doors, narrowly avoiding a skateboarder in an Andean wool hat. The youth made a whooping noise as he slalomed by, bringing Elliot to a sudden halt.

Something up ahead caught his eye. A face, framed in the molded plastic of a wing mirror. A woman. For a moment he thought it was the stewardess on the plane, the one who had known his name. But that was impossible.

She was sitting behind the wheel of a battered white Volkswagen Polo. Peering through the back window he glimpsed a head in silhouette, wearing a ski hat. She was speaking into a mobile phone.

Inside, the air smelled of floor polish and expensive perfume. Security men and porters lingered around the doorways. Professional women swept by in dark, crisply pressed suits. The girl behind the reception desk had ghostly pale eyes and short, white-blonde hair. She was talking into a headset when Elliot announced himself.

"Mr. Wallander will be down in a moment," she said, gesturing toward a sofa.

He sat and waited. A trio of porters were maneuvering a large bronze nude through an upstairs doorway. It was unsettling being back. He felt the extent of his fall anew—felt it physically, as a prickly heat on his skin. Across the threshold of the main auction room, a couple of women were conversing sotto voce. In one moment they both turned and looked at him before disappearing inside.

"Marcus! So you're here."

Cornelius Wallander was redder in the face and looser at the jaw than the last time they had met. He took Elliot's hand with both of his and shook it warmly. He was a big man, bald and bespectacled, irredeemably inelegant by the usual Bukowski standards. As a younger man, Elliot suspected, he had been shy. But with the years he had learned to satirize his own awkwardness, deferring with good humor to people—like Elliot— whom he considered more colorful or polished. The enthusiasm he brought to his work was also in his favor. Elliot had never seen anyone exude such pride in objects they did not own. Cornelius worshipped bold and beautiful things, as if those qualities, by their very proximity, somehow rubbed off on him.

"I so appreciate your coming. You look"—he took in Elliot's face, hesitating—"well, Marcus. Very well."

He sounded surprised.

"I appreciate the opportunity, Cornelius. It was kind of you to think of me."

Cornelius took Elliot's bags and tucked them behind the reception desk.

"Not at all, not at all. This job calls for something special. Not just the usual grunt work. I didn't know where else to turn. Plus I knew you were a fan."

"Yes, but how?"

"How?"

"How did you know?"

Cornelius grinned. "The international sale, autumn of '96? You were outbid on a Korvin-Krukovsky. The *Vase of Poppies,* I think. You had to settle for something smaller."

"The *Shchukin Mansion,* that's right. You've quite a memory."

Cornelius shook his head. "Just been working here too long." He showed Elliot into the lift, all bustle and small talk now, as if nothing had ever happened. "What became of it, by the way, the *Shchukin Mansion?* Did you sell it?"

Elliot watched the doors slide shut.

"I sold everything, in the end."

Cornelius blushed and pressed a button. "Of course, of course. I meant, did you sell it quickly?"

"After a year or so. To the Moscow Narodny Bank, London branch. Where are we going? Have they exiled you to the basement now?"

Cornelius chuckled. "I want to show you what we've amassed so far. You'd be surprised how word's got around. We've already quite a haul."

Elliot had anticipated that much. The upcoming auction, scheduled for early June, was not just a buying opportunity. It was a selling opportunity too, one not likely to be bettered for many years. Anyone who owned a Korvin-Krukovsky would be tempted to cash in.

"People want to be in stocks right now," Cornelius said. "I mean, new economy stocks. That's where the collectors of tomorrow will make their millions." He stared at the brushed steel doors, frowning at his blurred reflection. "Frederik Wahl says we must prepare for the time when even fine art auctions are conducted online. We're investing a fortune in new technology. Soon the catalog will be replaced by a three-dimensional virtual tour."

"Then you won't need people like me."

The doors slid open. The space beyond was dark, lit only by red safety lights. Cornelius clapped Elliot on the shoulder as they got out, steps and voices echoing.

"We will always need people like you, Marcus. The experts, the *initiates*. Every tour needs a guide."

Elliot had never been in this part of the building before. It was a kind of sub-basement, recently excavated or rebuilt, judging from the concrete walls and the cement floor. There was a steady hum of machinery: generators, boilers, and the complex of electrical systems that kept Bukowskis and its contents safe from fire, theft, and the ravages of climate.

Cornelius led the way along a wide passage, jangling keys in his jacket pocket, talking now about the inquiries he'd been fielding from Japan, the U.S.A., and Russia. The last exhibition in Tokyo, just five years back, had been a sellout. It was no surprise that there was interest from that quarter. American collectors were always a presence, especially where works had royal or imperial associations—as if there was something magic in regal blood, something their own world had irretrievably lost. It was the Russians, the newcomers to the market, that Elliot wanted to know about.

"As they see it, this work is a part of their history," Cornelius said. "And they want it back. You can't really blame them either, given what they've lost."

It was an argument Savva Leskov had advanced in his *Figaro* article: now that communism was dead, Russia could drift into the nihilism of ersatz Western pop culture, or find herself again through a rediscovery of what she had lost. Zoia, stylistically, historically, fitted the bill to perfection.

"Who are we talking about exactly? I read something about the Hermitage."

"The Hermitage, the Modern Art Museum in Moscow, plenty of private collectors too."

Cornelius pulled out the keys. They stopped in front of a pair of reinforced wooden doors. Electrical cables trailed out of socket holes on either side.

"This room isn't completely ready yet. But I've commandeered it, for private viewing purposes." He undid the locks. A smart-looking brass one required turning with a ship's wheel. "Plus I can't help feeling Zoia's work looks best in a plain setting, don't you think?"

The doors swung back on noiseless hinges. The space beyond was dark and smelled of wet cement. A runway of red carpet had been laid down the middle.

Cornelius went in. "Are you ready?" he said, reaching for a panel of switches.

Elliot stepped onto the carpet, wondering a little at the theatrics, wondering what Cornelius was doing keeping valuable paintings in a place where building work was still going on.

"So how many pictures do you actually—?"

The lights went on. And then he was looking at it, blinking, stunned. "Jesus."

An avenue of gold.

There were eighteen pictures on either side of the aisle, mounted on tall, gray panels. Different subjects, different styles, he saw them, felt them, as a single radiant whole. Cornelius had turned them toward the door, so that they could all be seen at once.

An ambush of celestial light.

"Quite a sight, aren't they? I've always wanted to do something like this. And there may never be another chance."

He had arranged them according to subject: still lifes at the front, landscapes at the back, buildings and human figures in between. All on gold, gold that seemed to turn to liquid as Elliot walked past.

He saw his own shadow, his own nebulized image. And then he was remembering something from his childhood, from the days when his mother was still alive. They'd been in Spain, driving through some dusty inland town. His mother had wanted to see the inside of a church she'd heard of. He remembered walking into the cold musty interior, and seeing it bloom before his eyes: a wall of gold behind the altar—panels, icons, crosses, figures—everything gold, shimmering in the candlelight. He remembered tugging at his mother's hand, wanting to understand what it meant, as she stood there motionless, captivated, serene.

"It took me forever to get the lighting right," Cornelius said. "Even now, I'm not sure that's even possible. With gold, you change an angle and you change everything. It's impossible to reveal all the possibilities."

It was true: looking in catalogs, you never got that sense of intangibility, the constant shift from light to shade. Photography revealed only one particular perspective, re-creating it in approximate yellows and ochers. The effect was dull, flat. Zoia's gold wrapped you in light, like a mirror, while the painted image floated free.

In his essay Savva Leskov had coined a name for this effect: "iconographic dissociation." He claimed the technique had been developed in Byzantine monasteries as an aid to the contemplation of the holy sphere, the Virgin and Child suspended between this world and the next.

The colors were vibrant. The paint was laid on in single strokes, composite hues visible in tiny eyelash curves. It was an exacting, perilous requirement of painting on gold leaf that once the paint was down, it could not be altered.

Cornelius's display played havoc with the chronology. From the historical point of view it was nonsense. It suggested a plan the artist could never have had, individual works subsumed into a posthumous statement, a valedictory summation. But it grabbed your attention.

"Of course these are just the big ones," Cornelius said. "We have others, smaller. Sketches too, and some costume designs for the theater. Rather good ones, I think. Of course there are some important pictures we haven't managed to track down. The Paris self-portrait, for instance. No one seems to know where *that* is."

Elliot leaned in closer to the *Sunflower with Birds*. The self-portrait was in storage in London, a fact known only to him and Paul Costa, the acquaintance who had logged it in for him.

"It's the whole Foujita connection," Cornelius went on. "It's a big draw, especially for the Japanese."

Most of her years in Paris Zoia had barely had the money for paint. But when she saw Foujita's work on precious metals, she had fixed on it with a strange determination. Foujita didn't take pupils. But he did have a certain penchant for round-faced girls with bobbed black hair— Europeans *à la Japonaise* was how Elliot thought of them. Maybe that was why the master had weakened in the end, sharing the secrets of his technique. The painting was a product of this time, one of the earliest examples of the painting on gold that was later to make Zoia's name. There was even speculation that the work had been painted by Foujita himself, at least in part.

Either way, the picture would have made the perfect centerpiece for the show: the only known portrait of Zoia from the all-important Paris years.

"We're hoping the National Museum will lend us the Oscar Björck portrait," Cornelius said. "But you know how they are."

"Maybe the owners will come forward nearer the time."

"If we knew who they were, we could approach them. They could make a lot of money. But I've asked around the dealers, and no one has a clue where it is." If he was being disingenuous, it didn't show. "Maybe you'll find something at the summer house, a settlement statement or something."

"The summer house?"

"Didn't I say? That's where her papers are. In Saltsjöbaden. Plenty in Russian, I gather. So your language skills will be needed. I've arranged for you to go out there. Get a little background for the catalog. Some biographical details."

The room felt cold. Elliot hugged himself.

"Okay. When?"

"Tomorrow." Cornelius smiled, shiny cheeks colored in the golden glow. "I'm sorry it's not the holiday time of year. But at least you won't be disturbed."

Cornelius was apologetic about the evening's arrangements, or lack of them. His sister-in-law was in the hospital, and he had promised to take his wife to visit, he said. On trips in the past, he and Elliot would have dined on fish and reindeer meat in some authentic restaurant, getting merry on beer and shots of absurdly expensive vodka. But Elliot wasn't wholly sorry to be missing out. There was only so much pretending you could do that everything was back to normal. And he wasn't sure he wanted to go over it all with Cornelius—even through an agreeable haze of alcohol—or whether Cornelius particularly wanted to listen.

Collecting his bags from behind the reception desk, seeing the receptionist's blank, perfunctory smile, it came to Elliot that certain limitations had, in fact, been deliberately defined. Cornelius had done him a professional favor, out of sympathy, out of respect for the good business they had done in the past. It was friendly, but it was not friend*ship*. It was not something that would be there for him, unconditionally. He had been given a chance. Somewhere down the line, he had earned that much. But that was all.

He stepped out onto the street. It was busier than before, office workers heading home through the light swirling snow, even some Bukowski people calling it a day. He looked around for a taxi, held up a hand as a pair rolled by without stopping.

The white Volkswagen was still parked there, twenty yards away. He saw the driver put down her phone, open the door, step out on to the road. She was wearing a parka, the hood pulled up. She was looking his way, checking the silhouetted figures that crowded the pavement around him.

She couldn't be looking for him. He'd never seen her before in his life. He looked around. The two of them were the only people standing there.

She started toward him, walking fast. Her hands were buried in her pockets.

A car horn made him jump. A taxi had pulled up beside him.

Elliot got in.

Initiates

4

---•---

St. Petersburg Province, July 1914.

Through a haze of summer dust. Dust drifting in sunlight. Sunlight falling in scattered rays across a shaded lane. This was how she pictured the last perfect moments.

Vladimir's mother had given him a kite. It was the biggest and most beautiful Zoia had ever seen. It was made of silk and painted like an eagle, with white pennants at the tips of its wings.

In a field outside the town, she and Vova—that was what everyone called him—ran across the mown hay, the kite held high above their heads. They tripped and fell on hidden furrows, tumbling over each other and landing in a heap of limbs and twine. They would stay there for a moment, breathing hard, feeling the unfamiliar weight of each other's bodies, before scrambling to their feet again and running on. Vova's face was tanned from the sun. There were freckles over the bridge of his nose, like constellations of stars.

"There's not enough wind," she protested as he charged off again for the fifth time. "It's hopeless."

He just smiled at her and shouted: "Come *on!*"

His voice was still high-pitched and boyish, though he was a year older than her. People said he took after his mother, Matilda Kshesinskaya, the famous ballerina, with his slim build, and handsome, delicate features. They never said he looked like his father, or, for that matter, who his father was.

She saw him reach the crest of a rise. The kite was trailing behind him, drifting out nine or ten feet, starting to make figure eights as it tugged at the line. Zoia was afraid its tail would snag in the grass.

The wind rose up behind them, gusting over the open fields. She sheltered her eyes as the kite tore away into the sky, jerking the spool of twine out of Vova's hand.

"Grab it!" he shouted at her. But she didn't move. The painted eagle was up above her, wing tips fluttering, climbing into the sky. She could feel herself growing small beneath it, a distant earth-bound thing, head longingly upturned.

Vova went tearing past, chasing the spool. His face wore an eager, elated smile. She saw his delight in this sudden moment of crisis.

"*Qui-ick!*"

She took off after him, bounding down the slope. The kite began to lose height. It looped toward the trees that lined the road, scaring a flock of birds that darted past their heads. Vova made a dive for the spool, but it was just out of reach. He slipped and went sprawling. Zoia jumped over his prostrate body and ran on, determined to be the heroine this time, no matter what it cost her in grazes and torn stockings. She laughed at the thought of her grandmother's good-natured scolding, the faces she always pulled when she wanted to look scandalized.

Vova was well behind her by the time she reached the roadside. She could hear him calling to her. But she was too busy to look around. The kite had drifted out of sight beyond the treetops. She wasn't sure if it had gone over them, or was caught up in the branches.

She ran around a corner, eyes fixed on the sky. It was more sheltered here, the foliage thicker. The sunlight was scattered into rays.

The stillness brought her to a halt. She was aware of something: a sense of straying farther than she should, like a child in a fairy tale.

Dust drifted by on the breeze. In the slanting light she saw patterns, swirls and eddies, infinite detail. She saw the world through a living veil.

The sound of an engine made her turn. It grew louder, then softer, then louder again. She couldn't tell if it was getting closer. Sometimes she saw motor cars parked outside Kshesinskaya's summer villa. Usually they signified the presence of important persons—Prince Dmitri Pavlovsky, the Grand Dukes Sergei and Andrei, General Sukhomlinov, the Minister of War, an old man with sad eyes who was always bowing. But it was rare to see them traveling about the countryside.

Vova's kite was lying in the middle of the road.

"Vova! Vova, it's over here!"

She ran toward it. Stopped dead.

A man was standing in front of her, barring her way. She heard a twig snap. Two more men were slowly picking their way through the bushes toward her. Big men. They moved stealthily, like hunters tracking prey.

She struggled to catch her breath. A voice in her head said *run*.

The first man wore a fat gold ring on his finger. He seemed to read her mind: "Stay where you are," he said.

She had seen them before. They had turned up in Strelna a couple of days earlier. They weren't wearing uniforms, but they were all dressed the same: in boots and long coats, with belts around their waists, although it hadn't rained for weeks. They didn't do anything in particular. They just walked up and down the streets, sometimes going into shops, sometimes lighting cigarettes and eyeing the people as they went by. Zoia had asked Vova's nanny who they were, these men in uniforms that weren't uniforms, but had received no answer. It was as if they were ghosts. No one wanted to look at them or acknowledge that their presence was anything out of the ordinary.

Finally a visitor from the court told Vova's mother the secret: the czar was coming to the area, to attend military maneuvers at Krasnoye Selo. The strange men were secret policemen. They always traveled ahead of the czar because of fears for his safety. Every town and village along the way was inspected for signs of an ambush.

Until then, it had never occurred to Zoia that anyone might want to kill the czar, especially not here, just thirty miles from the capital. Vova said it had happened before, that the czar's own grandfather had been blown up by a bomb as he rode in an open carriage, although he couldn't say by whom or for what reason. Zoia didn't say anything, but she wondered privately if he was making it up, if it was even *possible* that the anointed czar could be killed by an ordinary man. God had put the czar on the throne. So wasn't it obvious that only God could take him off again?

Vova was still calling her. He thought the game had changed now, to hide-and-seek. One of the policemen reached into his coat, eyes searching the road behind her.

Zoia pointed at the kite.

"It's ours."

The engine sounds were louder. In the distance she could see a dust cloud rising into the air. Vova appeared at her side, face flushed, mouth agape.

"It's *him*," he hissed, and at first Zoia didn't know what he was talking about. She had always imagined the czar on horseback, riding through the town as he had through St. Petersburg on the occasion of the Romanov tercentenary. She hadn't seen him—almost nobody had, because the whole route had been lined with ranks of imperial guards in their tall feathered shakos—but the souvenir photographs had been eagerly handed out at her school.

The policeman with the gold ring shouted: "Get off the road!"

They stepped back, seeing the motor car now, black, open-topped, moving toward them at a frightening speed, a huge vortex of dust rising behind it. The policemen kept watching them, as if they might be about to try something, but that didn't stop Vova from putting his hands over his head and shouting: "God save the czar!" at the top of his lungs.

And then there he was, unmistakably him, sitting in the back, staring ahead, motionless. If anything, he looked too much like the portraits and official photographs—the cut of his beard, his calm expression, his faraway, dreaming eyes—and it seemed somehow wrong to Zoia that there wasn't something more, even in those few seconds, something that made being in the actual presence of the living czar, different, better, in fact more *real*.

She blinked the dust out of her eyes. Vova was on tiptoe, determined to catch the last glimpses of the imperial automobile. Too late, he had found a handkerchief in his pocket and was now waving it over his head. The secret policemen had already vanished.

Zoia went to retrieve the kite. It was lying in the road, broken and torn. The czar's car had ridden right over it. She picked up the pieces and stood looking at them, smoothing out the fabric with the bird design on it.

"It's ruined."

Vova was still staring down the road.

"Maybe we can mend it," Zoia said, trying to look on the bright side. "The silk's all right. We can get some bamboo from the greenhouse."

Vova came over and inspected the damage, running his fingers over a broken strut.

"Yes, the greenhouse," he said absently, as if his mind was already on more important things.

•   •   •

The first time she went to Vova's house, there had been baby elephants in the ballroom. They were available for rides, to the end of the rose garden and back, and had come as part of the circus Matilda Kshesinskaya had hired for her son's birthday party. There were performing dogs doing back somersaults and walking about on their hind legs, dressed up as people. There were Chinese acrobats, magicians, and for the grand finale, an appearance by Vladimir Leonidovich Durov, the most famous clown and animal trainer in all Russia. He had traveled up specially from Moscow with a troupe of dancing monkeys and a large sow that read the newspaper between parachute jumps from the minstrels' gallery.

Zoia's parents hosted parties in Petersburg, but never anything like this. Theirs were smart affairs. The men wore medals, the ladies, sparkling jewel necklaces. Footmen in frock coats stood to attention at the doors, and the dancing was all minutes and Viennese waltzes. Usually Zoia was allowed to make an appearance, but not before her governess had tied up her hair and dressed her in her finest clothes. At one point in the evening she would be presented to the guests, after which she would recite a passage of French poetry, learned for the occasion. The guests would applaud, and her parents would beam, and then she would be escorted back up to bed, where she would relate her triumph to Mishka, her large toy bear.

That was what she liked most: seeing her parents smile, knowing they were proud of her, in spite of their long absences.

During the week she hardly ever saw them. They seemed to live in a different world. But at those parties, receiving the applause of a glittering circle, she had a sense of the gap closing. The approving smiles told her that one day she would marry well, which was the important thing, and bring sons into the world.

In Petersburg she had to dress up just to go outside. She would put on a cape and hat and long boots and follow her governess, Mademoiselle Élène, along the granite quaysides, past the embassies and private palaces of the aristocracy, with their austere, European facades. Sometimes her mother would come too, but even then Zoia had to walk behind her, by her governess's side.

She remembered trying to get close enough that her mother's sleeve might brush against her cheek.

At Vova's house she didn't have to worry about what her parents thought. She was free to do as she pleased. And there was always plenty to occupy her. There were animals everywhere: ponies, sheep, and lambs, the pack of terriers that followed Matilda everywhere, and some special pet pigs imported from the north of England. Musical soirées and dramatic performances were held several times a week. The house was always full of dancers and musicians and members of the court, who rode over from the czar's summer palace at Peterhof. They made a point of being nice to Vova and his young friends, joining in whatever party games had been thought up for the day, and engaging them in conversation. The year of the big maneuvers, Grand Duke Sergei, who aside from being the czar's uncle, was Inspector-General of the Artillery, took a whole day off from military planning to design a war game for them in the garden. He helped them build a wooden fortress in the middle of the ornamental lake—like the ones in Poland, that would keep out the Germans, he said—and two batteries of catapults that fired tennis balls.

One day it was announced that Grigory Rasputin would be visiting, accompanied by the czarina's friend Anna Vyrubova, and members of her circle. Vova had seen Rasputin before, and would refer to him only as "the smelly priest." He never washed, he said, and his beard and long hair were so dirty they were matted and stiff like a coconut. It turned out to be a strange day. Nobody came to play in the garden. Many of Kshesinskaya's regular guests stayed away altogether, and those that remained were mostly very quiet, and as if afraid of drawing attention to themselves. Rasputin spent most of the evening sitting in the drawing room, surrounded by his entourage, saying little. He stared at Zoia when she finally plucked up the courage to present herself, looking her up and down with glassy, mocking eyes. He asked for her name, and who her father was, but Matilda, to whom he had addressed these questions, only hesitated and changed the subject. It made Zoia wonder if the stories of Rasputin's mystical powers were true, if, as it seemed, there was some danger in his simply knowing your name.

The czar himself never came to visit, but everyone knew why that was. Once the young Nicholas had been in love with Matilda, but had been forced to break off the connection when he became engaged to the future empress. It was out of respect for the czarina that he stayed away. At school Zoia had heard it said that it was the czar who had built Kshesinskaya's mansion in St. Petersburg, and that there was a secret tunnel connecting it to the winter palace—although this Vova vehemently denied.

There was no tunnel, he said, and anyway his mother had paid for the house herself with the money she made at the Mariinsky Theatre.

If the czar was no longer in love with Kshesinskaya, the same could not be said of the Grand Dukes. Hardly a day went by without a visit from one or the other. The Grand Duke Sergei had reportedly built a *dacha* for her at Strelna, but it seemed to Zoia that Matilda loved the Grand Duke Andrei more. She was always glancing at him across busy rooms. And when she was beside him, her smiles seemed warmer.

The grown-ups who visited the house never spoke of it, at least not in her presence, but Zoia knew it was a subject of great interest. Whenever the ballerina rose to dance, or set off to pick berries or mushrooms in the grounds, heads would turn to see whose arm she would take. Zoia's mother always asked her about it when she got back home, although she couched her inquiries in general terms. Which of the Grand Dukes were present? How did they spend their time? And so on. It was only years later that she revealed what she knew: that the Grand Duke Andrei was, in fact, Vova's father.

Some things happened at Strelna that Zoia didn't mention to anyone. There were sensations she could not name. Like the time Matilda's young dancing partner, Pierre, came to play the war game. When a tennis ball hit him in the chest, he made a great show of being wounded, and then burst into song as he hit the grass, like a character in a tragic opera. Zoia was being a nurse that afternoon. As the battle raged on, with Vova leading an assault across the jetty, she knelt down beside the injured man, and dabbed his brow with a handkerchief. He let out a soft moan, his eyes still closed, then coughed pathetically. Zoia laughed and unfastened his collar. The flap of his shirt came open, revealing a triangle of smooth white flesh.

"Are you dead?" she asked. But Pierre did not answer.

She watched him for a moment, then, without thinking, reached inside the shirt and placed her hand against his heart.

She saw him look up and snatched her hand away.

He grabbed it with his. "Don't you know, fair princess," he whispered, "that only a kiss will save me?" He slumped back down again, letting his hands fall to his sides.

A small marble copy of Rodin's *The Kiss* stood on a bureau in Matilda Kshesinskaya's bedroom. Zoia had seen it there one morning while the maids were at work. One of them had giggled as she went over it with a duster. That night, while a dinner party was in full swing downstairs, Zoia had stolen up there with a lamp. Two lovers, naked. She had run her fingers over their perfect forms.

Now she sat frozen, breathless, not sure what to do, not even sure what she *wanted* to do.

Pierre's mouth was fractionally open. Through the parted lips she glimpsed his white teeth. She felt something intoxicating and dangerous well up inside her.

And then she was leaning over him, heart pounding. His forehead was damp. His skin sparkled along the hairline. There was a faint, sweet smell like almonds. She closed her eyes as his breath brushed against her cheek.

Only a kiss will save me.

She felt his lips even before she touched them.

"Got you!"

He laughed and grabbed her by the waist. She screamed as he rolled her onto her back, and jumped to his feet.

"Saved! Saved!" he yelled, and ran off to rejoin the battle, leaving her sprawling on the ground.

She remembered watching him go, bringing her fingers to her lips. She knew she should feel ashamed of herself, but strangely, she didn't.

At the water's edge Pierre looked back at her and smiled.

Pierre was twenty-three years old and handsome. The ladies watched him closely when he danced, their fans fluttering like butterflies in the sultry evening air. But he wasn't the only interesting man to show his face at the villa. There was a shy young violinist called Anton, not more than seventeen, who played once a week in the string orchestra. There were military cadets, who arrived in the company of elder relatives in their smart navy uniforms. And there was the boy who looked after Vladimir Durov's dancing monkeys. He was a little short, and had a gap between his front teeth big enough to pass your finger through. But the monkeys seemed to regard him as nothing less than a walking larder, which was the funniest thing Zoia had ever seen. They clambered all over him, rummaging through his numerous pockets for nuts, without the slightest regard for decorum. Buttons were no impediment to their nimble fingers, and on one occasion they even succeeded in unhitching his braces, so that his trousers dropped to his ankles, to the indescribable delight of all present.

Zoia began to notice how men looked at her, how the young ones would blush, and the older ones smile when she looked back. Sometimes she wondered why they didn't say anything, though, if they found her so interesting. Or why, if they did talk to her, it was always on some neutral subject like the weather or her schooling or the health of her relatives.

Standing one day before a full-length mirror, it came to her that their stares told them everything they needed to know. They could see *inside* her, and read the thoughts and feelings she tried so hard to mask. The idea was exciting, terrifying: that there was so much knowledge to be gleaned in seeing.

She placed an outstretched hand on her reflection, covering her face.

5

Stockholm, February 2000.

Early the next morning Elliot rented a car and drove south, skirting the gray waters of the Saltsjön, then turned east toward the Baltic along boulevards of ponderous grandeur and stone. Most of the last day's snowfall had been blown into cracks and crevices, etching the roof tiles and windows in white. Hunched pedestrians edged along the quaysides, squinting into a bitter wind.

A mile on, the nineteenth century gave way to the twentieth. Apartment blocks and silver chimneys stood sentinel among swathes of municipal woodland. He drove with a city map spread out on the passenger seat, flipping radio stations as the signals broke up or the music took a turn for the worse. Compressed, distorted voices leached through the static: German, Finnish, Russian. They screeched and babbled, drowning out the music on the classical station, then fading into background whispers. The nearer he got to the sea, the louder the voices became, something to do with freakish atmospheric conditions, he supposed. They crowded in, voice upon voice, beseeching, threatening. It spooked him, like walking through a graveyard and hearing whispers in the trees.

The horizon darkened as the city vanished in his rearview mirror. Oncoming headlights burned bright in the gloom, although minutes went by without him seeing any traffic at all. Four miles out on Route 228, it started snowing again, the flakes catching like fluff on the wipers. At a place called Fisksätra the map ran out. A mile on, the highway did too. He found himself winding through pine forest, passing entrances to private drives closed off behind iron gates.

With the snow, the road got slicker. On a hill he took a bend too fast, lost control, the car fishtailing, lurching to a halt against the verge. He got out to check if there was any damage. There were some nasty-looking scratches over the front nearside wheel, but nothing serious. He got back in the car, taking it slowly now. He wondered what would happen if the snow kept falling. In Scandinavia they were good at keeping their roads open, but he hadn't seen any snowplows. Maybe holiday resorts out of season were not a priority. Maybe you were just supposed to sit it out until the thaw.

Some time around the middle of the century Zoia had started spending her summers on the outskirts of Saltsjöbaden, an hour away from Stockholm. The town had been a resort for half a century, developed as a nautical playground by a member of the Wallenberg banking family. A Swedish Newport, Rhode Island, its sheltered position at the head of the archipelago had attracted the yachting and partying fraternities equally—although in later, more egalitarian times, its grand hotels had played host to political conferences, chess tournaments, and festivals of independent cinema. As the years went by, Zoia's stays there had grown longer and longer, perhaps because the peace suited her, perhaps because the city no longer did. There, at the top of the house, many of the gold paintings had been executed, painstaking labors of love the world was only ever allowed to see when complete.

It was a place Elliot had seen in his dreams.

The town didn't look like much at first. The little there was in the way of low-rent accommodation was situated on the landward side: youth hostels, a camping site, chalets available by the week, all shut up now and silent beneath several inches of snow. It wasn't until you reached the waterfront that the resort's upmarket orientation became clear. Elliot passed yachting marinas, whitewashed mansions, a grand, turreted hotel. But the yachts were huddled together beneath tarpaulins, and nothing moved on the promenade but gulls. Out on the water, rafts of gray ice drifted on the current.

Cornelius had typed the information Elliot needed on a sheet of Bukowski writing paper, complete with a schematic map of the town:

```
                    Dr. Peter Lindqvist
                    Lärkvägen 31
                    Tel: (08) 7170139
```

Lindqvist had been Zoia's doctor, and, in the absence of any family, it was to him that she had left the bulk of her estate, including the summerhouse and her private collection of pictures. Cornelius had been vague about the exact circumstances. The doctor had been in general practice and was now retired. He and his sister lived in Saltsjöbaden more or less permanently, and had tended Zoia in her declining years. It was he who had sent the collection—all of it, Cornelius believed—to Bukowskis for exhibition and sale. It was he who would benefit if the event were a success.

"You'll find him quite cooperative," Cornelius had said, as they were about to say good-bye. "But it would be as well to be discreet. I sense the man is anxious to maintain a low profile."

Lärkvägen was a winding street a good half mile from the shore. The houses were modest, befitting seasonal use, set back from the road and small, a mixture of clapboard and stone. Number 31 was a flaking gray building with a sagging tile roof and windows picked out in a sober shade of green. From a flagpole, a faded Swedish flag flapped in the breeze. Elliot pulled up beside an old black Mercedes. He'd seen models like it in South Kensington showrooms—flat, square radiator, boxy, perpendicular lines—lovingly restored to mint condition, and breathtakingly expensive. This one had blistered paint along the bottom of the doors and around the headlamp fittings.

He climbed the steps onto the porch. From somewhere nearby came the loud buzz of machinery. He knocked a couple of times, got no answer, then set off around the side of the house, following the noise, conscious of how inappropriately he was dressed: his leather shoes and gray city overcoat. He hadn't packed for a trip to the country.

At the end of a narrow yard a woman in a headscarf was feeding sticks into a wood chipper.

"Excuse me! Hello?"

The woman didn't look up, intent on the gaping metal mouth, as it yanked the branches from her hand.

"Mr. Elliot, is it?"

The voice was behind him. Elliot turned. A man was standing by the rented Volvo, carrying an armful of freshly cut foliage. He wore an oily-looking leather coat, and woolen trousers tucked into the tops of his boots.

"That's right. Dr. Lindqvist?"

Elliot stepped back down onto the driveway, trying not to slip on the impacted snow.

"I wasn't expecting you until this afternoon."

"I thought I'd set out early," Elliot said with a smile, glancing down the empty road. "Beat the traffic."

Lindqvist didn't seem to appreciate the joke. He turned to the Volvo. "You've some damage here. Did you have an accident?"

Elliot hadn't noticed it before, but the end of the front bumper had been bent out of position. He considered lying, but something in Lindqvist's demeanor told him that was a bad idea.

"I hit some black ice a few miles back. It's nothing serious."

He held out his hand. Lindqvist shook it awkwardly. His skin up close was raw and flaky, with spots of dried blood around his neck—the skin of a man who didn't believe in moisturizer or masculine grooming products. He wore a tidy gray mustache and glasses with the kind of heavy frames that would have looked postmodern on a film critic or an architect, but which on him looked impecunious and old. At certain angles the convex lenses gave him goggling, cartoon eyes.

"Well, I'll be with you in a moment. I expect you're anxious to get to work."

He walked off around the side of the house and deposited his load beside the chipper. He exchanged a few words with the woman, while the machine snapped and chewed. She looked back at Elliot with a look of polite welcome on her face that somehow fell short of a smile.

Dr. Lindqvist said he wanted to run the engine for a while. So it was in the Mercedes that they drove to the house, their breath still condensing in the cold air, despite the asthmatic heater at work beneath the windscreen. Behind the wheel, the old man became a little friendlier. He asked about Elliot's journey, and how preparations were going for the show.

"London seems a long way to come for something like this. I hope you find it's worth your while."

Lindqvist spoke English like a rural schoolmaster: grammar fastidious, accent heavy.

"Bukowskis is expecting a lot of international interest. There have already been some very promising inquiries."

It came to Elliot that he was sounding like an estate agent. Lindqvist frowned.

"Is that so? Well, well."

"Does that surprise you?"

The car went seesawing over a bump. They were heading east again, toward the sea. Elliot felt butterflies in his stomach.

"I don't know about such things—when an artist is *important,* when she isn't. Who can really be the judge of that?"

"Did you ever talk about these things? With Madam Zoia, I mean?"

Lindqvist looked around, the oversized eyes holding him for a moment. Then he laughed. "You obviously never met her."

"No, I never did."

"If you had, you wouldn't ask that question."

"Why not?"

Lindqvist changed down, gaze fixed now on the road. The snow hadn't yet been disturbed. The wheels skidded as they cornered.

"She wasn't part of that world. She never cared to be."

"What world?"

"Your world, I imagine."

Elliot forced a smile. "What do you mean?"

"Critics, academics. She wasn't interested in contributing to debates. About this school or that school. She couldn't have cared less about your aesthetic ideologies."

Elliot didn't argue, but in his experience dealers followed trends in the modern art scene in just the same way, and for just the same reasons, as brokers followed trends in the stock market: with an eye to a profit. They talked the critical language of the day, banked their 100 to 300 percent markups, and went home to their period houses in Chelsea. Ideology didn't come into it.

But then, he wasn't a dealer anymore.

"So . . . she never talked about her work? She had nothing to say about it."

Lindqvist's fingers tapped against the steering wheel.

"She was cornered from time to time. People turned up with cameras, microphones. She always said their questions were inept, pointless. They went away as ignorant as they arrived."

"Ignorant of her, or of her work?"

Lindqvist didn't answer. They were pulling up outside a wooden gate, held fast by a padlock. Thickly growing trees obscured the view.

"I've some spare boots in the back," he said. "The snow tends to drift here. So you'd better put them on."

They left the Mercedes in front of the gates and walked up the curving driveway, past fruit trees stiff with frost. The house lay on the far side of the slope. Stumbling through the drifts in boots a size too big, Elliot picked out details: a weathered red roof with a single eave, the end of a wooden balcony on the first floor, stone footings supporting creamy clapboard walls. It was a bigger house than Lindqvist's, but angled away from the road, as if reluctant to receive visitors. He had expected something different: white stucco walls, classical symmetry, ornamental gardens populated with statues—a villa on the Baltic. But this was just a lonely retreat.

Lindqvist fished in his coat for the keys, breathing heavily as he turned one lock, then a second. The lintel was carved with zigzag patterns and stylized floral motifs—Asiatic, Scythian designs, a kind that had been in vogue with Russian artists when Zoia was a child.

Lindqvist put his shoulder to the door and pushed. On the other side was a kitchen, dark and shuttered, but smelling unmistakably of stale provender and grease. Elliot saw copper pans hung up above a range, an old 1950s-style refrigerator, heavy oak cupboards with iron handles, a big table scored with knife marks. In the middle of the table, incongruously, lay a tin can with a bottle opener next to it.

Signs of life.

"There's no one still . . . ?"

Lindqvist found a light switch. A bare bulb went on over the table.

"Ah. Still connected. That's a bonus."

He closed the door and removed his gloves, briefly rubbing his hands together. The sound of the wind was fainter now. Elliot could hear the house creaking, like a galleon on a rolling sea.

"When was this place built?"

Lindqvist set off up a short flight of steps.

"About eighty years or so ago. It needs some work, but don't worry. It's sound. The papers are upstairs."

Elliot followed the doctor into a narrow hallway. A rug had been rolled up against a staircase. A glass vase by the front door was full of wheat stalks and dead flowers. Their footsteps echoed on bare boards.

"I suppose you plan to sell," Elliot asked, struggling to keep up as they climbed to the next floor.

All through the house there was a damp, woody smell.

"Of course. In the spring. Along with everything else. There are taxes to pay."

Halfway up the stairs was an icon. Four inches by four. St. George impassive on a white horse, reaching behind him with a long lance to slay the serpent, his ragged red cloak flying. The style and subject were of the Novgorod school, late-seventeenth century, although this was a copy at least a hundred years younger.

"So you're not keeping anything?"

There were windows on the landing, blocked out by shutters. In the summer it must have been airy and light, but in the damp-smelling darkness it was hard to picture it that way.

Lindqvist paused in front of a paneled door. "I suppose you think me unsentimental."

"Not at all, I—"

"Zoia didn't plan on leaving this house to me until a few years ago. I'm sure you've heard that from other people, and if you haven't, no doubt you will."

The big eyes blinked. Somehow Elliot had touched a nerve.

"The same thing goes for her paintings," Lindqvist said. "I expect she saw herself passing them on to close friends and family. In the event, none survived her. She had no children, as you know." He signed as he pushed open the door. "The fact that the closest person to her in her final years was her doctor is a sad thing. I have no wish to dwell on sad things. I respect Madam Zoia for her kindness, and I'm grateful. But I don't need to see her paintings every day to respect her memory."

"Of course," Elliot said. "I understand."

Lindqvist nodded. "Good."

He led the way into a sitting room. There was furniture under dust sheets, an upright piano, a porcelain stove.

The lights didn't work. Lindqvist unlocked a set of french windows and pushed back the shutters. There was a balcony outside, beyond it the gray sea, just visible through gaps in the trees. Gulls screeched in the distance. From the bay it was open water all the way to St. Petersburg.

This was where it used to hang, the *Chinese Princess in Paris*. Francesca, the art history student, had found the reference in a 1960s edition of *Vogue,* the picture itself partly reproduced in black and white. The fact that there was no official sale record, at a gallery or auction house, suggested Zoia had sold it right off the wall a few years later. Or given it away, the recipient Mrs. Hanna Elliot, née Carlson.

He scanned the walls, looking for the spot, and realized it was probably beside him, where the light fell brightest. He was standing where his mother had stood, two weeks from the end.

Lindqvist closed the windows.

"Over here. They're all here."

Over Elliot's shoulder, partly hidden by a sofa, stood a tall bureau bookcase. The style was Georgian, with a fold-down writing surface, drawers below and mirrored doors above, the silvering dulled behind veins of oxidation. It would have been valuable, were it not for the obvious signs of damage and inexpert repair.

Lindqvist fished out another key, a small brass one. "It took us a long time to find this. We almost gave up looking."

He undid the locks. The one on the lid showed signs of scoring, as if someone had tried to force it with a knife.

Lindqvist folded the lid down and opened up the shelves. Inside was a row of rectangular boxes: black cardboard, grey cardboard, metal. Some of them had labels attached to them, on the labels scrawls of ink, forming illegible words.

"Take a look," Lindqvist said. "It's what you came for."

Elliot reached up, ran his fingers along the shelf, stopped at a black metal box. A label had once been attached to the handle with string, but now only a scrap remained.

He took the box down and gently thumbed it open.

He caught a musty smell of old paper and gum. He slid a finger down the inside of the box, rolled back letters, envelopes, postcards. He pulled one out, saw French, written in a slanting, urgent hand:

I miss you so much, my little one. It feels like an eternity since I felt your mouth against mine. Can it be you have forgotten me . . . ?

At the top of the page: 1st July 1930.

A loud trilling sound brought his head up. Self-consciously Lindqvist reached into his coat and took out a mobile phone. It looked so incongruous in his hand, Elliot almost laughed.

Lindqvist said a few words, frowning at the reply. Apparently the signal was breaking up.

"I'd better go outside," he said. "Excuse me a moment."

He backed out of the room, leaving Elliot alone. Footsteps retreated down the hall.

Can it be you have forgotten me?

There was no signature at the end of the letter. No name at the beginning. It was the draft of a letter. Zoia at twenty-seven, nine years out of Russia, nine years from the Lubyanka. Nineteen thirty was the year she got it into her head to go to North Africa, for reasons that were never clear. Artistically it was an unproductive period, one that culminated in a period of serious illness, purportedly neurological. Most writings on her life had simply left it out. But one thing could be said for certain: her marriage to Karl Kilbom, her Communist rescuer, was as good as over by the time she returned to Sweden.

Elliot took down another box. The letter at the top was older, in Russian this time. The paper was coarse, almost powdery to the touch. The writer had set out to keep everything neat: straight margin, uniform hand, lines evenly spaced. But halfway down the page things began to fall apart: the writing became cramped and angled, the margins drifted, the lines converged as if beneath a crushing weight of feeling.

6th October 1926

Dearest Zoia,

    I don't know where you are. Did you come back from Paris?
Have you received my letter from Moscow? Tonight at eleven
we set sail from Odessa. I'll post this letter at the next port, which
is Sevastopol. Where are you, Zoia? Where on this stupid
planet . . . ?

He turned over the page and saw the signature: *Andrei.* A man Zoia must have left behind in Russia five years before.

Barriers of language and time. There was always a special delight in overcoming them. It was the thing that drew him to the study of languages in the first place, the feeling of privileged access. Even as a child, he saw pages of foreign text as walls to be broken down. It wasn't until he began to see art as a language that he was drawn to study that too.

He reached for the drawers, opened them one after the other.

More boxes, different shapes and sizes, but disordered this time. He flipped open a cigar box, found a stack of old photographs. From a cruise ship dining room a group of thirty-somethings raised their glasses in a toast. Flapper dresses and slicked-back hair. On the back of the picture was a stamp mark: *Stella Polaris.*

In 1933 Zoia started working on cruise ships in the Mediterranean, painting portraits of the passengers. Back then, it was the only way she could make a living.

Lindqvist was deep in conversation. Elliot could hear him talking into his mobile, trying to keep his voice down. It sounded like he was outside the house.

Another photograph: a blonde, handsome man, about forty. He was standing in a park, wearing a jacket and pale trousers. It looked as if he had his arm around someone, but that whole half of the picture was missing. Whoever he was with that day had been dispensed with.

He kept looking through the box. In the corner of his eye he saw a figure on the balcony. Lindqvist had found his way out there through some other room.

One print, seven inches by five, was of better quality than the rest. The paper was thick and the image had aged well. It was an interior shot, some time in the 1930s: Zoia in a studio with an easel on one side and a man in a pinstripe suit on the other. On the back, in pencil, was written: *Kristoffer and Zoia at work.*

The man was about Zoia's age, neat hair, tidy mustache. He wore a self-conscious grin on his face, and clutched a boxy black cine camera to his chest, as if it were a new toy. The photograph recorded a rare occurrence. Zoia did not invite visitors to her studio, unless it was to paint them. Whether in Paris, Stockholm, or elsewhere, she would not let anyone watch her work, a fact that undoubtedly contributed to her mystique. Off to one side there was a tall window, four panels of glass, divided by a cross. Light was falling full on Zoia's face, burning out the detail. She had moved during the exposure too: up close he could see blurring, in what was otherwise a pin-sharp print. It stripped the detail from her face, leaving it simplified, doll-like.

The french windows opened. He felt the raw, salty air against his face. "Have you any idea who this is? The man with the camera? Could—?" He was talking to an empty room.

"Hello?"

He went out onto the balcony. He could hear Lindqvist's voice, but Lindqvist wasn't there. He was down below, pacing up and down outside the front door, mobile phone still clamped to his ear.

The gulls had moved inland and were circling the house. Their cries were shrill.

Lindqvist looked up as he finished his call. "So. Have you found anything useful, Mr. Elliot?"

6

———•———

The Ibis Majestic was the only mid-price hotel in Saltsjöbaden that stayed open through the winter, a biscuit-colored block of 1980s off-the-shelf design. By half-past three, Elliot was standing in the empty lobby, listening to a sugary rendition of the *Four Seasons* while the receptionist ran a check on his credit card. Behind the desk a black-and-white CCTV monitor flipped from camera to camera, revealing empty interiors and empty streets.

"How many nights will you be staying, sir?"

The receptionist didn't take his eyes off the computer screen. He was young, maybe twenty-two, with a crew cut and pale, waxy skin.

"Two nights. Or three. I'm not sure yet."

"Shall we say three nights, for now? You can cancel the third if you don't need it."

On the monitor, a hunched figure went past the entrance to the parking lot, silhouetted against the snow. Elliot watched it disappear.

"Sir?"

"I'm sorry?"

"Shall we say three nights, for now?"

It looked like his credit was still good, despite the recent difficulties. Another step on the way back. Everything going according to plan.

The CCTV switched to a camera in the lobby. Elliot saw himself standing at the desk, both hands clutching his suitcase, like a refugee.

"All right, fine. Three nights."

"Very good, sir."

The receptionist started tapping keys. Outside, it was almost dark, everything a blanket shade of blue.

Three nights. Three days. It wasn't exactly what he'd planned, but Dr. Lindqvist hadn't given him much choice. He didn't want the letters taken away, said he hadn't *decided* what to do with them yet. As if nothing had been ruled out where they were concerned. As if he reserved the right to lock them all up again at any time. It meant he would have to work right there in Zoia's house, surrounded by her things, by the sights and sounds that were once part of her life.

The doctor's attitude was hard to explain. He had been left a load of paintings, and couldn't wait to sell them. He had been left papers of far less value and yet wanted to keep hold of them—wasn't keen, pretty clearly, on anyone even seeing them, except in as far as they helped Bukowskis pull in the buyers. It was strange behavior for someone anxious to guard an artist's memory. It was strange behavior for someone who didn't give a damn one way or the other.

He wanted to close the book on Zoia's life as quickly as possible, but *his* way. Take what you need and go. Like those television people who turned up while Zoia was alive, and left as ignorant as when they'd arrived.

The monitor flipped to a corridor, closed doors left and right, a fire extinguisher at the far end.

It came to Elliot that maybe what Lindqvist planned to do with the letters was destroy them. The idea struck him as consistent with the doctor's ambivalence. But why? One obvious answer: because that was what Zoia had asked him to do. It explained a lot, his attitude, his defensiveness. She had asked him to destroy the letters—as a very private person might—but instead he had kept them because Cornelius said they might be useful.

Poor Dr. Lindqvist, caught between honor and good old-fashioned greed. And touchy about it too, afraid of what people might say.

Cornelius had told him once how Nordic people got through the long, dark winters: the Danes ate, the Finns drank, and the Swedes gossiped. Lindqvist was obviously worried they were gossiping already.

It cast the whole operation in a different light. It wasn't simply research he had been asked to carry out. It was trespass, invasive and unwelcome—if perfectly legal, the dead having no rights to privacy.

He saw himself in Zoia's room again, riffling through her pictures. He felt the rush of cold air as the balcony windows swung open.

"Room 210. On the second floor."

The receptionist slid a plastic key across the desk. Elliot blinked.

"The lift is to your left."

•   •   •

Up in the room, he discovered someone had tried to call him on his mobile phone. It had happened over an hour earlier, but he hadn't heard the ringer. The number was one he knew by heart.

He threw off his coat and dialed the number on the hotel phone.

"Harriet Shaw."

Harriet was the kind of lawyer who always took her own calls. That was one of the things Elliot liked about her. She made every case she was handling seem like *the* case, even though it wasn't.

"Harriet, it's Marcus."

"Marcus, hi. Just one second."

He heard her firing off instructions to her PA, got a picture of her in her Holborn office, phone tucked under her ear, reaching across the huge desk with some fat document that needed faxing or copying. Besides the inevitable navy blue suits, she had a preference for shirts with high collars, usually set off with a clasp at her throat, a quasi-Victorian look that had Elliot wondering if she wasn't hiding some kind of postoperational scar. Sometimes she whooped things up a little with eyeliner and nail varnish that was a shade too red to flatter. Like him, she had married late, in her case to a German with "von" in his name.

A door closed.

"Thanks for getting back to me. Are you okay?"

"Yes, yes, fine. I'm in Sweden."

"Of course you are. How's Sweden?"

He could hear her riffling papers. In spite of the perfect line, he felt like he was talking to the other side of the world.

"Cold and dark. And difficult."

"The work?"

"There's more of it than I thought. More . . . to it. What's happened? Has something—?"

"I'm afraid so, Marcus. Something rather unexpected." Elliot gripped the phone. "The Ward of Court order. It seems your wife—I mean, Nadia—is trying to overturn it, ahead of the residency hearing. I was notified by Social Services this morning."

For the past two weeks their daughter Teresa had been with foster parents, Mr. and Mrs. Edwards of Turnham Green. They had a Victorian red-brick house in need of refurbishment, cupboards full of secondhand toys, and walls covered in kindergarten drawings and cut-out stars. Teresa was supposed to stay there as a Ward of Court until the residence hearing in March. Elliot could have contested the order, could have pushed the court for a provisional decision in his favor, but Harriet had advised against it. It would be useful in this situation to establish himself as the reasonable parent, the one who had some awareness of equity and, by extension, the one who could ultimately be relied upon to consider the best interests of the child. It might make all the difference when the real battle was joined.

It had been obvious since their separation that Nadia planned to make a fight of the residence issue. It was her way of extracting the most advantageous terms from the divorce settlement. The truth was she had never wanted a child, had still been too young at twenty-four to be a mother, she thought. Her options were being closed down, the Western world's delights being snatched away just as they were finally within reach. He had seen it in the way she fretted over each and every inconvenience of pregnancy. It had been a battle just to get her to give up alcohol, and he was pretty sure she cheated at lunchtime, dumping the empty bottles in next door's bin. He had been the one who researched her dietary needs, buying the pills and the supplements and setting them out on the kitchen counter every morning so she wouldn't even have to read the labels.

So it was a big surprise when she tried to abscond with Teresa. She had disappeared to Stansted Airport a few days after New Year. In Prague, she and Teresa would have been out of reach of the English courts. Elliot would have been hard put even to find them.

By chance he had called the flat that afternoon. Teresa had been due a vaccination, and he'd wanted to be sure Nadia didn't forget, the way she did almost everything. Inés, their once-a-week cleaner, had answered the phone. She said she'd seen Nadia and Teresa on the way out, Nadia dragging a big suitcase toward a waiting mini-cab. Apparently she'd told Inés that they were going away to visit family, which had struck Elliot as odd, given that Teresa was due back at preschool any day. So he'd asked Inés to take a look at the dresser by the bed, where Nadia kept her family photographs. Sure enough, they were all gone. Likewise her violin case, and the inlaid jewelry box her grandmother had given her for her sixteenth birthday.

That was when he'd called his lawyer.

It was amazing how quickly she'd gone into action. Harriet Shaw worked in the family law department at Mishcon de Reya, a blue-blood firm that would have been beyond his budget were it not for the fact that he and Harriet went back twenty years, to a student hall of residence at Edinburgh and an extracurricular Russian course (which she subsequently gave up). She had been on the phone to the High Court at two o'clock, and in front of a judge at half-past, applying for a Section 8 Prohibited Steps order, which had been immediately granted. A few minutes later the court staff were sending out alerts to all of London's international airports, and the Channel ports for good measure.

What happened then was still unclear. Nadia and Teresa had been boarding the plane when airport security found them. It was possible Nadia had been drinking. Like Elliot, she was nervous about flying, and a forty-minute delay would have given her plenty of opportunity to drown her butterflies in vodka and lime. It was also possible that in all the haste, the exact circumstances of the operation had not been passed down the chain of command. Some of the officers involved apparently thought they had been sent to prevent an abduction. In any event, a female official had allegedly taken it upon herself to remove Teresa by force. Nadia had repeatedly struck her in the face. A second officer was bitten on the hand. Nadia was duly arrested and charged with assault. By the time Elliot had arrived an hour later, Teresa was in the care of welfare officers. That night in a nearby hotel she had nightmares and woke up crying.

Harriet had told him to look on the bright side: this was drunkenness and violence in glorious Technicolor, played out before terrified witnesses. They had a real chance of winning now, a real chance of giving Teresa the future she deserved.

Only something had gone wrong.

"Apparently Essex police have dropped the charges."

Elliot was on his feet. "What? *Why?*"

Harriet sighed. "Well, apparently her lawyer came up with a witness who says the airport security people surprised her and failed to identify themselves. She perceived a threat to the child is the argument. I know it's rubbish—"

"Of course it's rubbish."

"Marcus, even if she *was* being charged, it wouldn't stop her petitioning the County Court. It just would have made things more difficult when she got there."

Elliot told himself to keep calm. The truth was, he'd never been comfortable with the idea of Nadia being branded a criminal, even if the odds of her receiving a custodial sentence were virtually nil. It had just been something useful to brandish in front of a judge at the residency hearing, another reason why Teresa was better off with him.

"All right. Okay. So what do we do?"

Harriet's breath pushed against the mouthpiece. Harriet was a top lawyer at a top firm. She wasn't supposed to be wrong about *anything*. She was supposed to be invincible.

"Well, I think we have to fight this every inch of the way. We can't afford to have the incident written off as some sort of harmless mistake. It's too important for that."

Elliot couldn't keep the sense of betrayal from his voice.

"I don't understand this, Harriet. A week ago we were home free. Now we have to fight for every inch. What the hell happened?"

"Marcus, I never said . . . Look, what happened is, Nadia got herself a new solicitor. Miles Hanson. Have you heard of him?"

"Heard of him? Why should I have heard of him?"

"He's a partner at Collyer-Bristow. He made quite a name for himself in a child abduction case. *Osman v. Harris?* Anyway, he's good."

"How good?"

"Let's just say, he won't be a pushover. He does his homework."

Elliot brought a hand to his forehead. He felt hot and shaky, as if he was going to be sick. It was something that had happened a lot since he and Nadia had split up. Sometimes he found he couldn't eat for twenty-four hours at a time.

"I don't get it. If this guy Hanson's so famous, how come Nadia can afford him?"

"I was rather hoping you'd tell me."

"I've no idea. I can't imagine where she'd . . ."

But he *could* imagine. Nadia had always turned heads. With the years, her beauty had become more fragile, more complex, but, if anything, deeper. There were plenty of friends in their circle—*his* friends—who had openly expressed their admiration for her. Then there were his old clients: men with deep pockets and an eye for an acquisition opportunity. In the days when Nadia worked at the gallery, it was clear many of them thought she was the best thing on show.

And then there was the guy she met at a party when he was away at

Maastricht. Laurent. The French guy she took home and fucked on the floor of the sitting room, and *said* she never planned to see again.

"You could never understand me, you're not capable," were the words that stood out from the ensuing row, a scene that was in all other respects so familiar from a thousand movies and TV dramas that the sheer banality of it still made him wince. But he remembered those words of hers with special clarity because they struck him as true. He had always suspected that there were sides to her life he knew nothing about, sides he never would know. Doors she kept firmly closed.

"Well, that's not important right now," Harriet said. "What's important is we don't allow Nadia to change the status quo. If Teresa is living with her mother when we get to the residency hearing, it'll be that much harder to convince the court it should be otherwise."

Elliot slumped back on the bed. "I understand."

"Don't worry, Marcus. The odds are still in our favor. The court found for us last time."

"That was before Miracle Miles came along."

Harriet laughed with disproportionate force, eager to seize on any hint of levity. "The Ward of Court hearing will be next week or the week after. I'll push for as late a date as possible. But I think it would help if you could be there. I want the court to see you're genuinely concerned about Teresa's safety."

He had pictured the scene a hundred times, the dread of it never lessening, even in the bitterest times: he and Nadia, in court together, just a few feet apart, but not speaking, not even acknowledging each other, a great, silent divide between them.

"I'll be there," he said. "Count on it."

Satellite TV didn't take his mind off the hearing. News of another bad opening on Wall Street barely registered. He thought about a hit of Mogadon, but held off, knowing he would pay a price for it later. Part of getting back to normal was sleeping when you were supposed to sleep, switching on and switching off, each day following the same pattern, whatever the needs of the moment.

Nadia had an expensive lawyer. And someone else was footing the bill. Maybe she had a boyfriend already, had already lined up the man who would take his place. Three years down the road, maybe less, Teresa would be calling him Daddy.

Three months after he had found the Zoia self-portrait, he had started talking to Nadia about having children. It was a subject they had barely mentioned before. But suddenly it was urgent to him, not so much a test of love—he still believed no test was necessary—but as a way to cement it, to make it permanent, irrevocable. Beauty trapped in amber. What followed still confused him: she had agreed to the child and *then* betrayed him. To this day, he couldn't make sense of it.

Unless, of course, Teresa was not actually his.

The thought had occurred to him more than once. It was a wise father, they said, who knew his own son, and he had not been wise. He had been trusting and frequently absent. But then he looked at Teresa, looked at those perfect details—the line of the parting in her hazel-brown hair, the curve of her eyebrows, like the brushstrokes of a Chinese calligrapher—and he could not bring himself to believe it.

Even thinking about it, he felt guilty.

He held off until half-four before picking up the phone again. A woman who wasn't Mrs. Edwards answered. There were children shrieking in the background.

"I'm Teresa's father," he explained. "Can I speak to her?"

"Not now, dear," the woman said. "She'll be at her play group."

"Her play group. Well, could you tell her I called? And that I'll call again later?"

Something got knocked over. There was wailing. The woman fussed and scolded for a moment, then picked up the receiver again.

"What was that, dear?"

"Could you tell Teresa I'll call again later?"

"All right. But she goes to bed at half-past six."

It had always been seven at their house, later if there were guests around. He liked people to see his daughter, to admire her.

Now it was in bed at half-past six. No exceptions.

"It's important they get their sleep at that age," the woman said, as if that was something he, as an absentee father, couldn't possibly be expected to know.

The Princess

7

St. Petersburg, August 1914.

When she traveled through the countryside, people snatched off their caps and bowed their heads. Old men with white beards knelt down and kissed her hand. Outside the churches peasant women shouted blessings, calling her "little princess" and holding out their hands to her, as if she were a saint and could somehow bless them in return. Inside, there were special pews or galleries set aside for her family, away from the ordinary people. Wherever they were, the priests gave them Communion first. On the way out, people bowed to Christ and the Virgin, and then to them.

In time, Zoia understood. She and her kind were closer to God than the common man. They were the ones who had been given the task of fashioning the world to His purpose, who lived in greater proximity to His truth, like the angels in heaven. But that meant they were more conspicuous to Him as well. All the rules she was forced to observe, the way her every moment was watched over, every lapse sharply corrected, this was the price of being visible, of living beneath the gaze of the all-seeing eye.

At boarding school in the Smolny Institute the demands of propriety were even greater. It was forbidden to speak Russian, the language of the village, except for half an hour in the afternoon. At mealtimes it was not permitted to speak at all. Running was strictly prohibited, and would have been impossible anyway in the long, heavy dresses they were made to wear, with their stiff white collars and cuffs. Even their daily walks were like military parades, two-by-two in long coats and fur hats, no matter what the weather. And always the same route.

Every once in a while priests in scented robes visited the school to hear confession. It was essential to tell them the absolute truth, to recount every sin: instances of jealousy and laziness, and the petty lies she told to stay out of trouble. Those who held back, it was said, would find they couldn't open their mouths when it came to Communion, or if they did manage that, they would choke on the consecrated bread. The body and blood of Christ would not enter a contaminated vessel. And if they died, they would go to God with their sins on their heads, to be cleansed by fire. Once, when her turn to confess had passed, Zoia realized there was one sin she had forgotten to mention. As the priest was leaving, she ran back up the aisle and threw herself at his feet.

It was strange, though: the next morning she felt like her life had begun again. She felt like one of God's angels, washed clean of all blame. And that was when her parents came to visit her, bringing gifts of flowers.

She was eleven years old when war broke out. When her father left for the front, she cried bitterly because he would not take her with him. This was the great adventure that everyone had been dressing up for, and she didn't want to be left out. Even the old man Sukhomlinov had turned up at Kshesinskaya's in a hussar's uniform, which, with his potbelly and spindly legs, didn't suit him at all.

"I could be a nurse," she shouted, as they headed off to the barracks to receive a special blessing from the Church, "or an adjutant."

Her father just smiled and brushed the hair away from her forehead. He was a tall man, and widely admired for his looks and his wit, or so her governess assured her. At parties it was always his stories that seemed to keep the guests enthralled. Only lately he had been more sober than usual, as if troubled by a future the rest of the household could not see.

"I could help send out your orders. Let me come."

"Maybe when you're older."

"How much older?"

"A year or two."

But she knew the war would be over long before then. She had overheard Grand Prince Sergei say they only had enough shells for a few weeks' campaigning, and only three factories to make new ones. Besides, no one, not even the British, had enough money to keep their armies in the field for more than two or three months.

"In any case," her father added, before she could object any further, "I need you here, to look after your mother."

And as he said it, she saw the smile fade from his lips, as if some dark thought had unexpectedly entered his head.

The streets were full of people singing patriotic songs. Bands of soldiers were moving toward the railway stations, being cheered from upstairs windows and passing trams. Every church along the way seemed to be holding a service, the congregations spilling out onto the pavement, icons and crosses held high. Zoia had not seen such crowds since the tercentenary, but these crowds were different. There were no parades or light shows to entertain them, no stalls selling beer and pies. People drifted about with their hands in their pockets, gathering around anyone with a newspaper, wanting to be part of the moment somehow, to swim in the great tide of events.

Zoia went with her mother as far as the Warsaw station. Her father refused to let them stay to see his train off. There were too many people on the platforms, and the crush was unbearable. Railway officials elbowed their way up and down, making inaudible announcements through tin megaphones. Everywhere women were weeping, or clutching at the outstretched hands of their menfolk. It seemed to Zoia that they were letting their emotions run away with them, until she saw the tears in her mother's eyes.

And then she was crying too. She fought the urge to throw her arms around her father's neck.

He gave some instructions to his batman, then bent down and kissed her on the forehead. "Be good, little one. And remember what I said: your mother needs you."

She swallowed hard, tried to make some reply, but he was already moving away. The last thing she saw of him was his hand, waving at them over the heads of the crowd. At least she thought it was his.

Fear stole into her heart one step at a time.

At boarding school, lessons were shorter. Time was set aside to make bandages for the Red Cross and tobacco pouches for the soldiers. Every day there were prayers for their safety and for victory. The bells tolled across the city hour after hour.

Three weeks in, a girl turned up for lessons wearing a black apron of mourning. Her father had been killed at the front. She sat at the back of the class staring into space, the tears rolling down her face.

German lessons were canceled. English lessons replaced them. The German teachers disappeared, and girls with German-sounding names were ostracized. The other girls made up cruel songs about them, and forced them to listen. Even the city changed its name, to purge it of its German taint. Petersburg became Petrograd.

The teachers would not answer questions about the war. Newspapers were not permitted either. What the children learned, they learned from visiting relatives: rumors of bloody victories in Galicia and defeats in East Prussia, where General Samsonov had shot himself after losing two hundred thousand men in ten days.

By December there were black aprons in every classroom, in every row of desks. From the barred windows on the top floor, they watched funeral processions go by on the way to the military cemetery. One of the girls had an uncle who worked at the Ministry of War. She heard him say they would soon have to call up the second levy of reserves, which meant there would be no one left in the Russian army with more than a week's training. There were ammunition shortages at the front and transport chaos in the rear, he'd said. If it hadn't been for Prince Lvov's volunteers, the war would have been lost already.

She heard him say at least a million men were captured or dead.

Zoia came home for the Christmas holidays. There were fewer servants in the house than when she had left. Some had gone off to fight, others had returned to their families. None had been replaced. Zoia tried to do as her father had asked her, but it proved difficult. Her mother was out all day, working for a women's committee, collecting warm underwear for the troops. Zoia gave up her best doll for a fund-raising event. Letters arrived from her father sporadically, and sometimes in the wrong order. The worst times were when they didn't come at all.

Without the parties and the guests, the house was silent and empty. Some afternoons, when no one was watching, Zoia would wrap herself in a coat and scarf and slip outside. Once she walked as far as the Nevsky Prospekt. She wandered through the big department stores and rode on a tram. It was something she would never have dreamed of doing before the war, a breach of every rule. But the taste of illicit freedom was hard to resist.

There were soldiers and sailors everywhere, some walking on crutches, others with their arms in slings. Zoia heard whistles as she walked past, although it took her a while to realize they were directed at her. As she crossed the Fontanka Canal, she saw a sergeant—a handsome man with a dimple in his jaw and a bandage around his head—walking slowly along the pavement with a walking stick. He caught her eye and asked if he could buy her a drink before he headed back to the front.

"Just over there," he said, nodding toward the frosted glass windows of a cellar tavern. From inside came the sound of voices, and music being played on a squeeze-box.

There was a sad, lonely look in his eyes.

Zoia recognized the insignia on his lapel.

"My father's in your regiment," Zoia said, not meaning anything by it. But the sergeant immediately straightened up and limped away.

The letter came when they were in Pavlovsk, almost exactly a year from the day she saw the czar's car pass by. It was a summer spent waiting for news, from the front or from her father. Every morning Zoia would sit by the gate until the mail arrived, her only company the insects and the long, sighing grass, and every afternoon she would cycle into the town to buy whatever newspapers were available.

They reported further heavy engagements in the Polish salient, where the enemy were attacking on two fronts, and a third enemy offensive in Lithuania. They reported the arrest and investigation of General Sukhom-linov, on suspicion of treachery. The great fortresses that Grand Duke Sergei had told her would keep out the enemy—Kovno, Grodno, Osowiec, Ivangorod—fell one by one. Standing in line to buy her copy, Zoia heard people mutter that the court was riddled with German spies and sympa-thizers, and that the czarina—the "German woman," they called her—was to blame. Across Russia there were strikes and demonstrations against the government's conduct of the war.

Sometimes people in the queue gave her hostile looks. Her governess warned her to dress more plainly when she went to the shops. She said that ignorant people were looking for someone to blame for the fact that the war was not won yet. She said it was not the time to draw attention to yourself.

Some of those summering in Pavlovsk tried to carry on as they had in peacetime. There were no plays or concerts to go to anymore, but they could still host dinner parties and dances. Zoia's mother went to a few of them, but then stopped, spending the evenings instead writing letters and playing the piano. She told a friend who visited that some kinds of people thought they could drink their way to victory. Zoia was disappointed. She loved to dance. When you were dancing you forgot about everything.

Sometimes her mother would appear at bedtime and brush Zoia's hair in front of the big mirror. She would brush and brush, the strokes getting slower and slower, as she stared at Zoia's reflection.

Once she said, in a faraway voice: "We must find you a good man when the time comes, Zoia. A man who deserves you."

Zoia thought of Pierre, the dancer, and the kiss she had given him by the lake.

Her mother rose to her feet, placing her hands on Zoia's shoulders. "Promise me you'll be a good girl until then."

Zoia felt herself blush. It came to her that her mother knew something, had heard something. Some years ago a girl at her school had been caught kissing a cadet from the Naval Academy. It was said her mother had taken her home and beaten her until she fainted.

"I promise," Zoia said.

Her mother smiled and stroked Zoia's cheek with the back of her hand. "A rich man with connections. A man who'll protect us."

The next day a letter arrived from the Ministry of War. Zoia stood by the gate, holding it with trembling hands. She could feel it burning her skin, as if its meaning were somehow leaking out, like poison. She looked up at the postman, hoping he might say there had been some mistake and take it away again. But he avoided her eye, turned his bicycle around, and rode away.

Her mother collapsed when she read the news: *Died in valiant service to His Imperial Majesty the Czar.* Zoia ran into the garden, not wanting to hear or see anything, wanting to hide in some dark place where the world could not touch her. She would never see her father again. It would not sink in. In spite of the black aprons, death seemed to her like a trick, an illusion. In her every vision of the future he was there. No one had even mentioned the possibility that his service to the czar might one day take him away from them.

She did not see her mother until the next day. She seemed suddenly older. There was gray in her hair and her eyes were watery slits behind swollen lids. She was sitting on the piano stool, staring out into the gardens. After a while she turned toward Zoia, and held out her arms.

Zoia ran to her, felt the unfamiliar, hard embrace.

"I still have you, Zoia," she said. "At least I still have you."

She said it over and over.

Two weeks later, Zoia returned to school. One Friday morning, during French, the principal, Princess Volkonsky, appeared at the front of the classroom. She told Zoia that she had a visitor, and that she should come directly. Normally visitors were only permitted on Thursdays and Sundays, in the afternoons, and certainly never in the middle of lessons. Zoia did not know what to think. Her mother was still in Pavlovsk, and she could not imagine who else might have come to see her. It would have to be someone important for the principal not to send them away.

She had a long time to consider the question, as she followed the princess through the empty corridors. The old lady walked slowly, with the aid of a walking stick, which clacked against the marble floors, a sound that always announced her approach minutes before she actually appeared. After a while, Zoia plucked up the courage to speak.

"Madam, may I be permitted to know who—?"

But the princess put a finger to her lips. It was a secret. Something that could not be spoken of. Zoia felt her pulse quicken. She wondered what she had done to deserve this strange treatment.

They stopped outside a heavy, paneled door. Princess Volkonsky reached out for the handle, hesitated as if about to say something, but then seemed to think better of the idea. She opened the door and went in.

Zoia heard someone get up.

"Zoia Korvin-Krukovsky," the princess said, then stood aside to let Zoia enter.

A male voice said: "Thank you, Your Highness," the words swiftly followed by a smart click of the heels.

Zoia looked up into the stranger's face.

He was an army officer, a captain or a colonel, tall and slim, with blonde hair going gray at the temples, and pale blue eyes.

Zoia swallowed. He was the most beautiful man she had ever seen. His face was like the faces on statues and commemorative medals: she saw resolution and fearlessness, and quiet pride. Standing before him, she felt small and ungainly.

Not knowing what else to do, she curtsied, lowering her eyes to his shiny boots.

"*Bonjour, Monsieur*," she stammered, assuming the ban on speaking Russian was still in force.

"*Bonjour*," he replied.

He studied her for a moment, then walked over and, to her astonishment, took her hand. She thought for a moment that he was actually going to kiss it, but instead he just held it in his own.

"Zoia, don't you know who I am?"

Slowly she shook her head. The principal closed the door behind her.

"I'm your father."

Zoia felt the blood drain from her face. It crossed her mind that this was a joke, except that the Princess Volkonsky would never have been party to such a thing.

"You're mistaken, sir," she said. "My father is dead."

The stranger slowly shook his head.

"He was your stepfather. I thought you knew that."

The man who called himself her father took a step closer. She swallowed hard and took a step back.

"My father is dead," she said again, fighting back tears now. Feeling the whole encounter like some cruel, undeserved punishment.

"You were three years old. The czar himself granted your mother and me a divorce."

"It's not true!"

She stood there, staring at the floor, arms folded against her stomach. She wished the teachers would come and take her away again. She didn't want to listen to this man.

She heard him sigh. She knew she had hurt him, but she couldn't help it. It didn't seem fair for this to be true: that her father should lose his life and then his place in *her* life not three weeks later.

She began to tremble. The room felt cold. For a moment she thought she was going to faint.

"It's something we thought you should know. Your mother and I. It's something we agreed."

Zoia began to tremble. She felt disgusted and ashamed. This was what the stranger had come for: to make her understand the duplicity of her world, the difference between what was seen and what was true.

She looked up at him again. In spite of everything, she wished he couldn't see her crying. She wished she could be at her best, so that he would see she was not just a pale, tearful child.

He put a hand on her shoulder. His braided jacket gave off a clean, comforting smell.

"They told me you were becoming a beautiful woman," he said. "I see they were right."

She did not move. She was afraid if she moved she might start to sob, and then the stranger would see how weak she was, and be disappointed.

"I'm leaving for the front tomorrow," he said. "I just wanted to see you before I left."

He looked at her for a moment more, then turned and walked out of the room. Zoia wanted to call him back, to say she was sorry, to have him tell her everything. But she couldn't move. She couldn't move, or speak.

The echo of his footsteps grew faint in the corridor.

She knew she would never see him again.

8

———————•———————

Saltsjöbaden, February 2000.

He closes his eyes, and all he sees is gold. It's moving now, like blistered skin, a membrane stretched over living tissue. Then, up close, it's different: congealed, granular, streaked with dirt and decay. He catches faces reflected in pitted metal.

His father hated the *Chinese Princess* from the moment he set eyes on her. The picture seemed to enrage him. He told Elliot's mother he didn't want it in the house. He told her to take it back where it came from.

He heard them fighting in the kitchen, screams that resonated in the walls, in the floorboards. He was eight years old, sitting on the stairs, too scared to come down. He could hear her crying, sobbing. He never thought her capable of that, capable of such terrible despair.

Something crashed against the door. Wood splintered. He covered his ears, trying to wish it all away.

"Stop it stop it stop it."

But they didn't stop. All because of a picture. A portrait on gold. Because of something it meant.

"Stop it stop it stop it stop it *stop it.*"

He shouted, tears streaming, but they didn't come to him. They didn't even hear. He didn't exist for them anymore. He was just a ghost on the stairs, a dream child, screaming, but making no sound.

He kicks off the sheets, throws himself on his back, sees a different picture now: the *Vase of Poppies,* the blood-red petals on their twisted stems, a woman in a fur coat bidding like she's going to have it no matter what, the rings on her fingers sparkling as she waves the rolled-up catalog above her freshly coiffured head.

Mid-auction. The moment he knows. That squeeze in his gut that tells him a corner has been turned. Somehow or other the word is out. A collectability threshold has been crossed. A star of French cinema—Isabelle This or Emmanuelle That—has a Korvin-Krukovsky in her Paris apartment, a fact recorded in *Paris Match*. It's hard for living artists to command good prices, hard to generate the mystique, but Zoia was always secretive. And she isn't going to be alive much longer.

Cornelius stands at the back of the room, bouncing up and down on the balls of his feet. A shiny grin lights up his face as the auctioneer smacks down the gavel on a Korvin-Krukovsky record. He's been quietly championing Zoia's work for years, has always seen its market potential. Now at last he's gathering it all up in the Bukowskis vault, vindication and generous bonuses in prospect, maybe even the cash he needs to set up on his own.

He wasn't at the funeral though. *Multiple organ failure after a battle with cancer.* There wasn't a window in his schedule for that final farewell. Strange behavior for an initiate, if that's what he really is. Or is that a sentimental view? From the dealer's standpoint, Zoia's long-awaited death is a cause for celebration.

He wishes the papers weren't still in her house. That he didn't have to work there, alone.

Without the covers it's cold. He squeezes his eyes shut, tries to listen to his breathing. But sleep won't come.

It was a mistake, skipping the Mogadon. Recently he's found it doesn't work so well, or at least works differently. Instead of unconsciousness he gets sweats and bad dreams that have him continually lurching awake. It was the same with the other benzodiazepines, the Tropium and the Somnite. At first oblivion, then growing restlessness, visions and dread pushing up through the narcotic foglike weeds through cement. He hoped the flight and the early starts would be enough to knock him out. He thought the fresh Baltic air would clear his head. But at the Majestic the windows don't open without a special key. And something about Cornelius's scheme has him churned up inside. He feels complicit in something without knowing what it is.

Cornelius had sent him money ahead of time: one thousand pounds to help cover expenses. Good old Cornelius.

Somewhere in the hotel a fan is on. The hum of the motor funnels down the hollow plasterboard walls. Elliot rolls over again and stares at the clock, thinking now of the room where the *Chinese Princess* used to hang, thinking of the small red mouth and the languid, watchful stare.

He wishes he had never found that picture—portrait or self-portrait, it's all the same. He wishes it had never existed.

9

He drew up outside the gate and switched the engine off. He sat for a long time, looking at the house through the tangle of swaying branches. The wind had worn the footprints on the driveway into faint depressions, as if years had gone by instead of a day. It gusted around the chimneys, making spirals of powdery snow that drifted past the eaves.

It seemed different this time: lower, hunkered down, blank gaze turned toward the sea. Just an empty house. Nothing in it but dusty furniture and boxes of old letters.

Dr. Lindqvist hadn't been at home that morning. He had been called away unexpectedly to Uppsala. Agda Lindqvist, who turned out to be his sister, gave Elliot the keys and written instructions on how to make the house habitable. That was the arrangement: Elliot would pick up the key every morning, and return it every evening. It was the only key he had, the doctor had explained, and he could not risk losing it.

The truth, of course, was that Lindqvist didn't trust him. But that was fine. Lindqvist struck Elliot as the kind of man who didn't trust anyone.

He grabbed his briefcase and got out of the car. It was cold, a couple of degrees below zero according to the dashboard thermometer. But this time he had equipped himself with a ski hat and a muffler from the sports apparel shop in the lobby of the Grand Hotel. He climbed over the fence, and picked his way toward the house. The snow had developed a crust that gave way without warning, plunging him up to his shins. He battled on, keeping up a good pace, wanting to get to work, wanting to focus on the job in hand.

A few yards from the kitchen door he stopped and looked up at the windows. The curtains were all drawn, except in the window beneath the roof, where Venetian blinds hung unevenly, bunched on one side and spread wide on the other. A draft had them swaying a little, the wooden slats tapping against the glass.

Elliot hesitated, then set off to the front of the house where Dr. Lindqvist had made his phone call, and found the place where he had walked up and down. A little drift of snow had gathered on the balcony above. Nothing stirred but the pines.

He hunched his shoulders and headed back toward the kitchen, turning the key over and over in his pocket. Beyond the trees, the icy gray sea slapped and rolled against the rocks.

He wondered if the place had changed much in thirty years.

As a boy he had believed in ghosts for a long time. For him they were as much a part of the real world as the planets and the Milky Way—not the ghosts of comic books or black and white films, the kind that wore sheets or period costume and glowed in the dark, but a different kind. These ghosts were people.

He hardly ever saw them. They could not be seen because they were almost never in the same room as you. They occupied the spaces you had left behind, or were yet to enter. They watched you from the shadows, and whispered to you in your dreams. And only sometimes—as in that split second between sleeping and waking—could you see them, standing before you with their backs to the light. You sensed their presence the way you remembered something important you had forgotten to do, with a jolt to the heart.

After his mother had died, he would run the taps in the bath, and then go to his bedroom. He would get undressed and put on his bathrobe, and by the time the tub was half full, and there was steam drifting out into the corridor, he would know that she was in there.

He would go and stand outside the door, open it an inch or two, enough that he could breathe in the smell of her pale skin and the perfume on her clothes, enough to hear the faint rustle of her dress. And if he closed his eyes, he could hear her humming gently to herself as she stood in front of the mirror, tying up her long blonde hair.

At night she would come and stand beside his bed when he was lying curled up under the blankets. He never turned to look at her, but he knew she was there. Sometimes she held a letter in her hand, the letter she had left on her dressing table, the one his father had burned before the inquest. In his dreams he took the letter and tried to read it. But the words were always unintelligible, and the harder he tried to read them the more violently he would wake up. It was a letter written in a language he did not have the means or the learning to interpret.

He never told his father about his mother's visits. He assumed he already knew about them, and that when he sat in silence by the fire, staring into the flames until the logs were spent, he knew she was there in the kitchen, moving back and forward between the oven and the sink. If he said nothing about it, it was because it was better that way. Ghosts were people you didn't speak about. In any case, he didn't live with his father for long. When he was nine years old, Elliot was sent to live with his aunt and uncle in Scotland.

There, for some reason, the ghosts would not follow, although there were times when he wished they would.

He went through the rooms one by one. Rugs had been rolled up and stored in the corners. The shelves and mantels had been cleared of ornaments, except for some pewter candlesticks and a bowl of seashells on a windowsill. There were dust sheets over everything. The white, sepulchral forms reminded him of childhood, of hide-and-seek in his grandmother's house, kneeling in the attic in the musty darkness, hardly daring to breathe, listening to the creak of floorboards draw closer and closer. In the dining room, a delicate green and white chandelier had been draped with muslin. One solitary upright chair, at the head of the table, had been uncovered—by Lindqvist, he assumed, the old man checking out his inheritance. Certainly the doctor, or perhaps his taciturn sister, had been back since the previous morning, because the tin can and the bottle opener he had seen on the kitchen table had both been cleared away.

Elliot drew back the curtains. First in the dining room, then everywhere. He hummed to himself, groping for a tune and not finding one. Little by little the house filled with pale winter light.

Zoia had wanted to make one last trip back to Saltsjöbaden a few weeks before she died. It was something Peter Lindqvist had said—or rather, had let slip—as they drove back from the house. She had wanted to go back for a day or so, but the doctors had forbidden it. Elliot had wanted to know more, but Lindqvist had declined to oblige, batting away his questions with a shrug and a shake of the head.

Elliot wondered if it had something to do with the letters, whether it hadn't been Zoia's intention to destroy them then. And when the doctors had told her it was impossible for her to go, she had asked Lindqvist to do the job for her. But, for some reason, he had let her down.

Zoia's studio was at the top of the house. Even from the landing he could smell the oil paint and the turpentine. She had another, bigger studio above her apartment in the city, in a building she once shared with Isaac Grünewald, the pupil and devotee of Matisse. But this was where she had worked in the summer months.

He climbed the last flight of stairs, saw bare, white walls and a skylight up in the roof. A big picture window looked out across the treetops toward the easternmost reaches of the bay.

He drew closer, saw his breath flare against the glass. Over the water the seabirds soared and dived, their cries catching like laughter on the wind. This was the forbidden room, the room where Zoia had worked unobserved. In Stockholm people sometimes called on her unexpectedly, and she was always too polite to turn them away. In Stockholm she had sitters. But not here. Here it was just the paintings and her. Conversations of a different kind. Initiates only.

He turned, found himself staring at the back of a large, sturdy easel. It stood square in the middle of the room, a wooden panel fixed in place. Behind it were tables and shelves crammed with bottles of turpentine, white spirit, and jam jars full of brushes. It was as if he had just walked into the frame, into the composition: *Portrait of a Man by the Window*. As if Zoia herself were standing there, brush in hand.

He went around the other side of the easel. The panel had already been gilded. Looking up close, he could just make out the square sheets of leaf—the traditional four fingers' width—that she had used. From a certain angle the overlaps made pale, jagged bars that ran the length of the picture. But there was no image, not a single trace of pigment. He looked up close, searching for marks or indentations that might reveal something about the intended subject. But there was nothing, just his own shadow moving over the glimmering surface.

The lowest of the shelves was crammed with old books and gallery catalogs. A battered English translation of Cennino Cennini's *Il Libro dell' Arte* was wedged between a tome on orchids and a monograph on Vincent van Gogh.

Elliot had come across Cennini's treatise as a student. It was thought to have been written in Tuscany around 1390. It covered everything from the preparation of surfaces, and the making of paints and brushes, to gilding, varnishing, mosaic, and wider issues concerning the artist's life. It was Cennini who had advised the young artist not to indulge too much in the company of women, on the grounds that it would leave his hand "so unsteady it will waver and tremble more than leaves in the wind."

Elliot flipped open the book, found himself looking at a passage underlined in pencil.

The painter must develop both imagination and dexterity, his purpose to discover things not seen, things hidden beneath the shadow of natural objects, and to fix them with the hand, presenting to plain sight what does not actually exist.

The oil-fired boiler was in a spidery lean-to at the side of the house. He was in there, trying to make it work, when Cornelius Wallander rang him on the mobile.

"Any luck with the Paris self-portrait? Did you have a good look through the papers?"

The papers were still in the bureau.

"No sign of anything so far. What makes you think she kept her business records out here?"

"There wasn't much at the apartment, that's all. We went right through the place. There were some sale papers, but not what we were looking for."

Elliot squinted at the instructions Lindqvist had given him. As far as he could tell, the boiler should have been working already.

"I'll keep an eye out. It's a big house. Maybe something'll turn up."

Cornelius sighed. "We could really use that picture. The whole Foujita angle's proving a big draw."

Elliot wiped the soot off his hands with a handkerchief. "What makes you say that?"

"I heard the Museum of Contemporary Art in Tokyo are planning to send a buyer. And the Hirano Masakichi have been making inquiries. They both have big Foujita collections. David Van Buhren has been sniffing around, and I already told you about the Art Institute of Chicago."

The previous November, at Sotheby's New York, a Foujita self-portrait dating from 1926—watercolor, oil, gold leaf, and ink on silk—had been sold to a private collector for $1.5 million. It was not a record. *Jeune Fille dans le Parc* had fetched $5.5 million at Christie's in 1990. But prewar Foujitas came on the market only rarely, and the success of the sale was bound to have raised interest in other artists of the Foujita circle, not least his one and only pupil. Just how far was only now becoming clear.

"You think the self-portrait's all they're interested in?"

"I hope not. But it would certainly be the crown jewel, as far as they're concerned. Especially with the doubts over attribution."

Elliot himself had no such doubts. As far as he could see, the Paris self-portrait was plainly the work of the pupil, not the master. True, the hands were Foujita hands, long white and slender, but the eyes—feline, watchful—could only have been Zoia's.

Elliot kept his opinion to himself.

"So have you found anything in the papers?" Cornelius said.

Elliot flicked the ON switch again, with the same result. He noticed a stack of logs and bunches of twigs at the far end of the room, and remembered the big stove up in the sitting room.

"Not yet, but I've hardly begun. There's a mass of stuff to go through, much more than I'd expected. Just sorting it into some kind of order'll be quite a job."

"Well, don't get bogged down. A little insight is all we're looking for. A little color."

"Yes, of course."

"The color in question being gold." Cornelius chuckled.

"That's what I want to focus on," Elliot said. "I want to know what drove her to paint on precious metals. I can't help thinking there was something compulsive about it."

Cornelius drew breath at the word "compulsive."

"Well, I thought that was clear, Marcus, wasn't it? You read the cuttings I sent you."

"Yes, of course, but—"

"And the Savva Leskov essay?"

"Yes, I read them. I'm just not sure . . . You see, I've always had this sense that . . ."

"That what?"

Elliot hesitated.

"Well, I was thinking: Was Zoia really so political? A torchbearer for the old Russia, and all that. I know that's how people talk about her, Leskov and the others, but did she ever make those claims herself?"

"Why should she? The artist creates; the critics interpret. It's a question of demarcation."

"But suppose the critics are wrong? Suppose her pictures aren't as . . . *public* as they seem?"

The wind gusted against the house. Timber creaked against timber. Whenever he closed his eyes, he could hear footsteps moving across the bare boards.

"Marcus, they're on gold, for heaven's sake. How much more public can you get?"

"The choice of medium doesn't . . . What if there's something *else* going on? Something—"

"Marcus, we don't have time for—"

"Something no one's seen yet? Wouldn't that be worth—?"

Above him a door bumped shut. Interference crackled on the line. Elliot was suddenly aware of how unprofessional he was sounding.

There was a pause.

"So . . . you want the Bukowskis catalog to say that Savva Leskov, and everyone else, have missed the point where Zoia is concerned." Cornelius was trying to make a joke of it, and doing even worse than usual. "That they are, in fact, completely wrong about . . . *everything*. And we have to start all over again."

The incredulity was straining his voice. Leskov, the scholar and critic of thirty years' standing, regaled with honors from Moscow to Massachusetts, versus Elliot, failed art dealer turned writer of catalogs. It was obviously not a contest.

"Zoia was married to a Communist for sixteen years. Surely that doesn't fit the profile."

"She married Karl Kilbom to escape from Russia. She didn't have any choice. And the marriage was a disaster. First chance she got she ran away to Paris, to Foujita and his crowd. Marcus, it's *all* in the articles, all the . . . *interpretation* you need."

Cornelius's impatience was surprising, disconcerting. It was as if he had some huge personal stake in tying Zoia as firmly as possible to imperial Russia. But then, with all that post-Communist money knocking on Bukowskis' door, perhaps that was exactly the case. In any case Elliot wasn't qualified to interpret Zoia's work. He lacked the authority. His job was to assemble and log: names, dates, places. The interpretation had already been taken care of.

Cornelius was an ally he could not afford to lose. And, when all was said and done, what did it matter what people thought? Living artists had an awkward habit of belying what was said of them, often willfully. They resented and resisted categorization, because the process, by definition, stood in denial of the very things they most prized in their work: its uniqueness, its individuality. But there was no danger of Zoia objecting to anything. She had only her papers to speak for her, and they were in safe hands, beyond prying eyes.

All the same, it was a special kind of oblivion to be remembered as someone you never were.

"You're right. All I meant was, it would be good to have it in the artist's own words: her love of Russia, her determination to preserve an ancient tradition."

"Which is exactly what I sent you out there for, Marcus. I'm glad we understand each other."

"Sure. Of course."

"So my advice is: start with Foujita. He's very bankable at the moment."

"Foujita. Right."

"And look, if you get lonely out there, just come on back to Stockholm for an evening, and we'll have dinner or something, all right?"

Cornelius was conciliatory now, as if sensitive to the possibility of wounded feelings.

"Thanks. I may take you up on that. It's a shame Lindqvist won't let me take anything away, though. I don't understand it."

Cornelius was already talking to someone else.

"Neither do I. Still, he's the client here, Marcus, when it comes down to it. And the client is always right, right?"

10

They were love letters. Letters and drafts of letters, in Russian, French, German, Swedish, English. They were written on postcards, on water-marked stationery, on pages torn from notebooks and diaries. They were scrawled on the backs of hotel bills and restaurant menus, or squeezed into the white space around theater programs. Some were signed, dated, and addressed. Others gave no clue as to the identity of author or recipient, as if written only for the sake of writing, with no intention that they should ever be read. Some affected detachment and *froideur,* like a dressing on an open wound, the pain and anger bleeding through. Others overflowed with desire, and hopes of a new beginning in some future time and place.

There were letters written on ships and in railway carriages, in hospitals and safe houses. There were letters written in bureaucratic type or gouged into the paper with an unsteady hand. There were letters from New York, London, and Moscow, from Paris and Berlin, from Kazakh-stan, Tunis, Algiers. They numbered in the hundreds, a secret archive of love.

Elliot had expectations of the letters. The moment Cornelius mentioned them, it had been like a piece snapping into place. In those boxes, in these papers, still unread and untranslated, he would find what he needed. The intangible would be rendered material. Zoia had infected his life, but now at last the nature and origins of that infection would become explicit, comprehensible.

He would sell the self-portrait as the final, cleansing act.

But the papers were older than he'd expected. Most seemed to have been written between the wars. What he wanted most were letters from the 1960s and 1970s—1970, above all: the year Zoia parted with the *Chinese Princess in Paris,* the year she sold it, leaving no record of the deal. But there was nothing from that time.

He ran through the boxes again, moving them one by one from the desk to the floor. The archive petered out with a clutch of printed invitation cards and newspaper cuttings from the 1950s. If there had been papers from later years, they had been removed.

He lit the stove using the wood from the boiler room and some old rags he found beneath the kitchen sink. At first it gave off just enough heat to keep his fingers warm. He pulled the dust sheet off a chaise longue and moved it closer. It was already getting dark. He watched the light of the fire play on the wall where the self-portrait used to hang. He pictured it there again, the seated figure fixed against shimmering, golden flames.

A figure in hell.

He fished a picture out of the cigar box: Zoia in a polka-dot dress and sunglasses snapped outside a casino, slick-haired men in livery looking on. Zoia liked casinos. She admired men who gambled audaciously. It appealed to the aristocrat in her, to live and not heed the consequences. Aristocrats were supposed to wear their fortunes lightly, and their losses too.

He pinned the picture to the wall. Zoia posed with marble calm, her chin slightly raised. Neither smile nor frown. Looking at her, he felt self-conscious, a boyish intruder in a grown-up world. How much money had she just lost at the tables? Or had the photograph been taken in celebration of a win? He looked into her eyes but he couldn't tell.

She was mocking him. She was mocking his simpleton plan. Zoia was born to the court of an emperor-god. She didn't leave the keys to her life lying around where anyone might find them. Bolsheviks thought the inner self was their legitimate province, public property to be managed, probed, dissected. To them, private thoughts were as suspect as private capital: individualist, bourgeois, prone to dissent and reaction. But Zoia was not a Bolshevik. She had only married one.

Cornelius had told him to focus on the Foujita angle; the 1920s, a decade Zoia spent in and out of Paris, a decade that gave birth to the paintings on gold. It made sense from all points of view, not just the commercial one. It was the decade that culminated in Zoia's one and only self-portrait, if that's what it was: a picture you could not see without knowledge, without being there when it was made. Except that no one was ever allowed to get that close.

Kneeling before the stove, he began to read, pale flames dancing behind the paper. He pulled down the lid on the bureau, and went on reading there. What he needed was a system, and space to work it. A system would reveal the patterns, and the patterns would reveal the artist. He would uncover what Zoia did not trust the world to understand. And he would be the first.

In the first box he found a collection of letters in Russian, written in a frostily elegant hand. They were from Zoia's mother: mostly from Moscow to Stockholm, some from the Crimea to Moscow. Some of them dated from a few months before Zoia left Russia. They seemed to be mostly about money, about what she was selling to stay alive, and how everything in Russia was getting more and more expensive.

He went back down to the boiler room and fetched a stack of logs. He piled the wood up neatly in the corner, then went back for more. He moved through the house making as much noise as possible, banging doors, pounding up and down the stairs. He wished he could put on music. He would have liked to have filled the house with sound.

He took the dust sheet off the table, folded out the leaves and lined up the boxes of letters along the back for ease of access. He plugged in his computer and took out the rest of the photographs and spread them on the desk.

Zoia, transfigured by motion and sunlight, stood by her easel, next to the man holding the cine camera. *Kristoffer and Zoia at work.* She was wearing overalls with the sleeves rolled up, and there was something sticking out of her top pocket, a knife of some kind, with a small, pale blade like a fang. There were dark smudges of paint all over her fingers, and up one of her arms. If it weren't for the lack of a carcass, she could have been mistaken for a butcher, caught in the process of plying her trade. Her friends had surprised her, perhaps wanting some share of the secrets she had learned in Paris and Florence.

Even back then, people sensed that she was holding something back. Zoia, every inch the Russian aristocrat: distant, egocentric, aloof, keeping even her audience at arm's length. She was everything the currents of her time were against, culturally, politically. She was an anachronism at nineteen years old.

He stared into her face. There was something surreal in the blur of motion, as if she didn't wholly belong to that one time and place. A spirit in transit.

Most of the other pictures were of men: young men, handsome men, posing in studios or captured outdoors, in the street, in cafés, on the decks of ships. They had flawless skin and bright, focused eyes. Some of the prints had stamp marks on the back, identifying the studio where they were processed. A handful had dates scrawled in ink. Only a couple had names: Alain was maybe twenty-one, with an olive complexion and dark, Levantine features. Jan was older, conspicuously care-worn. He stood outside a roadside café, his hands stuffed into the pockets of an ill-fitting suit, smiling doubtfully into the camera. The pictures of women were few.

He propped the pictures up along the back of the bureau, Zoia in the middle, flanked by her men.

Zoia was on her second husband by the age of eighteen. Yuri, a law student she married in Moscow, was the first, but that liaison only lasted a couple of years. Karl Kilbom, the Communist politician and agitator, came next. But the letters made it clear that there were lovers too.

A Russian poet called Sandro sent verses from the Caucasus. An English screenwriter called Jack Orton wrote jealously from film sets in London and Stockholm. An artist called Oscar—Oscar Björck, perhaps, whose portrait of Zoia hung in the National Museum—asked her to send him pictures of herself undressed. There was a Russian emigré called Kolya who worked in the restaurant business. He wrote of how he dreamed of escaping together to a place where the world could not find them.

And there were others. It was hard keeping track of them, even harder sorting one from the other. Correspondences overlapped. Sometimes there were only initials to go by, at other times only signatures illegibly scrawled. Nicknames and pet names were another impediment to clarity. Zoia kept drafts without names or dates. Elliot began making lists, then the lists became index cards, bearing dates and details.

In Biarritz, Zoia had a fling with an unnamed South American whose parents had sent him to Europe after a scandal involving a married woman. Alain turned out to be an art student Zoia had met in Paris. Jan was a German architect by the name of Ruhtenberg, a one-time colleague of Mies van der Rohe at the Bauhaus. There was a sculptor called Stig Bloomberg, who fell for Zoia some time before her first exhibition. There was Andrei Burov, a Soviet architect, whose haunted, jealous correspondence spanned the whole period.

Elliot read and skimmed. He compared handwriting and dates. He started logging the letters on the computer. The room at last grew warm. Expanding joists made bumping, scuffling sounds. A house coming back to life.

Jealousy and devotion. Hopes of reunion. Betrayal. Guilt. Zoia's lovers were men whose eyes had been opened, who could never again see the world as they had. She had awoken something in them, something time and distance could never fully extinguish. It was said Karl Kilbom saw Zoia only once before her arrest, when she was working as an interpreter for the Communist International. The second time they met, almost a year later, they were already engaged. Even Yuri, the student-husband she left for Karl, went on writing to her for years afterward, letters from sana- toriums in Germany and government jobs in central Asia.

Zoia exerted a kind of fascination. She entered men's lives and every- thing changed. There was something in her spirit, her complexity, they couldn't live without. Her love was transfiguring. It painted the world in vibrant colors. Solemn vows before God and the law didn't stand a chance.

Here was a reason to keep the letters close, a reason to destroy them too, if posterity was an issue: hers was a catalog not of love, but of betrayal.

How was that going to play with Cornelius and his Russian clients: Zoia Korvin-Krukovsky, guardian of Slavic culture and serial adulterer? How would that sit with a torchbearer of Holy Russia?

Andrei Burov's letters had been separated from the others. They were tied together with a ribbon, and wrapped in a brown paper envelope.

The pattern was different. The letters began when Zoia was still in Russia, and ended where the collection did. Months, even years went by in silence, but then the correspondence would begin again, passion undi- minished, if anything intensified by the knowledge of time already lost. When Zoia married Karl his letters were sarcastic and boastful. They were at their most ecstatic when her affections were supposedly unattached.

There was another difference: among Andrei's letters were letters Zoia had sent to him; not drafts or copies, but the originals. Somehow they had come back to her.

Andrei was more than an architect. His talents ranged into art direc- tion for the cinema and the stage. In the early 1920s he became a protégé of Vsevolod Meyerhold, the head of the theater department at the Commissariat for Enlightenment. Elliot knew of Meyerhold. A cultural ideologue of the postrevolutionary years, he had preached the gospel of symbolism, and his belief in the transcendent power of machines. He supported the Reds when they nationalized the theaters in 1917 and, with their help, launched a revolution of his own against the old naturalist conventions of Russian theater, inviting audiences onto the stage to literally tear down the fabric of the traditional proscenium arch.

Meyerhold said that actors should not look inside themselves for the truth of their characters, as Stanislavski had taught. That approach, he said, was sentimental bilge. They should abandon individual expression altogether, in favor of a standardized vocabulary of movement, like gymnasts, or production-line workers. Meyerhold fed the Bolshevik fetish for machinery and industrial production.

Andrei fell in with Meyerhold's ideas. He embraced the new aesthetics and the ideology that went with them. It seemed he was highly regarded by the commissars. They showered him with prizes and sent him on missions to Europe and the U.S.A. He shared their contempt for the old ways, and their enthusiasm for a world in which man and machine would move ever closer to harmonious union. The old ways were selfish, sentimental, and unambitious. The future would be one of heroic collective endeavor, mechanized, rational, chromium-plated. Capable of banishing every human ill with the sheer force of its efficiency.

It was hard to see where Zoia fit in. It was hard to see her and Andrei as anything but enemies. If Cornelius had it right, their assumptions, their points of reference, were diametrically opposed: the courtier and the Bolshevik, one devoted to the preservation of a mystical Russia, the other sworn to destroy it. Yet their letters, punctuated by time and distance, were full of love.

13th February 1928

Dearest Andrei,

Today is my Saint's day, and of course no one here celebrates it. So your letter, which I received this morning, was a wonderful and unexpected gift.

You ask what we should do about the time we have lost. I don't know how you guessed that this is what troubles me, but it does

*more than anything. Lying in bed at night, seeing myself as an
adult now, I look at the past six years and I'm filled with horror
and disgust. And not some passing feeling, but something hard and
cold that sits inside me, and never leaves me for a single moment.*

*Andrusha, at least I know your time has not been wasted. You
have your work and your ambitions, whereas about my work it's
better if I keep silent. I have wasted so much time. And all my life,
all my traveling, has changed nothing. When I stand before the
easel, this dark mood comes upon me and all I want to do is hide.
As for love, this is the one thing that never leaves me in peace—or
rather the absence of love. Because I search for it day and night,
and put into that search every ounce of strength I possess. And then
when I find it, I run from it, or destroy it, and so it goes on forever.*

*I know I should start over again, from the beginning. I know I
should start a new life. What I have lost has turned me into a
beggar, and that is at the heart of the disgust I feel. But how can I
build a life without foundations? Andrusha, can you understand all
the sadness and bitterness of this confession? I am so weak in my
heart and my soul. I have no strength to fight with life all over
again, although strength is what I need now more than ever.*

*Maybe it's useless. Maybe we cannot simply turn our backs on
all the wasted years, and it's pointless to try.*

*Andrei, you say I haven't replied to your letters, but that's not
true. I have, and I repeat that when I read of your success and
happiness, then I feel the same: I feel your youth and strength and
joy—the very things I need myself.*

*Andrusha, I want to believe that we will never be separated
from each other, that we will never lose what we share deep inside
ourselves, and that one day we will make of it something beautiful.
And then at last we shall be who we should have been, and the past
will be at rest.*

He woke suddenly to darkness. Somewhere a bell was ringing, an old-
fashioned electric bell, like the one his parents used to have on the side of
their house. It took him a moment to realize it was a telephone.

He got up, a stark dream clearing from his head—a picture of a young woman screaming behind a green paneled door. His heart was pounding.

The stove had gone out, but for a line of red embers in the grate. The room was cold again. He hit a key on his computer, bringing the screen back to life. It shed enough light for him to reach the door.

He stumbled out onto the landing, looking for the landline. He guessed it was Dr. Lindqvist calling, wanting to know what he was doing there so late, although it was strange he hadn't used the mobile number.

He found a switch. Yellow light filled the stairwell. He hurried down to the hall, thinking there'd been a phone down there, but when he got there, he found nothing.

The phone went on ringing, long single rings separated by even longer silences. He checked the kitchen, then the dining room. Zoia had put ringers on every floor. The whole house seemed to shake.

The phone was under a dust sheet on the sideboard, an old 1960s model with a row of clear plastic buttons along the top.

"Hello?"

There was nothing but the sound of dead air.

He tried a couple of buttons. "Dr. Lindqvist? Hello?"

But he was too late. The caller had already hung up. He put his finger in the cradle and heard the line clear.

He checked his watch: nine o'clock. Already too late to ring Teresa.

He took a deep breath. The caller had probably been a salesman or the phone company, wanting to know why the bills hadn't been paid. He headed back up the stairs, aware now of the silence, the sound of his own steps on the floorboards, the wind catching on the corners of the house. He felt a draft against his face. Somewhere a door or window had blown open.

He went back into the sitting room and disconnected the computer from the light socket. He was hungry and cold, and Dr. Lindqvist would be expecting his key back.

He screwed the bulb back in and stepped down from the chair, only then seeing it, only then realizing with a sickening jolt what had happened.

The desk was in chaos. Two of the boxes had been knocked down, their contents scattered, all order lost. Letters, read and unread, lay strewn across the floor.

He stood for a moment, feeling cold air against his neck, hearing the cinders hiss in the stove.

"Who's *there?*"

He only said it to hear the sound of his voice.

With a sucking noise one of the french windows swung open. Papers flipped over at his feet. Then it closed again with a shuddering bang.

Elliot almost laughed out loud. There was something wrong with the catch, that was all. He took a closer look: sure enough, the fitting had come loose. One of the screws that held it in place was missing.

Some sheets of thin blue paper were snagged in the jamb. He stooped to pick them up, saw handwriting in pencil, cramped, jagged letters punctuated with whiplike curls and laterals. Russian. Close to illegible.

A letter from Yuri, the law student Zoia had married at sixteen and divorced two years later. Her youthful mistake.

April 1924. Three years after the event, five years before the Paris self-portrait. It was a letter he'd set aside without reading.

. . . My dearest Zoia, you told me of the impact my letters have on your life. Believe me, since I got your first letter and was able to answer it, my life had changed completely too. Every sentence gives me another little part of you, and, like a child, I read it over and over, digesting, feeling every word. And you know it's not like me to feel anything so intensely. You say I should be stronger, and more resolute. And you are right. I am not strong—because of you. You are my weakness.

Whatever men strive for in their lives, whatever the direction, at the end there always stands a woman, whether alive or imaginary, flesh or idol. These two years of hardship, of self-denial and long toiling hours, I too have had in front of me the image of a woman. But until now, I was afraid to admit to myself whose image it was.

These days I am too practical a man to believe that destiny will take me step by step into the future I want. Your letters make me happy, and I want to show you what I feel, what I have been storing up for you all this time. But we are not children anymore, as we were in Moscow, imagining that somehow our future will take care of itself, because it is meant to be.

My darling, sometimes I tell myself how lucky we are. Just think of the horrors and the dangers we have left behind us, and how often our very existence—mine especially—was under threat. And look! At the end of it all we are still alive. But all the same, I'm haunted by the memory of what I did in Russia. And the worst part of it is the thought that you still reproach me too. My only hope is that you still return a small part of the feelings I have for you. Tell me I have your understanding and that you can forgive me.

11

The wind had veered around to the south, and sleet was falling. He put on the wipers, squinting through the smeary windscreen as they thumped back and forth. Beside the road the pine trees stood in ranks, symbols and numbers daubed on their fibrous trunks.

Knowledge was a force at his back. Already he knew what no one else knew. And it was just a scrap, a fragment of the whole. He was a traveler, stumbling on an ancient tomb, the seals unbroken, its secrets intact.

He reached Dr. Lindqvist's house, put the key through the letterbox, and headed back to the center of town. A gritting lorry was trundling toward the hotel as he approached, orange lights strobing the street. Elliot changed down a gear and moved out to overtake.

The gritting lorry hit the horn.

There was a car coming the other way, dim yellow headlamps barely visible through the sleet.

He tried to cut back behind the lorry, but he was already too far ahead. He braced himself against the wheel, hit the brakes, felt the wheels slide on ice.

The other car lurched to a halt. The truck slowed. Suddenly everyone was letting him go by, waiting there on the road, watching him: the idiot who couldn't drive.

He held up a hand by way of apology, but if there was any response from the other driver he couldn't see it. The car was a white Volkswagen Polo, one of the older models. As it drove away, he caught the silhouette of a woman in the mirror.

The receptionist emerged from the back office, chewing. A sour junkfood smell wafted across the lobby. The PA system was playing some song by The Carpenters, arranged for string orchestra.

"A good day, Mr. Elliot?"

The receptionist's complexion wore a waxy sheen.

"Yes, thank you. Do you know if there are any restaurants still open around here?"

The receptionist frowned and checked his watch. He hadn't changed his shirt since yesterday: there were grimy marks around the collar.

"They've stopped serving at the Grand by now. There are bar snacks in your room."

Peanuts and orange juice, chased down with vodka at eight quid a shot.

"Thank you."

Elliot headed for the stairs.

"Oh, Mr. Elliot, did you see the young lady on your way in?"

Elliot turned. "The young lady?"

The receptionist gestured toward the doors. There was a faint blush on his tapioca cheeks.

"She was just here a minute ago. She asked for you by name."

There had obviously been some mistake.

"For me? I don't think . . . What was her name?"

The receptionist shrugged apologetically, although there was a suggestion in his voice that the question was somehow unreasonable. "She didn't give her name. I told her you're not in, and she left."

"She didn't leave a message?"

The receptionist shook his head slowly. It came to Elliot that he had already reached the conclusion that the woman was a prostitute, and that for some reason the assignation had been botched.

Elliot's thoughts shifted to Cornelius. Was it possible he had sent someone over? Apart from Dr. Lindqvist, he was the only person who knew where he was. Was it possible the woman *was* a prostitute?

The car, the white Polo. He had seen it before: outside Bukowskis the evening he arrived. There had been a woman behind the wheel. And when he had come out of the place, looking for a taxi, she had come after him. She wore a parka with the hood up to hide her face.

"What did she look like?"

The receptionist seemed to think the question was funny.

"Well, pretty. Short hair, dark. Like, er . . ." He smiled again. "Like Jennifer Jason Leigh."

"Jennifer Jason . . . ?"

"Leigh. *Single White Female? Dolores Claiborne?*"

Elliot frowned. This was what the boy did all day when business was slow: he watched thriller videos in the back office.

"I think I know who you mean."

The receptionist grinned, obviously a fan.

"She plays these crazy women. Complicated, you know." He caught the look on Elliot's face. Slowly the smile vanished. "Anyway. That's what she looked like, sort of."

In the room, he went to the window without turning on the lights. He checked up and down the street. There was no sign of the Volkswagen. The thought came to him that this had something to do with Nadia and her expensive new lawyer: surveillance of the opposing spouse, all part of the service. But that was crazy. He couldn't be sure he had seen the same car twice. Probably he hadn't. The Jason Leigh lookalike was a friend of Cornelius's, or maybe of Dr. Lindqvist's. He watched a couple more cars go by, then pulled the curtains closed.

With the lights back on, he fixed himself a vodka from the mini-bar. Heightened states induced paranoia. It was something he had read. Alertness meant alertness to danger, and among dangers was always the possibility of betrayal. When Nadia's unfaithfulness had become known to him, for example, he had begun to see deception and conspiracy in everything she did. Worse than that, he had gone back and reinterpreted everything from their past in the light of that same betrayal; so that, in the end, it had become impossible to see their relationship as anything but an illusion. The con artist and the mark, one with secret knowledge, the other with a head full of dreams.

The trouble was, it was hard to dismiss feelings as paranoid without having access to the facts. Like when exactly Nadia decided she was going to leave, and take Teresa with her. It was a question he still couldn't answer.

He sat on the bed, the lip of the glass tapping against his teeth, breathing in the alcohol, going back over it all as he had a thousand times, searching for the truth, for that moment when Nadia and he had become enemies, when love had inexplicably turned to hate.

His arrest had nothing to do with her. He was pretty sure about that. The issue was: Who had told the *Evening Standard?*

The headline was one he would remember for the rest of his life: VAT MAN FOILS ICON CON. The five and a half column inches underneath were all it took to destroy him. Never mind that the charges were dropped for lack of evidence, or that misvaluation of imported works was an everyday occurrence in the antiques trade. The suggestion that he had been connected to the Russian mafia, that he had deliberately misidentified valuable works of art to evade export restrictions, was enough. In the time it took him to get back to business, his client base evaporated. Even items of incontrovertible provenance would not sell. A few months on, he was forced to dump his whole stock at auction, for much less than he'd paid for it.

The thing was, the VAT man didn't talk to the press when investigations were ongoing. And he hadn't been a big enough fish for there to have been money in leaking the story.

But Nadia could have leaked it. In the trauma of his arrest, he had called her and told her everything. He had assumed that this crisis somehow superseded their private difficulties, that they would close ranks in the face of an external threat—as if a doctor had just told him he had terminal cancer or something of that kind. A part of him had even believed that adversity might bring them together again. Nadia had expressed shock and disbelief, even distress. She had called a solicitor as he requested. And maybe she had called the newspaper too, in time to make the first edition.

Books he had borrowed from the self-help section of the library said irrational fears should be given expression, and wherever possible confronted. To live in a permanent condition of doubt was unhealthy. It was inimical to self-confidence, they explained, because self-confidence was inextricably linked to confidence in others. It was clear they viewed openness as an almost universal panacea, secrets as the seeds of pathogenesis—psychological cancer cells that spread and clumped and clustered into all-consuming tumors. And when openness was not enough, there were always serotonin-reuptake inhibitors, and the older classes of antidepressants. The books had encouraged him to be open about those too.

He finished the vodka and picked up the phone. Cornelius took a while to answer. There were voices in the background.

"Marcus. How are you? How's it going out there?"

A host's exuberance. Friends around for dinner.

"Fine. Good, actually. Listen, Cornelius, I just wondered if you—"

"Just a moment."

He heard Cornelius's hand close over the mouthpiece, his muted voice.

"I'm sorry, what was that?"

"There was a woman here, Cornelius. At the hotel. She asked for me. It sounds stupid, but I wondered if you . . . well, if maybe she was something to do with you."

"A woman?"

"This evening."

It seemed Cornelius didn't have a clue what he was talking about.

"I'm sorry," Elliot said. "It doesn't matter. Some kind of mistake, I expect. Never mind."

There was a pause on the line.

"Marcus? Is everything okay?"

"Yes. Of course. I've been in that empty old house all day, that's all. I think I'm a little spooked."

He heard an engine outside, pulled back the curtains. A delivery van rolled by.

"*Ja*, well . . . Have you found anything interesting?"

"Yes. Some things I . . . I definitely want to follow up on."

It was important to sound positive.

"About Zoia? What kind of things?"

Guardian of Slavic culture and serial adulterer. Elliot hesitated. "I'll tell you about it when I see you. How are things at your end?"

"Shaping up nicely. Of course the markets are a big worry."

"The markets?"

"Turn on the TV, if you can bear it." Elliot reached for the remote, pointed it at the screen. "Otherwise very promising. We've had some more inquiries from Russia. Apparently the retrospective was featured on an arts program there, on TV."

"We're talking private buyers?"

"Or their agents. Your old friend Leo Demichev, as a matter of fact."

Elliot lowered the remote. "Demichev?" It was a name he'd hoped never to hear again. "He's not my friend, Cornelius. Never was."

He heard Cornelius sigh. "Yes, yes, Marcus, whatever. This is just *business*, okay?"

"What was he after, did he say?"

"Just testing the waters, I think. He has some possible buyers lined up back home."

Most of Demichev's business went the other way, in Elliot's experience, Russian art and artifacts being shepherded out of the country and turning up in Western auction houses, or being sold direct to collectors. It was a trade fraught with restrictions, red tape, security problems, and bureaucratic obstruction. Which is why Demichev was able to charge outrageous commissions to make it happen.

"He didn't mention any names, I suppose," Elliot said.

"Oh, you know Leo, always sticks to the generalities where his clients are concerned. He asked after you, as a matter of fact."

"Me? How did he know I was—?"

"Well, I must have mentioned it. I hope you don't mind. Your name'll be on the catalog, Marcus, so I don't think you can keep it a secret."

Cornelius was sounding defensive now, touchy.

"No, you're right, of course. No harm done."

"He was delighted to hear you were back on your feet, as a matter of fact. He said so. He said we should all get together some time. What do you think about that?"

Elliot thought about it. For a couple of seconds there was nothing on the line but dead air.

When the call was over he turned on the TV. CNN was reporting a triple-digit fall on the Nasdaq. In a matter of hours the dot.com "boom" had been redesignated a "bubble," and the bubble had finally burst. The bulletin featured men in stripy shirts holding their heads in their hands or staring at their computer terminals in stunned disbelief. A bald sixty-something with elfin ears observed that, historically speaking, stocks across the board were ridiculously overvalued. Experts queued up to say they had seen it coming.

Elliot stared without seeing. His head felt heavy, but he was too churned up to sleep. He couldn't shake a sense of unpreparedness, of events in motion. There was something behind all the secrecy, something more than an aristocratic sensibility. But he lacked the vision, the knowledge, to see it.

Bukowskis wanted him to focus on Foujita and the Paris years, the years that culminated in Zoia's new direction. But there were no letters from Foujita among her papers. He had found hardly a mention of his name.

Zoia had lived a long time. She hadn't always been famous, but she'd always been working. He couldn't believe he was the first to get curious, the first to sense a hidden meaning behind the paintings on gold. Someone must have got close to her. Someone must have written something down.

Journals, newspapers. That was the next step. The National Library had complete archives. It should have been his starting point. Critics like Leskov opined, they interpreted and compared. But reporters dug out facts, they conducted interviews, they asked questions.

He turned off the TV and listened to the silence. He wondered if he was the only guest in the hotel. He opened his wallet and took out the photographs he kept behind his driver's license: one of Teresa, taken more than a year ago, when she was rounder in the face than now; one of his mother, an old passport photograph he had found among his father's effects.

He tried ringing the foster home. He wanted to tell Teresa he would be coming to get her soon. And then everything would be back to normal—almost everything. He wondered if she was missing him.

The line was busy.

The other photograph was in his jacket pocket. He had taken it from the house: Zoia in her studio, invaded by friends bearing a movie camera primed for use. He thought Zoia was smiling, but the blurriness of her image unsettled him. *Her spirit in transit*—like those Victorian photographs purporting to show the souls of the recently departed leaving their bodies. He got the same feeling when X-raying portraits, looking for underdrawing or for telltale mistakes since painted over—*pentimenti* they were called, literally things repented of. Sometimes you found a completely different image: a face *behind* the subject's face, two identities present in the same space. It was a feeling of displacement, something cloying, morbid.

He propped the photograph up behind the phone and got undressed.

Repentances.

He climbed beneath the covers, closed his eyes, saw Yuri's writing scrawled across a blood-red page.

. . . all the same, I'm haunted by the memory of what I did in Russia.

What had he done? What exactly did Zoia have to forgive?

He blinked awake again, but the tiredness was descending now, like a weight dragging him down.

He didn't want to think about Yuri. Yuri had nothing to do with Paris, or with art. He had nothing to do with the paintings on gold.

The Wolf's Tooth

12

Moscow, March 1919.

Sometimes her mother did secretarial work in a bank. A distant family member had contacts at the Commissariat of Finance. She was paid in ration stamps, although not enough for them to live on. To make up the difference they sold their clothes and jewelry on the street. Other times they joined the labor gangs digging up Red Square in return for a bowl of watery soup and a crust of bread so stale you could break a tooth on it. Survival became the sole preoccupation of every waking hour. Even hope was slowly squeezed out of their lives. Zoia's mother didn't talk about the czar anymore—even in whispers—of how he might return one day and set the world to rights. The czar had been shot, along with all his family, a fact joyously trumpeted in the state press.

Zoia's trips to the galleries were like coming up for air.

The hunting party was Count Orlov's idea. It was supposed to be a secret, but Zoia couldn't help herself. When Andrei asked what she was so excited about, she told him everything: about the lodge in the Sparrow Hills, the special provisions that had been stashed away, along with the rifles and ammunition, even the horse and cart that had been secured by arrangement with a friend in the mayor's office.

She was still talking about it when he placed a hand on her arm.

"Zoia, you shouldn't go. You should stay away from these people. I've told you that."

They were standing outside the gates of Morozov's mansion. Andrei had heard there were some new pictures on show there, but they'd found the place locked up.

"What are you talking about? They're my friends. Of course I'm—"

His grip tightened. "Keep your voice down, will you?"

A sentry appeared in the doorway of the gatehouse, buttoning up his coat. He eyed them steadily as they walked away, Andrei forcing the pace so that she almost slipped on the ice.

"Let go of me."

She yanked her arm free and marched on, refusing to look at him now, wanting to punish him for treating her like a child. Soon he was hurrying up alongside her, breathing heavily. Recently he had acquired a small mustache and a tall fur cap, which he wore far back on his head at what was probably supposed to be a rakish angle, but which caused his ears to stick out even farther than usual, going a raw shade of red in the freezing air.

"I'm serious, Zoia. These are not the kind of people you should be mixing with. It's . . . it's *unworthy* of you."

She stared into his long, lean face, trying to understand where all this hostility had come from.

"You don't even know them."

"I know enough. I know their kind: frivolous, irresponsible . . . *parasites.*"

Zoia turned away, hurrying across the street, her footfalls breaking ice in the muddy puddles. Count Orlov, the young Countess Maria and her circle—the truth was she *admired* their frivolity, she admired the spirit, the audacity it required to be frivolous in times like these. They came from good families and were damned if they would hide the fact. Their aim was to have fun, to breeze through the dark days in as much style as possible, chins held high. There were no balls to go to, no drinking clubs and tennis tournaments, no weekends at the *dacha*. But that made everything a challenge, every re-creation of the old life, however small, a victory. Zoia had only got to know them recently, but they had welcomed her as one of their own. They made a welcome change from the fractious society of painters and poets which Andrei Burov had introduced her to, men for whom art was all mixed up with politics, which had to be talked about and debated before it could even begin.

That was why she hadn't visited Andrei in over a month. She was getting tired of hearing his views on art, the way he appropriated every work, every artist for his various discourses on symbolism, futurism, imaginism. She had started going to the galleries without him, just so she could be alone with the pictures. When she was alone, she found she could do more than look at them. She could step into them, and be there in the artist's shoes. She could see the world with different eyes, see beauty and tragedy with an intensity that brought tears to her eyes.

Her new friends weren't artists, but like art they made her feel alive again.

"You don't know what you're talking about."

"I know a lot more than you think. Zoia, the Party is under attack, and the leadership has made its . . ."—in his haste to keep up with her, he lost his footing and had to steady himself against a streetlight—"its position very clear: either you're for the Revolution or you're"—his voice dropped to a hush—"against it."

The way he said *against it* you would think that was the darkest sin in the world, like eating your own children. But that was typical of him. Whenever he talked about the Revolution, it was as if his capacity for objective criticism—normally razor-sharp—went out the window. He became a babbling zealot incapable of independent thought. She was always tempted to poke fun at him.

"Admit it: you're just jealous because . . ."

"Because what?"

She didn't want to spell it out: everything Count Orlov's people had and Andrei didn't. She was about to walk on, when Andrei grabbed her by the arm again.

"When are you going to start listening to me?"

It startled her. There was something revolting in this thin, clever man resorting to force. Until that moment he had always been a reassuring presence for her, an anchor. He believed Russia was leading the world toward a bright new dawn, and, at times, his vision excited, even inspired her. But now he was trying to frighten her because he was jealous of people with more style and more panache than he had.

She began to pry his fingers free.

"Don't be a brute, Andrushka." She kept her voice cool and calm, because she knew how that maddened him. "It really doesn't suit you. At all."

The hunting party had been planned for weeks, and it was going to be something special. Nothing had been left to chance and no expense had been spared. Count Orlov swapped a diamond necklace for half a case of claret from the Kremlin cellars. Tatiana Argunov, a pretty, blonde-haired girl with rosy cheeks, traded a string of pearls for a kilo of dried fruit and some brandy. Everyone chipped in with something, although discreetly, so as to avoid unwanted attention. It was still possible to get food back then. The worst of the shortages had yet to hit. At dawn on a misty Saturday, they piled into a cart and headed for the northernmost slopes. Countess Maria knew of an old hunting lodge, deep in the woods, one that hadn't yet been ransacked. They would be alone up there, free from prying eyes. They would hunt rabbits and wild boar, and celebrate into the night without a care.

In the Sparrow Hills there was still snow on the ground. They breakfasted on biscuits and brandy and set off into the woods. Three men went ahead with the rifles, taking the path. Everyone else spread out among the trees, so as to drive their prey toward the guns. Someone said there were wolves in the area, that they had moved toward the city in search of food. Others said they were just dogs, abandoned and gone wild. It gave the whole enterprise an edge of danger, a danger different from the kind they had left behind.

She didn't get a proper look at Yuri until he pulled the big fur hat off his head and smiled at her. She had heard his name. He came from a good family and was said to be the best tennis player in Moscow. He was supposed to be studying law, perhaps with a view to following his father into academia. A lady who smoked, a friend of Countess Maria, had described him as "exquisite," as if he were a work of art.

That morning, she understood why. He fixed his gray eyes on her, and she was rooted to the spot. He had blonde hair and a pale, noble face, like a figure in an epic painting. Yet his smile was modest, beseeching her to overlook his invisible flaws.

"I've a confession to make," he said, as he came toward her. "Don't tell the others, but I don't really like hunting."

He said he had been watching her all the way from Moscow. He said he hoped she didn't mind. She felt the words go through her body like heat.

That was the start of it, the moment she fell. Looking back, it wasn't clever of her. The countess's friend was right. Yuri *was* just like a work of art: charming, beautiful, but fragile. And it was not a time for fragility. It was a time when strength was all that mattered; strength and cunning and a talent for going unnoticed. But up in the Sparrow Hills none of that seemed important.

They lost the others somehow. They were too busy talking to pay attention. They ended up on the edge of the woods, looking down the snowy slopes, their breath coming and going in swirling clouds. And it came to her that she was happy, the awareness of it a physical thing, like a pain that suddenly stops. Yuri made her happy. Even later, that was all she could say to explain her infatuation. There were better reasons to love Andrei or the poet, Sandro Kusikov. Kusikov was romantic and brave, Andrei brilliant and energetic. But when she was with Yuri, she felt complete. She felt that everything was possible once again.

"What are you smiling at?" he said. And when she refused to tell him, he gathered up a powdery snowball in his gloved hands and chased her down the hill.

She ran, although with the laughter it was hard to catch a breath. Yuri had a remarkably good aim. The snowballs missed by inches, whistling past her head, forcing her to duck and swerve. Several hit her square on the back. When distance allowed, she hastily scooped up some snow and hurled it back at him, though none of it seemed to reach him.

She ran shrieking into the woods. The others were there on the path, sharing the last of the brandy. Count Orlov had shot a rabbit, his friend Sergei Raevsky another. Zoia straightened up, brushing the snow off her coat, trying to regain a little dignity.

"Are you all right, Zoichik?" Orlov said, grinning. "We thought you'd been abducted."

"I was," she said, picking her way through the undergrowth. "But I escaped. I'm lucky to be alive."

At that moment, one of Yuri's snowballs hit Orlov square on the forehead. The ensuing battle lasted half an hour, Orlov leading one battalion, Yuri the other. When Orlov had finally surrendered, they all went to the old hunting lodge, and passed the remaining time singing and talking and making jokes with a fierce determination that faltered only now and then. In fact, sitting surrounded by Yuri's friends, holding his hand beneath the traveling rug, Zoia found it possible to believe that this was her future, a future secured with the bonds of love, and that the world outside—the fear, the suspicion, the hunger—would soon vanish like a bad dream.

When they reached the wine, the toast was to "eternal friendship." And Yuri was the one who proposed it.

Her mother was set against the marriage. Zoia was still only sixteen, old enough to marry at court perhaps, *if* the match was highly advantageous, but far too young in the present circumstances.

"What are his prospects? What are his connections?"

They were on their knees, scrubbing down the communal stairs. It was something everyone in the building took turns at, but the leader of the house committee had been pointedly critical of their efforts to date, and now they took her turn as well.

"His father lectures in law, Mama."

"Law? There's no law here anymore. So what good is *that*?"

Muddy water dripped down the steps. Her mother's hands were raw and scabby, her nails like weathered bamboo. Over recent months her whole body had withered, shrunk on to the bone, as if ravaged by disease. The radiant, bejeweled hostess Zoia remembered from her childhood seemed now like a creature from a dream.

"We must find you a man in the Party," she said. "Someone high up. Those are the circles you should move in. Not your wretched poets and tennis players. Do you want us all to starve to death?"

The Party had taken everything. And yet she was now supposed to marry into it, and raise good little Bolsheviks, presumably, who would despise everything they had once held dear, things her father and stepfather had died for. It shocked Zoia that her mother did not even have the strength left to hate.

She was leaning on her brush now, no longer working. Zoia had seen her do it before: stop in the middle of what she was doing, as if captive to some reverie. Then she would come around again, reality slowly enveloping her once more. Zoia saw the pain in her eyes, and knew she had been dreaming of the past.

Her mother looked up again, sniffed, pushed away a strand of loose gray hair from her forehead.

"The Party," she said. "You'll marry a man in the Party."

•   •   •

They didn't need permission. Not anymore. All they had to do was sign a register and it was official. All the same, Zoia wanted to be married in the eyes of God as well as the state, a second marriage that was unimpeachable, whoever was in power. And that meant a priest and a church.

She didn't dare tell her mother until it was all over. Participation in religious ceremonies was a crime. Most of the churches were boarded up. The clergy who hadn't been arrested had gone to ground, shaved off their beards and vanished among the nameless masses. Others had turned *agent provocateur,* holding secret services one day, informing on the congregation the next.

Even Yuri's friends said it was too risky.

"But it won't be right otherwise. It has to be *right.* This one thing, Yuri, if nothing else."

It hurt him, hearing her talk that way. He wanted to give her everything, to make up for what she'd lost. But the truth was, were it not for the Revolution, she would have been out of his reach completely. He had traces of noble blood in his veins, but Zoia was the Korvin-Krukovsky's only child, a future lady-in-waiting to the czarina. She would have met her future husband at court, a man with titles and estates, not a place at law school. Even aspiring to such a match would have brought derision, scandal.

This one thing, Yuri. If nothing else.

He couldn't refuse. He couldn't have her thinking their marriage wasn't real.

Planning it took time. Asking around was dangerous. Informers were everywhere. Just the mention of religion and people clammed up, as if the very notion of the supernatural was so distant and exotic as never to have entered their consciousness. After the state married them, Zoia moved in with Yuri's family. To have continued living apart might have led to questions. Yuri's mother gave him a gold brooch, which he had melted down for their wedding rings. But rings had to be blessed to have meaning.

Then all at once a service was arranged. They had just two days' notice. Zoia and Yuri were not even told where to go until the night of the ceremony.

They left the apartment under cover of darkness, taking the long way around, then doubling back on themselves in case they were being followed. It was a warm, still night, stars burning faintly behind a veil of

cloud. The church was on the far side of Arbat, a tiny, ramshackle building, weathered clapboard and brick, hemmed in between the railway line
and a burned-out apartment block. They went around the back and in
through a tiny door at the foot of the tower.

Yuri's friends from the hunting party were waiting, the men in their
battered dinner jackets so as to lend a little formality to the occasion.
Countess Maria announced that she would serve as Zoia's maid of honor.
Tatiana Argunov gave her a pretty lace shawl as a wedding gift. Count
Orlov produced a bottle of Krug and candles to light the incense-smelling
gloom.

The priest was an old man with a white beard. It was said he had once
been a hermit at Optina Pustyn, and had secretly given Communion to
the czar and his family on their way into exile. He had put on robes for
the occasion and a crucifix on a gold chain, but his hands were shaking
as he read out the Mass.

Afterward they celebrated in Yuri's apartment, drinking sotto voce
toasts to the happy couple. Countess Maria had tears in her eyes as she
held Zoia tight. Then Yuri's father insisted they go home. It wasn't safe to
gather in such numbers, especially in the middle of the night.

But it didn't matter. Zoia was Yuri's bride now, and that made her
happier than he had ever seen her. It was worth the risk of arrest to see
her sweet face as he took his vows, and swore to stay at her side forever.

For three weeks that summer they were happy. Then the soldiers
came.

13

Stockholm, February 2000.

At the Swedish National Library they kept the microfilm records on the top floor. Most of the books and journals had been cataloged on computers, but for the newspaper archives you had to spool through the celluloid in chronological order, page by page.

There were ten viewing machines. Earnest postgraduate types stared myopically into the gray-blue screens. The building had once been a royal palace, a neoclassical tribute to symmetry and reason. But its eighteenth-century elegance was now hidden behind fire walls, partitions, and rows of book stacks, rising level by level to the roof.

His starting point would be her exhibitions. Exhibitions would have been a hook on which to hang journalistic inquiry: interviews, profiles, critiques. He knew exactly when these took place from the catalogs and sales data Cornelius had given him, some of which dated all the way back to Zoia's 1929 debut at the Galerie Bernheim-Jeune in Paris. Not all arts pages were puff and eulogy. The reporter who had destroyed his business back in England wrote articles on theft and forgery between pieces on the Turner Prize and the latest from the sale rooms. It was possible someone assigned to write about Zoia, someone with a nose for a story, had looked beyond the press releases or the programs put out by the organizers.

He focused on three major newspapers, the ones with the best coverage of the art scene. He checked editions contemporaneous with Zoia's shows. Scrolling through the films, he soon got the hang of where the stories were, learned to skip the small ads, the birth and death notices, the sports sections, without having to backtrack. Headlines and photographs flashed past, big stories jumping out at him: bomb blasts and demonstrations, bodies under blankets, warplanes on a carrier deck—people and places newsworthy in blood.

It was an hour before he found anything: a profile in *Svenska Dag-bladet* dating from 1992. It recited the familiar facts and anecdotes. Only one new thing caught Elliot's eye: it said Zoia had been offered fellowships to universities in America, Japan, and Russia, specifically so that she could pass on her knowledge of painting on precious metals, but that she had never taken them up.

Elliot wrote a line in his notebook: *Gold—no students.*

He switched papers and went on searching: the Stockholm show in 1995, the big Tokyo exhibition the same year, London 1992, Helsinki 1990. He found nothing but the same unquestioning line: Zoia as the flame keeper for Holy Russia.

In the *Göteborgsposten* there was a short piece on the Kremlin exhibition of 1993: three hundred words of the usual biographical background, and underneath it a blotchy photograph of a middle-aged man handing Zoia a parcel while a group of men in suits applauded in the background. The caption below read:

> *Alexei Burov, son of the leading Soviet architect, Andrei Burov, presented Ms. Krukovsky with a collection of the correspondence which passed between his father and her over a thirty-year period. The Minister said the correspondence was evidence of the indissoluble ties that bound Russian people to the Motherland, ties that superseded even geography and ideology.*

The patriotic line, taking shape. The piece explained one thing, though: how Zoia's letters to Burov ended up at the house. Andrei Burov had kept them all his life. At the Kremlin exhibition, Burov's son had returned them to her.

Elliot ran through the 1980s, then the 1970s. After a couple of hours his vision began to blur. He checked out other possible hooks: Zoia at seventy, Zoia at sixty, Foujita's death in 1968. As he went back, the stories got fewer, like the exhibitions themselves. In the 1970s, the era of East–West détente, the political agenda behind Zoia's work was rarely mentioned. For most of the 1960s, it was as if she hadn't been painting at all. Back then, her work was too decorative, too consciously backward-looking to merit serious discussion. The focus was on art that deconstructed the very act of seeing.

By chance he found a reference in *Dagens Nyheter,* December 1969, in the diary section. It was the photograph that caught his eye: Zoia, small and pale in a dark suit, standing next to a woman maybe five years her junior. The younger woman was in a period costume and held a cigarette in a holder. The occasion was an opening night at the National Theatre, a production of Gogol's *The Government Inspector.* The caption read: *Cast member Hildur Backlin greets artist and friend Zoia Korvin-Krukovsky. The two met in the famous 1929 production, which starred Gösta Ekman.*

Hildur Backlin had made her debut in that production, the piece said, and Zoia had designed the costumes. Backlin had modeled for Zoia over the years that followed.

In Cornelius's strong room there had been a portrait of a young woman in a black dress, making herself up in front of a mirror, with light-bulbs around it, the kind that were found in theater dressing rooms. It was known only as the *Actress.*

Elliot wrote another line in his notebook.

He searched on into the afternoon. There was a problem with his approach, pegging everything to newsworthy events: the reporters stuck to their brief. They filed their copy and went home. If they even spoke to the artist, it was only so they could leaven their pieces with the occasional quotation.

He got the impression she did not care for their questions anyhow, that she found them banal. Some of the answers she gave were almost perversely matter-of-fact. She told them she painted what pleased her, because that was all she could do. She said she painted what was beautiful and nothing more.

But then newspapers gave only a surface impression. He needed to find more analytical sources. Five hours in, he abandoned the microfilms for the periodicals catalogs beside the Reading Room.

Elliot had dipped into the world of the cultural journal as a student, and then again as a dealer, occasionally seeking the insights of scholarship into the dustier corners of art history. With a few exceptions, the journals in question had survived for a dozen or so issues and then vanished, as their philanthropic backers grew weary of the inevitable losses. Some managed only a solitary launch issue before sinking beneath the financial waves. People were hungrier for art than they had ever been, hungry for any novelty of perspective, and equally willing to pay for it. But what they would not do was read about it. They wanted their art, like their music, to speak for itself.

In Sweden it appeared to be the same. The titles that survived were mainly about architecture, design, furniture. One journal he dug out was called *New Vision*. On the cover of its first issue in 1972 was a photograph of a huge curtain draped across the Rifle Valley in Colorado—one of Christo's more ambitious wrapping projects. But *New Vision* had lost its way by 1973, and disappeared from sight altogether one year after launch.

At a quarter to six a bell rang, warning of imminent closure. Elliot was up in the north wing, working his way through the shelves of bound periodicals. The smell of stale print and glue was making him feel nauseous. Zoia's name cropped up now and again when her work went on show, but analysis was as scant as ever. Zoia's life was still a work in progress.

A second bell rang. He could hear people in the corridors, filing out, feet traipsing on linoleum. A man in a uniform went past the door, jangling keys.

There were two volumes left on the shelf. Elliot grabbed them and flipped through, wanting to complete at least this part of the task. A cheaply produced English-language magazine called the *Baltic Arts Review*, dating from 1969, had been indexed. He took the volume into the light and ran his finger down the columns of blotchy type.

It was there that Elliot found the entry: *Korvin-Krukovsky, Zoia: the Mysteries of Gold [see also Foujita, Tsuguharu]. Vol. II, No. 1 (Summer 1969), pp. 13–17.*

The Mysteries of Gold

by Mats Heinemann

. . . The picture that began it all was Foujita's portrait of his wife, painted in Paris in 1917. A watercolor on gold leaf, it depicted the subject as a princess of ancient Egypt, and was strongly influenced by the tomb art of the Pharaohs, which was then in the process of being uncovered by archaeologists like Howard Carter. With its simplicity and elegance, the portrait is an early example of Foujita's attempts to steer a path between tradition and modernity, East and West.

The collector and *haute couturier* Jacques Doucet (1853–1929) bought the work, along with its companion piece, a self-portrait in the same style, and it was in his salon on the Rue de la Paix that Zoia first glimpsed it through the window. She could not afford to buy anything, Doucet's being the most exclusive establishment of its kind in Paris (Doucet numbered Hollywood film stars and royalty among his clients), but she would not leave until she had learned all there was to learn about the picture, and the man who had painted it.

"At the time I could not explain how this small picture cast its spell on me. Foujita had drawn his subject in profile, driving out all perspective. And yet it was there in the gold. This picture was perfectly complete and self-contained. It did not leave me thinking of any vanished time or place."

The element of adornment, even disguise, in the picture also touched a chord. Zoia has always had a great love of the theater, and designed costumes for a number of important productions in the 1920s and 1930s. There can be little doubt that gold's ability to dazzle, its intrinsic association with value and worth, has its attractions for her, as it does for her clients.

"Gold is a noble metal," she said. "It illuminates everything, and betrays nothing."

14

Hildur Backlin's debut in the 1929 production of *The Government Inspector* turned out to be the beginning of a long, if intermittent, career on stage and screen. That evening, standing under recessed lights at the back of a downtown bookshop, Elliot found Backlin mentioned in several reference works on Swedish theater. She had performed the classics—Ibsen, Chekhov, Shakespeare, Molière—all over Sweden during the 1930s and 1940s, between occasional forays into cinema and London's West End. In 1930 she had traveled to Germany, and appeared in some early talkies, most notably Leontine Sagan's homoerotic classic, *Maidens in Uniform.* The 1940s found her working under a stage name in Hollywood, where Greta Garbo and Ingrid Bergman had created an appetite for Swedish talent. But Backlin never made it beyond B-movie titles such as *Lost in a Harem, Spotlight Scandals,* and *Romance of the West.* She returned to Sweden and to the theater, and in the 1950s helped to found an acting school—attended by some of the regulars in early Ingmar Bergman films.

None of the reference books mentioned her death, but that did not mean she was still alive. She would have been more than ninety years old. But the prospect of hearing directly from one of Zoia's early models—one of her *first* models since she studied with Foujita—wasn't a possibility Elliot could ignore. Later subjects, the wealthy and powerful who commissioned portraits of themselves on gold, as if seeking the reverence normally afforded an iconographical saint, were far less promising sources. They sat, they paid, they hung their opulent images over the fireplace or the boardroom table, and that was it. They had not participated in the creation of the picture the way models often did. They had not *engaged.* But Hildur Backlin had been there at a vital time, when Zoia was fresh from Montparnasse, squeezing herself back into the role of a politician's wife after the liberation and excess of Paris. It was the time when she made her choices, when she found her way as an artist. And Hildur was her friend. There was no limit to what she might know.

There were only five Backlins in the Stockholm phonebook, and the third turned out to be Hildur's daughter. Pia Backlin seemed only too eager to help. Yes, her mother was still alive, she said, but for health reasons was no longer living in Stockholm. She had moved to a retirement home in the spa town of Södertälje. Two years earlier she had suffered a stroke that had left her partially paralyzed, but she had made a good recovery and was otherwise in reasonable health.

"I'm sure she'd be only too pleased to talk to you," Pia said. Elliot got the impression that she herself didn't visit as often as she should. "Who was it you said you were researching?"

"Zoia Korvin-Krukovsky. The painter. I believe your mother and her were friends. At least, that's what I read."

For a moment there was silence on the line.

"The Russian lady? The one who painted on gold?"

"That's right."

"Well. I don't think so."

"I read it in a newspaper. They were great friends, I believe."

"Really? Oh well. It's just I don't remember Mama ever mentioning her."

The Princess Christina Residential Care Home lay on the far side of the town, next to a lake, an old country house hotel of shuttered windows, porticoes, and dying ivy. There was evidence of a recent makeover: a series of bright blue signs directing visitors to the car park, a satellite dish perched awkwardly on one end of the roof, and a gift shop for last-minute purchases.

Elliot thought about buying some flowers, and went as far as the door before changing his mind. This was professional research, not a social call. He'd even splurged on a miniature tape recorder that morning, to save himself having to take notes. And there was something insincere, even sinister, about a stranger bearing gifts.

Two men in overalls stood smoking outside the kitchens, their free hands tucked under their armpits for warmth. There was a boiled meat smell in the air. The younger of the two, a lanky teenager with spiky two-toned hair, squinted at him as he went by, holding the end of his cigarette between his lips.

Hildur Backlin was waiting for him in what the staff called "the Orangery." An old iron conservatory, it looked out across an open-air swimming pool enclosed on three sides by colonnades, with white plastic sun loungers stacked up at one end. The pool was heated. Wisps of steam rose from the surface and spun away on the breeze. A solitary swimmer—a man with thin white hair swept back over a liver-spotted head—was doing lengths, exhaling loudly as he sidestroked through the water.

Birgitta, a chubby blonde from Reception, led him to a wheelchair that stood facing the windows. Elliot glimpsed a pair of beige nylon slippers peeping out from under a tartan blanket. Gnarled, arthritic knuckles were curled around the armrest. There was a stale flowery smell mixed with traces of disinfectant.

"Mrs. Backlin? Your visitor is here."

A phlegmy coughing noise, the old lady struggling to clear her throat.

"Half an hour," Birgitta said to him quietly, pulling up a chair for him. "She gets tired." She turned to the occupant of the wheelchair. "Anything I can get you, Mrs. Backlin? A cup of tea? No?"

Mrs. Backlin croaked something that Elliot couldn't make out. Birgitta bent down toward her, obviously unsure what it was herself. It crossed Elliot's mind that he was wasting his time here, that Zoia's friend was too frail and too old to tell him anything, let alone what had happened in Zoia's studio seventy years earlier. He wished he'd questioned Pia Backlin more closely on the state of her mother's mind.

"All right," Birgitta said. "You need anything, you just tell Mr.———"

"Elliot."

"Mr. Elliot here. All right?"

Birgitta bustled off, leaving Elliot smiling into a pair of cloudy green eyes. It seemed that Hildur had made some effort for the occasion: she wore lipstick and powder, and what was left of her eyebrows had been highlighted with black pencil. Her fine gray hair had been given a lilac rinse and stood up on her head in blow-dried waves that reminded Elliot of a Flash Gordon movie. Ermine or arctic fox was coiled around her neck, an accessory pointedly at odds with her nylon slippers and surgical stockings. Elliot could hardly recognize her, even from the photograph in *Dagens Nyheter* taken thirty years earlier.

"Mrs. Backlin. I'm Marcus Elliot," he said in his best Swedish. "Your daughter rang about my coming?"

She came back at him in English, her voice clucky and sharp. "Zoia, yes. I knew there'd be someone."

One half of her face remained motionless, frozen, connections to the brain severed by the stroke. She spoke through the side of her mouth, pushing the words out from under the dead weight of flesh, her sentences punctuated with short sucking breaths.

Elliot sat down. "I'm doing some research. On Zoia's work."

"She still owes me a painting. Did they tell you that?"

"A painting?"

"*My* painting. The one in the hat. With . . . the birds. She promised me I'd have it."

For a few years, before the war, Zoia got into the habit of putting birds in her pictures, small ones, sometimes colorful, sometimes drab. They had always struck Elliot as subversive, chirping away from the corners of the pictures like hecklers at a political meeting. But there were no birds in the *Actress,* as far as he could remember. Nor was the subject wearing a hat.

"This is a picture you posed for?"

"*Sat* for. A portrait."

"On gold?"

The old lady tapped a finger against her nose. "Oh yes. Worth a bit now."

Elliot smiled and nodded. Best indulge the old woman for a while.

"And she promised to give it to you? This picture."

"In her will. Told me at poor Nikolai's funeral. For your family, she said. But I haven't"—the breath hissed through her teeth—"heard a thing."

It was obviously something that had been on her mind. Still afraid he was wasting his time, Elliot reached into his pocket for the microcassette player, and pressed the Record button. A little red eye lit up beneath the microphone.

"Do you mind if I . . . ?" The old lady looked at the machine distrustfully as Elliot placed it on a nearby table. "Can I be clear? Did you know Zoia in her later life? Your daughter was surprised when I—"

"We were close once. We lost touch. A long time ago."

Elliot pressed his hands together between his knees.

"So . . . I don't suppose the name Hanna Elliot means anything to you? She was my mother. I'm not sure, but I think she knew Zoia too. About thirty years ago."

Hildur sighed irascibly.

"I *told* you. Zoia and I. We lost t-touch." She was watching the wheels go around on the cassette player. "But she . . . *promised* me that picture."

Pictures. It all came down to pictures; their power, their meaning. Statements that took on an extra weight and finality with the death of the artist, at least for those who understood them. And Hildur could still help him there. She could help him understand, if she wanted to.

For a few moments, the only sound was the wheeze of her breathing.

"Let's talk about the early days," Elliot said. "That's really why I'm here, Mrs. Backlin. Can we talk about that?"

Hildur pushed back a little, her chin dropping toward her chest.

"I read that you met in the spring of 1929. On *The Government Inspector.*"

"Ah, Gogol, Nikolai Vasilevich," she said dreamily, resting her head against the back of the chair. "The *great* satirist. Did you know, he turned to God in the end? Starved himself to death as an . . . act of penance."

"The theater was where you and Zoia became friends. Is that right?"

"She loved the theater. All that let's pretend. All those . . . m-masks. Behind a mask you can be yourself and not get the blame for it."

"The blame?"

Hildur didn't seem to hear him. "Of course, she could never have been an actress. Not in the true sense. Stanislavsky said, find the truth . . . *inside.* From your own experience. It would have . . . k-*killed* her."

Elliot leaned forward. "I'm not sure I . . . You're saying . . . ? What are we talking about, exactly?"

Hildur pointed a crooked finger at him.

"My first husband was Russian, you know. We met in Paris. Poor . . . Nikolai. The Reds took everything. He was a count, you see. They killed his little boy. You can't be surprised if people like that . . . if they take what doesn't belong to them."

Elliot frowned. There was Nikolai again.

"Mrs. Backlin? Hildur?" He waited until she was looking at him again. "I wanted to ask you about Zoia's work. Her paintings."

"What about them?"

"People say Zoia was concerned with preserving a legacy. A Russian artistic tradition, a mystical tradition. Did she ever say anything about that to you?"

Hildur made a disgusted face. "All that came later, much later. People wrote it in . . . n-newspapers."

"So it wasn't true?"

Hildur was shaking her head. "People say . . . People write." She pointed a finger at him. "People like you."

"It isn't true. Is that what you're saying?"

She made a tut-tutting sound. "Zoia, Zoia. Her Russia was a *dream*. A beautiful dream. The real Russia she *hated*."

"Hated?"

"She didn't talk about *that*. You won't find *that*."

"What about the cityscapes? She painted dozens of those. She painted every palace in Moscow."

Hildur waved a dismissive hand in front of her face, getting agitated now. "Dreams. Dreams. Where are the pictures of Sevastopol? Where's the *Crimea?* You won't find any of those—no, no, no. Those things all stayed"—she gulped down another breath—"out of sight."

It was a matter of record that Zoia had visited Sevastopol, probably more than once. Her family had taken holidays in the Crimea when she was a child, and her mother and grandmother were still down there when she was arrested in Moscow in 1921. And it was true: Zoia had never represented the city or the peninsula in any way.

"So you're saying her whole direction was simple escapism? Nostalgia at best?"

Hildur studied him with her pale eyes. "Do you smoke?" she said.

Elliot shook his head. "I gave up."

"I'm not allowed to. No one is here. Not even the ones who are"—she lowered her voice and eased forward—"dying."

A large woman in a bathrobe and a towel around her head came traipsing out of a steam room and headed for the pool. Hildur caught sight of her and slumped back in her chair.

"We could go for a stroll in the grounds, if you like," she said, watching the woman take off her bathrobe. Billows of white flesh strained at the fabric of a one-piece floral bathing suit. "I'm already wrapped up. They won't spot us out there."

Elliot frowned. "Are you sure you should?" he said. "You sound as if—"

"It'll do me good," she said flatly.

Passing Reception, he told Birgitta he was going to fetch something from the car, then walked around the side of the building to the service entrance. A minute later, he emerged a hundred krona poorer, but with four cigarettes and a box of matches hidden in his top pocket. He returned to find Hildur wearing leather gloves and a woolen scarf.

"We'll head for the lake," she whispered. "I know a place."

Glancing over his shoulder, Elliot wheeled her out of the Orangery, past the swimming pool, and down into the gardens. It was only one o'clock, but already the sun cast long shadows across the snow-covered lawns. Down on the water a handful of small black-and-white birds were scampering about on the ice, excited, it seemed, by the appearance of a small oval of water in the middle.

Elliot asked Hildur about Sevastopol, about why Zoia never painted it, but she mostly ignored his questions, instead chattering about the rules of the care home, which she found oppressive and unreasonable. She talked as if Elliot were family, not a virtual stranger. It was something people did when, as far as they were concerned, the whole world had put them at a distance. Friends, family, staff, strangers off the street, they were all the same.

The allotted half hour was down to ten minutes.

"You sat for Zoia how many times? Do you remember?"

"A few times," Hildur said. "Quite a few."

"And she painted you on gold?"

"Once. The last time."

Elliot took the cassette player from his pocket. The wheels were still turning.

"How did she work? What was the procedure?"

"Oh, she made sketches. Lots of sketches. That was the longest part. Then she . . . m-made the panel, with the gold. Then you had to come back a few days later while she applied the . . . p-paint."

"So the panel, the gold, that wasn't prepared ahead of time?"

"Oh no. No no no."

"Why not? Most painters prepare their surfaces before the subject turns up."

"Not her."

Elliot had always assumed that the gold was essentially a trademark, a background Zoia learned to work on the way most painters worked with canvas. But Hildur's account suggested that there were choices being made, not just about the scale of a picture, but in terms of the gold itself—its type, its appearance, its application.

As he walked, his shoes slipped on the impacted snow. He was glad to have the wheelchair to hang on to.

"So did she talk to you about this? Her way of working?"

Hildur wasn't listening again. "She used to stare at it for a long time," she said. "Long before she painted anything. Like an old friend. The gold was what she loved. Made it all possible, you see. That's why she wouldn't let anyone see her using it. Wouldn't let anyone into the studio."

"Is that really true? No one?"

"No one."

"What about Karl, her husband?"

"*Especially* not Karl."

"Why do you say that?"

Hildur tut-tutted as if this was fundamental. "Those two." She shook her head. "Like you English say: chalk and cheese. Oil and water. She never let him in on things like that."

"You mean, painting?"

"And living it up. Oh yes. She wasn't in Sweden two years before she upped and left for Paris. She always told me that was Karl's idea. That he pushed her into going. But I never believed that." She sat up suddenly. "Over there. *There.*"

She gestured toward a copse of birch trees around the edge of the lake. Elliot checked over his shoulder, half expecting to see men in white coats running down the lawn toward him. A sign ahead read: NO SWIMMING.

Hildur hunched her shoulders and looked back toward the house. "They can't see us here."

Elliot reached into his pocket for the cigarettes. He handed them to Hildur and lit one as she held it between her twitching lips. The others she quickly salted away beneath her tartan rug.

Elliot watched her inhale, saw the tension drain from her body as she slowly breathed out again. He was expecting her to start coughing, but it didn't happen.

She looked at him again, keeping the cigarette no more than an inch from her mouth.

"You remind me of someone I knew once," she said. "In America. Nice-looking boy. Tall." She wagged the cigarette at him, eyelids narrowing. "Zoia would have painted *you*." A darker thought seemed to cross her mind. "But then maybe not. She didn't always paint what she loved."

Elliot dug his hands into his overcoat. "Tell me about Karl," he said.

Hildur gave her head a spasmodic shake. "Typical bourgeois Communist. Ashamed of his . . . m-money. Guilty about not being poor. He was always telling her off for taking taxis and using the car, she said. Afraid his comrades would get wind of it."

"So you knew him well."

Hildur sighed. "Not so well. He didn't like theater people. He considered us decadent. Prone to depravity." She regarded Elliot steadily. "Sexually he was *desperately* conventional. You could tell that just by looking at him." She rolled her shoulders. "Still. He didn't deserve to be treated like that."

"By Zoia?"

"He saved her life, didn't he? Loved her once, I suppose." She chuckled, revealing a line of crooked gray teeth. "When she first turned up, everyone thought she . . . m-must be a revolutionary, like him. They expected Rosa Luxemburg. Of course, she couldn't say anything, for his sake. She couldn't say what she really thought of the"—her grinning head sunk down between hunched shoulders—"*fucking Reds.*" She laughed at the look of surprise on Elliot's face, her whole body rocking in the chair. "Not a marriage made in heaven."

"So she was unfaithful. That was why they divorced?"

The smile vanished from Hildur's thin, painted lips. She took another drag on the cigarette, staring at him disdainfully. "You need all this to sell pictures, do you?"

For a moment, Elliot was lost for words. "I just want to understand. It could be important, especially if there's . . . if she *intended*—"

"Well, if it's for *her*, then that's all right."

Hildur showed him a thin smile. She held the cigarette out to her side and got rid of the ash by tapping her whole hand against the wheel. "Zoia wanted passion. One all-consuming passion. Karl wanted a family. Neither obliged. *C'est tout.*" She shrugged. "Push me into the sun. I'm getting cold."

He got behind the wheelchair and began to push her through the tangled woodland. The far end of the lake was still bathed in sunlight.

"I know Zoia never had children," Elliot said. "But did she ever say why not?"

"No. My guess is, she didn't want them."

"With Karl?"

"With anyone."

"How do you know that?"

"I don't know. I observed. Artists are selfish. They live to feed their work. It's flesh and blood to them. It's who they *are.*"

"What did you observe?"

Hildur fell silent as she drew on her cigarette. Eventually a long white plume flared out in front of her.

"One time we met in a restaurant. Somewhere in Östermalm. The Källhagen, I think it was. It was summer. I remember because all the doors were open. And there was a school with a . . . p-playground opposite. The children came running out of the school and started playing in the playground, screaming and shouting, but nothing so much. Nothing you'd call a n-nuisance."

"And you were there with Zoia. Just the two of you?"

"I didn't think anything of it. But then Zoia suddenly stood up and *announced* she wanted to go somewhere else. We'd already *ordered*. The noise, she said. It was giving her a headache. But I think they just annoyed her, the children. You won't find *them* in her paintings either. Anyway, children would have complicated things. She might have lost some of her . . . p-power."

"Her power?"

"You'd have felt it if you'd met her. Men were always fascinated by Zoia. In those days. They tried to hide it, of course. But it ate them up inside."

"What men are you talking about?"

"Not just men. Women too. She seemed so fearless, you see. And they envied that. They wanted to be close to it. To touch that spirit."

They had reached the end of the lake. Hildur sat motionless in the wheelchair, arms on the armrests, the cigarette a curled inch of ash balanced on the filter.

"He told me about it once, tried to explain himself." She was looking out across the ice. "There was always a sense . . . a sense she carried something secret inside her, something you couldn't reach. It stirred an intense kind of lust, he said, a desire to reach that mystery *physically*. Expose it to the light."

She nodded, mouth set in a grim line. "A hunger you felt in your loins, he said. A desire to be reunited with the unknown. He said it was a Russian thing. A thing of the East."

Gently Elliot took the cigarette end from between her gloved fingers. "Who did? Who said that?"

Hildur sat up, seeming to realize she had said too much. And that was when Elliot knew: Nikolai was Kolya, Kolya the Russian emigré who'd worked in the restaurant business. Among Zoia's papers Elliot recalled passionate, guilt-ridden exchanges that hinted at an affair close to home. With Hildur away filming or on tour, there would have been plenty of opportunities for a liaison. Hildur's husband had fallen under Zoia's spell, and sometime later—maybe months, maybe decades—he had confessed as much. Even if the affair had happened before Hildur was on the scene, it could explain why the friendship hadn't lasted. It could explain a lot where Hildur was concerned: the curious mixture of bitterness and intimacy that colored her memories.

Something in her eyes told Elliot she knew what he was thinking. She pulled the rug tight across her lap, smoothing out the creases.

"Zoia ensnared a lot of men. A lot of fools. You're just the latest."

15

He drove back toward the coast, the cassette player playing on the passenger seat. It was starting to get dark, the freshly salted road winding wet and black across the snow-covered land.

On the tape everything was noisier than he remembered it. Background sounds he hadn't even noticed crowded into earshot: voices, footsteps, doors banging, the roar of a plane going over. Hildur's voice echoed as if in a church.

The great *satirist. Did you know, he turned to God in the end? Starved himself to death as an . . .*

The shallow, sibilant breath.

. . . act of penance.

A container truck blasted past, showering slush. Elliot gripped the wheel, fighting the impulse to swerve.

. . . Of course, she could never have been an actress. Not in the true sense. Stanislavsky said, find the truth. . . inside. From your own experience.

A little catching sound in her throat, maybe a cough, maybe a laugh.

. . . It would have k-killed her.

He let the tape run on, thoughts and impressions overlapping, connecting, breaking apart—through it all an unmistakable sense of something *there,* coming little by little within reach: a picture, a message. A key to understanding.

Hildur was a woman betrayed. Doubly so: by husband *and* by friend. Beneath the veneer of acceptance, the scar was still livid, even after all these years. Maybe the sudden interest in Zoia brought back the bad memories. Or maybe they had never left her.

He flipped on the windshield-wipers. Dirt and moisture smeared across the glass.

. . . They killed his little boy. You can't be surprised if people like that . . . take what doesn't belong to them.

She spoke of Kolya, but it was Zoia she was thinking of: Zoia the seducer, the adulteress, a woman who put art and sexual freedom before hearth and home. A woman who could not bear the noise children made in a playground.

He hit fast-forward. The tape screeched through for a few seconds. He let go.

... *The real Russia she* hated.

... *Hated?*

... *She didn't talk about* that. *You won't find* that.

Impatience at his lack of understanding, his lack of depth. Here was another one of those people who talked and wrote, but did not see.

Elliot got a flash of Dr. Lindqvist behind the wheel of his old black Mercedes, letting him know what a hopeless outsider he was, how he and his "aesthetic ideologies" were a waste of time where Zoia was concerned.

Hildur's voice was harsh, mocking.

... *Where are the pictures of Sevastopol? Where's the* Crimea? *You won't find any of those—no, no, no. Those things all stayed ... out of sight.*

Elliot felt the hairs come up on the back of his neck. He grabbed the cassette player, fumbled in the darkness for the Rewind.

—*You won't find any of those—no, no, no. Those things all stayed ...*

He snapped down on the Stop button. Somehow he hadn't picked up on it the first time, the implication of what Hildur was actually saying: not that Zoia had never painted the Crimea, as he'd first supposed, but that *the pictures were hidden.* They were hidden because they represented something Zoia could not bear the world to see.

Hidden work. *Core* work.

If the pictures were secret, then presumably Zoia never sold them. But if that was the case, they should have turned up in the private collection she left behind. And since Lindqvist was selling everything of Zoia's, why wouldn't he sell those too? He wished he'd tried harder to clear up the point, but he had a feeling Hildur wouldn't have obliged. Momentary lapses aside, she only said what it suited her to say.

Maybe she was just playing with him. Maybe she didn't know what she was talking about.

The road turned north. The sky above Stockholm was an orange curtain masking the stars. A steady procession of oncoming headlights swept across his windscreen, diffracting among the tears of moisture.

Hildur knew more than she let on. He was certain of that. She and Zoia had been friends once, close friends. Even now she was caught between bitterness and loyalty, between protecting and condemning. And she knew something about the gold. He had sensed the same ambivalence on that subject.

He picked up the cassette player again, flipped the cassette over, pressed Play. The sound was different now, the voices flatter, deader. In the background there was only the rattle of the wheelchair, the distant twittering of birds on the lake.

. . . Artists are selfish. They live to feed their work. It's flesh and blood to them. It's who they are.

. . . What did you observe?

The tone of his voice surprised him, the hunger, the urgency. As if he had to know everything while there was still a chance. It was how he must have sounded to the old woman.

Hildur started talking about the incident at the restaurant. He fast-forwarded again. A sign up ahead told him there were two kilometers to go before the turnings that would take him east toward the coast.

. . . a sense she carried something secret inside her, something you couldn't reach.

A Mercedes swept up behind him, lights blue-white. It stayed there a moment, then slid out to overtake.

. . . an intense kind of lust, he said, a desire to reach that mystery physically. *Expose it to the light.*

Something Zoia was supposed to have said back in 1969, reported in the blotchy pages of the *Baltic Arts Review:* gold, the noble metal, illuminating everything, betraying nothing. What did she mean by that? What kind of betrayal did she have in mind?

He rewound the tape, searching for the place, wanting to hear what Hildur had said exactly. It took several attempts to find it. Her complaints about the staff and their rules seemed to go on forever.

—*So did she talk to you about this? Her way of working?*

No answer. A bird call, far away. A gull. The breeze made a ruffling sound against the microphone.

Then Hildur's voice, distant in recollection.

—*She used to stare at it for a long time. Long before she painted anything. Like an old friend. The gold was what she loved. Made it all possible, you see.*

No bitterness this time, only sadness and wonder.

Cornelius was right after all: he had to focus on the Foujita angle. It was Foujita who had taught Zoia about gold. She was the only pupil he didn't turn away.

Elliot swerved off the exit lane and headed into the city. The Bukowskis reference library would be open for another three hours.

16

In July 1913, Tsuguharu Foujita, eldest son of a Japanese military doctor, graduate of Tokyo Art School and judo black belt, stepped off the SS *Mishima Maru* in Marseilles wearing a pith helmet, spectacles, and a white linen coat that, in keeping with the fashions of the day, stopped six inches short of the knee. Arriving in Paris a few days later, he went directly to Montparnasse and took a room at the Hotel d'Odessa, four hundred yards from the Académie Colarossi, where his old teacher, Kuroda Seiki, had studied in the 1880s. But Foujita did not enroll. Maybe he had never planned on going to classes, or maybe he changed his mind when he arrived. Instead of taking lessons, he went to work almost at once, painting, sketching, socializing, striking out into the demimonde of the Left Bank as if he had been born to it.

The earliest known photograph of Foujita from his Paris years showed him dressed like a businessman in a three-piece suit and a bowler hat. But the mask of conformity was soon discarded in favor of more exotic guises. Foujita fell in with the dancer Isadora Duncan and her brother Raymond. This was the time, the chronology revealed, that Isadora was in mourning for her two children, drowned in a boating accident. Foujita was attracted to the Spartan ideals of asceticism and natural living which the Duncans espoused. He took to walking around Montparnasse in handmade sandals, a headband, and an ancient Greek-style tunic made from cloth he had woven himself.

Women in particular were fascinated. Foujita was a great success at parties, and, having divorced the wife he had left behind in Tokyo, he embarked on a series of affairs. Later, tiring of Sparta, he took to wearing an oriental tunic, a Babylonian-style necklace and earrings, and a wristwatch tattoo. He cut his hair into a distinctive combed-forward bowl, in imitation of an ancient Egyptian statue, a look he kept for life.

People nicknamed him *Fou-fou* (*"fou"* being French for *"mad"*). But it didn't bother him. Foujita was a man who lived in his own world, one he fashioned to his liking. Of all the foreigners on the Paris art scene, he was the one for whom exile seemed the most liberating, the most happy. European exiles like Picasso were haunted by memories of what they had left behind. By comparison, Foujita was unfettered by his past.

In Montparnasse Foujita met Amedeo Modigliani, who had moved there from Montmartre several years earlier. Modi would come into Foujita's studio in the afternoons reciting Italian poetry, and quiz him on oriental painting techniques. In particular, Modi was drawn to the sinuous black lines with which Foujita drew his subjects, and the ivory-smooth surfaces which he prepared beforehand, surfaces which imparted a unique sense of translucence and depth.

Surfaces had to be prepared before they could be gilded. And that preparation involved applying coat after coat of gesso, a white plasterlike substance made of water, hide glue, and powdered gypsum or marble dust. In traditional icon painting, parts of the surface would be left ungilded, if only to save money, which meant any artist working in the field would have been familiar with the demands of painting directly onto gesso. The art history books were vague about how Foujita prepared his canvases. They mentioned his use of a "milky white ground," and his habit of mixing his paints with exotic substances—powdered glass, ground oyster shells—to achieve opaque, luminous whites. But the use of a ground was a gilder's technique, and the very fact that Foujita often used gold and silver leaf suggested it was one he knew well.

It must have been a part of what drew Zoia to him.

Foujita was a latecomer to the Paris art scene, but he was soon outshining everyone. He earned good money and was adored by the critics. His work was exhibited annually at the Salon d' Automne, and successful shows were held as far afield as London, Berlin, Milan, New York, and Chicago. In 1925 he was awarded the *Légion d'honneur* and the Belgian Order of Léopold I. By 1926 his paintings were being purchased for the national collection by the French state. When, two years later, Zoia went knocking at Foujita's door, he was the most successful painter in Paris.

For Foujita, the turning point came in 1917, the year he met and married Fernande Barrey in the space of three weeks, the year of the Egyptian portrait on gold. From that time on, Foujita never looked back.

Nowadays the *Portrait de Madam Foujita* and the self-portrait that accompanied it were hanging in the Angladon Museum in Avignon, where the bulk of Jacques Doucet's art collection had ended up. They were among the few important Foujitas on public display outside Japan. One reason Foujita's fame had dwindled since his heyday was the speed with which his best work had been snapped up by private collectors. Little had come on to the open market since. In the big national collections the critical mass of works needed to maintain wide public awareness was simply not there. For the same reason, there was little systematic scholarship on Foujita's work.

Despite its formal title, the subject of the Egyptian portrait was clearly Fernande Barrey, and not, as the oriental style had led some to believe, a retrospective picture of Tomiko, the wife Foujita had left in Japan. Fernande, an artist in her own right, even had the same thick, bobbed hair, with a fringe that reached over her eyebrows and into her dark, penetrating eyes. And there was another, more persuasive clue.

Fernande had married Foujita at the end of March. Soon afterward, according to one account, she took a handful of her husband's works across the Seine to the dealers on the Right Bank, hoping to raise some money. Caught in the rain at Georges Chéron's gallery on the Rue La Boétie, she exchanged two watercolors for an umbrella. A client took them at once, and a few hours later Chéron turned up at Foujita's studio, buying everything in sight, rooting through the corners with the aid of a cigarette lighter. He offered Foujita a seven-year contract, guaranteeing him an income of four hundred and fifty francs per month. That night, to celebrate their good fortune, the couple went out and bought a pair of canaries—canaries which appeared in the *Portrait de Madam Foujita*, delicately perching on Fernande's curled fingers. The picture, along with the self-portrait, was unveiled later that year at one of the two exhibitions held at Chéron's gallery, which was almost certainly where Jacques Doucet acquired it.

Looked at this way, the choice of gold, like the yellow birds, suggested celebration, a flourish of opulence, a statement of confidence in the future. Maybe it was this cocktail of the exotic and the exuberant that caught Zoia's eye: from the darkness of 1917, a year of slaughter and revolution, a shining image of a distant world.

In the library at Bukowskis Elliot pulled out everything he could find on the art of ancient Egypt. The craftsmen of the Upper Nile were the first to master the art of gilding, but beyond that it wasn't a field he knew much about. He pored over color plates of statuettes and figurines, jewelry and magic charms. One thing struck him at once: there were very few images of Egyptian princesses. They were found on the walls of tombs, illustrating dynastic history or woven into spells. But the female figures the sale rooms dealt in—the kind Foujita would have had a chance to see—were not princesses but goddesses. And the goddess that most resembled the woman in the female portrait was Hathor, the goddess of joy and love.

Foujita had painted Fernande as a goddess, and *that* was why the background had to be gold. In ancient Egypt, gold was the symbol of divinity. Only those related by blood to the royal house—the Pharaoh himself was a living god—were permitted to use gold on their sarcophagi. In sacred art, the connection was even stronger: gold, the element that never tarnished, that went on forever unchanged, represented the very flesh of the gods.

In one respect, though, Foujita's technique was inappropriate.

Elliot went back to the plates from Avignon. Even without the real painting in front of him, the difference was clear. The ancient Egyptians devised a technique known as water-gilding. Four or five layers of a clay bole—thin liquid clay, mixed with hide glue—were painted on to the gesso, and polished when dry. The gold leaf was then gently floated on shallow puddles of water. As the water sank into the clay it dragged the leaf down with it. The gold could then be burnished, the preferred instrument for the purpose being a canine tooth. In Egypt they used a jackal's fang, in Byzantium and Russia a wolf's. They made special knives, bound with twine, sharp enough to puncture flesh, and worked the gilt until it shone with the mirrorlike surface of solid gold. But Foujita had used a different technique. Mordant gilding involved applying an oil-based glue to the gesso, and placing the gold leaf on top of that. The advantage of the technique was the relative ease of it. The disadvantage was that the surface of the leaf was irrevocably fixed, and could not be burnished. That was why church artists in later centuries only used mordant gilding when depicting gold thread in sacred vestments, gold that was never meant to look solid.

Elliot went down to the front desk. The pale-eyed girl recognized him, and after a couple of internal phone calls, gave him the key to the gallery in the basement. He went down there, opened up the doors, turned on the lights.

Some of the bulbs had been taken out, but the pictures were there just as before, glowering in the half-light. From some directions, the gold took on a darkness like bronze, smoky depths flecked with yellow stars. He went from frame to frame, stopped in front of *The Summer Palace at Tsarskoe Selo.* In the foreground, almost lost beneath the massive blue and white facade, were a mother and child about to cross the street. He hadn't even noticed them before. The mother was holding out her hand, but the child was refusing to take it. He remembered what Hildur Backlin said: that children would have sapped Zoia's power, sexually, perhaps creatively too. She could not even stand to be near them.

He stepped closer, sucking up the detail, the million threads and wrinkles that ran through the gilt. From a few inches away it gave an impression of infinite complexity, hints of patterns and symbols, spiderweb filaments of light and shadow, connecting, repeating, radiating. You shifted your weight and suddenly the patterns changed.

Foujita's gold had a crystalline, mineral quality. It was particularized, granular, perhaps in conscious imitation of an ancient artifact, one where the underlying gesso ground had disintegrated, or the wood had split. But Zoia's gold was different. The patterns of burnishing, even the color of the gold, varied from picture to picture, but the gold itself was always whole, unbroken, like a barrier to infection, like skin.

Zoia had traveled to Florence in the 1930s to study. After the avant-garde world of Paris, it must have seemed to her contemporaries a bizarre move. But Florence was Cennino Cennini's hometown, the one place in Europe where water-gilding was still taught and practiced as it had been for centuries. Zoia needed that technique. She needed it the way Degas needed absinthe and Gauguin needed sex. Because it unlocked something. Because somehow it made creation possible.

He heard footsteps in the corridor. Cornelius Wallander, looking sweaty and flushed, bustled into the room carrying a big brown envelope. "Ah, Marcus, they told me you were down here. You got my message then."

"Your message?"

"On your mobile. This morning?"

Elliot pulled the phone from his pocket. He had turned it off the night before, to save the battery, and forgotten to turn it on again.

"Well, you're here now anyway," Cornelius said. "Here are plates of every major picture in the show, titles, dates, dimensions, and materials. Actually, some of the dates we aren't sure about. Maybe you can help us with those."

He handed the envelope over. Inside was a stack of glossy prints of Zoia's work, with the identifying information written inside the borders by hand.

"I'll do my best," he said. "But the letters I've read so far don't say very much about her pictures. Most of them are from other people."

Cornelius shrugged. "To be expected, I suppose. Listen, Marcus, there was something—"

The *Actress* was on the other side of the aisle. It was an early work, perhaps one of the earliest using gold. Unlike the pictures that came later, where the gold was in the background, creating a kind of ambience, here the leaf was used decoratively within the composition. The effect was self-conscious, gaudy, ironic. Like the subject with her makeup, it dazzled to disguise.

He leaned in closer, remembering something from his days of study. "Gold leaf is actually semitransparent. Did you know that?"

Cornelius frowned. "No, I didn't."

"Pure gold, I mean. Twenty-four karat. That's another reason artists put a clay bole over the gesso. Gold leaf on white takes on a greenish tint. You need a terra-cotta hue to give it warmth."

Cornelius nodded, wanting to get back to business. "Interesting. I always thought gold was gold."

"No. It's always been much more than that."

There was a big panorama at the far end of the room. *Stockholm Harbor* was one of a series of Stockholm cityscapes, wide panoramic views that were strangely mute in texture and tone. The use of filmy, translucent pigment for the water, allowing the gold beneath to shine through in submerged reflection, was interesting from a technical point of view. But Elliot couldn't think of the pictures as anything but an uncomfortable thank-you to the country that gave Zoia shelter all those years. And sure enough, most of them ended up on the walls of municipal buildings in and around the capital.

Zoia was always at her worst when working to order, something that happened increasingly as time went on. Some said she began to focus on the money, the artist as businesswoman. Others thought the obsession with materials and techniques led her into a creative dead-end—a fate similar to Foujita's. For twenty years postwar his pictures had been haunted by strange, doll-like figures with staring faces. Somewhere between mawkish and creepy. He had turned them out by the score, diluting his reputation and his sale-room value canvas by canvas.

Like the master, the pupil did her best work when she was young, during the years of wandering, before she found what she was looking for, or gave up looking.

He had to go back to the letters. He had to go through them in detail, hunt down every reference to materials and techniques, however fleeting. But that would take time.

He realized that Cornelius was talking to him, his voice low, confidential. "You mustn't say anything, Marcus, whatever happens. There are security considerations."

"I'm sorry, what did you say?"

"Well, it'll have to remain a secret until the show actually opens. Otherwise the whole place could become a target. Chechens and so forth."

"A target? Bukowskis?"

Cornelius stepped closer. "It would be part of the program. Apparently the dates coincide, and the ministry thought it might be a perfect occasion to round off his trip."

"Whose trip?"

Cornelius looked puzzled. Beneath the lights his eyes were lost in shadow. "Didn't you hear what I said? Putin's. Vladimir Putin. The President of Russia?"

"Putin. Yes, of course."

"He's due to visit Sweden this summer. Not a state visit, but his first since he was elected."

Elliot began to get a sick feeling in his stomach.

"I'm not really supposed to be telling you this," Cornelius said, "but we got a call from the Foreign Ministry, requesting more information. They sounded very keen. The symbolism of it all, you see. It's perfect from their point of view."

The symbolism. That was what everyone had been groping for, a transfiguring term of art that would give meaning and weight to the artist's life. Zoia, the flame-keeper, the patriot, her quiet devotion to Russia transcending ideologies of left or right. She was the perfect ally for a post-Communist leader with a card-carrying past. Recruited from the grave, suitably sanitized and packaged, she would now lend a hand with diplomatic relations and bilateral trade.

"Of course, they need to be assured that the event would be appropriate," Cornelius said.

"Symbolic."

He nodded enthusiastically. "Exactly. That's what they were hoping."

"And you told them—"

"Me? Oh dear no, they didn't speak to me. Frederik took the call. I was merely *informed*."

"Then what did Frederik tell them?"

"That it was a marvelous idea. Oh, all the screening and security will be a nuisance, I know. We shan't be able to *move* for black limousines and bodyguards. And we'll have to deck the whole place out in Russian flags, apparently, which is rather *outré* in my opinion, but one has to play along."

He looked into Elliot's face. "Raises the profile of the thing, Marcus. Good for you, good for all of us. And with what's happening to the stock markets . . ." He shook his head, momentarily speechless in the face of the unfolding catastrophe. "Well, we can't afford to look a golden goose in the mouth, if you know what I mean."

Elliot nodded. It was true. He needed the show to be a success as much as anyone. He needed it for Teresa's sake. With a stab of guilt, he realized he had hardly thought of her all day.

"Anyway, talking of you," Cornelius said. "There's something Frederik would like you to do for him."

"Frederik?"

He shrugged apologetically. "I assume it was his idea. He wants you to write something, a briefing, kind of an article. We may even be able to publish it in the newspaper. Frederik has contacts in the press."

"What kind of briefing?"

"On Zoia. On her work. Sort of preview of the catalog copy."

"He doesn't trust me with the job?"

"Of course he does, Marcus. Of course he does. But you're working all alone out there—which is fine. But now the whole project has taken on, well, a different dimension. You understand. Everyone needs to be sure we're on the same page." Cornelius put a hand on Elliot's arm. "We'd pay you something extra, of course."

Elliot nodded. Now they had him writing briefings for the Foreign Ministry, except that the briefing in question was as much about himself as about Zoia. They wanted to be sure he saw things the right way. He could say no, of course, but that would be the end of his involvement. Frederik Wahl would get him kicked off the project. There would be nothing Cornelius could do about it.

And then he would never know.

"Fine," he said. "Just tell me when he wants it."

17

Halfway to the coast the wind kicked up out of nowhere, hurling spirals of sleet down the road. A weather report on the radio said the thaw was temporary, and warned of icy conditions in the days ahead. He made the journey slowly, following a tanker truck most of the way to the Salt-sjöbaden turnoff, glad just to be moving, to be on the road. After the encounter with Cornelius he'd gone to the nearest café, aware suddenly of how little he'd eaten in the last couple of days. But the food and the coffee hadn't settled him as he'd hoped. Every time he'd looked at his reflection in the plate-glass window, he'd seen Zoia in her studio, the eyes blurred in motion, in flight.

He saw her at Jacques Doucet's salon, spellbound by the picture of Fernande Barrey as a goddess of the Nile, seeing something in it that Elliot knew he hadn't seen.

Was it possible Zoia recognized herself in the picture? Was that part of it? She bore a passing resemblance to Fernande: the deep-set eyes, the bobbed black hair, a provocative, girlish roundness in the face. Most of Foujita's women were like that, not least his third wife, Lucie Badoul, the one he renamed Youki, the Japanese for "snow." Elliot recalled the famous nude of 1924, *Youki, Snow Goddess.* Foujita had painted her, sprawled out pale and naked on a silvery bed, a black dog at her feet—another lover-deity.

It had come to him that the black dog was not a dog at all, but a jackal, and that the jackal was Anubis, the god who guarded the tombs of the Pharaohs. Anubis, the one they called the Keeper of Secrets.

Business was picking up at the Ibis Majestic. The car park was full of Saabs and Volvo sedans, and there was a large coach outside. A succession of businessmen with overnight bags and suit-carriers slung over their shoulders were making their way out, some of them a little the worse for wear. They lumbered down the steps, red-faced and vociferous.

At first, Elliot didn't see the white Volkswagen. It was coming out of a parking spot on the other side of the coach, reversing a couple of feet, nudging the car behind.

He slammed on the brakes.

He was sure it was her: the woman he had seen outside Bukowskis. No question this time. He could see the hooded head silhouetted against the lights of the hotel lobby.

He pulled over and sat watching from the other side of the road. The driver eased forward and then back again, indicator lights flashing. It looked as if she hadn't seen him; she had probably been sitting there all afternoon, waiting for him to show. Now, finally, she had decided to give up and go home.

Cornelius said the Putin visit meant there were "security considerations." Was this what this was, a ham-fisted screening operation? It made a twisted kind of sense.

He left the engine running and got out of the car. "Hey! Hey you!"

His voice sounded small in the gusting wind. "YOU!"

He set off across the road.

Without warning the Volkswagen lurched out into his path. Full-beam headlights dazzled him. He tried to shield his eyes.

Somewhere in the street a horn sounded.

The car surged forward. It was going to run him down. Of course. That had been the plan all along, *to get rid of him.*

He got a flash of Nadia. The blank, stony look she wore when she told him he could never understand her. This was how much she hated him.

His feet slipped as he tried to run clear. He caught a startled expression on the driver's face, heard the tires scrape over grit and slush. He banged up against the side of the coach, felt the car go by behind him.

It skidded to a stop, sat there a few yards away, exhaust plume dancing in a glare of brake lights. The coach driver stuck his head around the front of the coach, wanting to know what was going on, probably expecting to see a hooligan with a can of spray paint. "Are you okay?"

Elliot took a couple of deep breaths, nodded.

"You should be careful. Dark coat, dark night."

He shook his head despairingly and disappeared.

The door of the Volkswagen began to open. Elliot marched over.

"Who the hell are you? What do you want?"

The face that looked up at him was young. He'd expected someone older, a face exhibiting experience and purpose. But the girl was in her mid-twenties at most.

She pulled headphones out of her ears. She'd been listening to music on a portable CD-player. "I'm sorry. I didn't see you."

Short, spiky hair, brown eyes. A car went past, throwing a bar of light across her face. Her mouth was curvaceous and dark. It was the only really grown-up thing about her.

"Are you Mr. Elliot?" she said.

"What if I am?"

"I've been looking for you. My name is Kerstin Östlund."

She hesitated, then held out her hand. She was wearing coarse woolen mittens.

"I've seen you out here before," Elliot said. "What do you want?"

The girl put her hand back on the wheel. From inside the car came a whiff of tobacco. "I tried to call you at the hotel, but you were never there. I didn't want to leave a message. I even called the house."

"The house?"

"Zoia's house. I know someone at Bukowskis. She told me you were working out there."

"So?"

"I'm a reporter. For *Expressen*."

Elliot straightened up. "Sorry. I don't talk to reporters."

"Please, Mr. Elliot—"

"You're wasting your time."

He shut the door and walked back toward the car. She wound down her window.

"I was a friend of Zoia's. Mr. Elliot? There's something I have to tell you. Something you ought to know."

Elliot stopped, squinted back through the swirling sleet. Her eyes reminded him of Fernande Barrey's, of Zoia's. The darkness, the intensity. The crazy notion came to him that they were all in it together, all connected by something they knew.

Initiates.

"Park the car," he said.

• • •

The hotel was crowded with the overspill from a conference of commercial lawyers. They were queuing at the front desk, squaring up for two days and nights of networking and expenses-paid recreation. As Elliot escorted Kerstin through the lobby, they turned one by one to look her up and down. Not that she was giving much away. She wore a knee-length suede coat, with long, artificial fur around the cuffs. She was tall, a little square-shouldered, even statuesque, but the way she walked, shoulders hunched, hands dug deep into her pockets, made it obvious she wasn't comfortable under the gaze of strangers. She reminded Elliot of those girls he used to be wary of at student parties, the ones who wore masses of mascara and eyeshadow and were angry at the world.

The bar was the one part of the hotel that made an attempt at atmosphere. It was dimly lit, with booths all around the walls, and little orange lamps on the tables. A handful of lawyers had already settled in, toasting each other with shots of preprandial vodka. Gold cuff links and gold teeth glinted beneath the recessed halogen lights.

They took a booth in the corner.

"So you're on a story, is that it?" Elliot asked.

"Yes. Kind of."

"And, what? Zoia was one of your sources?"

"No."

The reporter reached into her coat and took out a pack of cigarettes. She spoke schoolroom English, accented, but grammatically sound, the way his mother used to speak.

"Do you mind if I . . . ?"

"What is it with Sweden nowadays?" he said. "Everybody smokes."

She slid the packet toward him. He shook his head.

"It's the winter." She lit up, showing him a fleeting smile. "People get lonely."

"And cigarettes keep them company?"

Kerstin blew out the match. "Something like that."

She looked better in the orange light. It disguised her pallor. In fact, if it hadn't been for the budget haircut and the puffiness beneath her eyes, she might have been pretty.

"So what did you want to tell me?" he asked.

She held the cigarette between her lips as she shrugged off her coat. "I used to work at Bukowskis. That's how I got your name. I still have some friends there."

"You? At Bukowskis?"

"I read art history at Stockholm University. Bukowskis was my first job."

"You must have done well."

"My grades were quite bad, actually, but one of my professors put in a good word. I think you call it pulling strings."

No embarrassment, no suggestion of apology.

"They put me in the domestic valuations department. This was about three years ago. Cornelius Wallander was in charge back then."

"Yes, I know."

She took a drag on her cigarette, watching him through narrowed eyes. Her manner was professional, streetwise, but there was something unstable about her too, an unsettling fragility.

"How well do you know him?" she asked.

"Cornelius? He's a professional contact. We go back quite a way."

"To when you were a dealer."

She knew that too. People had obviously been talking.

"That's right. To when I was a dealer."

"But you're not dealing now."

"So?"

She regarded him steadily. "I wanted to know if you're part of it, that's all."

First ingratiating, now insinuating. Elliot almost laughed. "Part of it? Part of what?"

One of the hotel staff was standing by their table, the same young man who was usually at Reception.

"Can I get you anything, Mr. Elliot? Miss?"

There was an extra smarminess about him this time, like someone in the know. One of the lawyers at the bar was staring at Kerstin, tongue working at the side of his mouth.

They ordered coffee.

"Suppose you tell me what this is all about?" Elliot said.

"Wallander witnessed the will. Zoia's will. That's odd, don't you think?"

Kerstin exhaled watchfully. As she lifted her head, the light caught a little depression in her forehead, a narrow but clearly discernible dent about an inch long, vanishing beneath the hairline. He wondered what kind of accident made a scar like that.

"I'm sorry, I don't follow you."

"I'm talking about the will that was drawn up a few days before Zoia died, the will that left almost everything to Dr. Peter Lindqvist, including all the pictures in her private collection. That's Zoia's doctor."

"I know who he is. So what?"

"Do you know who actually drew up this will? I'll tell you: Lindqvist's *lawyer,* that's who." She nodded, giving it time to sink in. "His name is Thomas Röstman. I found out he defended Lindqvist in a malpractice suit about eight years ago, in Uppsala."

"A malpractice suit?"

She nodded, eyes crimping as she took another drag on her cigarette. "I'm still chasing down the details. I heard some poor woman lost a kidney. A good one."

"So what are you saying? The will was a fake?"

Kerstin just smoked, watching him.

"Well, I hate to spoil your story," he said, "but aren't you rather leaping to conclusions?"

"I would be. If I didn't know what she *wanted* to do with her pictures." She said it like she really knew.

"I suppose you're going to tell me she wanted them destroyed."

Kerstin put her head on one side, frowned. "No. Why would you think that?"

"Nothing. Just something that . . . So what did she want to do, according to your theory."

"It's not a theory. It's what she told me. Some pictures were going to public galleries, in Sweden, in France. One was going to an art school in Italy, and at least one to the Montparnasse Museum in Paris. And there were individuals, people she'd promised to give pictures to."

"And Zoia told you this?"

Kerstin nodded.

"Why?"

She looked down at the cigarette packet, started pushing it back and forth between her fingers.

"I got to know her toward the end. She was very kind to me when . . ." She rubbed her temple with the back of her thumb. "When things were bad. We became friends."

Elliot tried to picture it: the wild child and the artist at ninety.

Kerstin looked up, caught the doubtful look on his face. "You think I'm making it up?"

"I'm just wondering how a girl like you would hit it off with a woman like her. I'm wondering what on earth you would have in common."

Kerstin smoked for a moment, watching him. "I didn't . . . It was a professional thing, to start with. I was sent out to go through these books and papers, for valuation purposes mainly. A tax write-off."

"What papers?"

"They used to belong to Zoia's ex-husband, Karl Kilbom. The politician?"

Elliot nodded. "The one who saved her life."

"Right. They divorced in 1937. Well, he left all his papers to a son from a subsequent marriage. Eventually the son thought they should be given to the national archive. So we went in there to sort them out and arrive at a notional value. That's where I came across her letters."

"Zoia's letters?"

"A lot of them weren't dated. So I thought it would be an idea to ask her to help us on that. Since she was still around."

Elliot put his head on one side. "You went to all the trouble of tracking Zoia down, just to get some dates on some letters she wrote—what?—sixty years earlier? What made you think she'd remember?"

The receptionist reappeared, setting cups of coffee in front of them.

"It wasn't just that." Kerstin reached for a sachet of sugar. "I thought the letters were interesting. I wanted to meet her. I always liked her paintings."

"And she helped you."

"Like I told you, she was kind. She made a lot of time for me, and that meant something. Because . . ." She tore open the sachet and dumped the contents into her cup. "Because she didn't have much time left."

She stirred the coffee. She had painted nails, bitten down to the quick. Elliot wondered what Zoia had helped her get through.

"Suppose all this is true about the will. What's it got to do with me? What can I do?"

Kerstin looked at him over the rim of her cup. "You've got access. To her papers, to her house. You could look around."

"For what?"

"Any information about the paintings. About who she planned to send them to. Maybe she corresponded with some of these galleries. Maybe there are letters that talk about what she planned to do."

"Even if there were, it wouldn't prove anything. A will nullifies everything that precedes it."

"All we need is evidence. Enough evidence for the authorities to look at the will again, look at the signature, look at the medical records. Maybe Zoia wasn't in a fit state to sign anything at the end. We've only got Lindqvist's word that she was, and he was the main beneficiary."

Outside, the coach was revving its engine. With a hiss of brakes it pulled out into the road. More lawyers were pouring into the bar: dark suits, tanned faces, a smarter clientele than the Majestic was used to. The sight of all that money, all those steady incomes, it always made him feel like an outcast.

"Let's just say I did find something. Then what? You get your story, and what do I get? The exhibition falls through. The sale falls through. And I lose a commission I badly need." Kerstin picked at a patch of hard flesh at the base of her fingers. "Of course, you're a reporter. You just want a story, right?"

"All that . . . all those things will happen anyway if the truth comes out."

"What Zoia *told* you may not have been true. Has that ever occurred to you? If she was so determined to give those paintings away, why didn't she just go ahead and do it? There was nothing stopping her."

Kerstin shook her head. "You don't understand. Her pictures were her savings. She sold one when she needed to, to raise money. She couldn't afford to just give them away. Besides, she wouldn't have lied about something like that. You'd know that if you knew her." She tamped out her cigarette in the blown-glass ashtray. Suddenly there were tears in her eyes. "The truth never matters to you people, does it?"

She reached for her coat, pulled it over her shoulders. Elliot didn't know what to say. He wondered who "you people" were supposed to be, and how come he was one of them.

In a moment she would be gone.

"Wait. Wait a second. Maybe I can . . . Maybe *you* can . . ."

"Can what?"

"There are things *I* want to know. About her pictures. If you knew her, maybe . . ."

Kerstin pushed back in her seat.

"What kind of things?"

He leaned across the table. "I want to know about the Crimea. Sevastopol. I want to know about some pictures that are missing. Apparently she kept them hidden somehow. Did she ever tell you about them?"

A frown crossed Kerstin's face, a frown that suddenly dissolved into a solemn blank. "Why does that matter to you? If you're not dealing anymore."

She *knew,*

"I'm curious. I want to understand."

"You want to understand Zoia, but you don't care about her."

"I care about the artist."

"But not the woman."

Out of nowhere he was angry: a chemical hit, an intravenous rush. "Look, maybe she was good to you. Fine. But let's not kid ourselves. This is not a saint we're talking about. Zoia Korvin-Krukovsky was a survivor. She used people, and she discarded them. Read her letters. Her whole life was littered with casualties."

"Casualties? What are you talking about?"

"You should know. Look at Karl Kilbom." The words seem to come from someone else. "He saved her life. He gave her a good home. He financed her career. And how did she repay him? She ran off to Paris. And that was just the start of it."

Hildur Backlin's words. And yet his own too. The vehemence of the betrayed.

"She had her reasons."

"Sure. I expect she thought Paris would be more fun."

Kerstin got to her feet, started buttoning up her coat. If she was angry, though, it was a cool kind of anger. "You don't understand Karl anymore than you understand Zoia."

Elliot held out his hands. "Then tell me where I'm wrong."

She put her head on one side. "What does it matter now? Karl, Paris. It's ancient history, isn't it?"

Elliot wished he'd kept calm. It was the pressure of a long day, of the nights without sleep. He should have apologized, but somehow he couldn't.

Kerstin took a pen from her pocket and started writing something on a napkin.

"I tell you what," she said. "You help me and I'll help you. Call me when you think you've found something. Then I'll tell you what I know."

She slid the napkin across the table.

Potemkin Village

What We Are Fighting For

In launching the October Revolution, the working class hoped to free itself. But the result has been an even greater enslavement. The police power of the monarchy has passed into the hands of usurpers, the Communists, who have brought to the laborers, instead of freedom, the constant terror of the Cheka and its torture chambers, the horrors of which have many times exceeded those of the czarist gendarmerie. Bayonets, bullets and the harsh cries of the *oprichniks* from the Cheka, these are what the toiler in Soviet Russia has won for himself after many battles and great suffering. The Communist authorities have replaced the hammer and sickle, glorious emblems of the workers' state, with the bayonet and the prison bars. They have done this for the sake of preserving a calm, untroubled life for the new bureaucracy of Communist commissars and officials.

But what is most rotten and criminal of all is the creation by the Communist of a moral enslavement. They have tried to get their hands even on the worker's mind, forcing him to think only the way they want him to think. Through their control of the trades unions, they have tied the workers to their benches, making labor not a joy, but a new serfdom. To protests by peasants, expressed in spontaneous uprisings, and by workers, forced into strikes by the desperate conditions of life, they answer with mass executions, and with a bloodlust alien even to czarist generals. Toiling Russia, first to raise the red banner of liberation, is drenched in blood.

149

18

Moscow, June 1921.

Karl Kilbom didn't believe Lindhagen's story, and neither did any of the other delegates. He'd taken a knock on the head, that was all. He'd suffered an episode of delusion while lying in the gutter, having his shoes stolen. Because nothing he said made any sense.

He'd gone missing on their fourth day in the capital, the day Leon Trotsky was due to address the Congress, and then shown up at lunchtime in the dining room of the Continental Hotel with a split lip, and blood down his shirtfront. Zeth Höglund, the leader of the Swedish delegation, had wanted to call the police, but Lindhagen had begged him not to. In Kilbom's opinion, this only confirmed his suspicions that the story wasn't true: at best an example of the young man's imagination running away with him, at worst a fabrication born of some reactionary epiphany.

Lindhagen was the youngest member of the group, and the only one with more than a smattering of Russian. Propped up on a dining room chair, glass of brandy in hand, he told them what had happened.

Lindhagen's room overlooked the back of the kitchens, which gave out on a narrow yard protected by high walls and iron gates. That morning he had risen at dawn and was shaving when he saw a team of women collecting the peelings and food waste, piling it onto a cart and covering it with a tarpaulin. They were just outside the yard when two children dressed in blackened rags—a boy and a girl—appeared from nowhere and jumped onto the cart, grabbing handfuls of refuse and shoving it into sacks as fast as they could. Lindhagen had put down his razor and leaned out of the window, disturbed at the sight of the ragged children furiously rooting around in the rubbish.

But what came next was worse. The women attacked, grabbing the children as they jumped down again, clawing, punching, dragging the boy to the ground—as if this were a pile of priceless treasure they were defending, not a heap of garbage good only for pig swill.

Lindhagen was horrified. He shouted from the window, but the women were too intent on their business to hear him. They were gathered around the boy now, kicking him, stooping to hammer down punches with a cold, hateful regularity, as if he were some vile insect, some pestilential vermin that had no right to exist.

One of the women elbowed a little space for herself, cast a glance around, then stamped with all her weight on the child's throat.

Lindhagen ran down. The boy was going to be murdered, if he wasn't already dead. In the corridors and kitchens, men in white aprons stared transfixed as he darted past. But by the time he found the yard, there was nothing but a few scraps of peelings and a greasy smear on the cobbles that might have been blood.

He looked around, spotted the women at the end of the alley, pushing away their cartload of rubbish past a policeman on patrol. There was no sign of the boy. He looked down and saw that he was still carrying his open razor.

He took a deep breath. It hadn't been as bad as it looked. The women had scared the child, not killed him. He had run off, chastened but alive, and was at that very moment probably licking his wounds in some nearby alley. He watched the cart slowly turn the corner, his heart still pounding, feeling a little foolish to have overreacted. He turned to go back inside the hotel, only at the last second catching sight of the emaciated, dirt-blackened limb that flopped down from under the tarpaulin.

He shouted to the policeman, pointing at the women and the blood, trying to explain what had happened. But the policeman took him by the shoulder and turned him back toward the hotel. He didn't want to know about the killing that had taken place under his nose. He just wanted the foreigner to go back to his room.

Lindhagen stood by the kitchen door for a minute, stunned, not knowing what to do. Everything he had seen in Moscow until that moment had filled him with hope. Despite the years of war, the economic dislocation, the virtual abolition of money (a subject about which there were still many arguments), he had been impressed by the order and prosperity of the capital. Everywhere he went—or rather, everywhere he was taken—he and his comrades were greeted by committees of well-fed and smartly turned-out workers. Even on the shop floors he heard singing, and expressions of sympathy for the proletariat of his country, who still labored under the yoke of bourgeois capitalism. People had put up pictures of Lenin everywhere, even above the doors of churches. He had already written home to his wife, delighted to be able to dismiss the reports of famines and peasant massacres as anti-Bolshevik propaganda. Yet he had just seen an urchin boy trampled to death for stealing a few handfuls of potato peelings.

That was when he spotted the girl. She was crouched down behind a gatepost on the other side of the alley, staring at him. Her black hair was matted and filthy. Her hollow cheeks made her cheekbones seem unnaturally high and round, like an old woman's.

But she wasn't looking at him after all. Her gaze was fixed on something a few feet away. He turned, realized that something had been left behind in all the commotion: a scrap of bread, already covered in dirt, but half the size of his fist.

At this point, Zeth Höglund interrupted the story. All around them, people from other delegations were craning their necks, wondering what their Swedish comrades were whispering about. Kilbom and Frederik Ström took Lindhagen back to his room, while the others went looking for a doctor.

Lindhagen sat down on the bed while they cleaned him up, still talking as they dabbed at the wound on his head.

He'd tried to go after the girl, he said. He wasn't sure why. She was a witness to the attack, and she was hungry. He'd wanted to help her. But as soon as he took a step toward her, she'd run off, darting down the alley, ducking into the shadows of an old arcade where the shop fronts were hidden behind huge red banners. He'd thought she was frightened by the sight of the razor.

He'd kept after her, shouting for her to wait. But she'd run on, dodging around a line of disused stalls, before disappearing down a winding alleyway that led behind a church.

He wasn't sure how long he'd kept running. Maybe it was just a few minutes. Even for early morning, the streets seemed surprisingly empty. A sign on the corner of one big thoroughfare read HUNTER'S ROW. It had once been a big shopping and trading area, but almost everything had been boarded up. Private trading had been illegal for the past two years, and the recent policy reversal announced by Lenin had clearly not taken effect. But it was as if a cordon sanitaire had been thrown around the central district. Lindhagen got a feeling he had strayed into a part of town he was not meant to be in. When a car went by, manned by Cheka soldiers—the same soldiers he had seen on guard at the front of the hotel—he instinctively ducked into the shadows.

He thought he had lost the girl, but as he was turning back he caught sight of her again at the far end of the street. She seemed weak now, dizzy. As she walked she kept steadying herself against the walls. Lindhagen had followed her, keeping his distance. Beneath her rags, he could see that she was little more than a skeleton.

Somehow he'd ended up by the railway. On the other side of a collapsed fence he could see the track, the nearest set overgrown with weeds. Peering through the gap, he saw a line of crumbling brick sheds crammed together beneath a bridge. That was where the girl was heading. He followed, passing beneath the arches, covering his nose and mouth against the stench that seemed to rise up out of the earth. There were flies everywhere. They bumped against his face, his mouth, they buzzed frenziedly in his ears as if trying to burrow into his brain. Part of him wanted to turn back. Part of him wanted to see.

He stumbled over a pile of rags, saw the rags move, jumped back thinking: *rats.* It had to be rats. But then there were eyes, human eyes, looking up at him, mucus slits between swollen lids, yellow skin stretched over bone, pulled back from the mouth in a savage, desiccated leer. As he stared, his thoughts were of shrunken heads, of some horror from an anthropological museum.

He staggered on, spun on his heels, and then, there they were. Children. He couldn't tell how many. Scores, hundreds. They lay coughing, shivering, faces filth-blackened, many hidden beneath the compound mass of rags. Some were too weak to even turn their heads. From the stench and the flies he thought some were already dead.

And in the middle of them all, watching him now, was the girl he had followed. She began walking toward him, seemingly no longer afraid. Lindhagen felt himself rooted to the spot, fascinated, repelled. She was just a few feet away when she grabbed the hem of her skirt and pulled it up to her face. He saw her pale naked flesh, the emaciated bow of her thighs, and then, above the ruddy shadow of her pubis, the pregnant bulge of her womb.

Run. That was all he could think of doing. But suddenly there were other girls pulling at him, trying to strip the clothes off his back. He'd yanked himself free, staggered back toward the street, hurled himself through the fence. And that was the last thing he could remember. He'd woken up on the other side of the street with no shoes on, and a pair of street sweepers staring down at him. One of them had laughed as he'd gone through his pockets.

"Lucky for you this isn't the South," he'd said. "They'd have cut you up for meat by now."

Lindhagen read Dostoevsky. He had a copy of *The Devils* by his bedside with a brown-paper cover. Kilbom hadn't read it, but he knew it was full of unsound ideas. All Dostoevsky's work was infected with the same misguided messianic questing. Lenin had dismissed the book as reactionary trash, which should have been reason enough to leave it alone. But Lindhagen said he liked Dostoevsky for the understanding with which he wrote about ordinary people, beggars, outcasts, criminals. Dostoevsky saw beauty at the heart of every Russian soul.

Religious ideas were polluting Lindhagen's mind. His upbringing had been strict Protestant, and that kind of indoctrination had a habit of resurfacing in later life, undermining rational convictions. Lindhagen thought all of central Moscow had been artificially sanitized and dressed up, a huge fake like the Potemkin villages that once stood in the Crimea and on the banks of the Dnieper, with their stage scenery houses and casts of richly costumed peasants. As if the leadership had time for that kind of thing.

The truth was, he'd been foolish enough to chase an urchin into an alley and had been assaulted. The rest was a fiction-fueled nightmare that had invaded his brain while he slept, and which now he mistook for fact. And even if it was fact, what did it prove? The Revolution was a work in progress. The Bolsheviks couldn't be expected to win a civil war and cure all Russia's social problems at the same time.

Kilbom went off to the Kremlin that afternoon to hear Trotsky speak on the prospects for world revolution. It was something he had been looking forward to. Trotsky gave his speeches in German—the official language of the Third International—which Kilbom understood, and he peppered his remarks with jokes, which even Lenin could never manage. But as he sat in the crowded hall, listening to an analysis of the state of international proletarian consciousness, he found his mind wandering back to Lindhagen's story. He found himself dwelling on remarks, rumors, reports that he had given little heed to at the time.

Lenin had said the forced requisition of grain from peasant villages had inevitably led to "abuses." It was a remark that had cropped up in several of his recent articles and speeches. Abuses. In years of drought and heavy frosts, what constituted an abuse? Just how much of their food were the peasants compelled to give up? And exactly how was that compulsion enforced? According to some American delegates, desperate appeals for food aid had been going out in their country from prominent Russian citizens, including Maxim Gorky, the writer and friend of Lenin. Yet there was no mention anywhere in the Soviet press of famine, and certainly no sign of it at the Congress.

There were doubts about industry too. The factories he had toured looked like models of discipline and fraternal harmony, but Frederik Ström had been told by a Russian friend that most of the factories had been on strike a few months earlier, and that many workers had been killed in demonstrations.

Then there was the revolt at the Kronstadt Naval Base. No one ever talked about that, nor how the revolt had been crushed. It was almost as if it had never happened, although it unquestionably had. The thousands of sailors who had escaped across the ice to Finland bore testament to that.

It took an effort of will for Kilbom to stop dwelling on these things. In his mind a picture of the little prostitute, her white naked belly, mingled with Trotsky's denouncements of doctrinal heresy. The German and Dutch delegations were upset that the Soviets were trading with the capitalist West, instead of actively exporting revolution. Kilbom pictured the boy being trampled to death, the boots splintering his brittle bones.

He reminded himself that part of his purpose in Moscow was to get money from the Russians. The Swedish party needed support for its newspaper and its organization, especially now the economic climate had improved. The revolution was about making the world anew. It required patience and discipline and, above all, vision. He looked around the room and he could see it—in the upturned faces of the Russian delegates, intense and eager. The present was already history. It was the future they were fighting for, the rebuilding of mankind. The child prostitute and the urchin were the detritus of the old world, at worst a regrettable by-product of a transitional phase. Because it was objectively and scientifically impossible that they could exist in the socialist state once completed.

He took a small leather notebook from his inside pocket and wrote a line in pencil: *Central Committee—Lindhagen—motion to expel.*

19

The interpreters were all daughters of the bourgeoisie. They wore starched white blouses and pleated skirts. They spoke with soft, unassuming voices. Kilbom watched them across the banqueting halls and meeting rooms, educated ladies playing handmaid to the dictatorship of the proletariat. There was something pleasing about it, something exciting. Like having a princess kneel to clean your shoes.

He wondered if they secretly harbored resentment, having to serve men who would once have served them. If so, they hid it well, going about their duties diligently, even enthusiastically. He decided it was welcome evidence that even those who stood to lose from revolution could learn to embrace it, just as he had done. It was something he wished people back home could see.

At a dinner for the Communist Youth Movement, a bearded Russian delegate called Potresov caught him eyeing a pretty brunette. The state of education in Russia made the employment of the "former classes" unavoidable, he explained in execrable English, just as it was in the civil service generally. But this was just a temporary fix. In time, the organs of the state would be purged of opportunistic and inappropriate elements, and these genteel, pale-skinned girls would be packed off to do some real work—on their knees or on their backs, he said. And at that he laughed, blowing rank breath in Kilbom's face.

The brunette was about eighteen, exactly half Kilbom's age. She was petite but curvaceous, with firm, girlish breasts that stood high up on her chest. She had dark, piercing eyes, with pupils that reminded Kilbom of black glass. He went on watching her while Potresov told a story: how the Soviets in the city of Vladimir, in their zeal to nationalize the means of production, had declared women over eighteen to be state property, and demanded that they register with the Bureau of Free Love. He said he'd been trying to get to Vladimir for the last six weeks, but the railways weren't running, as usual.

Kilbom attempted fraternal laughter, but his heart wasn't in it. There was something reckless in the way these Russians talked, something wanton. Too much death had hardened them.

Potresov's eyes narrowed. His speech was starting to slur. There was champagne available at the banquet, but he'd done nothing but knock back vodka all evening.

"So that's your type," he said. It took a moment for Kilbom to realize Potresov was talking about the girl. "Demure, but expensive."

"Expensive? What do you mean?"

"Her family used to own the Moscow railway. She'd have been lady-in-waiting to the czarina, they say. If we hadn't shot her."

Kilbom could see it now: the way she sat, a little straighter than everyone else, the way she brought her hands back to her lap when she wasn't using them. There was something cultivated in her manner, something utterly out of keeping with revolutionary times.

The girl looked up, caught Kilbom's gaze, looked down again. He felt his heart jump.

"And now? What about now?"

"Now she has a clerk's job at the Ministry of War, and a husband just out of the madhouse."

"A husband?"

Potresov leaned closer. "Informer for the Cheka. Ratted on his friends."

He made a lazy cut-throat gesture with his finger.

A member of the Indian delegation, a man called Roy, was sitting next to the girl, talking as he chewed. He had his hand on the back of her chair. Kilbom saw the girl edge forward, shoulders gently hunching to avoid contact, smiling as she did it, so Roy wouldn't notice.

The waiters put plates of roast duck in front of them, with puréed potatoes and cabbage.

"Looks like you've got competition," Potresov said. "I heard he sent flowers to her room. Flowers, mind you!"

"What's her name?"

"Her name, her name . . ." Potresov grabbed the bottle again. Kilbom tried to cover his glass, and got vodka poured over his shirt cuff. "I don't remember. But if you want her, you'd better take her, before somebody else does." He took a sip, wrinkled his nose. "Girls of her class all end up screwing for their rations. It's just a question of who. And how often."

The girl looked up at him again. She had noticed him. She was making her assessment, those dark eyes scanning his soul.

One of Roy's fingers was making circles on the back of her neck. He bent down and whispered something in her ear, something that made her instinctively, if almost imperceptibly, wince.

From that night on, he watched her. At the meetings and the dinners he observed her listening, talking, smiling (when smiles were called for), the way her eyes narrowed when she laughed, the fetching way she tucked her hair behind her ear when someone leaned over to speak to her. There was still a touch of the schoolgirl in the brittleness of her manners: the prefect on Inspection Day. But there was something else, something practiced in her disposition, a poise in the company of men that a pretty face alone could not account for. He could see it, how men felt awkward and transparent in her presence, how they fumbled and flattered, anxious for her approval.

He pictured her pale fingers parted over jeweled fabric, the decorous courtesan of Western art. The czar's mistress had been a ballerina. Maybe that would have been her fate too, if the czar hadn't been overthrown. High-born ladies who fuck. He pictured her in corsets and lace petticoats, feet pointed skyward on a gilded chaise-longue, being ridden hard by an archduke with a handlebar mustache.

But there were moments, when no one was looking, when all the play-acting stopped, when her eyes would glaze over, and she was far away. He thought he could see the glistening of tears, caught her more than once swallowing hard, trying to drag herself back to the present from whatever dark reverie had taken hold of her. Sometimes he felt a ripple of anger that occasions of such significance did not command her complete attention, that she should allow herself to be anywhere but in this company, this company of men who were remaking the world. At the same time, he found he wanted to know where she went.

He gave himself reasons for watching her, for the anxiety he felt when she was nowhere to be seen.

Potresov was wrong about her: her attractions had nothing to do with class. She outshone the dusty anachronisms of the Russian aristocracy. She had been fashioned by forces more fundamental than circumstance. Her qualities were innate.

The next day they were taken on a trip to an architect's studio. A twenty-foot model of a monument to the Third International was on display, a huge steel and wire tower that reminded Kilbom of a fairground helter-skelter. Roy, the Indian delegate, was much in evidence. He kept badgering the girl, paying no attention to the architect as he tried to explain his vision, always touching her on the arm as he spoke. As they all filed out at the end of the visit, he put an arm around her waist, as if she didn't know which way to go.

Karl wished he could rescue her, but whatever the pretext for intervention, it would have been obvious what he was up to. Everyone was watching her, and thinking the same thing. He resolved to risk a smile next time she looked at him—a polite smile, an acknowledgment, no more. But the next time never came. It was as if she had already seen all she needed to see. As the chances came and went, her failure to look at him, her *refusal* to look at him, began to anger him too. It was unbelievable, but behind the downcast eyes and gentle smiles, she still thought she was too good for him.

Kilbom believed in the refinement of the masses. But most of his Russian comrades seemed to revel in their coarseness. He wanted to show her that he was not like them, that he understood her distaste. It was not easy being an educated man in the middle of a proletarian movement, working for the triumph of the working class without succumbing to its vices. He wanted her to understand.

Then, unexpectedly, his chance came. They were due to meet some Russian officials to discuss the issue of financial support. Zeth Höglund said they would need a dedicated interpreter, one who spoke French, and so that night the whole Swedish delegation tramped down to the first floor of the hotel to find one. It was there, in a bedroom next to the bakery, that he found himself looking at three girls. And she was one of them.

The girls hadn't been expecting visitors. One of them covered herself with her blouse. Another, a blonde called Tatiana, whose short curly hair was pinned tightly to her scalp, didn't bother. She stood there in her stockings and chemise, an accommodating smile on her face. The brunette was the only one fully dressed, although two of the top buttons on her blouse were undone, revealing a little gold crucifix at her neck.

"My apologies, comrade ladies," Höglund said, but before everyone could leave again, Kilbom stepped forward.

"We need an interpreter for a few days. Would you be willing . . . ?"

He wondered if the brunette recognized him, if she knew he had been watching her. He felt his face grow hot.

She held out her hand.

"My name is Zoia," she said.

He remembered for a long time afterward how her hand felt strangely cold.

That night at the theater he sat beside her. It was hard to focus on the play. Having her there so close set his nerves on edge. He felt a trembling in his stomach and a swelling, needful ache in his groin. He imagined her mouth pressed hard against his, having her right there in the theater, their forms writhing in silhouette.

The production was a political comedy, a mixture of slapstick and music hall and triumphal songs. The bourgeois characters all had white painted faces and held their noses with disgust whenever they were obliged to address a member of the proletariat. One of them wore a top hat and was followed around by a chambermaid with a bowl of water and a towel. It turned out he was supposed to be a politician. Every time he was forced in the course of electioneering to shake a proletarian hand, he would turn smartly to his maid and wash himself up to the elbows. The audience loved it, the Russians in the stalls in particular. They laughed and jeered, getting to their feet and shaking their bony fists.

When requested, Zoia translated into German. Everyone in the delegation was impressed by her fluency. Most of the interpreters had only French or broken English. Kilbom was credited with having made a good find.

An hour into the play, Höglund excused himself and left, followed by Frederik Ström and a couple of the others. Kilbom turned to the girl, determined to say something.

"How long have you . . . ?"

A banal question. It stuck in his throat as she turned and looked at him. He thought he saw her smile.

"You work at the Ministry of War, don't you?"

"In the telephone exchange. I've only been there a month."

"And before that?"

"I was studying to be an artist."

On stage a proletarian set fire to a priest's long gray beard. The stage filled with purple smoke as he ran around in circles. The audience roared with laughter. Potresov had told him that in the countryside the Cheka did that for real, only with a touch of petrol to help things along. Then they cut the priest's tongue out and gouged out his eyes, for the benefit of the congregation. But then Potresov liked to shock people, especially foreign delegates who were yet to be bloodied in the revolutionary struggle.

"Is this difficult for you?" Kilbom said.

He felt her eyes turn on him again. This question surprised her.

"English is the hardest. I can manage French and German, but—"

"I didn't mean the languages. I meant . . . everything. All this. They told me your family are . . ." He shrugged, not knowing how to avoid sounding hostile.

"Bourgeois?"

"Noble, actually. Aristocrats."

She turned away, pushing out her chin in a contrary way. "Who said that?"

"Some nobody with a drink problem. Nothing to worry about."

If she was scared, she hid it well.

"Is it true?" he said.

"No. There weren't any titles in the family."

"No titles . . ."

"My grandmother had a big estate in Tambov, and my father owned a printer's and some textile factories. And my stepfather was a soldier. He had an estate too, near St. Petersburg."

"So you were very rich."

Something on stage seemed to please her. She smiled. "Oh yes, very rich. And I would have had it all in the end. I was the only child. But then the Revolution happened."

"And now?"

"Now we're poor, like everyone."

No bitterness or self-pity. Just a statement of the facts. He couldn't help admiring it. There was an implicit strength in her acceptance, as if none of what had happened really mattered very much.

He leaned closer, resting his elbows on his knees. "It doesn't bother you then? Having lost so much?"

"If I hadn't lost something, I would be the only one. I would be alone in all Russia."

"And you don't want to be alone."

She didn't answer. Another peal of laughter went up from the stalls. In spite of her words, he had a comforting sense of power, of being in control. It was the opposite of what he usually felt around beautiful women.

"So where are they now? Still in Russia?"

"Who?"

"Your family. You don't mind my asking?"

"I've only my mother and my grandmother. I left them in Sevastopol."

"Sevastopol? What were you doing down there?"

Her head dropped. She didn't answer.

"I'm sorry. I'm curious that's all. I was afraid I wouldn't get another chance to talk to you."

Down in the stalls they were applauding the final proletarian victory. The bankers and priests, by now in their underwear, were being carried upside down to their destruction by a crowd of workers and Red Guards.

"You can talk to me any time you want," Zoia said. "I'm paid to be at your disposal entirely."

The audience were cheering and stamping as the actors took their bows. Before Kilbom could say anymore, the lights were going up and the crowd was heading out of the theater.

Lying awake that night in the creaking four-poster bed, head swimming with vodka and warm champagne, he ran through her words in his mind, searching for some clue as to their meaning, some hint of a subtext.

Potresov's ugly face bloomed out of the darkness. *Girls of her class all end up screwing for their rations. It's just a question of who. And how often.*

Was that what her words were, a plain statement of fact? He had only to summon her to his bed and she would come, in return perhaps for some money or a bar of soap, or a grateful word in the ear of her superiors. Or was it the exact opposite? A formal statement of their respective professional positions, a reminder that they *were* professional, and would stay that way no matter what.

What was it about this girl? There were more beautiful ones back home. But thinking about them didn't send the blood to his groin the way she did. What if he went down there again, to her room, right now? He could tell her something for appearance's sake. *There's something urgent I need you to translate. Upstairs.*

He had a feeling one cold, loveless fuck wouldn't be enough. He would want more. And what if he had misunderstood her, and word of his attempted seduction got around? Kilbom abusing his hosts' hospitality, embarrassing the whole delegation. His chance of leading the party again would be gone forever.

His desire for her was compromising, dangerous. She had him thinking unproletarian thoughts: thinking he was better than Russian comrades who had made the revolution and defended it with their blood. She undermined his faith in the supremacy of politics.

He threw back the covers and went over to the washstand, lifting up his nightshirt. Maybe empty balls would get his mind off her for a few hours, at least until morning. It was either that or a night without sleep.

Bars of yellow light swept across the ceiling. A motor car was pulling up outside. He edged back the curtains. Across the square the clock read a quarter to three. He heard doors slam, saw men in caps and leather coats march across the cobbles and into the hotel. They kept the engine running.

He wondered what could be going on so late: some kind of important official business, because only officials had cars—officials and the secret police. Someone coming back from a late-night meeting, perhaps, a meeting rounded off with a session of heavy drinking. Some delegations were more in with the current leadership than others.

The engine turned, three pulses to the second, the fan belt singing almost beyond the range of hearing. Somewhere, from inside the hotel, he thought he heard voices, a door bang.

He felt suddenly giddy. He let his nightshirt drop and went back to bed, pulling the covers up over his head. He would make her his, one way or another. He would show her she had met her match. And then they would make love the way it should be done.

But still he saw her on the chaise-longue, petticoated legs upraised. He hugged the pillow as the car pulled away outside.

Next morning Zoia was nowhere to be seen. She did not come down to breakfast, and when Kilbom and Höglund went up to her room they found it empty. The manager of the hotel looked shifty. He said he had no information. The men who guarded the front door said the same thing. Kilbom made a phone call to the Foreign Ministry, just in case she had gone back to her job, but they knew nothing of her whereabouts. It was only when they ran into Tatiana outside the Congress that they learned what had happened.

"They came for her last night," she said, as delegates jostled past. "She's been arrested."

"On what charge?" Kilbom demanded, but Tatiana just looked at him, as if she didn't understand the question.

He grabbed her by the arm. "What'll they do to her?"

But the girl wouldn't answer that either.

In the afternoon a phone call came through from the organizing committee, confirming what had happened. Their interpreter had been mixed up in a counter-revolutionary plot in Petrograd. Another would be found for them.

Höglund was furious. "She was the only one with decent German," he protested. "We needed her. We've important meetings this evening."

The official said they should raise the matter with the Cheka and hung up.

Kilbom knew what he had to do. Here was the test.

"Zeth, there's been a terrible mistake," he said. "That girl is innocent."

"Innocent?" Höglund said. "How do you know?"

"I just know. She's not interested in politics. She's . . . she's an *artist*."

Roy was probably responsible. He was angry that Zoia wouldn't sleep with him. There were bad apples in the Cheka who would arrest anyone if the price was right.

Höglund looked unconvinced. "We shouldn't interfere. It's none of our business."

But before he could say anymore, Kilbom had elbowed his way to the phone.

Moscow, 16th March 1922

My dear beloved Zoia,

At last we have another letter from you. I was so worried about your long silence, and even sent a telegram to your husband, but received no reply. Finally I got a call from the Swedish consulate, saying they had a package with my name on it, and I went there very early this morning and collected it.

Thank you for the magazine with the photographs of your apartment in Stockholm. Your husband Karl looks very handsome, and you too look quite beautiful. As for the flat, it seems very pleasant, spartan but pretty in the Nordic style. Granny is happy with the kitchen which I'm glad to see you've kept tidy. Remember though that everyone here is going to look at and talk about these pictures, and that it would be as well not to appear with your hair all messed up and styled in such a dowdy way.

Your first letter made me so sad I wanted to cry. Why is Karl so determined to change you? Why does he think you need to be changed? I expect you have been exaggerating, and it's not as bad as you say. In the end it's up to you. If Karl loves you that should mean he'll do whatever you want. All you have to do is be sensible and you will have everything you could want in life. Just think about last year, that terrible year, and how it so nearly ended in disaster. That was what a life of independence did for you. I thank God that you are no longer in Moscow. All the same, it's difficult for me to read that you are unhappy, that Karl is pressuring you so much, and that you do not feel you are mistress in your own home.

Dearest, what you must realize is how empty your life was before, how unhealthy and insubstantial. If you only sit back and think about what it's put you through, and why, then you'll feel better about things. At last you have a suitable husband, a good home and a position in society. What else could you possibly need? You should turn your thoughts to family matters now. You don't need anymore than you have. You simply need to hold on to it.

I know you and Karl come from very different backgrounds. But at least Karl is not Russian, and therefore has some manners. He needs to keep you on the straight and narrow, and if he does, you will be the healthier for it. Last year was so dreadful because you did not listen to me.

I'm sad not to have met Karl yet. I hope I will see him in the summer. In the meantime, tell him he must be mindful of your weak heart.

> *Your loving,*
> *Mama*

20

———•———

Saltsjöbaden, February 2000.

Lying in the darkness, Scotch and benzodiazepines churning in his stomach, he plays the tape again, holding the speaker close to his ear. The batteries are getting low, Hildur's voice deeper now, and slower.

—*Not a marriage made in heaven.*

She was talking about Karl and Zoia, but it might as well have been Marcus and Nadia. Two brides with material agendas. Two husbands duped.

Expediency on the one hand, delusions on the other.

Right on cue, melodious church bells ring out the hour. Twelve midnight. His shoulders shake with bitter, masochistic laughter.

Of course, neither marriage was legitimate in the eyes of God. Maybe *that* was the problem. Zoia was divorced and remarried by official decree, a matter of filling in forms and bribing officials. Marcus and Nadia went to the Westminster Register Office on the Marylebone Road. Nadia specifically said she didn't want a big, expensive affair. In retrospect it was a preference entirely consistent with a view of the union as purely temporary.

—*Artists are selfish. They live to feed their work.*

Before they were even married, Nadia was probably thinking ahead to the divorce. Perhaps that was always the plan, or at least *a* plan: quick in, quick out, collecting a British passport and a useful financial settlement on the way. And it would have happened that way too, if she hadn't weakened and allowed herself to get pregnant.

Hildur said Zoia didn't like children. She could have said the same about Nadia.

. . . *children would have complicated things. She might have lost some of her . . . p-power.*

Power being power over men, power over the desiring other. It's harder spinning dreams with a baby at your breast. It's harder to get attention.

The day Teresa was born was the happiest day of his life.

Laughter and well-oiled bonhomie echo in the street. The commercial lawyers are back from dinner at the Grand, climbing out of minibuses and taxis. He remembers the disdainful look on the reporter's face as she told him he had it all wrong about Zoia. Kerstin Östlund. He could not *hope* to understand. He was outside the loop, a blind man where the female psyche was concerned.

She said he didn't understand Karl either. But at least that's a temporary problem. He has the politician's letters.

He saw a picture of Karl in Zoia's house. He was leaning over a balcony, pipe in hand, burly arms folded, wearing a shirt without a collar. Every inch the working-class hero—Zoia's hero anyway. The man who had saved her life. Her husband for sixteen years. Being inside *his* head will open Zoia up. Zoia betrayed him, and betrayal bestows a unique perspective. It forces you to see things as they are, instead of how you want them to be. Betrayal is a flayer's knife, laying bare the ugly, pragmatic truth behind the shining picture of love.

Zoia betrayed Hildur Backlin, somewhere along the line, years ago. And there's been clarity ever since. Hildur saw through the masks in the end.

His head feels heavy. In his mind, the faces blur. Zoia and Nadia, Nadia and Teresa. He hears his daughter's laughter crossing the room beyond the end of his bed. She's running toward the window, wanting to see the snow falling.

"Sweetie?"

She loves snow. She loves to pick it up and throw it into the air.

A truck has stopped outside, engine still running. The red glare of brake lights plays over the misty window.

They start the engines to mask the sound of shooting.

He sits up suddenly, awake. A bar of streetlight is falling across the bedside table. But there's no truck after all. From the microcassette player comes the dead hiss of blank tape. He hits the Stop button and lies down again. His daughter and his mother stare out of the filmy window of his wallet, propped open by the phone.

Why did he put them there, together like that? It strikes him that the symbolism is all wrong. Teresa is a normal, healthy child. She isn't going to grow into his mother. She's going to lead a happy life, and want for nothing. And she won't have mood swings that culminate in self-destruction.

Then it comes to him that this is what he wanted to say: *Look at what I made after you were gone. Look at what you missed.*

Nadia gave him the child—unwillingly, grudgingly perhaps, but she did that much. And, for a time, it was like starting again. He basked in the glow of familial responsibility, refocused, grounded. A pity it hadn't lasted. A pity Zoia hadn't let it last.

He was dealing in her pictures by that time, in a small way, introducing them to carefully chosen collectors. He felt a degree of entitlement, explaining the influences on her work, and its allure. Looking back, though, it was a masochistic exercise, a futile attempt to master what he did not understand. A dealer was just a dealer, a bridge between the artist and her audience—a bridge with a toll at both ends. He was not an initiate at all.

He looked at Zoia's gold and he knew Nadia still wanted to be free of him.

Once, he found Teresa on the kitchen floor, hoarse from crying. Nadia had passed out at the kitchen table with the vodka bottle right there in front of her. Half-past five in the afternoon, friends coming around at six. He remembers the feeling of unpitying rage.

After he'd seen to Teresa he carried Nadia upstairs and dumped her on the bed. He brought the bottle up too and set it on the bedside table, along with the Waterford crystal, wedding-present glass. A moment of cruelty that marked the beginning of the end.

In London nothing worked out the way he thought it would. His women friends maintained a distance from Nadia that went beyond the usual English reserve. It was as if, after fighting shy of commitment for so many years, they were disappointed with his final choice. The men were not much better. They made few allowances for her poor grasp of English, forgetting that she and Marcus had mostly spoken German to each other in Prague. Nadia smiled and said little, reinforcing the idea that she had, in fact, nothing much to say.

"Your friends don't like me", she said one day, and they argued about it.

"Of course they like you. What could they possibly dislike?"

"I didn't say they *dis*liked me. Just that they don't *like* me."

Someone was having a Christmas drinks party and she didn't want to go.

"Go on your own," she said.

He realized with a spasm of dismay that part of him wanted to do just that. He wanted to see his friends without worrying whether she was having a good time or not.

"How's that going to look, for God's sake?"

"Just say I'm ill or something. You always think of something."

In the end neither of them went.

She joined an amateur music group and started making her own friends, friends she didn't seem in any hurry to introduce to him. She spent hours on the phone to Prague, talking to people he didn't know.

Nadia made phone calls. Zoia wrote letters. Extramarital communications to worlds left behind, worlds which their husbands could not share.

She started spending money. It was something he felt happy about, at first. There were things she wanted in England, that gave her pleasure, and he was providing them. When she wanted to move out of the flat into a house, he went ahead, stretching himself financially in a way he'd never done before. He worked harder, took more risks, and was away more often so that she could have the house of her dreams, so that she wouldn't wake up one day to the rudeness and the noise and the sheer brute ugliness of London, and wonder if leaving Prague hadn't been a terrible mistake.

Guests turned up from the Czech Republic, most of them Nadia's age. Some of them stayed for weeks. The days of her cooking dinner, rarely a triumph gastronomically, were no more. He found himself eating fewer cooked meals than when he had been single. As for his business, her interest in it, which had once seemed so strong, withered away to nothing. She even stopped helping out at the antiques fairs, which meant they spent even more time apart.

There were times when it didn't bother him. There were times when they laughed like they used to laugh, so that the time in between shrank into a kind of sad, ridiculous joke. Laughter put things into a perspective that he liked, a perspective he wished he could hang on to, but never could.

It was less than two years into the marriage when he started talking about children. She said, what was the hurry?

"I'll get fat and have stretch marks. Plenty of time for those later."

"Younger mothers bounce back faster. It only gets harder as you get older. I thought you really wanted kids."

"Of course I do," she said. "It's just a question of when."

They had more or less the same conversation a dozen times. He mistrusted the freedom she seemed so anxious to keep hold of. He could not see it as anything but the freedom to leave.

Then suddenly her mother fell seriously ill and everything changed.

He remembers driving back from the hospital after the mercy dash to Prague, still wearing the same clothes he'd had on at work when the news of her heart attack came through. It was 3 A.M. He remembers the empty streets of sooty grand buildings, the ghostly white bands of light rolling over Nadia's face. It had been touch-and-go. Her mother remained in a coma for six hours before the shots brought her around.

In those moments, for the first time, he saw the city as he imagined she did: as a home she had left, as something she belonged to and was apart from. He felt the mass of it, pulling with the force of gravity, like a dark star.

He remembers how she put her hand on his. There was sadness and distance in her eyes. She held on so tight he could feel the nails digging in.

"She'll be all right. Don't worry," he said.

She didn't answer. Then out of the blue she said: "You're right. Let's not wait anymore." As if they had been talking about nothing else all day.

He didn't ask her why she had changed her mind. He thought she wanted a child for her mother's sake, while there was still time, in case the next heart attack was fatal. He saw it as a decision she had finally made, after years of secret equivocation: that she would stay with him for the rest of her life.

They drove back to the flat in silence, holding hands. He didn't see the truth: that the child was not for her mother, or even for them. As she sat in the hospital corridor, waiting for a verdict while the doctors worked in the intensive care unit, Nadia had found herself staring into a chasm of loneliness, had glimpsed it somehow in her future. In her panic she had reached for an answer, a guarantee that, whatever happened, she would never be alone again.

In his dreams he too sat in that corridor, waiting for the doctors to return. He waited while the rest of his life slowly fell into ruin, his business, his family, his last chance at Bukowskis. He waited and waited in hope of understanding, an understanding that would set him free.

21

Zoia's ship sailed into Stockholm harbor two days before Christmas, the city skyline looming up out of the dawn fog, gray on gray, street-lights strung out along the shoreline, like pale stars. It had been two weeks since she had left Moscow, traveling on Karl Kilbom's passport. Most of her friends and family had no idea she was leaving. There hadn't been time to tell them. Even those who knew had stayed away when the time came to see her off. She left the land of her birth without a single good-bye.

Elliot read the letters at the kitchen table, a new 100-watt bulb suspended from the socket above his head. The letters were piled up around him—on the chairs, on the floor, on the worktops. The laptop computer was plugged in behind the cooker, an extension cord snaking across the shiny stone tiles.

The mass of detail no longer daunted him. Everywhere there were flashes of illumination, beacons in the sea of words. In his time away, pictures had begun to form—chronologies, sequences, connections. He was still far from a point of understanding, but as he read on, even what was missing or unexplained became clearer. The gaps in his knowledge were being compressed, fact by fact, line by line, into simple, definable questions.

He worked without respite, feeding on sweetened coffee and rolls taken from the hotel dining room. Every letter told him something, helped him refine the picture. Sometimes he was forced to question an assumption, or throw it out completely. He entered as much as he could into the computer, but whenever he went back to the screen, it was always out of date, lagging behind his current thinking. The story was coalescing under its own power, a living thing. He began to perceive what was not said as well as what was. He could recognize in the letters elements invisible to the casual reader: silences, evasions, pretenses, lies.

These were perspectives denied to him in ordinary life—denied perhaps to anyone. He was discovering Zoia from the inside, seeing the world through her eyes. No woman had ever granted him that kind of access. Perhaps no woman ever could.

Zoia's archive was the fruit of her loneliness. It was isolation that had made her such an assiduous collector. These letters, a record of passions long dead, gave ballast to her life. They told her who she was.

Two letters from January 1922 told the story of her arrival in Sweden: one from Zoia to her mother, just returned to Moscow, the other to Yuri, her first husband divorced in absentia. Elliot found them among a bundle of correspondence tied up with string. The paper was brittle and yellowed. Some of the pages were stuck together. He had to steam them apart. The ink left reverse images on the paper facing, lines of writing crisscrossing, one letter invading another. They were all in Russian, to or from Moscow mainly, delivered via the Swedish consulate, but often constrained, conscious of probable interception. Fitful communications across the battle-lines of the international class war.

Karl had grown up on a small farm sixty miles north of Stockholm, near a town called Österbybruk in the province of Uppland. He had gone into left-wing politics while still a student, though much of his career was marred by divisions—Communists from socialists, revolutionaries from democrats, pro-Moscow factions from anti-Moscow factions. By 1921 he had somehow accumulated money and contacts. For Christmas that year he gave Zoia a gold watch and diamond earrings. He arranged for her to have private drawing lessons with Edward Berggren, one of Sweden's leading artists. He told Zoia they couldn't buy a car because it might not look good to the party rank and file. But in their flat they had two live-in maids.

Elliot had a good idea where the money came from.

Sweden had enjoyed mixed fortunes in the Great War. Arms manufacturers got rich, supplying guns and explosives; other industries were hit hard as their markets disappeared. Two years in, there was unemployment and hunger. Bread was rationed. In the spring of 1917 demonstrations turned to violence. All across Europe, the masses were taking to the streets.

Radicals like Kilbom kept busy. Sweden was a convenient conduit through which to move funds internationally, without fear of interdiction. Money raised by sympathizers in the U.S.A. and elsewhere reached the Bolsheviks via Swedish bank accounts. Several of Kilbom's colleagues were indicted for breaching foreign exchange regulations. After the Armistice the flow of money went the other way. Kilbom made secret trips to Germany and Italy, helping to establish Communist cells. He and his party were the bankers of world revolution.

Kilbom was not an insurrectionist where his home country was concerned. He believed he could work the parliamentary system. Ministers came to dine at his apartment on a regular basis, Zoia reported. He wanted to start a newspaper that would educate the working classes, and prevent them from being bought off with bread and circuses, or set at each other's throats by the capital-owning bourgeoisie. He dreamed of being elected to office by the will of the people, without recourse to revolutionary violence.

He was a passionate believer in the moral necessity of labor. Idleness was vice, whether it was the idleness of the rich, the kept woman, or the *lumpenproletariat*.

His courtship of Zoia had been swift. Of all the Swedish delegates in Moscow, he had the best contacts in the Cheka. The deputy chief of the organization, a Russian Pole called Vyacheslav Menzhinsky, was an old friend.

Following her release from the Lubyanka, Zoia had written to Kilbom, thanking him for his efforts. Kilbom had written back proposing marriage. On his return to Moscow everything—a state wedding and a divorce included—was settled by official decree. All it took was a couple of days.

But as a politician's spouse, Zoia was a disappointment from the start. It was there in every letter, the taint of grievance and recrimination. In April 1922 Karl wrote to his mother-in-law in Moscow, a woman he had never met, listing her daughter's shortcomings. She wrote back to Zoia, gripped with fear that the union was doomed.

What your husband complains about are precisely those aspects of your character that I have always sought to change, although you

*have never listened to me: you are capricious, lazy, and untidy—
and very ungrateful. In all of this I'm afraid he is quite correct.
Secondly, he says, you do not care for his friends or talk to them.
This is awful. They are important people and necessary to him, and
that you should behave badly before them makes me ashamed of
you. I can imagine people saying that your mother didn't bring you
up properly, and didn't teach you any manners.*

*The root of all these evils is your laziness. I can just imagine
how untidy and chaotic your house is, and even at this distance, it
makes me ashamed. Another thing: you love dresses, but you never
look after them.*

*All this, my dear, is simply the truth. So please do not be angry
with me for upbraiding you. Your husband is a foreigner, and so all
of this can only seem strange and unwelcome to him.*

*And then it seems that you went to a party without him. This
is beyond criticism! I accept what you say, that you and he are
different people, but you simply must act in accordance with the
rules of society. Carry on in such a shocking way, and you risk
losing the respect of everyone. You must think of your husband's
position and confine yourself to company that is suitable.
Dispense with your old Moscow antics—nothing good can come
of them. Such is the life of a coquette, which is a very sad life and
a short one.*

*Above all, I must also entreat you not to write to Yuri. I know
he is still in touch with you, and you with him. I have been told as
much. But I have to tell you that if you write to him just once more,
you will never receive another letter from me ever again. You would
see how reasonable this is, if you knew something of the gossip,
problems, and insults I've had to endure. You cannot imagine how
terrible my life is now, and if you did, you would not give Yuri the
time of day. The insults and humiliations I suffer every day at the
hands of acquaintances and strangers alike, and all on account of
that damned wedding—which, like everything else, is laid at my
door, as your mother. I am trying to avoid running into anyone, for
fear of what they will say.*

*So I ask you, if you love your mother, send Yuri's letters back
unopened. I wanted to telephone his father and put an end to his*

*correspondence, but I am too disgusted about it all to even go near
a phone.*

Elliot opened a new file on the computer. He wanted every reference to
the preceding year isolated and logged. He needed to build a picture of
that particular period: Zoia in revolutionary Moscow, midway through
the civil war, the time of Zoia's *Moscow antics,* and *that damned wedding.*

Even in wartime, Zoia relished her freedom. She went unescorted to
bars and cafés, seeking out the company of poets and painters. She toured
the galleries with Andrei Burov, and enrolled at Kandinsky's experimental academy. For her, the collapse of the old social order had its compensations: for a brief, exciting time, she could enter circles forbidden to any
future lady-in-waiting. She learned to drink and argue and make love.
The new aesthetics of the inner self worked on her like a spell. It held out
the promise of an even profounder liberation.

Then the Reds started shooting poets too.

He wondered how much Karl Kilbom knew of this time, how much
Zoia would have put in letters to a stranger. Karl had always had fixed
ideas about what his wife would be like. One meeting and a few letters
later he had decided on Zoia. He needed her with all the mysterious passion of love at first sight. She needed a way out.

In Stockholm she wrote clandestine letters to the husband she had
just divorced. She kept letters from men in Russia who admired her, letters laced with bitterness and mockery. Andrei, the disciple of Meyerhold,
told Zoia's mother he planned to visit Stockholm in the summer. She
wrote to Zoia on 22 February:

*I do not like Andrei. I think I even hate him. He told me your life is
like a nonsense poem written by a poet who usually lies. It upset me
to hear him talk like that. Please don't write to him, in case he tries
to blackmail you as he did at the high school. He has been boasting
all over Moscow about his relations with you. It's something I can't
stand to hear.*

Always she wrote with fear that Karl would grow weary of his new
spouse and abandon her. She urged Zoia to behave, to be the kind of wife
he wanted. At the same time she implored Zoia to demand an official

church marriage, recognizable under Swedish law. The reason was obvious: a Swedish marriage would confer citizenship. It would ensure that Zoia could not be deported. Karl was their lifeline, their hope of safety. But there were things he could not be allowed to know, secrets that could never be spoken of. Madam Korvin-Krukovsky's greatest fear was that they were not secret enough.

At noon on the fifth day the lights went out. Elliot checked the fuse boxes below the stairs, but everything was dead. The power had been cut off.

Even with the shutters open, there was not enough light in the kitchen. The sitting room was cramped and full of furniture. The obvious place to work was in the studio at the top of the house, where the big picture window looked out across the bay.

In town he bought a pair of storm lanterns and four boxes of candles. He hung the storm lanterns from the rafters beneath the roof, and set the candles in jars on the landings. With the last of the kindling, he set a fire going in the little iron stove in the corner of the studio, then went outside to look for more. He wanted to light all the stoves in the house, to drive out the cold and the smell of damp.

Below the house, on the seaward side, there was a path that led through the trees, a winding carpet of flat snow that zigzagged through the bracken. The ground beneath was mossy and yielding. He went slowly, looking for fallen timber, gathering what he could. He stopped to listen to the wind as it gusted through the tops of the pines. This had been Zoia's way down to the shore. Her footsteps had flattened the earth beneath his feet on a thousand solitary walks. It was said she only came to the coast in the summer. But he knew that wasn't true. She had come out here in winter too, alone, without telling anyone, to walk in these woods and gaze across the restless sea.

22

Dr. Lindqvist opened the door in his dressing gown. He was stooping, and behind the heavy lenses his eyes were bloodshot.

"Still here, Mr. Elliot? I'd have thought you'd be finished by now."

Elliot dug his hands into his pockets and smiled affably. "Almost. How was Uppsala?"

Lindqvist wiped his nose with a folded handkerchief. "Cold. It's always cold in that damned city. You'll be wanting the keys, I suppose. Here, come in a moment."

Lindqvist disappeared, leaving Elliot to wait in the narrow hallway. From inside he heard voices, Lindqvist's sister scolding him, telling him to get back to bed before he caught his death, Lindqvist replying with an irritable *ja ja ja.*

On the walls there were pictures in varnished wooden frames, watercolors with big skies turned brownish with age, old black-and-white photographs of sailing ships, large and small, evidence of a passion past or present. Tiny black thunderflies were trapped beneath the glass.

Lindqvist came back, coughing.

"So you're almost done, you say?" he said, handing over the keys.

Elliot shrugged. "Yes, another day or two . . ."

"That's good because I really want to empty the place out soon. The furniture, the books. And the papers. Some people are interested, so . . ."

"In the papers? They want to buy the papers?"

Immediately Elliot wished he hadn't sounded so concerned.

Lindqvist looked at him warily. There was a thick medicinal smell coming off him—throat lozenges or disinfectant.

"You think they should be given to the National Archive, I suppose."

Elliot shrugged again. "Ideally."

Lindqvist opened the door. Cold air flooded the hallway. "That was not her wish," he said, subject closed. "So have you found anything of interest up there? Anything new?"

The way he said *up there,* it was as if he preferred to keep away from the place, given the choice.

Elliot put the keys in his pocket. "Some family history. Background mainly, you know. But it all helps."

Kerstin Östlund was in Elliot's mind now, telling him how Lindqvist had changed Zoia's will or forged it, telling him about a malpractice lawyer called Röstman who helped him do it.

Lindqvist grunted, like he wasn't surprised at the lack of revelations. "Everything's on schedule, though, for the exhibition?"

"Absolutely. There are still some early works we're trying to trace. But that won't hold anything up."

"Good. Well . . ."

Lindqvist waved a perfunctory farewell, and made to close the door.

"Oh, Dr. Lindqvist?"

Lindqvist had the handkerchief over his mouth. He held the door ajar.

"There was something I wanted to ask you," Elliot said. "I don't know if you can help me. I've come across some references I can't work out."

Lindqvist pushed his glasses up his nose and sniffed hard. "References?"

"To some pictures, sketches perhaps, I'm not sure. Of the Crimea, of Sevastopol. Or painted there possibly, although that would mean . . . You see, I think they may be important."

Lindqvist was frowning at him, the handkerchief still pressed to his lips.

"I was wondering if Madam Zoia ever said anything about them. Anything at all."

The doctor was very still for a moment, then shook his head. "I can't help you there," he said, and closed the door.

Lindqvist was coming down with the flu. With luck it would keep him away from the house for a few days, if not longer. But that didn't mean he would continue to grant access. Elliot got the impression he was quite capable of saying no at any time.

He drove back to the hotel, found the receptionist alone as usual at the desk. The last of the commercial lawyers were checking out, the conference over. Elliot nudged his way to the head of the queue.

"Ah, good morning, Mr. Elliot," the receptionist said, looking up from the computer screen. "Still with us then?"

Elliot caught irritated mutterings from the men behind him. He leaned across the counter. "I need to know if there's a locksmith somewhere around here."

The receptionist looked at him uncertainly. "A locksmith?"

"That's right. I need to copy some keys."

23

———•———

From accumulation to extrapolation. Up in the studio he worked chronologically, transforming the room into an exposition of Zoia's early life,
turning every surface into a collage of images and words. In a cupboard
he found a stack of large sketchbooks. He pinned the leaves along the wall,
then stuck the photographs on top of them, along with pictures torn from
catalogs and the plates Cornelius had given him. On the white spaces he
made headings, adding dates and places, names and notes. Most of the
letters had to go on the floor. Two columns: letters from Zoia on one side,
letters to Zoia on the other. Where a letter was referred to but missing, he
inserted a blank sheet of paper, writing on it what he had reason to believe
it contained. Only key letters went up on the walls. He drew diagrams and
made labels, like a detective assembling clues. He built up the record five
years at a time. Five years took him from one end of the room to the other.
He weighed the letters down with stones from the beach. He attached
Post-It notes bearing references and summaries of content.

The gilded panel stayed in the middle of the room, where Zoia had left
it, as if waiting for her return. Sometimes he stopped to stare into its shimmering, illusory depths. He tried to imagine what Zoia had planned to
paint, the subject of what would have been her last work. He tried to read
it in the crooked overlaps of light, the pale, almost imperceptible bars.

But he could not see it.

Without power, the laptop was no use. The battery could only hold a
charge for an hour at a time. He preferred to build the picture physically
in any case. He could see the flow of words, the gaps, the silences. He
could gauge Zoia's state of mind from the shape of her writing and the
character of her language. He was making a map of Zoia's life. He was
dragging her secrets into the light.

What was it Karl didn't know? What was it he could not be told?

There was one scandal attached to Zoia's name, if you could call it a scandal. It was a story she had finally come out with in 1938, the year after her marriage to Karl ended.

In Moscow in 1919, Zoia said, she had met and fallen in love with a law student named Yuri. In spite of opposition from both families they had married the same year in a secret church service. Though his family were academics, it seemed the bridegroom moved in aristocratic circles, young people of good birth who were determined to carry on the old way of life as best they could, however reduced their circumstances. They held picnics by the river and a hunting party in the Sparrow Hills, where Napoleon had surveyed Moscow before its fall.

One night, a month into their marriage, soldiers came to the flat where Zoia and Yuri were staying. They searched the place, pocketed the jewelry Zoia had carefully hidden, and took away any papers that weren't in Russian. They took Yuri away as well.

For three weeks Zoia heard nothing. She tried to find out what had become of Yuri, where he was, if he had been charged with anything. But no one would tell her. Friends urged her to stay away from the Cheka at all costs, to wait, and keep silent, like thousands of others. Zoia ignored their advice, touring police stations with a photograph of Yuri, showing it to anyone who would look.

Then, without warning, Yuri reappeared. He was evasive about what had happened to him. He had been interrogated, he said, about his studies and his family, and that was all. He couldn't explain why the process had taken three weeks, didn't want to talk about it. And then he announced that he had managed to get himself a new job in a government department, although he was vague about that too. Just a pen-pushing job, he said, without explaining how he had come by it within hours of his release.

For a while life got a little easier. All of a sudden they had more food. But at night, Zoia said, Yuri paced the rooms for hours at a time. Every time someone came to the door, he jumped and started shaking.

Two days after Christmas he was arrested again, although this time the soldiers were more polite than before. As they took him away, Yuri was shaking so badly he could hardly walk.

Zoia soon learned that there had been other arrests that night. All Yuri's friends from the hunting party had been rounded up. The wife of one of them gave Zoia the cold shoulder. The word was out that Yuri had been recruited by the Cheka. He had been acting as an agent provocateur, and had betrayed them all. He had only been arrested the second time so as to deflect suspicion. In the days that followed, everyone in the circle but Yuri was charged with involvement in a counter-revolutionary conspiracy, and executed. Yuri was transferred to a special prison for the mentally ill. He was finally released in the autumn of 1921, a few weeks before Zoia left for Stockholm.

That was when he told her he had done it for her. The thought of never seeing her again had been more than he could stand.

A traitor in the family was something to hide. It was even a reason to run away to the Crimea, away from the cold stares and the wagging tongues. Zoia said she'd known nothing of Yuri's deal with the Cheka, but maybe that was not true. Maybe he told her everything, and they had been in it together from the start. The Reds had gone on to give her a cushy job at the Foreign Ministry. She had ended up marrying a Communist. For some that was enough to prove where her sympathies lay. And she carried on writing to Yuri even after his treachery had been revealed—had been seen with him indeed, driving around Moscow after his release from the asylum. Madam Korvin-Krukovsky wrote to Zoia in February that they hadn't a friend left in Moscow, except for a girl called Rosa, and even Rosa reported hearing the cruelest rumors: that Zoia had been behind the plot, that her mind had been poisoned by the company she'd kept, people like Andrei Burov and his modernist friends. They said she had turned traitor for the money, to satisfy her taste for luxury. She had screwed her way up the Party hierarchy and thence to a life of ease in Stockholm, where even the money Lenin sent she blew on minks and chauffeur-driven cars. They called her a Jewish whore—because by now it was known that her father had been Jewish, and it was common knowledge that Jews and Bolsheviks were one and the same thing. Madam Korvin-Krukovsky thanked God her daughter was no longer in Moscow, where people would have spat at her in the street.

The story of the hunting party might have surprised many people in Sweden, but not Karl. He had friends in the Cheka. He was in a better position to know the truth than Zoia herself. Besides, why would he care what Yuri had done, or Zoia for that matter? In the war against the bourgeoisie, he was in the opposing camp.

Zoia's mother just wanted Yuri out of their lives. He had brought disgrace to them all. Only Zoia still pitied him, answering his faltering, heartbroken letters.

Moscow, 4th January 1922

My dear darling Zoisich,

You have been gone six weeks, and I haven't heard a word from you. Are you upset with me for not coming to say good-bye at the station? If so, please don't be angry. It was just too difficult for me. I didn't think I could bear it. Please write to me. Tell me how you are at least.

I still have my pictures of you. I've hung them up on the walls. Your beautiful eyes look down on me as I write, although I try not to look at them too much, because it makes me sad to be reminded that I cannot kiss you anymore, nor show you the tenderness I feel. Tell me the truth: do you really love this husband of yours? And don't you have any love left for me? I want so much to see you again. If you only knew.

I kiss you, my beloved—although not mine—but still closest to my heart, and still loved.

Beneath the letter there was what looked like a reply. But it was only a draft. Elliot could not be sure Zoia had sent it, or that it had ever arrived. The hand was hurried and obscure, the lines bunching as they streamed across the page.

I have been thinking about writing to you, Yurevich, but it has been very difficult for me, you must understand. Your letter touched me very much, because it told me how you are thinking of me. It also reminded me how impossible it is to be angry with you. In any case, as far as my departure from Moscow is concerned, it was so hurried I didn't have time to reflect on why you did not come to say good-bye.

I am fine now. My life is fine, although there are some difficulties I don't know how to overcome.

We got to Stockholm on a steamship from Tallinn, just like the one you and I used to dream about. Do you remember? I hated the trip and was so seasick I thought I was going to die. At the customs house they wanted to take Mishka away from me, but they laughed when I explained why I needed a teddy bear . . . We were met by a car, because they don't have carriages in Stockholm anymore, and taken to the apartment, which has a good feel about it, and has been decorated with some style. Karl's office is lined with red wood and the dining room in black oak. We have two maids and a dog, and I have already started painting lessons. Karl wants me to exhibit this autumn, and says he will use his journalist contacts to help get me noticed, although I don't think I'm anywhere near ready. He's even lined up some important politician for me to paint a portrait of. He is already planning my career very seriously, as you can see.

Karl seems to have a great many acquaintances. Some are very interesting. And some are not. In fact, I find the Swedes rather pedantic and particular about things, and they much prefer to have meals at home than go out. Over Christmas I found it quite a strain. Karl seems to know everyone in Stockholm, and the formal dinners seemed to go on forever.

Karl dotes on me, and I love him back, of course. He does not have what you would call an easygoing nature. He is always telling me what to do, like a mentor more than anything, but he is generous too. I received gold and diamonds from him at Christmas, and a silver dinner service from some of his friends. One of them arranged for me to go to a party where the Swedish royal family were present. And that was very thrilling. The only sad thing is that the doctors have told me I cannot have children, and Karl is in a terrible state about it.

The draft ended there, abruptly, like something brittle that snaps. Elliot searched through the whole bundle, but found nothing more.

He pinned the letter to the wall, trying to picture the sequence of events. Zoia had gone to the doctors in Sweden. Karl would have insisted, given the diseases she must have been exposed to in Russia. They had examined her and pronounced her incapable of bearing children.

Hildur Backlin told a different story, the story about the restaurant in Östermalm. The sound of children playing had been too much for Zoia. She had got up and left in the middle of the meal. But Hildur had been wrong about the reason. Zoia's childlessness was not a matter of choice. It was a condition, a physiological condition probably, given the state of medical knowledge at the time. Something malformed in her reproductive organs. Malformed or damaged. It had to be one or the other.

For a while it seemed the doctors were wrong. On 14 May 1922, Zoia's mother replied to a letter she had just received from Zoia.

> *Tell me what your husband thinks about your condition. Is he happy about it? Does he want this baby? You have written about it very briefly and I can hardly understand a word. So, my darling, please write more often as your letters only come once a month, and such intervals are unbearable.*
>
> *Maya visited me recently. She is happy you're going to have a baby. She wants to have her own so much she gets excited even at the news that someone else is expecting. She says your baby will be gorgeous as both you and Karl are beautiful and clever.*

Elliot found another mention of the pregnancy at the end of the month: Zoia's grandmother was knitting baby clothes. The child was due in the winter. But then the references abruptly ceased. In June Madam Korvin-Krukovsky replied to another letter from Zoia, which she referred to as "full of despair." Zoia said she planned to leave Stockholm, to travel. By July 1922 she was in Germany, sometimes with Karl, sometimes alone.

The doctors were right, after all.

On 6 August, while in Berlin, she wrote to an old friend, the poet Sandro Kusikov. She asked him to send her some of his old poems about Russia, and the landscapes of the Caucasus where he was born.

Early the next morning, Elliot sat down at the kitchen table to write the briefing Cornelius had asked him for: just a couple of pages on Zoia's life and work, why it would make a suitable centerpiece for the visit of a Russian premier and former head of the KGB. The laptop had enough battery power for that.

He sat there a long time, watching the wind blow granules of ice across the window. No words came.

24

————•————

Back at the hotel he pulled the mobile phone from his coat pocket and found it was dead. He rummaged in his suitcase for the charger and the adapter, and plugged them into the electric shaver socket in the bathroom. He entered his code number and waited for a signal.

His complexion was yellow in the neon light. He leaned toward the glass, turning his head this way and that. He couldn't see it anymore, what it was that women used to say made him handsome: the friendly brown eyes, the strong chin, the retiring smile he didn't use often enough. His face looked shapeless now, swollen, bruised.

Zoia painted on mirrors of gold. Everything around them was touched with a sacred radiance. But they were still mirrors. They cast back only the light that was brought to them. The painted image floated in a version of your world, not in its own.

The ringer made him jump: he had voicemail. He picked up the phone and immediately it lit up in his hand. The display read: 7 *Missed Calls*. He pressed the playback key. The faltering digital voice told him he had five messages.

—Monday, 1:21 P.M.: *Marcus, it's Harriet Shaw. Can you give me a call as soon as possible? There's been . . . Well, I need to talk to you asap. I'll be in all afternoon.*

"Damn."

The message was two days old. The phone had been dead all that time.

—Monday, 8:34 P.M.: *Marcus. Paul. I haven't heard from you. Are you okay?*

Paul Costa, electrician, medicinal supplier, stop-gap business associate.

—*Everything's taken care of at this end. Paperwork etcetera. So do I send the picture over or what? Gimme a call.*

—Tuesday, 10:47 A.M.: Nobody spoke. Elliot pressed the phone against his ear, waiting for a message. It sounded like traffic going by on a busy street. He heard a footstep, a sharp intake of breath. A woman, he thought. Then whoever she was hung up.

—Tuesday, 9:45 A.M.: *Marcus, it's Harriet again. Um, I really have to speak to you, sort of urgently. There's been a development. So please call me as soon as you get this, okay? I'll be waiting. Oh my number. Maybe you've lost it. It's—*

Elliot knew the number. He hit the key for the next message.

—Tuesday, 2:35 P.M.: *Hello, Marcus. Cornelius here. Have you turned your phone off again?*

Elliot could hear the irritation in his voice, a touch of disappointment, as if Elliot were shutting him out of something.

—*Anyway, I just wanted to talk to you about that briefing I asked you for. Frederik says it's essential we have something by next week if we're—*

Elliot didn't wait to hear the rest. He hung up and dialed Harriet Shaw's number. The phone rang for a long time. He checked his watch: 8:57 P.M. One hour behind in England. He prayed Harriet hadn't already gone home. "Come on, come on."

"Hello? Harriet Shaw's office."

An exasperated voice: Deborah, the PA, leaning across the desk, coat on, one foot out the door, dying to be gone.

"Is she in, please?"

Hesitation. A hand over the mouthpiece. "Who's calling?"

"Marcus Elliot."

"I'll just see if—"

Harriet took the receiver. "Marcus. Thank God. I've been trying to reach you for days."

"I'm sorry, Harriet. It's this damned phone. What's going on?"

He heard Deborah bustle off. A door closed.

"Nadia's petition. To overturn the Ward of Court order? We have a date for the hearing. It's sooner than we wanted, I'm afraid."

"How soon?"

"Tomorrow afternoon. Half-past two."

"*What?*"

The charger landed in the basin with a bang. Elliot turned, realized he had yanked it out of the socket. Fumbling, he picked it up again and shoved it back in the wall. When he put the phone to his ear again, Harriet was still talking.

"I did the best I could, Marcus, I did. But Hanson has contacts and he really put on the pressure. He said the child—I mean, Teresa—was being traumatized by separation from her mother."

"And how would he know that?"

He heard Harriet sigh.

"Because he asked the foster parents. Mr. and Mrs. Edwards? He got them to say she was . . . suffering."

"Oh, Jesus."

"There wasn't much I could do. You have to understand, Marcus, this is all about perceptions. It just wouldn't look good demanding a later hearing just because you're on a business trip in Stockholm. This is supposed to be about the welfare of the child."

Elliot brought his hand to his forehead. Once he would have reminded Harriet that *of course* this was about the welfare of the child, that every penny he had spent, every ounce of effort, his whole damned *life* was about the welfare of the child. But not this time.

"Okay. Then I'll just have to get there."

"I really think it would help. You know what they say: possession is nine-tenths. If Nadia gets your daughter back, it'll be that much harder to get her away again. Your flying back specially will score us some valuable points."

"I understand."

"Good. I had Deborah make inquiries. There's an early flight tomorrow morning. Stockholm Västerås to London Stansted. It should get you here with at least a couple of hours to spare. Time for me to prep you. Can you make that?"

25

He made instant coffee with the toy-sized kettle on the minibar. He drank it black, chasing down a couple of the Preludins he kept for emergencies, feeling them kick in as he stepped out into the night, everything opening up, the world growing harder and sharper before his eyes.

Half-past 4 A.M., stealing out of town along empty, snow-cushioned roads. He sat hunched over the wheel, the heater blowing cold air. The outside thermometer read minus eight. Goose pimples came up on his arms. He felt physically exhausted and blindingly alert.

He looked in his mirror as he climbed from the shoreline: rooftops, streetlights, beyond them the formless, ink-black sea. In the sky above Zoia's house there was a yellow smudge of moonlight. He saw her by the window, young and beautiful again. Wide-eyed Zoia, bewitching, lonely. The maker of masks. She was watching his car disappear among the trees.

Can it be you have forgotten me?

Everything in the house was just as he'd left it. Her letters were open on the studio floor. Pictures, notes, and photographs were pinned up all over the walls. Work begun but not completed. Like an open wound.

The idea of someone walking in and finding it was unbearable. It was the middle of a process, one that had to be finished before it could be interpreted or appreciated. Just as Zoia had done, he dreaded interruption, the intrusion of uninformed minds. He could have gone back himself and cleared up, but there was a desecration in that too.

He saw her standing by the unused panel, the gold turned greenish in the moonlight. She had brushes in her hand.

"I'm coming back," he said out loud. His voice came out cracked and boyish, like the voice of a stranger.

•   •   •

He found a petrol station open on the outskirts of Stockholm. A bleary-eyed Asian attendant was mopping up a spill behind the counter. Elliot bought biscuits and iced tea and breakfasted behind the wheel. Preludin killed hunger, but he'd been caught that way before, almost passing out before it occurred to him to eat. He watched the snow as it swirled past the lights of the forecourt. It was coming down more heavily now, the flakes like duck down, drifting in the gutters, smothering everything. Gusts of wind tugged at the signs advertising engine oil and tires. He turned on the radio, hoping for a weather report, but all he could find was music. The thermometer told him the temperature was rising. He turned on the engine and moved out onto the road, wanting to get to the airport before things got any worse.

Through the suburbs of Stockholm they had trucks out clearing the snow, their orange warning lights lighting up the house fronts. Half-past five and he got his first bulletin. It said a storm system had picked up speed, veering in from the southeast, bringing weather along a two-hundred-mile front. It urged drivers to use caution and to think twice about unnecessary journeys.

Västerås-Hässlö was a regional airport, recently opened to international traffic, forty-five miles inland along a major highway. Elliot crawled behind a convoy of snowplows and sanding trucks as they tunneled through the storm. Sometimes the only thing he could see beyond the beating wipers were warning lights and the shortened beam of his own headlamps. Ten miles out he passed the scene of an accident. The convertible had skidded on a ramp and smashed into the barrier. Another car stood a few yards away, hood and chassis comically buckled. Medics were tending someone on the ground.

He reached the airport with twenty-five minutes to spare. At first he thought the terminal building was on fire. A towering plume of snow was being whipped off the roof by the wind. Everywhere cars and buses were maneuvering, jamming up the forecourt and the way into the car park. A pair of policemen in Day-Glo jackets were trying to keep things moving.

He parked a hundred meters away and hurried toward the terminal, suitcase in one hand, computer in the other. At least two hours to spare, that was what Harriet had said. He could afford a two-hour delay. His feet slipped as he ran.

Inside, the place was full of lost-looking people making phone calls. Luggage was everywhere. A crowd was besieging the little breakfast bar. The check-in desk had been abandoned. A notice written in felt pen announced that his flight had been delayed for an indefinite period.

They would not let him check his bag. The airline's telephone number was permanently engaged. The exasperated woman at the information desk had her hands full just directing people to the bus stops. The airport remained open. Up on the board, flights were announced in cascades of fluttering metal—arriving, departing—only to disappear again. Slowly the schedule disintegrated, until there was nothing left but an empty statement of what should have been.

Elliot stood in the middle of the crowd, watching the minutes go by, calculating and recalculating the time still available for him to reach the court. He left a message on Harriet Shaw's voicemail, telling her what had happened, asking if there was any way she could ask for the hearing to be postponed, knowing the answer was probably no. He thought about driving back to Stockholm, to the international airport, and taking the first flight out, catching a connection at Copenhagen or Amsterdam or Paris. But at the last minute it would cost money his credit card just wasn't good for anymore. And still it wouldn't get him there in time.

Outside it grew light. The snowfall let up a little, but the wind blew harder. Slowly the airport emptied. Eight o'clock came and went, then nine, then ten. At a quarter past, Elliot looked up from his seat in the arrivals hall and saw that the notice had been changed. His flight was now officially canceled. He thought about calling the airline again, booking himself on another flight. But what was the point, if he was too late for the hearing?

He pictured the proceedings: Nadia in the Armani suit he had paid for, black hair swept back beneath a band, pale, austere, and beautiful; Harriet going in hard about her drinking, her disregard for the authority of the court, her episodes of instability—a prelude to the heavier broadsides she had planned for the main residency hearing. It was funny, disturbing, given what was at stake: part of him was relieved to be missing it. He didn't want to look into Nadia's face when Harriet called her a threat to their child.

Seven years ago—it felt like the blink of an eye—they had been strangers. Seven years from love to war. And a dirty war at that.

They met in Prague, the summer of 1993.

His first time there had been twelve years earlier, before the Wall came down, when Prague was still sealed off from the West. Back then even tourist dollars were eschewed in favor of ideological purity. The handful of tatty coaches grinding their way around the sights were full of East Germans and Poles. Elliot and a school friend bought visas in London and railed it over the border from Vienna, curious to see how long it would take before they were thrown out again.

Old Prague was a storybook city caked in grime: ancient, soot-blackened. History lived in every detail: in the deerstalker rooftops and the blue-sparking trams. He wandered the streets in disbelief, photographing everything, images from Kafka crowding into his head. With the turn of every corner it came back to him: the special kind of frisson you get behind enemy lines.

They were followed. Their hotel rooms were searched, occasional items stolen, a tube of toothpaste run through repeatedly with a needle for some reason, so that when he squeezed it, the contents came out in his hand. They were approached continually by black marketeers, offering to buy Western money at four times the official rate. The authorities sent them to a different hotel every day, even though all of them were virtually empty. But it didn't matter. He felt like a prince in this place, an ambassador from the West—the West not as he knew it, but as it was imagined by those who had never been there: a place of heady freedom and effortless prosperity.

Communist or not, it was how Karl Kilbom must have felt in Moscow, the year he fell in love with Zoia—if it was love. The ennobling power of wealth and security. The effortless superiority they conveyed. Men sought affirmation of their newfound condition. They found that affirmation in beautiful things.

Everything had changed by the time he returned to Prague. Shiny German cars jammed the roads where the trams had been. Coca-Cola parasols had all but taken over the Old Town Square. The buildings had been pressure-sprayed to an even beige, or hidden beneath scaffolding and plastic sheeting. Even the sky was a different color: a hard, artificial blue. Kafka had thrown away his diary and opened a souvenir shop on the castle steps.

The magic city wasn't free. It was gone. Along with the soot and the secret police.

He gave up on the bars and the foreigners' haunts. He went looking for something the Western world hadn't yet dragged into its hard commercial light, something he could still make his.

He was staying on a converted houseboat, the only accommodation available. One Sunday morning he got up early and set off across the river. He ignored the castle and headed south into an area of low yellow houses and yards shaded by willows. It was there he heard the music. At first he thought it was coming from an upstairs window, but as he drew nearer he realized it was actually coming from the little baroque chapel. He stood listening in the cobbled alley, not sure if what he heard was just a recording or a woman singing for real.

That clear perfect sound echoed high above his head.

He followed the voice around the corner. A pink notice on the church door was written in Czech, the words printed over a gray treble clef: Mozart, Schubert, Richard Strauss; a recital by students of the Prague Conservatory. He slipped inside, taking a seat halfway down the aisle.

Three girls. One singing, one on the piano, a third seated next to her, turning the pages. Elliot couldn't place the song, though it was beautiful, or the language either. The audience numbered less than twenty, mostly old people and a smattering of what Elliot took to be fellow students. Light streamed through the tall windows onto freshly whitewashed walls.

Nadia was the one turning the pages. She had dark shoulder-length hair secured with a band, and slender white arms. She followed the score with care, only occasionally looking across at the audience. Elliot felt the moment she noticed him, felt it at his throat: her green eyes holding on his.

Every time she turned a new page, she glanced his way, probably wondering who he was, this music-loving stranger in a hand-tailored suit. Every time she returned to the music, he looked back at her, slowly taking in every detail: the curve of her neck, the contours of her mouth.

She was priceless. The thought had come to him as clearly as if he'd read it in a catalog. When she smiled at him, it made him giddy: the thought that soon she might actually be his.

*　　*　　*

The phone jumped in his hand.

"Hello? Harriet?"

But it wasn't Harriet. It was Cornelius.

"I'm just calling to see how you're getting on."

"I'm stuck at the airport. I'm supposed to—"

"The airport?"

"Something came up. I was supposed to get back to London this afternoon."

"Well, there's no chance of that. Haven't you heard? Nothing's flying until tomorrow at the earliest. They had a plane come off the runway at Skavsta."

The phone let out a series of loud beeps. Already the battery was low.

"Cornelius, I'll have to—"

"Get back to Stockholm, and come around for dinner. That's what I rang for, to invite you."

"That's very kind of you, Cornelius. But to be honest—"

"I have an ulterior motive, of course. I want a progress report on the catalog. You've been so mysterious about the whole thing, people are starting to talk."

Behind the good humor, impatience. Elliot covered his eyes with his hand. Here was the truth: Frederik Wahl was demanding proof of progress. The only problem was, Elliot didn't have any to show him.

"And what about the briefing? How's that coming along?"

"It's almost done," Elliot said. "Almost."

"Good. You know we really do need it—"

"By next week. Yes. I got your message. You'll have it, I promise."

There was a pause. Then Cornelius was back to his ebullient self. "So I'll see you later then? At my place?"

"Yes. I'll be there."

"Excellent. There's someone coming I think you should talk to. About Zoia, I mean."

"About Zoia?"

But before Cornelius could say any more, the battery died.

26

One of the pay phones in the terminal was out of order. There were queues at the others. When he finally got to one, he found it wouldn't accept his credit card, spewing it out immediately, without explanation, as if it were obviously no good for anything. He tried using change, but it turned out he didn't have enough for an international call. Behind him people sighed and pursed their lips as he went back to the credit card with the same result.

He got back in the car, paid cash for a day's parking, and headed back into town. The highway was closed but for a single lane, the traffic nosing its way forward through the blinding wind, bunching and slowing as it drew nearer the city, ending up in a single jam that went on for miles. He stared at the clock on the dashboard as the minutes ticked by, trying to picture events in London. Nadia would be in front of the full-length mirror by now, getting ready for court, following tips from her lawyer on how best to look: soft, pretty, and appealing for a male judge; sober and unthreatening for a female. Harriet Shaw said male judges were generally more sympathetic to a father's case. Many of them were fathers themselves. But Elliot couldn't help hoping there was a woman on the bench. Nadia always got what she wanted where men were concerned. It was something even her friends back home had told him. The fact that someone was now paying her legal bills was only the latest proof. She took what she wanted, and when that wasn't enough, she moved on.

In the early days of their marriage he had believed their differences lent their passion a clandestine edge. Their assignations took place in cozy restaurants and bars cocooned in darkness. In England, at dull summer drinks parties, they would sneak off into secluded corners of the garden and kiss with the hunger and urgency of teenagers. But other aspects of his behavior, observed dispassionately, betrayed an awareness that the relationship was essentially transactional. The way *providing* became so important, especially after his father died, and the Paris self-portrait was back in his life, hanging on the wall in his office. The way he felt responsible for every aspect of her life, for the fulfillment of every desire. She was his wife, but conditionally. For better and for richer, yes; but for poorer or for worse, probably not. Deep down he had known this, but had been powerless to change it. Even Teresa, even his wanting a child, was little more than an attempt to make Nadia need him more.

It was dark again by the time he reached the city center. He left the Volvo in an underground car park and rode the escalators into a shopping mall. In the mobile phone shop a girl with plum-colored hair took ten minutes to find a battery that would work in his old phone, and another ten to find the price. The Preludins had worn off by this time, leaving him feeling hollow and shaky. He ate a round of meatballs at a stand-up counter on the top level, then fitted the new battery and turned the phone back on. There was a message from Harriet Shaw. It was several hours old. It said she was going to the hearing and would report back when it was over. She told him not to worry.

He set off on foot toward the Old Town, where Cornelius lived, wanting to be moving, to be doing something. He reached the waterfront, walked around past the Grand Hotel and the opera house, then crossed over onto Helgeands Island with the royal palace floodlit above him. The mist and snow closed in around him as he walked through the little park, hiding the distant lights, masking the traffic noise, so that the city seemed like a small town, a few lines of lampposts spaced along the shoreline, just as it was the day Zoia arrived on that steamship from Tallinn, the juvenile bride with a teddy bear stuffed with icons, and secrets even her husband could never be told.

He had been in this place before, at the age of three or four. It was one of the few memories of Sweden he had retained throughout his childhood: the palace on the other side of the water and, more clearly still, the small, copper-plated lighthouse beside the bridge. It all came back to him: crowding into the elevator with his mother and father, the ride to the top, his father holding him under the arms so that he could see the view. He remembered woolen mittens with a red, zigzag pattern, and the sweet smell of candy bought from a shop with yellow shutters. It was the smell of an enchanted time.

He was still on the island when Harriet called.

It was bad news.

"Social Services didn't put up much of a fight, I'm afraid, what with the whole airport incident in doubt and everything." She sounded hurried, brisk. "Frankly, I think they saw an opportunity to save money, free of risk."

The judge had ruled that Teresa should go back to her mother, pending the final residency hearing the following month.

In his stomach Elliot felt the panic rising. "But what's to stop Nadia taking off again? With Teresa. What's to stop her trying again?"

"You can relax on that score. Your daughter's passport is to be lodged with the court. Nadia can go where she likes, but Teresa must stay in the U.K. until the hearing. They fought that one too, I might add. They presented a deposition from a doctor in Prague."

"A deposition? Saying what?"

Harriet sniffed dismissively. "Some sob story about Nadia's mother being taken ill. A cardiac *episode*, whatever that is. Your wife claimed that was why she dashed off to Prague without telling anyone. She claimed she was planning to come back."

"Come back? But she took Teresa without—"

"There wasn't time to do anything else, she said. She thought her mother was dying. The judge almost believed it."

From where he stood, Elliot could see the traffic rolling over the big road bridge before heading south and east toward the sea. He remembered Prague. A taxi rumbling through cobbled streets, bars of light rolling down Nadia's face as they rode back from the hospital. The night she changed her mind about a child.

"She's all right, though?" he said.

"I'm sorry?"

"Nadia's mother. She's all right."

There was a puzzled pause on the line. "Well, yes, I suppose so. You can be sure Mr. Hanson would've used it if she'd . . . *expired*."

"Yes, of course."

"Anyway, they didn't get away with it. That's the main thing. It's a disappointment, obviously, but the residency hearing is only a few weeks away, and I don't think it'll hurt us that much. The court order still happened. We can still use it. And it's not as if we don't have other ammunition."

He heard Harriet shuffle papers on her desk. It came to him that Miles Hanson had annoyed her. He was making her look second-rate, and she didn't like it one bit. He sensed that winning had become an objective in itself, a matter of professional pride.

When she spoke again, Harriet's voice was lower. "Talking of which, I have something else to report. You know the researcher we hired?"

Harriet called him a researcher. The man himself, a retired police officer, preferred to be known as a "litigation support specialist." To Elliot he was a private investigator, hired to watch people and follow them, and rummage through their dustbins if called upon.

"Yes, I know."

"He found something. Look, Marcus, maybe this should wait until you're back here. Maybe it's not something to—

"Harriet, tell me. It's okay."

She took a deep breath. "Okay. Well. It seems Nadia *does* have a friend."

"Laurent? The French guy?"

"No. Someone else. A musician, of sorts. One James Edward Barrett."

Elliot closed his eyes. Even now, after all that had happened, this was something he could hardly stand to hear.

"It's not clear yet how long it's been going on, Marcus. We'll find that out. But he has a past, that's the main thing: a conviction for criminal damage, charges of assault, *and* possession of a controlled substance. No convictions there, unfortunately."

Elliot laughed bitterly. "I take it this guy doesn't play the cello."

"Bass guitar, I think. Anyway, the court won't like the look of him, I'll see to that. They won't like him, and they won't like his lifestyle. And if we can establish that your wife was seeing him prior to your separation, they won't like that either. Beside the two of them, you're going to look like a saint, Marcus, I promise you. A saint *and* a victim."

27

The Wallanders lived in a narrow, gabled townhouse overlooking a small cobbled square. Trees stood at the corners, bare branches fat with clinging snow. Streetlights buzzed in the misty air.

Most Swedes of Cornelius's age would have moved off the island long ago, exchanging the quaintness of the Old Town for garages and gardens in the suburbs. But Cornelius and his wife had stayed. Their two children were grown up and gone, and the district offered convenience and tranquillity, most of the streets being too narrow for cars, let alone buses or trucks. The house itself had compensations too: molded ceilings, leaded glass, a wine cellar. In the sitting room there was an original limestone fireplace. A pair of puppetlike human figures flanked the mantel, their faces worn smooth with age.

Cornelius came to the door wearing a dark gray roll-neck sweater, and carrying a poker.

"Marcus! I thought you were stuck in a snowdrift somewhere."

He led the way upstairs. A buttery cooking smell drifted through the house. There was art on the walls, gold-framed and individually lit, self-consciously modern stuff, mostly ugly, but nothing of great value. Cornelius's circumstances were modest compared to most fine art dealers his age. But then, Cornelius was an employee, and always had been, and in the art business that was not the way to get rich.

A log fire was burning in the sitting room. Modern jazz trumpet seeped from the loudspeakers like something being slowly strangled. A German called Martin Burkhardt was introduced to him, a tall, gangling thirty-something with huge hands. His firm was based in Munich and produced art books by the warehouseful. There were voices in the kitchen, someone keeping Nelly Wallander company while she prepared the meal.

"So you're working on the Korvin-Krukovsky papers," Burkhardt said eagerly. "How's that going?"

Elliot found he didn't want to talk about it, not yet. There was too much he still needed to know.

Cornelius handed him a glass of wine. "Yes, how *is* it going?" He looked back at the German. "He's been promising us all kinds of new insights, but try getting details out of him."

"Isn't that the mark of a true scholar?" Burkhardt said. "That he wants to be sure of his facts before going public?"

"But we're *not* the public," Cornelius insisted. "We're the insiders, the *players*. Martin is thinking of a monograph for the German market, what with all the interest." He arched his eyebrows significantly, as if to underscore the importance of this opportunity.

There was a loud laugh from the kitchen, forced but hearty. Elliot felt the blood drain from his face.

"Marcus! There you are, *tovarish*. Long time!"

Leo Demichev, ex-Soviet diplomat, Anglophile, lecturer in communications, alumnus of Moscow State University, Stanford, and the KGB (or so it was whispered). In the latter Brezhnev years he had popped up on Western television as a kind of unofficial spokesman for the Soviet regime, urbane, affable, and formidably media-savvy. He'd made such a welcome change from the usual truculent automatons wheeled out by the Ministry of Information that even *Newsnight* and *24 Hours* had started treating him like an independent commentator, inviting him to debate with the likes of Caspar Weinberger and Henry Kissinger. After a period of post-Communist obscurity, he had resurfaced in the 1990s as the right-hand man to Vladimir Beloy, one-time Party bigwig turned media tycoon, until the latter was blown to pieces by a car bomb outside a Moscow nightclub—a fate which Demichev himself would probably have shared had he not been ill with bronchitis on the night in question.

Demichev enveloped him in a hug. Elliot stood rigid, breathing in cologne, recalling in flashes the boozy all-nighters in which the Russian had tempted him with easy money, dressing up his scheme as a cultural rescue operation. It was only when it all went wrong that he had suddenly become uncontactable and untraceable. In fact Elliot had never heard from him again, until now.

Demichev held him at arm's length and looked into his face.

"You're well, are you?"

"Very well."

"Good. *Good.*" He smiled his familiar smile. A wolf's smile. *The better to eat you with.* "I had a feeling I'd find you somewhere on the scene. Not one to miss a chance, eh? Smart fellow."

Cornelius had set a trap. He was well enough connected to know that Demichev was mixed up in the icon scandal, even if he didn't know the details. He knew how Elliot felt about him. Yet here he was, trying to effect a reconciliation, as if Elliot was being a tiny bit unreasonable harboring all that resentment, a tiny bit *immature.* Dealers broke the law all the time, was the underlying assumption. Dishonesty and secrecy made them rich. And it came to him with a pulse of cognition, that behind the smiles and the enthusiasm, Cornelius was jealous. He was jealous of the partners and the collectors and the dealers, people he had served faithfully with his expertise for thirty years. He was fed up with watching them shop for artworks the way he did for shoes, only with even less concern about what they cost. He should have been made a partner years ago, but somehow other people—younger, pushier—always got there first.

Kerstin Östlund said Cornelius had witnessed a forged will. The whole Zoia show was a scam.

Lindqvist, Cornelius, Demichev. He pictured them around the graveside. An official visit for appearance's sake. Greedy old men. In old Russia, the Russia Zoia was born into, you were supposed to put bread inside the coffin, or by the headstone at least. Bread was the link to the next world.

Demichev steered him back into the room, firing questions now at Burkhardt about his interest in Russian art. Elliot felt hot. The fire was way too fierce. For a moment he thought he was going to be sick. He could taste the bile, feel it burning at the back of his throat. He took a gulp of wine.

A thing Kerstin said to him that night in the bar: *I wanted to know if you're part of it, that's all.*

From a deep leather armchair Demichev held forth on cultural issues, one hand gesturing languidly, the other swilling ice cubes in his whisky glass. He had a professorial face: kind eyes, swept-back gray hair, cheeks that sagged in a melancholy way, somewhere between Richard Nixon and a bloodhound. In conversation, his range of references—historical, cultural, political—was daunting. He gave the impression of having read *everything*, and in the original. Over the years he had deployed this erudition profitably, expounding his particular brand of moral relativism for the benefit of various paymasters. According to the Demichev worldview, there was no such thing as good or evil. There were only different sets of values, priorities, and perspectives. The challenge for cultured people was to understand them, not to sit in judgment, which was an indulgence for tabloid newspapermen and soap-box politicians. Worse than that, judgment gave rise to moral imperatives, which in turn promoted conflict, as well as being personally inconvenient.

Unlike Elliot, Demichev had prospered since the icon debacle. The cut of his suit established that. Beside him Elliot felt like a down-and-out, with his crumpled jacket and dirt-spattered trousers. He gulped the wine, the alcohol starting to hit him with surprising force. He thought about Kerstin Östlund, where she was at that moment. He pictured her sitting behind the wheel of her beaten-up Polo, staking out a building somewhere—perhaps this building—blowing on her hands as she looked up at the lights in the windows. He wondered if she was any closer to getting her story.

"Marcus?"

He looked up. Cornelius was standing over him, bottle in hand.

"Another glass?"

"Thank you."

Cornelius poured. Across the room Demichev was in full flow.

"Russia stands on a precipice." The accent was part Slav, part West Coast America: Stalin on a surfboard. "Marxism was a materialist ideology—and as such completely alien to Russia—but at least it *was* an ideology. Without it, we are staring at nihilism, at the destruction of community by the forces of commercialism. Everything we call civilization is under threat."

Burkhardt sat upright on a sofa, holding his wineglass between his knees. He frowned behind rectangular spectacles. "But do you think anything can be done?"

"We must pick up where we left off. We must return to those questions that preoccupied Russian artists during the nineteenth century, after Napoleon was vanquished by the Russian masses—the masses, mind you, not their westernized masters. Namely, what does it mean to be Russian? What is Russia's place in the world? Culturally, *spiritually.*"

Burkhardt nodded like this all actually mattered to him. "Difficult questions."

"Certainly." Demichev smiled, eyes glistening in the firelight. "But there were great minds who thought they could be answered. And, who knows, maybe their time has come at last. Maybe the world needs their message today more than ever."

Elliot watched him, trying to detect a hint of self-consciousness, finding none. One day Demichev trumpeted the importance of Russia's cultural heritage. The next day he sold it under the counter for cash, no questions asked.

Burkhardt wanted to know about the message.

"You need to understand Russia," Demichev said. "You need to know how it was forged. You see, Russia got its Christianity from Byzantium, not from Rome. In Russia, church and state were united, not divided as they were in the West. Religious ritual was all-pervading and all-embracing and much of our nation's greatest art and music was poured into it."

Cornelius eased himself on to the sofa, like a latecomer at the theater.

"More important than that, the theology is different," Demichev said. "Western theology is based upon a reasoned understanding of divinity. The Russian Church has always believed that God cannot be grasped by the human mind. For the Russian, God must be *experienced,* the way an emotion is experienced."

Demichev's art-historical perspective had evolved over the last three years. It had taken on a curiously religious aspect, enough to make you wonder if he hadn't seen the light himself, except that in Russia it was supposed to be suffering that awakened spiritual consciousness, and suffering was something Demichev would do anything to avoid.

"This is where the icons come in," Cornelius added helpfully. "Isn't that right, Leo?"

"Of course. The icon is not a decoration. Nor is it an instruction for the poor and illiterate, as religious art has always been in the West. It is a gateway to the Holy Sphere." Demichev wagged a finger. "Russians have always prayed with their eyes *open.*"

Elliot thought of Zoia, a child, dressed in white, staring wide-eyed into the depths of the radiant image: the Holy Mother and the Christ child. The blue and the gold. It was icons she had taken with her from Russia, and almost nothing else. And yet so far he had found little evidence of churchgoing in her letters. Demichev was shooting in the dark. The iconographic connection was a coincidence, pure and simple. It was a sales pitch for the spiritually bereft.

Burkhardt pushed his glasses up his nose. "So this message you mentioned," he said. "It's essentially mystical."

Demichev nodded. "Mystical, holistic, fraternal." He caught Burkhardt's frown, and leaned forward. "What unites us more than the contemplation of higher things? A man standing before the universe soon forgets his petty ambitions, his earthly squabbles. It's not a question of denomination, sects, creeds. Such preoccupations are for Roman Catholics. Russia's mission in the world, like the artist's, is to open our hearts to the beauty and mystery of existence."

Burkhardt was buying it. The whole spiritual-historical angle was one he could use. There were New Age connotations that brought it vaguely up to date. "And Zoia," he said. "This is the essence of her appeal, you think, and her importance."

"Indeed," Demichev said. "Her work taps into the subconscious, the collective memory of the Russian people. Her appeal goes beyond artistic appreciation. It's the appeal of history."

Elliot felt sick. The more Demichev talked about Zoia, the more he reduced her to abstract concepts, the more dead and buried she seemed.

"One could say Zoia's work is a bridge then," Burkhardt ventured, "between the past and the future. She spans the materialist age."

Demichev made a low, appreciative noise, as if he had just sampled an especially rich and complex Bordeaux.

The German turned to Elliot, seeking further affirmation of this metaphorical insight. The others did likewise, deferring to the scholar of the moment. This was his cue, his reason for being there. He cleared his throat. The fire was cooking him. Beneath his shirt, sweat trickled down his flanks.

Where are you, Zoia? Where on this stupid planet?

He looked into the faces and caught something troubling: Cornelius, Demichev, Burkhardt, they were no longer looking at him—they were *staring*. It took a moment for him to realize that his hand was shaking violently, the wine making discernible slopping noises in the glass. He watched helplessly as it spilled over the lip and ran down his knuckles.

And then they were all talking again, as if they couldn't see the drips landing on the polished parquet floor, and nothing at all was wrong.

He gripped the glass with both hands.

In the bathroom there was a window he could open wide enough to stick his head out. He gulped cold air, feeling snowflakes on his face, tickling as they brushed against his lips. He leaned out further, saw an alley, the backs of houses black against the streetlight haze.

One thing was clear now, for the first time: the real reason he had been hired. It wasn't his knowledge Cornelius needed, or his languages. It wasn't even his interest in Zoia's work. It was his complicity. This wasn't about scholarship. This was a commercial opportunity, a marketing exercise requiring careful stage management. There was no room for awkward truths.

His breath plumed in the darkness, catching the beams of a streetlight at the far end of the alley. The town was stooped over in darkness, going about its business behind shuttered windows, in secret conclaves. The flesh of his face felt anaesthetized, heavy.

He'd always thought Cornelius took a charitable view of his business failure, believing it was an injustice that had brought him down. He thought his old friend had wanted to help for that reason. But he had been thinking wishfully. Cornelius had sought him out not because he believed in his innocence, but precisely because he believed in his guilt.

He closed the window. He drank some water and splashed it over his face. He stood braced against the washbasin. Gradually, the shaking stopped.

The attractions of a world without judgment. Demichev's philosophy had its appeal. Hide yourself in worlds where anything goes, if you can hack it, where the only crime is not to be exotic. Know this, though: that the hardest judgment to escape from will always be your own.

Cornelius met him coming out of the bathroom. "Are you all right, Marcus? You look a little off-color."

"I'm okay. It's been a long day. Plus the booze, you know."

Cornelius looked at the empty wine bottle in his hand. He was struggling to sound sympathetic. "Of course, of course. Stupid of me. Let me get you something else."

He led the way into the kitchen and opened up a big old-fashioned fridge. The others were in the dining room by now, voices booming in the narrow paneled space. A banker and his wife had joined the party, and some sleekly dressed divorcée who owned a gallery.

"You never said why you had to go back to London so suddenly. What happened?"

"My daughter. It's a long story."

Cornelius pulled out a carton of orange juice, and stood for a moment, miming grave concern. "Teresa? I hope she's all right."

Elliot accepted a glass. He wasn't going into the whole Ward of Court business now. "Yes, she's all right. False alarm, you could say."

"Well, I'm glad to hear it." Cornelius dived back into the fridge. "You heard about poor Peter Lindqvist, I suppose."

"Lindqvist? What about him?"

"He was taken to hospital yesterday. With pneumonia. He's not in danger, they say, but we were worried for a while there."

Elliot remembered the last time he had seen the old man, the stoop and the big, bloodshot eyes. He remembered his reluctance to hand over the keys to Zoia's house.

"You've known him for some time, haven't you?"

Cornelius became very still. He looked round. The fridge cast a ghostly light across his face. "Did he tell you that?"

"No. I just assumed . . . "

Cornelius turned away again. "I was thinking about the sale, that's all. Awful of me, I know, but you can imagine how it would complicate things if the old fellow died on us."

From the dining room Demichev's voice rang out. He was talking about Zoia again, her "stoical patriotism," and the "profound tranquillity" of her work. Nelly Wallander interjected that when she first saw a Korvin-Krukovsky in the flesh she had broken down and wept.

He wanted to go in there. He wanted to walk in, grab hold of the tablecloth, and yank it off the table.

"What the fuck is he doing here, Cornelius?"

It just came out, no plan behind it.

Cornelius took out another bottle of white. They were on to the cheaper Italian stuff by this time, now that no one would notice the difference.

"If you mean Leo, he's being useful. I'd have thought that was obvious."

"Useful how? Don't tell me he brought Herr Burkhardt along."

"No. I did that. It's not all that important, but it's something. Something for *you*. You've heard of royalties, haven't you?"

"Cornelius, the man's a crook."

"Martin Burkhardt?"

"*Leo Demichev.* How do you even know him?"

"Of course I know him. If you hadn't been"—he reached for a corkscrew and drilled it into the cork—"out of circulation for the past two and a half years, you'd know. He's done quite a bit of business at Bukowskis. For your information, he's highly thought of."

Elliot saw Demichev lean over a little so he could see into the kitchen. He wanted to know what all the sotto voce was about.

"You still haven't answered my question. What's his angle?"

"His *angle* . . ." Cornelius lowered his voice still further. "He deals. He's been helping us gather pictures. A fair number of the works in the exhibition are actually his now."

"Buying low, selling high."

"Isn't that what dealers do? The smart ones anyway?" Cornelius blushed. "I'm sorry, Marcus. I didn't mean to . . ."

"So how much is he in for?"

Cornelius wrenched out the cork with a loud pop. In the dining room Demichev made an amusing remark.

"There's a lot more to it, Marcus. The whole Putin visit. Whose idea do you think that was? Who do you think set it up?"

In the dining room amusement turned to laughter. Cornelius stepped closer. Elliot could see the beads of sweat on his blotchy forehead.

"I'll tell you something else." His breathing was tight and fitful. "It was Leo who suggested we bring *you* on board. It was Leo who wanted to give you a helping hand. Me? To be honest, I didn't think it such a good idea, so soon after your . . . *illness.*"

The laughter crescendoed in the dining room, a chorus of wild hilarity.

Cornelius reached up to put a hand on Elliot's shoulder, then took it away again.

"But I'm glad I listened to him. I know you're going to do a great job." He put his head on one side. With the smoke and the alcohol his eyes were red-rimmed and angry. "Unless, that is, you'd prefer it if we found someone else."

He waited for the remark to sink in.

"Now, I think it's time to rejoin the party, don't you?"

His car was the only one left on the deck. It stood surrounded by empty bays, like something forgotten or unclaimed. The overhead strip lights flipped lazily on and off.

At Cornelius's house the party was still in progress. Elliot was glad to be gone, knew as he had walked away, in fact, that this was another place he would never return to. Demichev and Cornelius would confer, of course. They would be concerned that he was going to let them down, that he could not, after all, be relied upon to complete the simple tasks he had been given. Because he was still too messed up, because he harbored grudges over a venture that had failed through no one's fault but his own. They might even share their concerns with Nelly Wallander and the other guests, tell their version of the whole sad story. *You wouldn't think it, but he used to be such good fun.*

Yes, he had always been good fun. He had always been the life and soul, eager to please. Too eager, it turned out.

In England, Teresa would be back with her mother now. No more Mr. and Mrs. Edwards of Turnham Green. She would be asleep in the bed he had found for her, with the pretty mother-of-pearl inlays in the head-board, her arms around her blue elephant, which had pride of place among her soft toys. Almost certainly he wouldn't see her again now, not until the residency hearing, which Harriet Shaw was still confident she could win.

Harriet was always confident.

He sat behind the wheel, trying to picture the moment of victory, try-ing to bask in its imagined warmth. But for once, nothing came, nothing at all.

Growing up in Prague, Teresa would forget him. He would become to her like some distant foreign uncle who spoke a language she could not understand, his very existence an awkward subject, best avoided.

Worse than not existing at all.

Despite his anger, despite everything he had done to fight it, he had a sense that it was always going to happen that way. Like the one that had gone before it, this Elliot marriage was broken before it was made.

He started the engine and headed for the ramp. It wasn't until he was out on the street again that he knew where he was going.

28

Life went on as if nothing had happened. Kerstin Östlund read the latest edition of *Expressen* at a coffee shop inside the central railway station. She often stopped there on her way into work. It was a bustling, noisy place, full of solitary travelers killing time.

There was a piece in the Arts section, next to a photograph of Zoia's paintings, lined up like banners in one of the "vaults" at Bukowskis. Cornelius Wallander was shown looking on appreciatively, talking to a representative of the Hermitage Gallery in St. Petersburg. The piece said the exhibition would travel to Russia, Japan, and the U.S.A. before returning to Stockholm for the big sale. Russia might not be a rich country, but certain Russian buyers had expressed their determination to ensure a "homecoming" for at least part of Zoia's work. Apparently, it was now an issue of national prestige.

Kerstin reread the piece, a cup of cold coffee in her hand.

There wasn't a word about the last-minute will, not a single subtextual hint that the rightful ownership of many pictures might be in doubt. The Arts editor hadn't even bothered to tell her about the piece, to ask if she was any closer to getting the proof she needed.

One thing she had learned in the course of her investigations was that the editor-in-chief's brother-in-law was a partner at Bukowskis. It was possible the word had gone out to spike her story, whether there was proof or not. Stockholm was a small town, and Zoia had been a foreigner, and most of the people and institutions being ripped off were foreigners too. The attitude was never far from the surface: we are a small country in the frozen north. We do what we must to keep the trains running and our houses warm. Morality begins at home, and ends at the front door.

When people looked at Zoia, all they saw was gold.

It was the same when Kerstin's baby had died. The world got by on willful blindness. The doctors said he would be fine. A mild episode of cardiac fibrillation had passed without recourse to treatment. There was no need to keep him in for observation. Kerstin knew they were short of places in the pediatric ward. They were under pressure to bear down on costs. She had even overheard the consultant say as much to one of the junior doctors outside the pediatric intensive care unit. But she had done as they had advised, and taken her baby home. So when his heart stopped that night, there had been no one there to save him.

The child's father had long since disappeared to London, to pursue an acting career. Theirs had been a brief, disastrous affair. She hadn't even told him when she had discovered she was pregnant. But in those first few days out of hospital, in her desperation, she had thought about trying to contact him again, before the sheer pointlessness of the idea struck home.

After four weeks the hospital sent her a letter expressing regret and explaining that they were in no way liable for the unfortunate turn of events. Normal clinical procedures had been observed. She called the consultant, just wanting to hear it for herself, hear his voice as he explained himself. But they just kept her on hold for ten minutes and then cut her off. She left messages by the dozen that were never returned.

She wasn't looking for compensation. She wanted someone to tell her *why*, that was all, to explain what had happened that should not have happened. It was the only thing she could think of to staunch the pain. She got nowhere. At the Health Department she filled in forms. No one actually concerned with the clinical decisions ever came forward. She dealt with administrators and officials, people who had to call up computer records to know who they were talking to. More than once she stood outside the hospital, hoping to recognize one of the doctors coming out. She didn't care if they thought she was crazy. She felt like screaming at the passersby, just so they would know, just so they would feel a tiny splinter of what she felt. But it soon became clear that there was not enough indignation to go around. In the end she went to a lawyer who said it would be expensive even to research the case, and highly doubtful she would win it. He observed that she was young, and could make a fresh start. He said she should try and put the whole episode behind her.

All that was two years ago, before she met Zoia. Looking back, she wondered if she would have got through that time without her. Again and again she had retreated to the artist's world and its memories.

She folded the paper away and sat staring through the smeary plate-

glass window. It was half-past nine in the morning. Well-wrapped com-
muters were streaming by on their way to work, the pace was a little
brisker than usual, the frowns deeper thanks to the ongoing stock market meltdown. Already the new millennium had a bad taste to it, like stale
champagne. There was to be no easy getaway to a bright new age. The
path was littered with unfinished business and unsettled scores. The
future was colored with uncertain menace.

At the office she spent a couple of hours in front of the computer,
working on a feature article about the Russian navy, and the dangers from
its leaky nuclear reactors. Apparently there was enough uranium in the
northern fleet to kill every fish in the Atlantic. She asked to see the Arts
editor, but he was in meetings all morning. At lunchtime she went out
again, bought a bunch of lilies from the florist on the corner, and took the
Green Line three stops north to Odenplan.

The Russian Orthodox Church was on Birger Jarlsgatan, a long, tree-
lined avenue of hotels and expensive shops, all welcoming golden light
and sweet smells. Shoppers paraded in the latest winter wear—leather
boots and padded suede that buttoned across the shoulder in a quasi-
military style. Kerstin lit a cigarette for warmth, catching sideways glances
from waxy-faced blondes and schoolmasterly men in field-green over-
coats. In the dry air, the smoke tasted poisonous.

The caretaker recognized her and opened up the gates. His name was
Dmitri. Zoia had once told her his story. He was from St. Petersburg, and
had defected from Russia twenty years back, seizing his moment in
Helsinki where he was interpreting for a trade delegation. No one knew
if he had left any family behind, although it was a fair guess that he had,
given the way the Soviets did things. He had a handsome face, but thin
and deeply lined, with long, vertical creases in his cheeks, a face aged
more by sorrow than by time.

He was out of breath from sweeping the path. "I thought we'd see you
again soon," he said, standing back to let her pass, the big broom in his
hand.

She used to come every week, but it had been more than a fortnight
since her last visit. "I've been busy," she said, walking through.

He nodded knowingly. "On a big story, I'll bet. An investigation."

With his thick Slavic accent, she could never quite tell if he took her
seriously or not. There was always a twinkle of satire in his eyes.

She smiled. Like Zoia said, you could always talk to Dmitri because hardly anyone else took the time to. People said he was a drunk, but that was nonsense. If he carried a flask of vodka in his coat pocket, it was only to help drive out the cold.

"I haven't been getting very far, to tell the truth," she said. "Not very far at all."

Dmitri opened his mouth, as if about to offer some encouragement, but then seemed to think better of the idea.

He closed the gate. "She'll like the lilies," he said. "They're beautiful."

He shouldered the broom like a rifle, and walked alongside her on her way to the grave. The central path had been cleared most of the way across the graveyard, but as they turned off toward the east wall, their feet sank into virgin snow. "I cleared all this just two days ago. You'd never think it. Mind how you go now."

Dmitri usually came with her to the grave, then left her alone there. It had become a routine, as if he were saying: *look who I've brought to see you, Madam Zoia.* Once Zoia started painting portraits of royalty, a lot of people took to treating her with that kind of deference, as if she were royalty herself. Zoia herself seemed to rather enjoy it, although Kerstin suspected this had nothing to do with wanting to feel superior. What Zoia really valued most was the distance it engendered, the ability it gave her, even in her last, failing years, to pick and choose who should be admitted to her life, and who should not.

The close gray sky threw faint shadows across the snow. Iron crosses stood half buried, some leaning like the masts of foundering ships. As she approached Zoia's grave, Kerstin found herself walking in someone else's footsteps. The stride was a little longer than her own, but every few yards the steps would close up, as if the man who made them had stopped to get his bearings.

"I meant to tell you," Dmitri said. "She had another visitor yesterday. Someone I haven't seen here before."

"Who was it?"

Dmitri shrugged. "He didn't tell me his name."

The steps went to the side of the grave. It looked like the foot of the cross had been cleared by hand. Kerstin stooped down, placed the lilies in the small stone vase. Tucked away behind it, she found something wrapped up in a white cloth, about the size of a library book.

"I thought he must be a Russian," Dmitri said. She looked up at him, not understanding. "It's bread. Take a look."

It was a loaf, rye bread with a square pattern cut across the top. She held it to her nose, caught the sour, comforting aroma.

Dmitri laughed. "Only a Russian would do something like that."

"Did you talk to him?"

"I just told him where to find her. It's funny though. I thought he was an Englishman at first. The way he talked. He *seemed* English." He took his broom and began to sweep away the snow from around the stone. "I did ask him if he was family, by way of conversation. He just said he was a friend."

Kerstin wrapped up the loaf again and placed it by the cross. "Elliot."

Dmitri stopped brushing. "So you know him then?"

"We've met. And you were right the first time. He is English."

Dmitri nodded slowly, then went back to work.

Common sense said he was in on the whole scam. Her friend Silvia, the receptionist at Bukowskis, had passed on the available intelligence, and none of it inspired confidence. Elliot was a man who had lost everything. Once a specialist dealer in East European art, he had been implicated in a smuggling case a couple of years back. Russian icons from the Novgorod school, sixteenth-century examples of great value, which it was illegal to export, had disappeared from the cellar of a museum. The circumstances were unclear. Some said they had been sold to raise money, others that they had been stolen following a flood. A year later they had turned up at an English port, part of a larger consignment, purporting to be works of lesser value. A customs official had grown suspicious at the stated age of the icons—and, presumably, their taxable value—and called in experts from London. Elliot had escaped criminal charges. He claimed to have been duped, to have known nothing of any wrongdoing. But the scandal finished him as a dealer, and his marriage had gone down with the ship. He had lost a lot of money in Russia. Even those parts of the shipment he had legitimately owned were sent back there, and remained under lock and key, pending further inquiries. He had spent a fortune on lawyers, and there were further court battles to come. He was a man who needed money, no questions asked.

Yet when she looked at him she didn't see a swindler. Of course it was the first requirement of a swindler that he shouldn't look the part, but all the same she had doubts. His curiosity about Zoia's work seemed genuine. His determination to unravel it, to understand, spoke to her of other needs besides money. And now there was his visit to the grave. The observance of a ritual. Where was the money in that?

She thought about it as she walked back through the graveyard. The principal beneficiaries of the scheme, financially speaking, would be the people who owned the major paintings. Their investments were climbing in value already, a fact verifiable in sale-room records. Since Zoia's death, her pictures had been changing hands at a growing pace, commanding higher and higher prices. It was a discreet trend, but clear evidence of speculative buying. Anyone in-the-know would have had a head start.

Dmitri waved to her through the bars of the gate. Kerstin raised a hand and walked on, an unlit cigarette between her lips. Her visit had been different this time, different from any of the others that had gone before. Usually she told Zoia what was happening, ran through the principal developments and what she planned to do next. In moments of clarity it came to her what Zoia would have said in reply—her mind as sharp as a razor until the day she died. But today it hadn't happened. It was as if they were not alone. There was Elliot in the frame as well, a presence, just as if he had been there in the graveyard with them. And all she got from Zoia were promptings of faint memories, a picture of how Kerstin had found her that first summer's day in Saltsjöbaden, sitting beneath a parasol at the edge of the woods, sketching the shoreline and the sea.

The funny thing was, he was discernibly Zoia's type. There was strength in his face, but confusion too, a misfit's vulnerability. Zoia had always been drawn to men on a mission, men who searched not out of curiosity, but out of need. She felt an instinctive communion with them, and they with her. There were patterns in the world, visible only to those who looked for them. At least that was how Kerstin understood it. There were connections spanning geography and time. And in their recognition lay a special kind of peace.

All she had was the memory of Zoia above the shore, sunlight on the water, a path of shimmering light all the way to the horizon. She had not felt so alone since Zoia died.

. . .

The afternoon traffic was building, headlamps burning yellow in the twilight. By the entrance to the underground station she took out her mobile
phone and dialed Bukowskis. Silvia picked up.

"It's Kerstin. Can we talk?"

"Just one moment, please."

Silvia's voice was a model of professional correctness, a sure sign that
she was not alone.

The switchboard beeped. Kerstin found herself listening to a burst of
Mozart. Inside the entrance to the station, a busker with a mouth organ
started blowing a tune, as if determined to provide a little competition.

The line beeped again.

"Kerstin?"

Silvia's voice was little more than a whisper now. Kerstin pressed the
phone close to her ear, covering the other with her hand.

"Is this a bad time, Silvia?"

"What's up? Are you okay?"

"I'm fine. I just wondered if you saw the piece today, in *Expressen?*"

"I saw it."

"Is it true? They're taking the show around the world?"

"I don't know. All I can tell you is plenty of people have been coming
to take a look: Russians, Germans, Japanese. Some big names. Cornelius
looks *very* happy."

The busker started stamping his foot, his whole skinny body lurching
up and down to the music. He had a raggedy ginger beard and a grubby
brown hat with earflaps hanging down.

"What about Marcus Elliot? Have you heard any more about him?"

"He was here a while back, using the library. He looked ill."

"But he's still here, in Sweden?"

"I think so. Why?"

"No reason. I'm wondering if I should try and talk to him again,
that's all."

"Forget it. Whatever you say will go straight back to Cornelius. I told
you, they're old friends."

People bustled by, heading down into the station, giving the busker as
wide a berth as possible, or marching by resolutely, eyes front.

"You're right. I know."

"Of course I'm right."

"I just . . ."

"What is it?" Silvia made a canny, knowing noise. "Don't tell me you *like* him. Because that's a different matter."

"No, I don't *like* him. I just want to tell him to mind his own business."

Silvia was talking to someone now, giving them directions. Kerstin waited, feeling stupid, wishing she hadn't called. But Silvia was the only person who really believed her story, the only person who thought her being fired from Bukowskis was, if anything, proof that it was true. Talking to Silvia reassured her that she wasn't going mad.

"Kerstin?"

"Thanks, Silvia. I'll talk to you soon, okay?"

"Okay. Hey, before you go, there's something else. Nothing much, but it's got Cornelius excited."

"What's that?"

"They've been looking for this self-portrait Zoia did when she was young—you know the one."

"The Paris self-portrait? The *Chinese Princess*?"

"That's it. Well, apparently the owner just stepped forward. A fax came through this morning. From London."

Kerstin straightened, realized she was still holding the unlit cigarette in her hand. "London. Well, well. What a surprise." She stuck the cigarette in her mouth and reached for matches.

"You sound disappointed."

The busker finished his tune and looked around for something: applause, appreciation, acknowledgment. No one gave it.

"Listen, Silvia, is there any way you can find out the owner's details: name, telephone number? There's something I need to check."

. . . I saw something in the street today that reminded me of you, and I thought I would write and let you know, while I have a moment to myself. It was a little white cat, so soft and sleek, in spite of its sharp claws, that I was filled with sentimental feelings and wanted to pick it up and stroke it, though there was no sense in it— and even a risk of infection. Still, it was beautiful for all that, and I couldn't take my eyes off it. Anyway, I thought of you and about our plan to meet in Vienna. I think it will be possible for me to get there, but I have been extremely busy, not least with a couple of design competitions (which I'm glad to say I won). One of them is for the largest power station the Soviet Union has ever built. I've also been working on the design for an epic movie called Battleship Potemkin, about how the Revolution started. In fact, just about everything you see in this movie is mine. I hope you can catch it on a big screen in Sweden soon. (It isn't polite to write so much about oneself, is it? But then this isn't a polite letter; so I'll continue.)

I'm glad to hear that you've been working again, and especially in the theater. I've no doubt you'll feel comfortable around the stage since your whole life you've been trying to portray an image of yourself, like the perfect little actress you are. To tell you the truth, if we are to meet again now, I don't know if we'll even recognize each other. It's crazy, this thing between us. We are absolute opposites in everything. Poles apart. What do people always say about that? They say opposites attract. Well, it seems that isn't always true after all.

29

He took the spare room at the northwest corner of the house, where two small casement windows looked out beneath the canopy of the trees. He slept on the narrow single bed beneath his overcoat, and the blankets he found in the wardrobe.

He took the dust sheets off the furniture. He rolled out rugs in the hall and on the landings. He wound the clocks in the sitting room, the kitchen, and the hall. He didn't bother with Dr. Lindqvist anymore. He came and went using his copied keys, leaving them always in the locks, just in case.

In her bedroom he opened the windows, cleansing the room with the salty, pine-laden air. He dusted the surfaces and put a winter bouquet in the vase on the mantel. There wasn't much he could do about the walls. She had owned a number of works by other artists, including some Foujita sketches, but these had been taken away to be sold, all except the icon on the stairs. Zoia had never liked putting up her own paintings. They had been made for other people to look at, she was reported to have said. The exception was the *Chinese Princess in Paris*. She had kept that painting for forty years, sometimes exhibiting it, but never selling. For initiates like Cornelius Wallander, it was further evidence that the picture held some special significance for its creator, as a self-portrait might.

But if that was the case, why had Zoia parted with it after so long? There were other pictures she could have sold, if it was just a question of money. Had she grown weary of it? Did it remind her of times and places she suddenly wanted to forget? Cornelius thought so. His private theory was that memories of lost youth grew painful for a woman approaching her seventieth year. She no longer wished to gaze on the beauty she had once possessed.

Elliot had never taken issue with Cornelius's theory, though he considered it simplistic, verging on absurd. The truth was, Zoia's motives in parting with the portrait had always been as opaque as the picture itself. All the same, he could not believe she had simply grown tired of it. A gesture of such weight had meaning and purpose. And that purpose had changed his life, accidentally or deliberately. The proof was that he was here, that she had brought him here, just as surely as if he had been summoned.

One hundred letters in, he reached the Paris years: 1923 to 1931. He spread them out on the studio floor, not in parallel lines this time, but outward in a spiral from the center of the room. It was a more economical use of space. It gave him a sense of events unfolding from a single point of origin.

A glance at the headings revealed three protracted stays in the French capital, possibly four. In between, Zoia was mostly in Stockholm, or in Biarritz chasing portrait commissions. She smiled out of a small photograph taken in San Sebastian in 1927, posing against a big, twenty-seater charabanc in a flapper dress and a straw hat. Early in 1931 she went to Tunisia, falling sick on her return with what the doctors said was cerebral anemia.

They were years of frantic activity for Karl. He wrote to Zoia from Italy, Germany, and Russia. He was risking his life, siphoning Soviet money to Communist cells under threat of extermination. At least half the time they were apart.

Most of Zoia's letters appeared to have been written in haste. The drafts were frequently illegible from first to last. She and Karl corresponded in German. Almost everything else was in Russian. This was not a woman making a clean break with the past. This was a frightened child, clinging to the motherland through the men who had loved her. She turned from one to another, writing in secret, collecting her mail from the post office the way people did in Russia, then hiding it away where it could not be found, perhaps at the house of a trusted female friend.

She was suffocating in the West, drowning. For her, the Russian letters were like coming up for air.

After she lost the baby in the summer of 1922, the pattern of her life seemed to fragment. She made plans to escape, plans that were never realized. Her letters were full of them. By this time she was nineteen years old. First she wrote to the poet Sandro Kusikov, now in exile. He answered by trying to arrange a meeting with her in Berlin, although in the end no meeting took place. Then it was Yuri again, in spite of the promises she had made to leave him be. She wrote to him at his sanatorium on the German-Polish border. By 1924 he was nearing the end of his treatment, doing translation work in Berlin, making plans to return to Moscow. His feelings had not changed.

> *... I cannot forget you even for a single moment, my dearest. I think about you all the time. All I want is to have my feelings returned, even in some small way. My whole life has shrunk to this: to writing to you, and reading your letters over and over. I don't know what kind of relationship you have with your husband, and I don't care. But believe me, pretty Zoia, these feelings I have for you, you will never find in anyone else.*

They made plans to meet but they also came to nothing. Yuri was expelled from Germany. Even there, his connections to the Soviet secret police had become known. He returned to Russia, to a government job in Central Asia. There were a handful of letters in 1926 and 1927, then silence. If Zoia was still writing after that, her letters did not arrive.

After Yuri, it was Andrei Burov. In 1926 the letters started coming thick and fast again. His resentment, stark and ugly in the aftermath of Zoia's departure, began to crumble. He told her of his work on *Battleship Potemkin*, of the accolades and prizes he had won. He set out his ideas about art, the courtship all too evident in his boasting and theorizing. Then that autumn, aboard a Black Sea steamship—Elliot had pinned up the letter on the wall of the studio—he revealed the feelings he could no longer hide. He wanted them to meet, in Paris, in Vienna, in St. Petersburg, to pick up where they had left off eight years earlier. Sometimes Zoia agreed, but when the time came she could never go through with it. In spite of the loneliness, she was still loyal to Karl.

Elliot could predict the response. Burov was proud, and always had been. When disappointed, his love turned swiftly to anger.

> *... I've no doubt you'll feel comfortable around the stage since your whole life you've been trying to portray an image of yourself, like the perfect little actress you are.*

• • •

But Zoia had other reasons to stay away. Her mother and her grand-mother were still in Russia, and she needed Karl's contacts to get them out. But that wasn't all: against all the odds, Zoia was still trying to make her marriage work. She was still trying to be the wife Karl thought she ought to be.

He lit stoves on every floor, learned to keep them burning low so that he didn't get through the logs too quickly. There were more old lanterns beneath the stairs, made of tarnished gray metal. It seemed the electric-ity supply had once been sporadic, making alternatives a necessity. He cleaned up the lanterns and set them in the rooms, except for the oil burners, for which he could find no fuel. When he got too tired to work, he would lie in the semidarkness, watching the flames dancing on the walls, listening to the house warming up. Instead of the damp, fungus smell there was the sweet catch of wood smoke. The place was coming back to life, becoming again the private refuge it had always been.

He hid the car around the side of the house. The shutters facing the road he kept closed. Only the chimneys betrayed the fact that anyone was there—if you could see past the trees. And he was careful to use the old-est, driest logs, which smoked the least. He made omelets on the kitchen stove, and ate them with slices of rye bread, then burned the packaging in the fire. He studied the letters a handful at a time, stuffing them in his pockets as he went about the house. He read them outside, on his trips to gather kindling and dead wood, brooding on the grains of detail they contained, letting the feelings behind the words reanimate inside him, hearing the voices as distinct and personal.

There were other things to do. He fixed the catch on the french win-dows. The guttering had come loose on one side of the house, and there were tiles missing further up. He found a ladder and some tools and set to work, thinking of it as a payment in kind, a recognition that he was only a guest in Zoia's house. At mid-day, and in the evenings, he would take the lanterns up to the studio and try to fit what he had learned into the bigger picture, updating his records as best he could, reinterpreting what he thought he knew in the light of new information.

Sometimes he slept there. He took the mattress up, and bedded down in the middle of the room, next to the small metal stove. It felt good, breathing in the smell of oil paint and turpentine, the smell of Zoia's industry. The smell was fresh, as if she was in the middle of something, and planned to come back. He could hear her sometimes, moving around the rooms below: the creak of the floorboards, the occasional gentle thump. If he closed his eyes, he could follow her progress, step by step, across the hall, up the wooden stairs, across the landing to the other side of the studio door. He would open his eyes at that moment, half expecting to see the handle turn.

Two hundred letters in, the crisis deepened. Zoia's resilience began to break down. Elliot found loneliness and fear, and a yearning for some long-lost innocence. It was something deeper and more punishing than nostalgia. There was a consciousness of corruption, a sense of complicity in the evils of the past. It was there beneath the surface in everything she did, and everything she wrote—everything, in fact, except her work. Her early painting was what they called "naive," a step toward the sunny uplands that came later with the advent of gold. But this skin of naiveté was stretched across a life in torment.

Her teacher, Kandinsky, had preached the gospel of expressionism. He had been to painting what Stanislavsky had been to drama. He taught his pupils not to represent the external world, but their responses to it. He had worked on developing languages of color and form that spoke to the subconscious mind.

Zoia said later that she had been too young to understand Kandinsky's theories. What she'd needed was to learn about line and form and technique. But she had absorbed the central proposition. Later she wrote to Andrei about her search for expression, her struggle to place something truthful and sincere in her paintings. (She only wrote to Andrei about things like that. To Karl, she wrote about how much she was selling, and for what kind of money.) That much of Kandinsky's teachings had stayed with them both.

Elliot put the prints up around the walls. The flatness of the reproductions was insulting. The pictures were frozen, like stills from a movie. He stared at them one after the other, going around and around the studio, lantern in hand if it was needed, until he could do it in his head with his eyes shut.

Where was Zoia in these pictures? Where was the private truth in all those bright-colored utopias?

He stared and stared, and still he could not see it.

Three hundred and fifty letters in, something else changed. It was 1928, the year Zoia saw Foujita's portrait of Fernande Barrey on the Rue de la Paix. Infidelity was suddenly possible. Elliot found the first evidence in a short letter from Andrei Burov, written on 17 March.

> I've just got back to Moscow, and was happy to find your latest letter, although in the event, it brought me only pain and sadness to read that you seem to have fallen in love with someone new. In fact, as I look at it again—all your recent letters in fact—it seems to me that they read like the reflections of a diary, and, as such, are written not for me at all, but for yourself. One thing I know is true though: when you are in love, Zoia, you are not at peace. It's just as you say: you love only to destroy. You are on a quest that will never end. But I urge you to remember that I am only flesh and blood, and to spare me this cruelty.

Elliot followed the trail. Zoia spent most of that year in Paris, working at a studio on the Rue Faubourg St-Honoré. She was experimenting with a range of subjects and techniques, the result an eclecticism that the critics of the time saw as a sign of immaturity. There were few clues as to the identity of the man she had fallen in love with. To a Russian friend in Stockholm she wrote that he had come from South America.

> . . . He has been sent away by his father to avert a scandal. He was having an affair with a married woman and the father was determined to put an end to it. He hasn't enough money for us both to live, and what he has he gambles away. But he is so attentive toward me: he sews my buttons back on, he polishes my shoes. He even likes to powder my face.

A few days later she wrote to Karl, asking him if he wanted a divorce, even telling him she planned to go back to Russia. Karl was in the middle of an election campaign. He wrote that he was too busy to even think about such things. He told her not to be stupid and to focus on making a name for herself.

The affair with the South American did not last. By October Andrei was congratulating Zoia on being alone again, "without any lovers." But Zoia was different now. There was a new recklessness about her private life. In the months that followed there were letters from other men that hinted at more than flirtation. The filmmaker Jack Orton wrote to her of his love and his jealousy when he thought of her with other men. They had first met in Stockholm in 1927, when he was working as assistant director on *Sin*, an adaptation of the play by Strindberg. There was a Portuguese nobleman, several students of painting, a man who sent postcards from all over Europe, and who signed himself only "Le Petit Marquis." There was the restaurateur called Kolya.

For each man Elliot created a file. Into the file went every available detail. He wanted to know why *these* men, what it was she saw in them. He wanted to understand what she needed.

The Kolya letters were few: five in all. But they burned with an intensity greater than any before them.

> . . . *Do you remember those timeless minutes when we were first close to each other? Just thinking about them I become breathless. It's an extraordinary thing, to love someone so strongly that it becomes physically painful. To consume each other as though we're starving, and to give ourselves to each other unreservedly, without limits. I kiss you, my only one, ceaselessly. I kiss every part of you, and every line of your face, and every one of your wrinkles. I am afraid I've been poisoned by your tenderness, utterly addicted, and will not be able to live without it. I just hope that in Stockholm I can take myself in hand again, and bury what I'm feeling in my work. But I don't hold out much hope, because everything that was between us was so dazzling and so right.*

Right, but not enduring. In the summer of 1930 Zoia was in love with a sculptor, a man with a wife and a son. She wrote letters from a hotel in

Södertälje, where she was alone, waiting for him to join her, letters guilt-ridden but livid with desire.

Each infatuation was deeper and more desperate than the last. Each one seemed to end with more pain and self-loathing.

In the spring of 1931 she was seeing an art student, Alain. He was seven years younger than her, of North African extraction. It turned out he was the reason she went to Tunisia. At least, that was what she told him again and again in letters that reproached him for his neglect.

Alain was handsome and overtly masculine in the dark way of the classical world. He was anxious to embrace the artistic life, to taste its secrets and its pleasures. He was drawn to Zoia after the success of her exhibitions in Paris and Stockholm, but his letters spoke of aimlessness and dissatisfaction. A mutual friend called Louis wrote to Zoia that Alain had never loved, that he was incapable of it.

There were more letters to him than to any of the others. Zoia had made copies of everything she sent him. His replies were brief and few, and dated mostly from before her visit. She embraced the affair, clung to it, while knowing all along that it was doomed.

> . . . *So much is against me, but still I dare to be here and to love you. It is a wonderful thing and a wretched thing as well. Even God is against me. I went all the way to the church yesterday and found it locked up, in spite of what I was told. And when I went back again today, and managed to get inside, I found it utterly silent, as if God refused to speak to me, or offer me any word of comfort. When I walked out again, all I could see were couples, young couples, walking by arm-in-arm, looking contented and at peace. And I couldn't bear to have them look at me, because I knew they would be able to see the sadness in my eyes, and the fear. And what could I have said to them if they had greeted me, when the only words I could get past my lips, the only words in my head were all about love?*
>
> *Bring me close to you, hold me, put my sufferings to rest, talk to me as only you can. Tell me gentle words, words I can cling to for a while, words which I can recall when you have left me, words which will stay in my mind and bring me courage and peace.*

•   •   •

On Wednesday afternoon Elliot was up in the studio, reading Zoia's letters to Alain. Some were written from the Hôtel Zephyr in La Marsa, a small beachside town just to the north of Tunis. One day she wrote to him three times. In the same stack were some unusual items, in particular telegrams from the Swedish consulate in Tunis to Karl Kilbom. It seemed they had heard news of his wife that gave rise to concern.

It was a day of sun and shadow, heavy clouds rolling past the sun, showers of rain and sleet rolling in from the west. He went to the window, turning the pages to the light.

At the sound of an engine he looked up. A car was coming around the corner. Outside the gates it slowed and stopped.

It was Kerstin Östlund's car.

His tire tracks had mostly weathered away by now. The stoves had been burning all day. Any moisture in the wood was gone. She would have to come closer if she was going to see any smoke.

The driver's door opened. She got out. The long suede coat, the untidy black hair. Had she come here when Zoia was alive? Had she come here since?

She stepped uncertainly across the slushy ground, put a hand on top of the gate. Her gaze drifted up to the top of the house, to the big window. Elliot couldn't tell if she could see him or not.

You help me and I'll help you, she'd said.

But he didn't need her help.

She was looking around the side now, checking for any sign of a vehicle probably. It crossed his mind that she planned to break in, to steal the papers she thought could help her. Maybe she wanted the story that badly. What would happen if she found him there? He wondered what he could possibly say that she would understand. At least she'd be in no position to call the police.

Part of him wanted the house to himself. Part of him wanted to ask her in.

Out over the water the gulls were shrieking, as if trying to raise the alarm. Kerstin Östlund hunched her shoulders and went back to her car. Elliot watched her drive away.

Parnassus

Stockholm, 16th October 1923

Dear Zoia,

I am not at all happy with your letters. They are full of stories about visits to cafés and nightclubs. There is only one thing missing: <u>*how you are working, when you are working, what you have painted, what your teachers are saying about your work, what your school is called,*</u> *and so on. You don't say a word about this, which is supposed to be the reason you went to Paris. I don't understand it at all. I don't understand how anyone can be like that. Do you know that exactly at this moment, as I write this letter, a telegram has arrived from you requesting money—for what? To visit more cafés? If you can't account for yourself a lot better than this, then I cannot continue to send you money.*

And your letters! In one you write that it is no good being surrounded by people, and that you are going to start work again seriously. Then in the next letter to me—<u>*written on the same day*</u>*—you say you have been out again, instead of being at your classes. Have you finished with school? How and when can you work if you spend your nights in cafés, dancing, etc. etc.? I understand your need to socialize with these people, but to be with them so much? That I do not understand. You must remember that they have already spent years studying and learning. They have made a name for themselves as artists. Whereas you are only a student. You are in Paris to* <u>*learn,*</u> *not to drift around. How many have you done now? You have been in Paris a month.* <u>*How many hours have you studied? How many objects have you drawn or painted or whatever?*</u> *Now I demand that you go every day to school and study seriously at least* <u>*five hours*</u> *per day. You must do this or you will not see one single penny more from me. If you want* *to be somebody, Zoia, you must work. I have explained this to you a thousand times. There is no other way forward. This you must understand now, otherwise you will only come to understand it later, when it's too late.*

I am saying this because I love you, and I do love you, even if it's in a way you cannot understand—not so that I allow you to do every silly thing you want to do, but in such a way that you will become somebody, through and through: somebody who is talked about and respected. If you come back to Sweden now, as you suggest, everyone will know you have achieved nothing and laugh at you. You let too many people know of your plans to come crawling back now. Be warned, little Zoia, that there are a number of Swedish people in Paris, and all of them write home about what is going on there. So everyone in Stockholm knows exactly what the Swedes there are up to.

I spent a couple of days recently with Comrade Teuchler. He was married to a Russian, but now they are divorced. He said that in the long term it's impossible for a Swede to stay married to a Russian, because Russians are <u>too lazy.</u> I protested at this, and told him that all Russians are not the same. Is this the way it is, my dearest? Just imagine what would happen if I came to the realization that this was true? Well, I should be one cherished illusion poorer, for one thing. I hope you will not allow me to experience such a disillusionment.

I have to finish now. I have a cold, I'm tired, and someone needs to speak to me.

I kiss you several times, but what I have said is very serious. Either you work properly, or you can return home and clean the floors, or whatever else you can find to occupy yourself.

Working for us both,
Your Karl

30

Paris, May 1929.

Alain Azria, nineteen years old, lean tanned face and blue eyes, stood posing with a cigarette beneath the statue of Marshal Ney, while his friend Louis went scouting for a table at the Closerie des Lilas. Alain preferred the artier places further down the Boulevard du Montparnasse—the Dôme, the Rotonde, the Coupole, and the Sélect—but these were always full of Americans (the Dôme and the Coupole even had American bars), and were consequently expensive. Visits there had to be rationed, especially in daylight hours when the artists and models were either asleep or at work in their studios.

Louis used to work at the Closerie, washing dishes. That was before he got the waiting job at La Jungle. Louis had no one to support him financially. His father had been killed in the war. Louis had to pay for his own art classes, and frequently couldn't. But all the same, Alain couldn't help envying the access, the fleeting contact with the in-crowd Louis's jobs gave him. Louis was living a true bohemian life, starving for his art, living in something very like a garret, spending more on paint than food or fuel. He was finding his way around the Parisian demimonde that had inspired so many great painters, and already he knew all the famous people by sight, even if they didn't know him. By comparison, Alain—over from Tunis for his second summer—felt like a tourist.

The Closerie was packed, the tables spilling out across the pavement, beyond the hedge that marked the official limits of the *terrasse,* and around the chestnut trees at the bottom of the Boulevard Saint-Michel. A party of Englishwomen, clutching catalogs and large, ugly handbags, had formed a queue to one side, and were debating in loud voices issues related to tipping. Alain saw them eyeing him, some no doubt admiring his Valentino looks, others clearly suspicious that he might be about to try and sneak in ahead of them. Alain grew self-conscious. He dug his hands into the pockets of his linen suit and strolled across the way to a kiosk, where he bought a newspaper and pretended to read it.

A poster caught his eye. It was plastered lopsided to the side of the kiosk. In bold type across the top was written:

AVEC LA COLLABORATION DE
FOUJITA

Foujita was the kind of artist Alain wanted to be. It wasn't the style he liked especially, with its delicate, feminine lines. But his career, that was a different matter. All the most beautiful women posed for Foujita, sooner or later. Even titled ladies wanted him to paint them nude, and not because they wished to be immortalized, as people were fond of saying, but because they wanted to prove worthy of his attention. Foujita's mix of ancient and modern, of Orient and Occident, his whole persona, in fact, had an almost magical appeal. The art world had seized on it like a drug. His work had mainlined into its very bloodstream, seductive but unsentimental; simple, but never stark. It sold like nothing else. Foujita had given up his garret long ago. He had a large four-story house on the Place Montsouris, which was regularly featured in society magazines. His wife, Youki—in Paris the artists seemed to get away with renaming their women whenever they pleased—was driven around Paris by a chauffeur in a yellow Ballot automobile.

The poster announced a gala afternoon at the Bobino theater, on 30 May at three o'clock: a variety show by the artists of Montparnasse, put on to raise money for "*la Création d'une Caisse de Secours Alimentaires aux Artistes.*" Foujita topped the billing, along with Kiki, the famous model and nightclub singer. Marie Vassilief would perform traditional Russian dances, accompanied by the orchestra of La Jungle and its *Danseurs Noirs.* Kiki's friend Thérèse Treize (formerly plain Thérèse Maure) would lead a troupe of chorus girls, made up of favorite models. There would be turns from other artists and performers too, and the whole thing had been organized by Henri Broca, the journalist behind the launch of *Paris-Montparnasse* magazine. Clearly, anyone who was anyone on the Paris art scene was going to be there.

Alain checked the date at the top of his newspaper: 30 May. He looked at his watch. It was already half-past two.

He threw the newspaper away. Louis appeared at his shoulder, looking pleased with himself, no doubt anticipating a good meal. He was taller than Alain, but not as handsome. He lacked cheekbones, and his long, gray teeth had filaments of yellowish color running through them, like flawed marble.

"There's a table inside. They're holding it for us."

Alain pointed at the poster. "Why didn't you tell me about this?"

"I heard it sold out weeks ago. Anyway, it'll just be a lot of clowning around."

"Maybe we can still make it. We'll take a cab."

Alain strode out into the street. A taxi went by without stopping, the driver staring ahead like he didn't want to know.

"I told you, they're sold out," Louis shouted.

A second taxi pulled up. Alain opened the door. "The band members are from La Jungle, aren't they? Just talk to them."

Louis looked back toward the Closerie, swallowing hard. "But what about . . . ?"

Alain climbed inside. "We'll go to the show, and then we'll have dinner at Le Boeuf. All right?"

It turned out the Bobino had seats to spare, but only in the upper circle where the crowd was mostly foreigners and old men with time on their hands. Alain wasn't satisfied. He wanted Louis to take him backstage, to mingle with the performers and musicians. It was just a question of striking up a conversation with the right person, of being in the right place at the right time. And then he would be where he wanted to be: on the inside. He was tired of sitting around in cafés and bars, waiting for something to happen, being *at* the scene, but not part of it.

"You don't have to come with me, if you don't want to. I can manage without you."

Louis just looked at him stupidly and stayed put.

The show had already started. The master of ceremonies, dressed in a cowboy outfit, had delivered a long monologue that had been greeted with cheers from the partisan audience in the stalls. Some of them had brought champagne and glasses into the auditorium. Thérèse Treize and the Montparnasse Girls, among them Kiki looking big and blowzy, were in the middle of their routine. Five or six years back, at the Jockey, when Kiki used to sing bawdy songs and dance, it was said she did a can-can the old-fashioned way, lifting her frilly underskirts high enough to reveal she wore nothing underneath. But this performance was not so risqué. It was part country dance, part chorus line, and the girls hardly showed anything at all. These days you had to be an artist or a photographer to see Kiki naked, although apparently she would still flash her backside at any tourists she caught staring at her. Alain slipped out through the side exit, down the stairs, and into the alley that led to the stage door. He bought a bunch of flowers from a vendor outside the foyer and slipped inside. He had no definite plan. He could say he was delivering the flowers if someone challenged him. Flowers for Madam Vassilief. That was as far as it went.

He was at the end of a corridor. The walls were nicotine yellow and peeling. Bare bulbs burned unsteadily, brighter then dimmer. A powdery perfume scent mingled with the fug of stale tobacco. He took a few steps. Doors went off to left and right—dressing rooms, he guessed. Voices and laughter came through the walls.

He listened. One of the dressing room doors was ajar: women talking, exchanging confidences hushed and scandalous. He glimpsed a bare arm. One of the women was standing in front of a mirror, fixing her hair. She turned away, the hem of her slip swaying against her thigh.

He went by slowly, trying not to attract attention.

Applause. Back here, it sounded like waves breaking on a beach. You had really made it as a painter when people paid money to hear you sing or perform a comic turn. It was a higher level of celebrity than just being known for your work. He had a sense there was a trick to it, getting your hooks into the consciousness of the public. There was a kind of alchemy you could learn, given the right teacher.

A door opened. A man in a clown costume appeared, carrying an umbrella and a crumpled top hat. He wore glasses and an ill-fitting wig, bald on top with tufts of red hair at the side. He gave Alain a myopic stare and waddled off into the shadows. The band struck up with "I can't give you anything but love."

Alain followed at a distance. He turned a corner. The passageway was wider here, but darker, a single red light screwed into the ceiling. The stage was close. He could hear creaking and thumping. Whoops and whistles echoed overhead, an ecstasy of congratulation. He felt his heart beat faster.

He inched open a heavy door, was instantly flattened against the wall. The Montparnasse Girls came hurrying through, all chattering at once, heading back to the dressing rooms. He held the door open, but they didn't see him. There was Kiki, there was Thérèse Treize, there was sultry, Hispanic-looking Siria, who danced the best. They were more beautiful up close, more seductive anyway: all women, all different, but all up for a can-can when the mood took them. They were proud of their bodies, unashamed, *delighted.* It made him dizzy to think about it, the power it gave them. Respectable ladies could say what they wanted in the dull safety of their drawing rooms. They were weak, insipid creatures next to these. They had never lived, and never would.

The last girl through—her name was Clara, according to Louis, and she modeled for Jules Pascin—stopped and hitched up her skirt to adjust a stocking. He held his breath, watching her stoop, her delicate fingers working their way around the silk, her limbs exposed as if for his appreciation, all the way up to her frilly panties.

She looked up, said: "Thank you, monsieur," then smoothed her skirt down again and hurried away. It took Alain a long time to realize he was still holding open the door.

Steps led up into the wings. The clown was there, a silhouette against the glare of the stage. He was holding an unlit candle now, as well as the umbrella. In the corner, an acrobat in a mask and a harlequin leotard was warming up. He looked too good to be an amateur, doing handstands and mid-air somersaults, and landing without a sound. Overhead, stage-hands went back and forth on narrow boardwalks suspended from the roof. There was a small crowd of people in the wings opposite, their faces picked out in reflected light. Alain could see the whites of their smiles.

The cowboy was out front again, telling jokes. There was laughter and jeering. The audience sounded uncomfortably close now, the noise almost threatening. The cowboy held up his hands, adopting a tone of mock gravity, calling for silence.

"And now, it is my singular honor to introduce the one and only Légionnaire of Montparnasse."

The band produced a burst of the "Marseillaise," played triple time.
"The wild man of the East."

The clown turned and looked back over his shoulder. He was staring at Alain now with his big glasses and his fixed, painted grin. It suddenly came to him that this was Foujita. Foujita was the clown.

A stagehand in a cap came hurrying over and lit the candle. Foujita leaned over, said something in his ear. The stagehand turned, fixed on Alain, came striding over.

"The honorable Léonard Tsuguharu Foo-jitah!" the cowboy shouted.

The stagehand looked like a boxer with his flattened nose.

"What do you want?" he said.

Foujita waddled onto the stage to a howl of applause.

"Flowers for Madam Vassilief," Alain replied, trying to look like it was nothing to do with him.

The stagehand put a heavy hand on his shoulder and turned him around the way he had come.

"That way. Third door on the right."

Marie Vassilief was Russian, an artist of some kind, but more famous for the canteen she used to run, off the Avenue de Maine. She had set it up during the war to help the city's starving artists, and it had quickly become the closest thing Montparnasse had to an arts club, with all the big names showing up and bickering with each other over stew and wine at ten centimes a glass. She was middle-aged now and nothing to look at, and that was why Alain thought of her. He thought she might be pleased to get flowers, whereas Kiki and the Montparnasse Girls would have them by the armful by the end of the night.

He headed back down the corridor, listening to the laughter and the voices. It felt good being here, if only for a moment, at the center of everything. The poster said the show would include the proclamation of *La Reine de Montparnasse*—which would surely be Kiki, what with her memoirs in Broca's magazine, and him being in love with her. And that meant there was bound to be a huge party somewhere afterward. He wondered where it was, and if there was any way he could get in.

He counted the doors, knocked, got no answer, knocked again.

"Yes, *yes!*" The voice was impatient, distracted.

Alain turned the handle and peered in, found himself staring into a deathly white face.

"Excuse please."

Red lips framing yellow teeth. The woman was Japanese, painted and dressed like a geisha.

"Ex*cuse* please."

Alain stepped back. The geisha nodded and shuffled past, heavy silk skirts gathered in one hand. On the other side of the room, Marie Vassilief stood surrounded by mirrors and bathed in electric light. She wore a strange, exotic dress, white, belted at the waist, stiff with embroidery, but with baggy, peasant sleeves. The patterns were Asiatic, zigzags and squares, a flavor of the Steppes. A pretty young Chinese woman stood behind her, adjusting the delicate lace cap that rose to a point and hung down by her ears.

The two women conferred, speaking in a strange language that was neither French nor Mandarin. The sound of the show came squawking through a loudspeaker on the wall.

Marie Vassilief turned. She had sharp, fragile features set in a pouchy face: thin lips and eyes piercing like a bird of prey's. She squinted at him through the glare. "What is it?"

Alain's hands were trembling as he held out the bouquet. "Flowers for Madame Vassilief."

The Chinese woman murmured something. The language was Russian, of course. He looked at her more closely. And it came to him that she wasn't Chinese at all. It was just the way she had made herself up, and cut her hair, and the Chinese silk dress she wore.

"Flowers," Vassilief said. "Well, how nice. Who are they from?"

Reflected light played over the young woman's pale skin. She turned away, busying herself with clips and pins.

"My friend and I, we're painters. I mean, we're studying to be painters. We thought after all you'd done for . . ."

Marie Vassilief smiled. With the extra wrinkles she looked kindlier.

"Well, that's very kind of you, monsieur. Very *gallant*. Just put them on the table, would you?"

He walked over. The young woman glanced at him in the mirror. He wanted to know who she was, if maybe she was a model too, undressable at forty francs a time. Paris was full of Russian emigrés. Many were aristocrats who had fled the Bolsheviks, and now lived in penury off their last pieces of jewelry, the women descending step by step into prostitution, if they could face it. Louis told a story of one Russian woman who had walked into the Tour d' Argent, ordered champagne and a plate of *marennes,* the expensive, delicately flavored oysters, and then, halfway through the meal, taken out a revolver and shot herself in the head.

The young woman let out a gasp. There was a little blob of blood on her finger where she had stuck herself with a pin. She put the finger in her mouth, then froze for a second as her gaze met his.

Some of the emigrés were Bolshevik spies. Apparently even Marie Vassilief had once been interned.

The girl's tongue flicked against her lower lip. She went back to dressing Madam Vassilief. Alain put the flowers down and turned to go, wishing he'd at least had the courage to tell her his name.

Weeks went by, and he didn't see her again. He enrolled for lessons at the Académie Paul Ranson, and was complimented on the energy of his drawing. Two afternoons a week, models were produced for the life class, but they were not like the sultry girls who turned up at the Dôme and the Rotonde, with their taut bodies and little breasts, looking to get noticed by a fashionable artist. These women were not after adventure, an escape from the confinement of petit-bourgeois life in some small provincial town. They were on a different circuit, the academic circuit, and most of them had been posing for years. In the studio they were silent and still as statues, and nothing about their nakedness was to Alain either stimulating or sexual. In fact, as he surveyed their swollen, degenerate forms, he found himself going from disappointment to anger, and then to a state he could not name, but which suffused his sketching, the work of his pencil and charcoal, with an energy that was new to him. He kept thinking of Soutine's *Carcass of Beef,* versions of which he had seen at Leopold Zborowski's dealership on the Rue Joseph Bara. The eviscerated, headless carcasses were daubed onto the canvas in fleshy pinks and arterial reds. You could sense the slaughterhouse, its repulsive, energizing brutality. It was that sense of the processes, the truth *behind* the subject, that he found himself reaching for.

Some of his classmates thought the results were ugly. Their faces puckered when his sketches were placed before them. A mousy American girl said they were cruel. But he didn't care. Pascin, Kisling, Foujita, they painted the models that excited them. The sexual charge was there in their work. Sex and desire were the truth, the truth behind the relation-ship of these artists to these models. Here, in the life class, that relation-ship was very different, and that difference had to be reflected. It was a lie to make of every plump matron a nymph, and every bony spinster a Venus.

After a while, he stopped going to the popular cafés, except when he had been working especially well. Instead he made evening trips to the bars on the Île Saint-Louis or to Montmartre. Sometimes he would ride to Pigalle, where the prostitutes stood in the doorways, smoking ciga-rettes. Louis was always embarrassed. He shuffled along with his hands in his pockets, trying not to catch anyone's eye. What was the point of being there, he complained, if they weren't going to buy? But the point was to observe, to feel. So much of what the world was about was compressed into these narrow streets: sex and greed, beauty and horror. You couldn't run away from it and call yourself an artist.

Sometimes he wondered about the Russian girl, if this was the kind of place where he might one day find her.

He didn't see her again until the summer was almost over. And it wasn't in Pigalle, but in La Jungle on a teeming Friday night.

Up to that point he had spent a disconsolate evening at his hotel, tak-ing dinner in his room, lying on the bed, thoughts churning. His parents had enrolled him at a law school back home, and were demanding he return in time to start. They were determined he should have a solid pro-fession. But that wasn't what upset him most. The last few weeks at the academy, he had been trying his hand at painting in oils. His teachers had looked at the results and pronounced him unready for that medium. They said his efforts were unstructured and indulgent. He had more work to do with pencil and chalk, they said. Their remarks had cut him to the bone.

They had told him to be patient, as if simply growing older would bring him some kind of clarity.

All evening he had paced the room, swigging eau-de-vie from the bottle, listening to the noise from the street, feeling that he was at a cross-roads. It was a warm night, the city coming alive. Cars and taxis queued on the boulevard, engines throbbing. Music drifted up from a café on the Place de Rennes.

Pencil and chalk. The worst of it was, they were right. He didn't know how to paint anything, because he didn't know how to *feel* about anything. That was the problem with too much education. It left you with a head full of other people's perceptions, a wealth of secondhand wisdom. It didn't tell you how to discover your own.

At half-past eleven he couldn't stand it anymore. He had a beer in the crush of La Coupole, where he ran into a couple of students from his art class; then they moved on to La Jungle.

Louis was working there as usual. He managed to get them a table, squeezed in between the lavatories and a large, wilting date palm. The place was heaving. Beneath a smoky cone of light, the band, in white dinner jackets, were screeching their way through wild Egyptian jazz. The clarinetist wore a Pharaoh's headdress, and everywhere people were dancing, not just on the tiny dance floor, but on the stage, between the tables, *on* the tables. Across the ceiling their shadows convulsed like demons triumphant in hell.

Louis brought them a jug of the house punch and warned them to go easy on it, the spirit being something out of a quart bottle with no label. They sat watching the crowd, the alcohol and the poison fizzing in their veins.

An accordionist stepped into the spotlight. The band switched to a tango. It wasn't a dance Alain could do, but he remembered his sisters taking lessons when he was a child, stalking back and forth across the flat roof at the back of their villa to the sound of a wind-up gramophone. And here there were women dancing together as well, holding each other close, cheek-to-cheek where the steps allowed, the swell of their breasts touching, brushing past each other. And that was when he saw the Russian girl again.

She was dancing with a blonde woman in red. The blonde was leading, smiling as she marched and pivoted her partner through the narrow spaces, leg sliding over leg in the sensual *sacadas* and *ganchos* that had always made Alain's sisters giggle.

One of his companions nudged him while he watched. The blonde woman's nipples were standing out hard beneath her dress, pushing out through the silken fabric. The Russian girl closed her eyes as she danced. She was wearing earrings and a delicate-looking necklace that sparkled.

Alain grabbed Louis as he went past. "Who is she?"

"The blonde?"

"The other one."

Louis squinted at the dance floor as the music ended and the couples separated to a smattering of applause.

"Oh *her*. She's a painter. Exhibited at the Bernheim Jeune last May. I've seen her here with Foujita."

"*Foujita?*"

"Zoia, she's called. Zoia something or other." The blonde woman led her away, an arm draped over her shoulder. Louis smiled. "Too bad, eh?"

Alain smoked a cigarette and watched her across the room. One good thing about being stuck behind a date palm was being able to see without being seen. And that was what he did. He watched the Russian painter until, an hour later, she and her friends got up and walked past his table on the way out. He tried to follow, but outside they climbed into a taxi and disappeared up the Boulevard Raspail.

He stalled his parents, told them his studies were going brilliantly and that he was planing an exhibition. He told them there was real money to be made. His father responded by cutting his allowance. In the daytime he studied and made trips to private galleries, especially when something by Pascin or Foujita was on show. At night he frequented the famous cafés once again, in spite of the tourists, who were a lot less numerous in any case, now that the summer was over and a crash on Wall Street had sent thousands of Americans scurrying home. He would sit there, trying to make a *café crème* last forty minutes; sketching, if only to keep the waiters from bothering him. And then he would head down the road to La Jungle and learn from Louis if there was any sign of Zoia, which there never was.

"Maybe she's left Paris," he said one day. "Try and find out, will you?"

Louis insisted she hadn't. She had a studio somewhere on the Rue Faubourg St-Honoré, on the Right Bank. But that was a long street, and though Alain walked up and down it several times, he never got a glimpse of her.

Louis said she had taken lessons from Foujita, and that he had taught her certain techniques he had developed using silver and gold, techniques known only to him.

He gathered the facts, one by one. Zoia had studied on and off for five years at the Académie de la Grande Chaumière, at the heart of Montparnasse. She had a husband in Sweden, a Communist, but was, at the same time, friendly with certain members of the Swedish royal family, in particular the Crown Prince Eugene, who had attended her exhibition at the Bernheim Jeune, and bought a number of her works. He heard rumors that she had been sleeping with Tsuguharu Foujita—some said behind his wife's back, others as part of a ménage à trois. In Montparnasse anything was possible.

Traditionally Russian artists met at La Coupole. Alain went over there, struck up conversations, but didn't learn much more. It was clear Zoia did not move in Russian emigré circles. Either she was too much of a snob, or she was afraid for some reason. One man he spoke to, a stiff, supercilious aristocrat, who sat at the edge of the company, smoking and saying little, ventured a curious remark as he went on his way: Alain should keep away from her, he said, if he knew what was good for him. But he wouldn't say why.

Louis thought Alain was being foolish, fixing his sights on a woman like her. Even if she wasn't a lesbian, she wasn't going to waste her time on a student, not when she could mix with the likes of Foujita. Alain knew he was probably right—except for the way she had looked at him that night at the theater. She had looked at him as she sucked the blood from her finger. And he'd been sure at the time that she wanted him.

One Monday night in November he was walking back from an exhibition on the Right Bank. It was raining hard. He ducked into a café for shelter, across the street from the Madeleine. It wasn't a cozy establishment. The tables were heavy iron with marble tops, and the lamps were high up on the whitewashed walls, casting a sallow, even light. The place did most of its business at lunchtime, and by now it was more than half-empty.

Zoia was sitting in the far corner alone, a steaming cup of tea in front of her, an empty shot glass beside it. She was at work on something, although Alain soon realized she wasn't sketching, but writing. She wrote continually, without stopping, her gaze never leaving the paper. Alain ordered a brandy and sat watching her, now and again looking down at the gallery pamphlet for the sake of appearances.

He couldn't let her get away a third time. He needed a plan, a way to introduce himself that wouldn't look impossibly gauche.

He finished the brandy, and ordered another. At last an idea came to him. They were close to the Gallery Bernheim Jeune. He could pretend that he'd seen her exhibition there, and was curious to know about the costs and the commissions. Artist to artist. He would go over and ask her, and at the same time compliment her on the work he'd never seen.

He downed the second brandy and called for the bill. He gave the waiter the money, reached for his coat and got to his feet, running the words through in his head. *Excuse me for troubling you. I just wanted to say how much I admired your work.*

But Zoia had gone.

He spun around, caught a glimpse of her going out the door, hat pulled down low, fur collar held tight around her.

The next thing he knew he was out on the street. Water was sluicing along the gutters, dripping in beaded curtains from awnings and rooftops. She was walking quickly. She dodged a couple of men pushing bicycles, and disappeared around the corner.

Alain followed, keeping his distance. He couldn't accost her in the street, but maybe he could find out where she lived. If he knew that, he might bump into her. He could even *arrange* to bump into her, if the geography of the area was on his side.

They headed west, toward the Ministry of the Interior, past apartment blocks with stately facades, then south, along a narrow street lined with small shops. Every few yards he would lose sight of her as she turned a corner, or as he passed beneath the glare of a streetlight. He would pick up the pace, spot her again, fall back. She walked quickly, purposefully, never looking around.

Soon they were on the Rue Faubourg St-Honoré. It was an unusual place to have a studio, colder and grander than either Montparnasse or Montmartre. It was a choice suggesting aloofness, a need to be apart. The strangeness of it hadn't really struck him until now. Maybe the rumors about Foujita's secret techniques were true, and this was Zoia's way of keeping them secret.

By the church of St. Philippe de Roule she took a right turn and was suddenly gone. Alain stopped at the corner, squinting down the empty street, listening for the sound of her footsteps. But there was nothing, just a rumbling from the metro beneath his feet.

"*Shit.*"

A taxi went by at the far end of the road, the sign showing "Libre." He looked up at the building on the corner. Offices. Dark windows, no curtains. She had simply vanished, as if he'd been following a ghost.

The church bells clanged the half hour. He pulled up his collar and turned.

She was standing in the shadow of a doorway, watching him.

"Do you make a habit of following women? Or am I getting special treatment?"

He could just make out her mouth, a curl of hair against her cheek.

She lit a cigarette, still watching him. By the flame, the gemstone darkness of her eyes seemed infinite, supernatural.

"I thought you were going to come over in the café. But you seemed more interested in your brandy."

"I was *going* to come over. It just took me a while to . . ."

"Work up the courage? Or were you afraid of looking foolish?"

The end of her cigarette hissed softly as she inhaled.

"Both."

"Well, you're looking pretty foolish now, aren't you?"

There was something childlike about her, for all her sophistication. Innocence held prisoner by harsh experience. The mixture was unstable, intoxicating.

"Yes. I suppose I am."

She stepped out of the doorway, the dark eyes turned away disdainfully.

"Then it's just as well you're good-looking. It makes up for it a little."

And she walked right past him up the Rue Faubourg. It was a few moments before Alain understood that he was supposed to follow.

31

The studio was two attic rooms above the corner of the Rue Cézanne. The bedroom was ten foot by twenty, with a sloping glass roof that framed a view of a water tank. The bed was a mattress on the floor, with cushions and a traveling blanket spread over the top. Zoia said she sometimes slept there when she was too tired to go back to her hotel. There was vodka and a bottle of cloudy lemonade beside the washstand, and a vase of poppies in the corner that turned out to be made of silk.

Bands of rain rolled across the city. He could hear them approaching across the rooftops. They would beat against the glass for a minute or two, then drift off again. A small iron stove was going in the other room. Flames danced behind the grille.

She didn't say much. She seemed to know all she needed to know about him. And the questions she did ask, he felt sure, were only for appearances. Where was he studying? What did he think of the teaching there? Which artists did he most admire?

He chattered nervously, saying the first thing that came into his head. He admired Jules Pascin and Chaim Soutine. He said he liked them for their honesty.

"You want to paint nudes, I suppose."

She poured him a drink, mixing the vodka with the lemonade. Once you got past being disconcerted, her frankness was exciting.

Artist to artist.

"If I can get beautiful ones, yes."

She laughed, shaking off her coat. "Then don't paint me."

"Why not?"

"I wouldn't measure up. I'm too small and too plump."

"You're not plump."

"A model should be tall. That way everything stays in proportion."

She walked past him, hung her coat on the back of the door. She wore a patterned dress underneath: tiny flowers on black. "Or if not tall, then lithe, like Paquita."

"Paquita?"

"One of Pascin's girls. Almost no breasts at all. An adolescent's body. *Une gamine*."

"Do you know Jules Pascin? What's he like?"

She brought the glasses over. "Older than he wants to be. And sadder. Cheers."

She clinked her glass against his.

"And Foujita?"

He was sounding like a tourist, but he had a sense she might tire of him at any moment, just as Louis said, and turn him out into the night.

She sighed, went and sat down on the mattress, curling her legs up underneath her. "What about him?"

"Is he . . . I don't know, sad too?"

She laughed. "If *he* is, then God help the rest of us." She brought the glass to her lips. "Are you going to stand there all night in your raincoat? Come here."

She took back the glass while he fumbled with the belt and the buttons. It was hard keeping his hands steady.

"It's a shame men don't pose." Her head was on one side as she watched him. "It's a shame they aren't painted anymore. I mean, the way women are."

"You mean, without their clothes on?"

He knelt down, took the vodka from her hand and drank.

"In Montparnasse painters are only interested in women. Women and sex. That's what makes them happy. For them, a man's body isn't a very interesting subject."

She looked at him. Their faces were close now. He could smell the musty sweetness of her hair, see the moisture glistening on her lips.

"It's all about pleasure here. Everything's about pleasure." She reached up and pushed her fingers into his thickly growing hair. "But then I think you already know that, don't you?"

He wasn't sure how long it was before she got up again to unbutton her dress: five minutes, ten. The unfamiliarity of it all obliterated any sense of

time. This was her world, and here he was in her power. And if his desire
was still his own, it was a desire she knew well—knew perhaps better than
him, its nature and how best it could be satisfied. Even the way she kissed
him was different. She teased and goaded, exploring him inch by inch,
describing circles on his skin with lips and fingertips. Her gentle bites
sent shivers down his spine.

In Tunis, the Arab girls were off limits completely, and the Jewish girls
his family clumsily nudged his way were too sheltered and respectable to
be any fun. Some French girls had kissed him, but only in stolen
moments, when no one was watching. Mostly they could only *be* kissed,
allowing him the privilege when softened by alcohol and moonlight. The
previous year, in Paris, he had twice been with prostitutes, who did not
kiss at all, and a tall American girl from the art school called Joyce. Joyce's
parents were something in the theater, and though she wasn't a beauty, it
was clear she regarded having a lover as an essential part of her European
education. Yet when they were alone in his room, she became strangely
passive and silent, allowing herself to be undressed, but taking almost no
part in it, or in anything that followed. So that in the end, it was like making love to someone in a coma. Just the sight of her legs hanging limply
over the edge of the bed made him feel predatory and slightly disgusted
with himself. And it didn't help that she clung to him afterward, as they
walked off together for a drink, her head canted over onto his shoulder
at an angle that couldn't possibly have been comfortable.

Zoia's kisses were hungry, searching. It was a revelation that he could
be the object of such carnal appetites. Like she said, it was all about pleasure, and knowing that, knowing there was no other point to it, made
him want her more. Every button down the back of her dress teased him.
Every strap was a frame for her smooth, pale flesh. She watched him as
she undressed, pleased to have his complete attention, chuckling as she
rolled down her stockings to reveal fine, delicate legs. She turned away to
take off her shift, turning back to him with her hands covering her
breasts, an expectant look on her face.

Alain swallowed. He loved how she showed herself to him. It was different from the bordellos, where the pleasure was all the client's. This was
like a secret shared, something exquisite and rare.

"Not like that," he said. "Put your hands on your hips. And your head
back a little."

She smiled and did as he asked, dropping a hip the way Kiki did for Man Ray, looking into his eyes the way she looked into the camera. Her breasts were fullish and widely spaced, with bold, dark nipples. He gently grazed them with the back of his fingers, then made her turn to the side, one way, then the other, so that the lamp threw shadows across the contours of her torso.

"I want to sketch you. I want to paint you."

He meant it, too.

"Don't paint me," she whispered, taking his hand and pressing the palm against her mouth. "I didn't bring you here to paint me."

Lying down on the mattress he caught his reflection in the glass high above, saw Zoia in silhouette as she pulled his clothes off and straddled him, her body working purposefully. And then she looked up too, saw what he saw, and smiled, as if this was all part of the attraction, that they should fuck and see themselves fucking at the same time—fucking *and* watching, watching and fucking in a weird, mesmerizing cycle. Until nothing else was left. With the brandy and the vodka, it made him feel giddy.

He rolled her over, not wanting to see the reflection anymore. He drew up her legs and began again, bringing his face close to hers this time, wanting to look into her dark eyes, to see himself *there*.

But her eyes were closed now. And they stayed that way until he was done. And though she returned his kisses, one for one, he had a sense that a spell had been broken, and that he had somehow led her in a direction she did not want to go.

He awoke at two to the sound of bells. Zoia lay with her back to him, curled up against the wall, one hand pressed flat against the plaster. He propped himself up on his elbows, checked that she was really asleep, then eased himself off the mattress.

There was a book beside the lamp, a cheap paperback edition of verses by Baudelaire, small enough to fit inside the palm of his hand. She had carefully covered it with pink paper. He flipped through the pages, saw a passage from "Le Guignon" underlined: *"L'Art est long et le Temps est court."*

He knew the aphorism. It had been up on a classroom wall at the Lycée Carnot in Tunis. But the implication had always struck him as onerous: the artist's life might be brief, but his work would be there forever, a permanent testament that could never be amended or improved. Surely this was the reason so many artists wanted their work destroyed before they died. Better oblivion than to be remembered for something false or second-rate. It made the artist a prisoner of posterity. But then, as the art master had said, maybe that was the point of art, the very source of its power: to the living from the dead.

He pulled on his shirt and trousers and went over to the washstand. He splashed water on his face and gulped down some lemonade. It was getting cold. The stove in the other room had burned down to its last embers. It was in there that Zoia worked, there that Foujita's secret techniques were employed, if the stories were true. He stood for a moment, listening to the silence, then walked through.

There was glass in the roof here too. Bright moonlight slanted across the shadows, catching on an easel and the corner of a canvas. He glimpsed dark swirls, like contours, around what might have been a face. It looked like preliminary sketchwork, coarse at that, executed in charcoal or diluted oil paint.

The face, if it was a face, seemed to him to be sleeping, curled up in the darkness just as Zoia was at that moment. The cold made him shudder.

Her materials were on a table at the side of the room: tubes of oil paint, brushes, turpentine, the usual things. There were jars full of pencils, charcoal, chalk, and a strange kind of knife with a small white blade like a fang. There were bags of a white powder that glistened faintly on his fingers.

The table had drawers. Carefully he opened them, saw something shining, realized it was metal: a book of gold leaf, about three inches by three, each square separated from the next by greased paper. In the moonlight it shone with a greenish tinge.

The fire popped. He closed the drawers, looked around for fuel, found half a bucket of coal, next to it scraps of paper screwed up tight into fire lighters.

He got to work refueling the stove, blowing on the embers until it made him giddy. At last the papers caught. By the light of the flames, he saw that they had sketches on them too.

He reached into the grate, picked out a couple of scraps, smoothed them out, leaning close to the flickering light. He was curious to see what it was Zoia had decided to destroy.

The images were strange. A group of figures were gathered in a semicircle, masked faces staring down. Their forms were twisted, malformed, but recognizably human. A second sketch was a detail: a sharp, angular mouth caught in mid-scream. Hastily he pulled out a third piece, burnt his fingers in the process, stamped out the embers on the floor. Up close, half lost in swirling darkness, were puffy, swollen eyes closed in sleep or death, a chalky whiteness beneath the rims.

What were they? Studies for a work she had abandoned? Sketches from a gallery, inspired by another artist's work—Goya perhaps, or Edvard Munch? They made him think of human sacrifice, some dark religious rite.

But that made sense. These were visions of a primal past, conjured up the way Stravinsky had conjured up *The Rite of Spring.* He nodded to himself, pleased at his analytical powers. It was an act of *homage,* the following of a Russian artistic movement, an exploration of technique, that was all.

There was something terrible in that screaming mouth.

He heard steps behind him and turned. Zoia was standing in the doorway.

He threw the papers back on the fire. "Sorry if I woke you. I was cold."

She came and stood by him, placing a hand on his shoulder. She was wearing a silk robe, tied at the waist. In the darkness, with her hair all untidy, she looked younger. He found he could picture her as a child.

She stood there in silence, watching the sketches curl up and burn.

"What were they?" he asked.

"Dreams," she said. "My dreams."

She left Paris ten days later. Alain saw her before she left, but they were hurried meetings, arranged at his request. And it was always she who cut them short, alleging some important engagement she could not afford to miss. She told him that people were watching, and that they had to be careful, but that only made him want to be with her even more.

Their last evening they were sitting in the café opposite the Madeleine, drinking Irish coffee. He asked why she was leaving. So far she had been evasive about it. She said it was her husband's idea. He was anxious she should capitalize on her recent success with an exhibition in Stockholm. She had told him she wasn't ready, but he had ignored her. Already he was lining up portrait commissions with well-connected people, enough to keep her busy for months. She had to go. It was a question of money, as much as anything else.

"But he's a big-shot politician. Surely he's got plenty of money."

She shook her head. The Swedish Communist Party had split over the issue of obedience to Moscow. Karl had led the anti-Moscow faction, she said, because he was disgusted at Stalin's dictatorship. There was no more financial support from that direction. He'd planned to launch a newspaper, had already invested heavily, but with all the bad economic news, nobody else would step forward. He was already talking about mortgaging their house.

Alain reached across the table and took her hands.

"When will you be back? There's so much I want to ask you. It's not fair. You're not like any woman I've ever met, and already you're going."

She smiled at him, a warmer smile, he thought, than any yet.

"You remind me of someone."

"Who?"

She lit a cigarette, holding it to her mouth with two fingers, the way only women did. "A friend. It doesn't matter."

"Tell me."

"His name's Andrei. We met at school in Moscow. I haven't seen him for years."

"And I'm like him."

"A little. He always wants to understand everything, see how it ticks." Her smile faded. "So he can change it, I suppose, make it better. Make *us* better." She looked up. "He's very brilliant, though."

"I hate him."

She laughed. "He'd feel the same way about you, I'm sure. You're much better looking, for one thing. He'd hate that."

Alain leaned in closer. "And what about your husband? Am I better looking than him too?"

"That's different. He's my husband."

"Meaning he owns you. He owns you and you can never be free again for the rest of your life."

She was very still for a moment. He knew he had said the wrong thing, even before she drew back from him.

"Listen." He tried to change the subject. "Why don't we go to your studio? Show me what you've been working on. I really want to see it."

She shook her head. "There's nothing to see."

"That's not true. You've been working on something. I saw it. Tell me about the gold."

Her eyes locked on his. He thought she was going to be angry with him, but then her expression softened.

"It's beautiful, that's all. It's . . ."

"It's what?"

"Everlasting. Perfect." She shrugged. "But I don't know how to use it. I haven't found the way. Not nearly."

"But I thought Foujita showed you all that."

"He taught me a lot. But not enough."

"I don't understand. He kept things back from you?"

"No." She started doing up her coat. "Foujita was generous with me, and patient. But even he can't make something true that isn't true. That's what he told me, and he was right."

A few moments later they were walking out of the café. Zoia had to be somewhere in twenty minutes, she said. It was good-bye.

"Come to Tunis," Alain pleaded. "Please. You must come." He couldn't keep the panic from his voice.

As a taxi pulled up she brought a hand up to his face and kissed him on the mouth. He saw her look back as she was driven away.

. . . I've been sitting here a while with my sketch book, and I've had a lot to drink. I should go, but I keep remembering the time we were here together, you sitting over there writing—just where another woman is sitting now—and then we got up without a word, and left, left to make love. It's something I can't stop thinking about . . .

Some friends just spotted me. They want me to sketch the woman they're with. They want to impress her, I suppose. They want an entrée. I don't want to do it, but I told them I would. Now they're waiting. I've had a lot of women. I know what they want and expect. It isn't hard to work out. They can be very sweet as well. But I can't forget what we had, what we started and never finished. This place, where we sat opposite each other, our conversation that was only with our eyes, with glances . . . and then in your apartment that night, in the studio . . . I can't think about this anymore. It's too exciting, too painful. I have to stop now. They're all waiting for me. The girl is waiting.

32

His father told him that if law school did not appeal, there was a junior teaching position vacant at the Lycée Carnot. He was friendly with M. Auclerc, the director of elementary studies. He could work at the school for a year or so while he thought about what to do with his life. Alain had no choice but to give in. At least he would have the summer free. He could go back to Paris then, and take up with Zoia where they had left off. And when he was ready, she could introduce him to the dealers and critics who could put a young artist like him on the map.

They began to exchange letters regularly. He told her she should come to Tunis, for the light, for the peace, for the desert. He reminded her of Delacroix and his *Women of Algiers,* and how inspirational that picture had been for Matisse and Picasso. He told her of the artists' colony in Hammamet, where Paul Klee and August Macke and Louis Moilliet had all worked. She wrote back that she would come as soon as she could. She had dreamed of him, standing in a wild desert landscape, with the ruins of Carthage at his back. She had dreamed of him riding a white horse.

The dream wasn't the only strange thing about that letter. The handwriting was erratic too: one minute upright and clear, the next slanted, cramped, almost illegible. Often the changes happened midsentence.

She asked him to send her a photograph of himself, so that she could be reminded, she said, of how beautiful he was. He decided to send a photograph *and* a sketch, a self-portrait in a mirror. But when his sisters found it, they said it made him look like a bookworm and a sissy. So he sent only the photograph.

He thought about telling her he loved her, but in writing it always came out weak and pleading. He decided it would probably put her off anyway. Love was such an unsophisticated emotion, and so ordinary in the Parisian context. Visit the Louvre, climb the Eiffel Tower, sit around in cafés, fall in love. Anyone could do that, and they did, by the thousand. But not everyone could unlock the world with the stroke of a brush.

Montparnasse was a different place by the time he returned. The whole scene had moved on. Arriving at the station, Alain went looking for the latest issue of *Paris-Montparnasse* magazine, only to learn it had ceased publication. Broca, the publisher, had been in love with Kiki, and his jealousy had driven him insane. There were no more costume balls and cabarets, put on by famous artists. Most of the famous figures had gone. The great collector, Jacques Doucet, was dead. Jules Pascin had strangled himself using a door handle and a necktie. Foujita was being hounded by the tax authorities and had fled to Japan. Other painters had moved to the country or the suburbs. In the bars and cafés there were only tourists, and fewer than ever of them.

Louis was still there, working in the kitchens at the Hôtel des Écoles. He had even found himself a dealer, but had yet to sell any pictures. His job used up all his energy, he said. He could not afford a studio, but it was difficult to work in his little rented room because of all the noise the neighbors made. Alain said he should come out to Tunis, because you could live there for next to nothing. He told him Zoia had promised to come, at which Louis's jaw had dropped in disbelief.

He went back to the Académie Paul Ranson. He wrote to Zoia, telling her that he was waiting for her. After a long delay, she wrote back, affectionate still, but distracted and unhappy. Her life in Sweden had become complicated, she said. She did not know when she would make it to Paris. She said her past was driving her mad, if she wasn't mad already. He would be better off forgetting about her.

Alain could read between the lines. Zoia had moved on from Paris too. Montparnasse was no longer a community. It had become instead a diaspora. But that did not mean it no longer existed. The network was still there, with its own language and discourse. Only now, it was more exclusive and impenetrable than ever.

He wrote back that he could not forget her, and that if her life was complicated, then she should remember what was important, and focus on that. He wrote that they were destined to be together. If she fixed on that, then she could forget all the rest. It was risky language, as good as a

declaration of love, although he managed to avoid the word. But risks
were required. He posted the letter on the Boulevard Montparnasse,
thinking that, in all probability, he would never hear from her again.

She arrived in Tunis in November, almost a year to the day after they first
made love. Alain hurried into town, wearing a linen suit and a brand-new
panama hat. It was a hot, humid afternoon, the breeze drifting in from
the desert, the sun turning red behind a veil of dust. He bought her
pomegranates, and lilies with pale, creamy petals.

He stopped at the corner of the Avenue Jules-Ferry, took a bottle of
cologne from his pocket, and splashed it around his neck. He hadn't
dared do it at home. Zoia was a married woman—married *and* divorced.
Just dressing up had been risky enough. He'd had lies at the ready, in case
anyone asked him where he was going, but lies could be discovered, even
if you didn't trip over them yourself.

His mother was petrified of scandal. She thought the merest whiff of
it would spell perpetual spinsterhood for his sisters. His father was less
predictable. Probably he would throw him out of the house, or exile him
to some minor administrative post in the interior, where he would die a
slow death from boredom and alcohol. And it would be that or nothing,
because the lycée would fire him without a second thought. His heart was
in his mouth as he crossed the road and hurried up the steps of the Hôtel
Grand Saint-Georges.

He found her standing out on the balcony. The room had a view
across the Quartier Lafayette, looking east toward the sea. Around the
fringes of the city, the calls to prayer had begun, faint echoing voices just
audible above the beeping and yelling in the streets.

She had changed. Her hair was short, fashionably perhaps, except that
there were no curls around her ears or temples to soften the effect. His
first thought was that she had been ill, that in some institution they had
shaved her head to keep her clean. She had lost weight too. There was
extra definition in her cheeks.

She ran to him, flung her arms around his neck. It was something she
had never done in Paris.

"I wasn't sure you'd come," she said.

He knew her smell. At least that was the same. He buried his face in her neck, drinking it in. For him this would always be the smell of secret pleasure.

"What are you talking about? I've waited all year to see you."

She smiled, holding him at arm's length now. For a minute or two they made small talk, about the journey, about Paris, about the places she had to see around Tunis. She put the lilies in a red vase and helped him off with his coat. With the heat and the anxiety he had begun to sweat. His shirt clung to his chest and his back. But the sweat was starting to cool now that he was safely inside the hotel.

He felt her arms circle him again, her face press against his back. For an instant he saw her sleeping in her studio, fingers splayed against the wall, as if trying to escape into some imaginary place.

She was very still.

"What is it? What's the matter?"

She laughed, but the laugh was brittle. "Nothing's the matter. I'm just so glad to see you. I'm glad you summoned me."

"Is that what I did, summon you?"

"Yes. And I should have come earlier, instead of wasting my time on . . ."

"On what?"

He turned.

"On *what?*"

She went and sat on the bed, reached for a cigarette, but couldn't find her lighter. She fussed through her bag, then tipped out the lot onto the covers. Among the banknotes and cosmetics he spotted a cardboard packet of Luminal.

"Here."

There were complimentary matches on the dressing table, next to the complimentary cigarettes. She lit up, smoking nervously.

"I told you things got complicated."

"In Stockholm."

"Well, they got worse. All my fault. My grandmother always said keep away from people's husbands. Even your own."

He felt a tremor inside. So this was the reason she hadn't come to Paris: a married man.

She was watching him closely now, trying to gauge his reaction. Her eyes spoke of experience broader and deeper than any in his little life. He knew he had no right to be jealous. She had never promised to be faithful. She had never promised anything. But then why the honesty? What was he supposed to feel? He wondered if jealousy, that most vulgar of emotions, was a trap, and she was waiting to see if he fell into it.

She reached for him. "It was madness, and it's over. I just want to forget about it now."

"Then why tell me?" He tried to sound like he didn't care either way.

"Because it doesn't matter anymore. It's in the past."

She pulled him closer. For an instant he was back in her studio, looking down at her as he had done that night. Except that this time, it was his home, and it was she who had followed him.

They made love in the twilight, the darkness stealing over them little by little. At first it felt strange, to be writhing naked on a hotel bed just a mile or two from his parents and his sisters and his colleagues at the Lycée Carnot, with their unassailable propriety. He felt alternately guilty and gleeful: guilty at the thought of them knowing, gleeful at the thought that they never would, that he had fooled them utterly. But after a while he forgot about Tunis, and everyone in it. He forgot where he was. He was making love to Zoia as he had a year ago, only with a greater consciousness of pleasure, and everything that stood between then and now was compressed into a passing thought. Even when it was over, and they lay beside each other, dazed and breathless, those months felt diminished, insignificant, merely an interruption in the real business of living.

That was the dream of Montparnasse: to live for the moments of the greatest intensity, to find in them a truthful inspiration, and to hell with all the rest.

The next evening he was yards from the hotel entrance when he ran into an old colleague of his father's. The man recognized him and stopped to exchange pleasantries. Alain had to walk past the hotel and wait around the corner, to avoid being seen going in.

He told Zoia it would be better if she moved out to the coast. He recommended La Marsa, to the north. It was the furthest of the Tunis resorts, but a train would get him there in half an hour, and they wouldn't have to worry so much about being observed. She would have peace to paint there, and the bathing was some of the best in the country.

Zoia checked into the Hôtel Zephyr, a grand, colonial-style building of fluted columns and sweeping staircases, with night-scented jasmine growing thickly in its shadow. The rest of the town was less imposing, a sprawl of boxy houses squeezed in between the beach and a crescent of low, sand-choked hills. Stumpy date palms grew by the side of the main road.

Visiting proved more difficult than he'd thought. Sometimes he didn't finish at the lycée until half-past six, and by the time he caught the train out to La Marsa, it was often after eight, giving him barely an hour before the last train back. Usually there was time for a drink or two, for hurried love-making, but nothing more. The guards on the train began to recognize him. They gave him knowing smiles as they clipped his tickets and wished him a good evening. He lied to his mother, telling her he was having dinner at the lycée, and organizing activities for the boarders. She was surprised, given that he had always said the food there was disgusting.

Sometimes he thought they should spend the time talking instead of just fucking. He wanted Zoia to tell him about her painting, about Foujita, about what it took to make it as an artist. They discussed his drawings, about which she was complimentary. But her priorities were clearly different. It was passion she wanted from him, not conversation, and the proof of his passion was to be found in bed.

She was still holding back from him, shutting him out. He always thought making love to a woman was a sure way of getting through to her, but not with Zoia. She was determined to live for the moment, she said. She admired gamblers, men who would chance everything on the turn of a card, for the thrill of it. But Alain wasn't convinced. All that hedonism was an escape, a drug, like the drugs she took to sleep. And if this was her true creed, then why the daily visits to the post office, to see if she had mail? Why were there bundles of letters in Russian, French, and Swedish hidden in her suitcase?

The things she did not trust him to know.

Sometimes he made love so it hurt her, although it never seemed to hurt her much. She moaned as much in pleasure as in pain. At times he would screw his hands up into fists to keep from slapping her across the face.

He found other ways to punish her. A couple of times he stayed away, left messages at the front desk that he was busy. He found that worked quite well. The next night, there were always tears in her eyes when he left.

One weekend she said she wanted to sketch him. He went and sat by the threshold of the balcony, a bedsheet wrapped around him. He struck a brooding pose, a fist curled under his chin, but Zoia told him to change it. She placed him on the edge of the settee, looking straight ahead at her, his arms planted at his sides, chin dropped slightly.

Sunlit curtains billowed behind him.

"Is that how they pose at your art school?" she said after a while. "With a loincloth? How quaint."

"No. The models pose nude."

"Then why not you?"

"Because I'm not a model. Besides, I might be recognized."

Her hand moved over the paper in long graceful movements, not at all like the fast, jagged ones he had come to use. Foujita's influence, perhaps.

"You mean you're not ashamed to be a painter of nudes, but you're ashamed to be one?"

"It would just be hard to explain, that's all. Me, with you, naked. People wouldn't understand."

"People?"

"You know what I'm talking about."

She fell silent, switched from pencil to pen and ink. The nib made harsh, scratching sounds. He saw her lips purse with irritation.

"That's a pity," she said. "It just means I shall have to draw your cock from memory."

"*What?*" Alain jumped to his feet.

"Sit *down.*" He stopped in front of her. "I was only joking."

Reluctantly he returned to the settee. She lit a cigarette.

"Although it is a very handsome cock. It deserves to be included, in my opinion. Much more interesting than a length of cotton, even Egyptian cotton—it is Egyptian, isn't it? I certainly hope so."

Alain resumed his pose. A shaft of sunlight caught Zoia's cigarette smoke, obscuring her face.

"I thought this was a portrait," he said, "not a life study. If you want a model, you can pay for one. The boys around here'll do anything for money."

"You disapprove."

"That depends."

"*I* can pay you, if it'd make you feel better."

"Don't be ridiculous."

She pouted as she drew.

"I rather like the idea. Then we'd both be whores, wouldn't we?"

And she went on that way, needling and complaining, until the work seemed to take her over and she was silent, focused completely on what she was doing. Alain watched her, beginning to envy the depth of her concentration, that ability to be somewhere else altogether than where you physically were. It was something he had never had, an alternative world so real he could enter it at will. For him, art was a conscious effort, a calculated deployment of styles and forms. Only momentarily had he experienced the suspension of reality that was supposed to happen when the artist became one with his art.

This was the place Zoia went at night, when she turned her face toward the wall. He wanted to know what kind of place it was. He wanted to know who else, if anyone, was to be found there.

After an hour or so, she got up without a word, put down her pen, and walked into the bathroom. Alain heard water running in the basin, the sound of washing. He got up, glimpsed her in the mirror, bent over the wash basin. He went over to see what she had done.

The picture came as a shock. It wasn't him at all. There was a resemblance in the face, yes, but that was it. This wasn't the portrait of an artist, but of an athlete, a warrior, a gigolo. It was all hard muscle and fixed, staring intensity. He was an animal, beautiful perhaps, but purely, overwhelmingly physical.

So much for artist to artist.

Zoia came out of the bathroom, drying her hands on a towel.

"Is this how you see me?" he said.

She looked at the sketch in his hand, and then at him. "You don't like it."

"Answer the question."

"Why should I? When you already know the answer."

"Tell me anyway."

She flung the towel over her shoulder. "It's how I saw you when I drew you. What else could it be?" She stepped closer, put a hand against his face. "Isn't that the point? Isn't that what it's all for?"

He pushed her hand away. "I don't care what you saw. It isn't me."

She stared at him with her dark eyes. "No, you're right. The real you has a cock. Whereas this has a discreet area of shading."

And before he could say another word, she took the sketch from his hands and tore it into little pieces.

Something changed after that. Zoia changed. Her moods were darker and less predictable, although at other times she was more loving than ever. She seemed torn between teasing him, abusing him, bringing him down to some earthier level, and subjugating herself to him completely. Once, when he slept over, he heard her crying in the bathroom, sobbing so violently it scared the life out of him. He was going to knock and ask if she was all right—stood, in fact, before the closed door, his knuckles inches from the wood—before another, more cautious instinct changed his mind.

As far as he could tell, she did no work at all.

Seeing her was the best thing in his day. Next to her, everything else was staid, dull, routine. But the lies were mounting up, elaborating beyond the point at which he could cut his losses and admit to them. There were fictional friends by now, and fictional house parties, and no end of fictional responsibilities at the Lycée Carnot. The burden of his fictions grew heavier every day.

One thing began to worry him: what if Zoia became pregnant? What would happen then? Maybe she was just crazy enough not to have thought about it. Or maybe she didn't care one way or the other.

Zoia told him to relax. It wasn't an issue.

"What do you mean, it's not an issue? What if your husband knew it wasn't his? What if he filed for divorce?"

They were out on the terrace, overlooking the sea, speaking softly so as not to be overheard. Zoia looked at him over the lip of her coffee cup.

"Suppose I did have a baby. What would you do?"

Just hearing the words brought the hairs up on his neck. "I'd have no choice. I'd have to run away with you. I couldn't stay here, that's for sure."

"But you'd do that? You'd stay with me?"

He tried to swallow. It was difficult. "Of course. Of course I . . . Only I think it would be better just the two of us, don't you?"

Suddenly she was laughing, covering her mouth with her fingers. "Poor Alain. Look at you. Did I scare you *that* much?"

He joined in the laughter, wondering if that cleared up the matter, and deciding it probably didn't.

They went wandering along the beach, toward the headland, he carrying the parasol, she splashing barefoot through the water. She was already talking about coming back in January or February. It wouldn't be a problem, she said. A painter needed light, and there was no light in Sweden that time of year . . .

"But you don't paint. Three weeks you've been here, and nothing."

She had pinned up her skirt so that her legs were bare to the knees, catching glances from passing couples.

"Why don't you take your shoes off and come in?" she said.

"Seriously. You're an artist. I thought you lived for your work."

She turned away, wading deeper into the water. There was a rosy blush on her cheeks from her days touring the city. It made her look younger.

"I thought I could, but I can't. Even when it's pretty, it disgusts me."

"What are you talking about? The National Gallery is buying your pictures, for God's sake."

She dragged a foot through the water, kicking up the spray. "They like that kind of thing. It cheers them up. Sweden is so gray and cold sometimes it makes you want to scream."

"I'd be proud to do what you've done."

She shook her head. "No. You wouldn't."

She was staring at the sun reflected on the water, frowning. It came to him that she really meant what she said.

He stopped. "You're not giving up?"

She didn't answer.

"You can't. Not now, not just when . . ."

She drew up her arms, hugging herself as if she were cold. He had noticed this about her, that she seemed to get the shivers even when it was perfectly warm. It was another aspect of a fragility she seemed to have acquired since Paris.

"Let's swim," she said.

"I haven't brought a swimsuit."

"Neither have I."

She was already unbuttoning the front of her dress. He looked up and down the shore. The couples they had passed were a hundred yards away now, but there were others in the distance. Farther up the beach a trinket seller was dragging his camel across the sand.

"What are you doing?"

She came striding toward him, pulling her arms out of her dress, the rivulets of salt water running down her calves. She took away the parasol.

"You look ridiculous carrying this, by the way."

She reached up and tugged at his tie. Then pulled him closer and planted a heavy kiss against his mouth. Over her shoulder he glimpsed pale figures approaching.

"You're crazy."

"Well, I warned you about that, didn't I?" She tossed the parasol aside. "Come on. You must be cooking in that stupid suit."

He laughed. "Stop it. Get off me."

"You know, sometimes you're awfully conventional for an artist."

She began unfastening the knot.

"*Stop it.*"

She didn't stop. She stripped the tie from his neck and snapped open his collar. He pushed her away, but she came back at him, grabbing his shirt, pulling it open. He seized her by the wrists, but she wrenched herself free, not smiling now, but determined, angry.

"I told you, stop. People are coming."

But she was out of control, grappling, clawing. He pushed her away again, harder.

"Zoia, for God's sake."

She went for his face. At least that's what he thought she was doing when he swiped at her.

He connected with the heel of his hand, felt the impression of her teeth against his skin.

She stopped dead, drew her hand across her mouth. He had cut her lip. Blood smeared across her cheek.

"Zoia, I'm sorry. I didn't mean to . . ."

She just watched him. When he tried to get closer, she backed off into the water. There were tears in her eyes.

A wave washed over his best leather shoes.

"Zoia, please . . ."

She threw her dress onto the sand, her eyes still fixed on him. Her slip followed. She was naked underneath.

"What are you doing? Zoia, you're going to get us arrested."

The flesh on her breasts was goose-pimply, the nipples dark and hard. She turned away and waded into the sea. He shouted after her, but she didn't look back.

A couple with a child between them. A little girl in a sailor suit. They were close enough for Alain to hear their voices.

"Damn it, Zoia! You can't swim!"

It was something she had told him. She had never learned to swim. Where she grew up, it was not considered necessary for ladies to learn.

She was up to her waist already. She rolled over and looked at him, then turned around once more.

"*Damn* it."

He tore off his clothes, and dived into the water. He had to swim hard to reach her. She was already striding through the surf, making for a sandbank a hundred yards from the shore.

When he finally got there, he was almost too out of breath to speak.

"We should go in a little. There are currents here. They're dangerous."

She came over to him, wrapped her legs around him, kissed him on the mouth. He tasted blood and salt water. It had to sting like mad. Her flesh felt slippery and warm.

On the shore, the little girl in the sailor suit was standing, staring at them. Her mother hastily took hold of her hand and dragged her away.

33

The one discernible measure of Alain's feelings was the interval between his visits, intervals that grew longer and longer: two days, three days, a week. Always with a cast-iron excuse, though: obligations at the lycée, obligations at home. His lies, if they were lies, were skillful, tinged with just the right amount of resignation and regret. She felt guilty taking up so much of his precious time.

They made love in silence, each in their own place. She watched him watch other women on the terrace of the Hôtel Zephyr. When she talked of her feelings for him, she could see his whole body tense. Her devotion was a disappointment to him in some way. His preference was for implicit love, love that had to be inferred, like meaning in a picture. Statement was banality. And if there was one thing an artist could not afford to be, it was banal.

She had told him all about herself by this time. He seemed to take it as a slight that she could keep anything back. So she gave him what he wanted, answering his questions with absolute honesty, hoping it would put their love on a more solid footing, hoping that it would spell a new beginning for them both.

She came back in January 1931, and stayed for a month. She met Alain's friend Louis, broke and starving in Hammamet. She gave him money. He wrote to her that Alain had never loved anyone in his whole life, and probably never would.

From Sweden the news was bad. Factories were closing almost every day. Her mother was living with them now, working as a cleaner to help pay her way. Zoia painted portraits at cut-price. Some were so stiff and lifeless, she was ashamed to ask for payment. The faces of her sitters mocked her as she slept.

She bought gold when she had the money, experimenting in her tiny studio. She didn't tell Karl. He thought her paints were expensive enough.

Besides, she had nothing to show for it. No golden pictures saw the light of day. In the gold she saw shifting images, faces, memories, but the touch of her brush distorted and defiled them. She longed to make her peace with them, somehow.

Her last trip to Tunis came at the end of April. She wrote to Alain again and again, but it was several days before he came to see her at the Hôtel Grand Saint-Georges. He told her he planned to study further in Paris, and that his father had agreed to pay for it. He said she should go out to La Marsa as usual, and that he would visit her there.

The staff at the Zephyr were glad to see her again. Business was slow for the time of year, slower than it had been for years. They watched her with special interest, the Russian lady with the handsome young lover.

She spent most of the days in her room, working. She told the chambermaid she needed pictures for the Stockholm exhibition. Her husband was counting on the money from a good few sales. Sometimes she took the train to a nearby Arab village, with a sketchbook under her arm. Once she made a trip to the market in Tunis, returning with a small packet, wrapped in vellum, and a pair of wooden panels. She worked late into the night, appearing for meals less and less often. Some mornings she slept until noon.

The handsome lover did not appear. Several times Zoia went down to the train station, dressed in her best summer clothes, but each time she returned alone. Stories began to circulate. Some of the other guests, men especially, made discreet inquiries. It was whispered she was a Romanov princess, traveling incognito. Some said she was a revolutionary, on the run from Stalin's assassins. The local police received more than one tip-off that she was a spy.

One morning a chambermaid was passing her door, and found it open. She knocked a couple of times and went in. The room was a mess. There were empty bottles and glasses everywhere, a painter's easel on its side, charred and screwed-up papers scattered across the floor. Madam Zoia wasn't there. One of the wooden panels she had bought lay on the bed, the surface scratched and scored. On the dressing table, the maid found smudges and smears of what she thought was blood. In the bathroom, empty packets of Luminal lay screwed up in the basin.

She went out on the balcony. Two floors below, on the main terrace, a waiter was preparing the tables for breakfast. It was a still morning, the sun rising clear above a green sea. There was no one on the beach, just a solitary bather wading out through the water. She wondered where Madam Zoia could have got to with a stomach full of barbiturates.

The waiter spotted her and gave her a wave. She was one of the younger females on the staff and, as such, a target for the attentions of almost every man in the place. She had learned to adopt a manner of haughty indifference to them all.

There were items of clothing scattered across the beach, not in a neat pile as she would have expected. One of them was washing back and forth at the water's edge.

She searched for the bather again. She was beyond the sandbar now, no longer moving. As the maid watched, her head disappeared below the surface.

Stockholm, 16th January 1931

My dear dear Zoia,

A thousand thank-yous and kisses to you for your long letter, which reassured me that you are happy, that you are able to work, and that you are finding inspiration in your surroundings. This is surely the kind of atmosphere you need. I can see that you are in love, and no wonder, in a place where the air is so thick with erotic mystery and sensuality. Mon Dieu! Mon Dieu! I knew you would get caught up in some passionate adventure among people so charged with the sweetness and temptation of the Orient. Relish it, be happy—and show that happiness in your work. I know you are working over there for another exhibition. Bravissimo! I'm delighted because I know you will surprise the world, and no one will be prouder than I, because I believe in you and always have done.

The other day, I was at a dinner party with your husband and your mother. Early on I became embroiled in a bit of an intellectual battle, which became heated, with all of us being curious about each other and rather obnoxious too. I studied Karl, with you very much in mind, and both understood and felt intuitively that he was not the man for you. He is distinguished, but he has neither your spirit, nor your capacity for love—nor jealousy either, for that matter. But I could see that he is very useful to you for support and for practical advice. I know from your mother that he gives you money, so that it is possible for you to stay over there and work. He clearly wants to make something of you. And he has his own ambitions too, evidently. I'm glad he's kind to you, that he is not petty, and that he wants to be proud of you. All in all, it was a very interesting evening.

So, Zoia darling, when you taste the delights of the Orient, think of me. Oh how I wish I could get lost in that country. Listen! Bring me perfumes from there, and if you find any Arabic books— in French—keep them for me. And in the markets I would like you to find me some incredible silk for a summer dress. In brown, sand, black, or white. But only if you happen to find any. Don't go to too much trouble. I know there is a type of batik or silk that's very pretty and decorative.

I must say I am lonely without you. I'm preparing for a trip myself, for six weeks—I don't know where to, but I am dying to be among some different race and mentality. Here everything is so plain and straightforward! The diplomat I told you about is nice, successful in his work, but not a strong character and very nervous all the time. Mrs. Troencken has returned and she invited me to dinner this week, but I declined—why?—out of loyalty to you. I had a feeling you would not want me to go. So! You see, you have quite some influence over me. I am doing some sport, skiing like crazy, to help forget this melancholy. It exhausts me completely.

I will write again soon.

With love,
Monica

34

Saltsjöbaden, March 2000.

Limbs already heavy, she stumbles into the sea. Ankle-deep, she falls, grazing her knee so it bleeds. She rises, coughing salt water, holding herself against the dawn chill, telling herself the Luminal will take her soon, and it will be over. Her legs and feet are glassy green beneath the surface, already one step removed from living flesh.

Up in the studio Marcus Elliot sees it all like a memory.

Near Sevastopol she did the same thing. She ran away beyond the outskirts of the city, trying to reach some place she remembered as a child, some place of villas screened by cypress trees and cedars, though she didn't find it. She ended up on a scree of sand and pebbles, staring at the waves with her chin on her knees. She pictured the waves from underneath, imagined lying there on the sea bed, watching them scour the shore, washing away the dirt and filth of human things, turning everything to sand.

That's when it should have happened. That was the perfect moment, an end she could have embraced like poetry. All she's done since is postpone what's inevitable and just. A worm on a hook, she's convulsed and wriggled, all the while working the point in deeper—thinking, of all things, that art could save her, that art could reach in like a surgeon, cauterize the wound and close it. Let her begin again. But the surgeon's blade is dirty, like the art is dishonest. Every cut spreads infection. It spreads to those around her, even those she loves.

She didn't have the courage that time. She didn't have the drugs to dull her fear. Typical of her, to fall down on the planning. She just dived in and struck out toward the horizon, fighting the swell, though that was against her too. When she finally got out of her depth, she found herself surrounded by flotsam. She grabbed hold of a piece of timber, and didn't have the courage to let go. It washed her up again like a pile of rags.

This time it's easier. There's no swell. There's helpful undertow. All she has to do is go out a little and the current will do the rest. An arc of brown smoke rises high into the sky from a tiny speck of a ship in the distance. All she has to do is keep her eyes on the smoke, and keep moving forward.

She hasn't left a note. She wants people to say it was an accident. Accidents are always tragic, where young artists are concerned. All that talk of promise, of genius waiting just around the corner. The obituaries will make everyone proud, as she herself can never do in life. She sees Alain's face as she told him she loved him, that stifled look of disappointment and disgust.

Dark shapes move through the water beneath her. She feels them brush against her skin. She probes downward, checking for depth, expecting to hit sand. She hits nothing. She holds her breath and dips deeper, opens her eyes, glimpses a murky patchwork twenty feet below. There's an old rusty anchor on its side, what looks like the skeleton of a boat. Strands of weed catch on her legs. She spins, sees the sea floor vanish into lightless depths.

She comes up gasping. Better to die in the shallows than be swallowed up by that menacing shadow. But she can't feel her arms anymore. Her whole body is becoming a dead weight. Even the flesh on her face seems to be dragging her down. It's too late to go back now, even if she wanted to.

It's calm on the surface. The sky is a deep, distant blue. The rising sun paints the water gold.

She rolls onto her back, takes a few deep breaths. The golden water laps across her body, robing her in beauty. She lets her head drop back. Her heartbeat slows. There is some strange peace here, between the shadow and the light, a perfect sense of completeness. She wants to stay forever, where the light is welcoming and warm.

The last thing she hears before her eyes close are distant voices on the shore. She wishes she could answer them.

Two of the kitchen staff dragged her from the water. Another minute and they would have been too late. They laid her on her side on the sand, and pulled her shoulders back to force the water from her lungs. She came to, spewing milky white vomit. They put her in the back of the night manager's car and raced her to a hospital in Tunis, where they pumped her stomach and plumbed a saline drip into her basilic vein. They went through her room, found her passport and telephoned the Swedish consulate. The consul went to the hospital, spoke to the doctors and sent telegrams to Stockholm. There was concern about the possibility of a scandal. Karl Kilbom was a political leader and a member of parliament—a useful one in many eyes, with his split from Moscow. Somewhere along the line it was decided not to involve the local police.

Communications with Stockholm were couched in diplomatic language. Suicide was not mentioned. Kilbom's first impression was that his wife had suffered some kind of migraine attack as a result of sunstroke. The doctors examined her, and suggested she was suffering from a neurological disorder, possibly a result of meningitis. It was agreed she should leave the country as soon as possible.

Zoia drafted letters to Karl, in which she tried to tell him what had happened. The letters she actually sent him concealed it, to judge from the replies. Karl was caught up in a libel action brought by the government. He could not leave Stockholm until it was over. She left for France at the beginning of June, for a sanatorium in Juan-les-Pins. She stayed there for six weeks, alone.

Elliot's hands were shaking again as he bundled up the Tunis letters. He was coming down with something. His face felt hot, but the rest of his body was cold. He put the letters back in their box, and put the box back in the desk. He knew he should enter the essential information into the database. And there were still letters from 1931 that he hadn't read. But he was in no state to do it now. There were other priorities. He had to get medicines and get warm.

The logs were all spent. He needed more fuel or he would freeze to death. He found a hatchet in the boiler room and marched out into the woods. It was late afternoon, the sun a red smear on the horizon. The snow lay in crusty, wind-blown patches. He pulled his coat around his neck and stumbled toward the shore, hearing it crunch beneath his boots.

On the rise above the beach there was a pine, bent over and dead, the trunk weathered to gray-white. He planted his feet and started swinging, gripping the hatchet with both hands.

The wind was light but changeable. It gusted around the headland and into the path of the waves, making a slapping, rippling sound. A minute in the freezing water and it would feel as if his skin was on fire. He would die in the glow of illusory warmth.

Branches caught on his sleeve. They gouged his face, as if trying to fend him off. He swung blindly, the blows coming faster and faster. He struck wildly, losing his balance, tripping over the mass of roots that reached up out of the earth. His face burned with fever and exertion.

One minute, they said, was the difference between life and death. He heard the onlookers reflecting on this fact, as if there was something salutary here, something you could actually learn from. As an adult, he observed that it was always this way: tragedy and near tragedy bringing detachment and lucidity, if briefly. The world did not work to a discernible plan. The forces of chaos could intervene at anytime, for no reason. But then everyone moved on with a shrug, because, after all, there was nothing to be done about it.

But the first time he heard it he had not been old enough to move on. He had been eight years old.

Go and tell your mother her program's starting.

He had deliberately dawdled on his way up to the bathroom. That was what it had all hinged on. He'd wanted to see the program too, especially the beginning, which he loved. But his father had said it wasn't a children's program, and it was past his bedtime anyway.

On the landing he'd stopped and sulked. If he was going to miss it, then his mother could miss some of it too. He'd sat there looking up at the clock on the wall, waiting for the music to start.

He'd sat there for about a minute.

He never told anyone afterward. His father never asked him why it had taken him so long to raise the alarm. He never said much at all. But Elliot remembered the paramedic on the scene shaking his head as they took her away: *One minute sooner and she could have been saved with mouth to mouth.*

He knew at once what they meant: it wasn't the pills that had killed her. In the end, she had drowned too. She had done what Zoia tried to do, only she had done it right.

His hands were bruised and swollen now. His fingers were locked around the hatchet, joints fused. He couldn't free them if he wanted to. He swung again and missed and almost buried the blade in his knee.

The water lapped against the shore. Black, insensible oblivion, a few short yards away. Inevitable, after all. Nothing to be afraid of. The thought was like a finger, tapping him on the shoulder. But he wasn't going to make that journey until her secrets were his. He wasn't going until he understood.

He worked on steadily until darkness fell. There was nothing left of the tree but a splintered stump.

The wood was damp. Soon the house was full of stinging smoke. He opened the windows in the studio and the hallway, and watched the clouds spiral upward through the house. In the sudden draft the candles guttered and died. The lamplight flickered in the rooms and on the landing, throwing fitful shadows across the ceilings. Cornelius called him on the mobile three times. Elliot let it ring.

He slept that night in the sitting room, in front of the big stove. He saw Zoia on the sunlit water, as she drifted toward death. He saw her shaved head in the sanatorium, where they diagnosed her with cerebral anemia.

He was there with her, alone in a cell with a barred window high up on the wall between them, though the sanatorium wasn't supposed to have cells. She looked younger than twenty-eight. She looked like a child. He started telling her about the pills he had been using, and what it was Paul Costa said about how to use them. But when he looked into her face, he saw she wasn't listening. She was gazing at the window. The little square of light was reflected in her eyes, flecks of gold in circles of black.

At the back of his mind was the thought that she might try it again. Suicide. Why else would they have her in this cell, with padded walls and a mattress for a bed? They were afraid she would hurt herself, and why not? Unless something had changed.

Make conversation. Be upbeat.

"Where are you going after this? Have you made plans?"

It came to him that Bukowskis were going to have the shock of their lives when they learned that she was still alive. To say nothing of Dr. Lindqvist. He'd have to give back all the paintings, and the house too.

She stayed looking up at the window. "Italy," she said.

"Italy? When?"

"As soon as possible."

It didn't sound like a whim. There was purpose in her voice.

"Why Italy?" he asked. "Why there?"

She gave him a pitying, disappointed look. The child seducer.

"You know."

Her voice was so clear and loud, he was sure someone had been speaking to him for real. He sat up sharply, eyes blinking open, expecting to find he wasn't alone.

A draft brushed past the curtains. On the stairs the boards squeaked.

He was covered head-to-toe with sweat. Even the blankets were heavy with it. But the fever was gone. His limbs felt weak and shaky, but his head was startlingly clear. Sleeping without drugs. He still wasn't used to it.

The clock in the hall struck seven.

He went into the bathroom and pulled off his clothes. He stood shivering in the bathtub, rubbing himself down with cold water and hard Ibis Majestic soap.

He caught sight of himself in the mirror and stood staring in disbelief. He was deathly pale and haggard, almost bearded, greasy hair gathered into a scarecrow heap on the top of his head. One of the branches had opened a cut beneath his right eye. There was a purple, crescent-shaped scab, about an inch long. There were more scabs on his forehead. He looked down at himself and saw that his hands and forearms were covered in scratches.

This was the only mirror left in Zoia's house. It was screwed into the wall. It was frightening how quickly you could forget what you looked like when there was no way of judging it.

It came to him that what he looked like most was a madman. One of those sad cases you avoided in the supermarket, the ones who wore secondhand clothes and mumbled to themselves. Was that what he had actually become? Was that what living in Zoia's house had done to him?

He'd heard it said you weren't really crazy until you started hearing voices. The trouble was, that wasn't always an easy thing to judge. Sometimes you got so wrapped up in a memory, so deep in thought, it was hard to be sure where the words came from. Like the voices that woke you from a dream. In the end, it was all in your head anyway. Hearing was not a passive thing, any more than seeing. Every sight and sound was filtered through a mesh of precognition. To be without understanding was to be blind, like a man who stands before an allegorical painting unaware of the symbols or their meaning. Things not understood were invisible things.

Italy. You know.

"What do I know?" His voice boomed in the empty space.

After France, Tunis. After Tunis, Italy. Along the way, attempted drowning and the ministrations of an insane asylum. People said Tunis was a sterile period. They said it fell in the middle of an unproductive stage, marred by sickness and creative stagnation. But what if Tunis was a culmination, a turning point? What if, out there in the water, seconds before death, Zoia had become a different person, an artist who saw the world with different eyes?

It was a while before she made it to Italy. She needed to save some money first. Karl wasn't giving her much, and the art market was in a slump, like everything else. She worked on cruise ships around the Mediterranean, doing portraits for cash. The *Stella Polaris* was one. But she was only waiting, marking time. Since Tunis something was different. She had acquired patience, the patience of someone working to a plan.

There were no more affairs, either, at least none that could be identified. She was on a different path, one she could only travel alone.

Elliot dressed in dry clothes and headed up to the studio with a cup of black coffee. Italy was where Zoia had learned the gilding techniques of the Renaissance, once reserved for sacred images alone. Italy was where she had learned to float gold on water, to create infinity in a skin of metal less than one-four-thousandth-of-a-millimeter thick.

It was said Karl Kilbom's disillusionment with Soviet communism contributed to his wife's sense of nostalgia. Kilbom even encouraged Zoia to write a memoir of her life in Russia. The Revolution had been betrayed, just like the Kronstadt sailors had said, and to expose the brutality of traitors was something good. Little by little, Zoia the artist turned back to Russia.

The public journey and the private one. What if one was simply a cover for the other?

Something Hildur Backlin said at the retirement home, as she stared out across the steaming water of the swimming pool: *She loved the theater. All that let's pretend. All those masks.*

Zoia liked masks. But her pictures were all naive simplicity, visions of a faultless world. The visions of a child. Except that Zoia didn't have time for children, apparently.

He pulled out Cennino Cennini's book, thumbed through it until he found the chapter on water gilding. It was light outside now, but not enough to read by. He fired up one of the storm lanterns, and stood turning the pages beneath the radiance of its pulsing yellow flame.

A piece of paper fell out and landed at his feet. He recognized Zoia's handwriting. It was just as if it had dropped through a letter box from the other side of the grave. And she had sent him up there to find it.

On the piece of paper were instructions. They were written in English.

35

It was exactly the evidence Kerstin Östlund had been looking for: a list of the paintings in Zoia's private collection, and who was to receive them on her death. It had been drawn up in 1993, when Zoia had turned ninety, and all the names the reporter had mentioned were there: the galleries in Russia, the National Museum in Stockholm, the Montparnasse Museum in Paris. The *Actress* was to go to Hildur Backlin, just as the old lady had claimed. The biggest painting, *Stockholm Harbor,* was to be given to a local charity. And no less than four other pictures, among them *The Summer Palace at Tsarskoe Selo* and the *Portrait of Hermine von Essen,* were earmarked for the children of someone called Monica Fisk. The addresses were there. The names of the curators were there. Even phone numbers. It was a document Zoia had taken trouble over. And the fact that she had written it in English, the lingua franca of the art world, as of all business, suggested an intention that everyone concerned should see it. The list didn't prove that the Lindqvist will was a fake. But it did show a last-minute change of heart had taken place where the fate of her collection was concerned. And maybe that was enough to interest the authorities.

His first impulse was to call Kerstin Östlund. He could still picture her face as she slid the napkin across the table in the Ibis Majestic bar, with her number on it, written in blotchy black felt pen. *You help me and I'll help you.* But she hadn't said *how* she would help him. He'd sensed she knew something about the Crimea pictures. But the fact that they were not mentioned on Zoia's list made their existence more doubtful than ever. Perhaps Kerstin Östlund had nothing to tell him, because there was nothing to know.

It was just like a reporter to make empty promises—of anonymity, of discretion. It became a habit. Muckraking bred cynicism, and cynicism bred lies. Besides, if he told Kerstin about his discovery, there was a danger events would run out of control. Stories might appear in the press overnight. Interested parties might intervene before his work was done. If the sale was canceled, he would lose his right of access to Zoia's papers, and to the house. Dr. Lindqvist would see to that. It was something he couldn't risk.

Driving inland the next morning, down empty roads brown with slush, he breathed a sigh of relief that he had resisted the urge to call. Kerstin had a certain appeal. A little more effort and she would have been pretty. And that crust of journalistic toughness she affected, it excited him, just as it made him wary—because there was clearly something behind it, some vulnerability, some wound. But it would have been wrong to turn to her now, an act of desertion, like walking away from a conversation in mid-sentence.

He laughed at that. But it was true: Zoia was a good companion. She was fascinating and infuriating. She lied and dissembled, then bared her soul in torrents of pain and ecstasy that took his breath away. Yet there was always more to learn. She was unpredictable, moody, proud, and elusive, but always she held out to him the promise of enlightenment, of a final unifying revelation. A homecoming. And she was always there, in her papers and in her house, waiting for him. Always.

He was driving toward a place called Bollmora, on the southernmost outskirts of Stockholm. It was a place on the list, the place where Monica Fisk's children lived. It was the one part of the document that was obscure to him, that he could not explain. That was why he had to go.

Monica Fisk. At first the name meant nothing to him. He'd searched his records for references, and found just a handful. Zoia had received letters from her in Tunis. She came across as a woman a few years younger than the artist, and seemingly under her influence. But among the letters that bore no signature, or which were incomplete, Elliot found others written in the same style. She had been a female confidante of Zoia's, and that made her a rarity. Zoia's relationships with women were scant and unstable, perhaps because her way of life was unconventional, perhaps because her reputation was tainted with scandal. Low church, bourgeois Sweden was a long way from Montparnasse. But Monica Fisk had been excited by Zoia, and by her art. She found Sweden suffocating, conformist, dull. In her mind, Zoia represented everything that was adventurous and exotic.

Sixty years later, with Monica herself apparently dead, Zoia had planned on returning the compliment with a sizable gift to her children, Klara and Martin. It was a stone worth turning over.

Elliot had heard of Bollmora. His mother had lived there as a child, although he himself had never been to the place. Little would have remained of the village she knew in any case. Since the early 1960s, the area had been a focus of large-scale, state-financed housing development. Waves of apartment blocks—low-rise, medium- and high-rise—had invaded the rolling, wooded landscape, and with it industry in search of manpower. Among his father's effects Elliot had come across a couple of small black and white photographs purportedly taken there: his mother in a floral print dress, eleven or twelve years old, standing with a bicycle in a leafy lane, squinting into the afternoon sun, some unnamed child companion at her side. In the background you could make out a bulky prewar car, and somebody's front garden in bloom. By now the lane would be a highway and the garden an office block or a car park.

He drove in from the west, past lines of warehouses crouching behind straggling, unkempt hedges. It was mid-morning, but most of the street-lights were still burning dimly. He snaked his way around a series of roundabouts and one-way systems that were clearly designed to deal with a greater volume of traffic than there was, and found himself in a residential zone. Set back from the road, the newest generation of tower blocks—mid-1970s versions, to judge from the white, minimalist exteriors—stood starkly against the gray sky, surrounded by wide skirts of grass. It was hard to get directions. Everyone he spoke to was vague about the location of the street, and vaguer about how to reach it. There were roadside disagreements everywhere he stopped. Something about Bollmora—the spaced, man-made landscape, the nomenclature of the streets—made the geography difficult to memorize, to pin down mentally. Even the inhabitants had given up trying. Elliot searched in vain for landmarks his mother might have recognized.

After an hour of driving around in circles, he pulled up outside an S-shaped low-rise, hemmed in between a football field and a motorway embankment. There was a small playground at the front, boasting two man-made hillocks, a range of battered slides and swings, but no children. It was a school day, Elliot reminded himself, and with the beginnings of the thaw, the wind had taken on a chill damp edge.

There was a bank of buzzers by the entrance to block C, but the buttons seemed dead. The door had been left ajar. He pushed it open and entered a narrow hallway, his eyes adjusting to the dim interior. There was a smell of mold and disinfectant. He began to climb the stairs, taking in the peeling paint and the pitted cement walls. Somewhere up above him a TV was on, the sound of muffled voices and applause echoing. A child's tricycle lay on its side, the front wheel missing, beside it an empty can of cooking oil. He began to wonder if he had come to the right place, whether Zoia hadn't made a mistake about the address. He couldn't see her in a place like this at any time of her life, she who had been educated alongside princesses, whose family had owned factories and railways.

But then, anyone could fall. He had fallen, *was* falling by any objective measure. Maybe this was what he had to look forward to. Maybe this was the real reason he was here, to get a glimpse of his future. It was a crazy idea, but it was there now, hard and indissoluble, like a stone in his gut.

There was no number on the door of what should have been apartment 9. He knocked hesitantly, aware of a child crying, then again, louder. Something moved behind the peephole.

"Mrs. Palmgren?"

Both Monica Fisk's children were called Palmgren, a name they must have taken from their father.

There came a squeak of sneakers on linoleum. The door opened. A woman's face, waxy and pale, appeared behind a chain.

"Excuse me. I was looking for Monica Fisk's daughter, Klara. Is this the right address?"

The woman had a baby slung over her shoulder. A bare pudgy leg, clad in a dirty cartoon sock, hung down across her chest.

"She's not back yet."

He wondered if this was Monica's granddaughter. She was about the right age, twenty-five or so. She had a handsome, open face, but there were dark circles under her eyes, and her short blonde hair was clumped and greasy. Elliot himself had made an effort for the occasion. He had shaved, even washed a shirt, ironing it at the kitchen table. Only the cuts on his face looked out of the ordinary.

"I'm here about a friend of her mother's. Zoia Korvin-Krukovsky. The artist?"

The girl's face registered nothing.

"It's about some paintings."

The infant moaned. A tiny hand clawed drowsily at the girl's chin. It was obvious she had no idea what he was talking about. Suddenly Elliot felt ridiculous. Out of touch. What had oil paintings to do with a place like this? What was their relevance? The girl probably thought he was crazy. Some crazy man who had wandered in off the street.

"Perhaps you could tell Mrs. Palmgren I called. Here."

He fumbled in his pockets for his notebook and pen, thinking the best thing was to leave his mobile number. But before he could start to write, he heard labored footsteps on the stairs beneath him, then a woman's voice, muttering irritably to herself.

"This is her," the girl said, and took the chain off the latch.

Klara Palmgren seemed anxious to help. She was in her sixties, overweight and matronly, with bleached blonde hair fixed in poodle-tight curls on the top of her head. She sat opposite Elliot on an orange sofa, while he explained about the research he was doing, and the big exhibition that was planned for the summer. She didn't betray any obvious signs of thinking he was mad. Rather, she listened, nodding politely, her hands rubbing and plucking at the fabric of the sofa, like someone used to smoking. On a table beside her, glass paperweights mingled with a scant collection of family photographs: a skinny-looking boy with a bad 1970s' haircut, standing by a swimming pool; Klara in a yellow dress with a little girl that was probably her daughter. There was one black and white photo: a studio portrait of Klara herself, taken maybe forty years ago. There was a singular lack of men: no wedding pictures, no happy couples. If there had been significant others in Klara Palmgren's life, they were no longer in the frame, literally or otherwise. The fact that she had retained her maiden name was further evidence of the fact.

He held back on mentioning the will. He was afraid the possibility that a fraud had taken place might influence what she had to say. She might claim to have been closer to Zoia than she really had been.

"Do you remember her well? I know she was a close friend of your mother's."

Klara frowned. "Remember . . . ?"

"Zoia. Zoia Korvin-Krukovsky."

She shook her head. Her daughter had retreated to the kitchen, ostensibly to make them a cup of coffee.

"Are you sure? She certainly seems to have remembered you. And your brother."

"My brother? Martin?"

"Martin, yes."

She glanced toward the smeary double-glazed windows. "Martin lives in the country now," she said, as if that explained something.

Elliot tried to jog her memory. These were valuable pictures, a big part of Zoia's collection. She wouldn't have wanted to leave them to strangers.

"Why don't you tell me about the last time you saw her? Start with that."

"The Russian lady?"

"Zoia, yes."

"I don't know if I ever saw her." Klara shrugged helplessly. "Maybe when I was a child. I don't know."

It came to Elliot that she had actually no idea what he was doing there either. She had never *heard* of Zoia Korvin-Krukovsky. He had mentioned her mother, Monica, and she had let him in because he didn't look like a criminal, and maybe because she didn't get many visitors. But that was as far as it went.

She must have read the confusion in his face. She gathered her hands in her lap, lowering her voice. "You see, my mother and I were not close. Not for a long time, anyway. My brother and I, we were raised by our father, Kristoffer Palmgren."

"Your father? May I ask why?"

Klara thought about it for a moment, then shrugged. "She . . . left us. When we were quite small. Three or four, I was. Martin would have been six. She went to France. Had an affair there, I believe."

"You don't know with whom?"

Klara shook her head vaguely, as if she wasn't sure if she knew or not. "I never heard a name. It didn't last anyway."

"You said France. When was this, exactly?"

"Just before the war." She put her head on one side, thinking about it. "I don't think she had a happy life, my mother. She always wanted excitement . . . a different kind of life. My father said she fell under bad influences when she was young."

"Bad influences?"

"Immoral people. Extravagant people. She had some money back then, from her family. But she spent it all."

"Did she ever come back?"

"To Sweden? Oh yes. When she was older. We saw her then, a little. Martin saw her more than I did. Before she died."

She gazed down at a worn patterned rug on the floor, nodding slightly to herself.

"How did she die?"

Klara stayed looking at the rug. "Cancer. February 1981." She looked up brightly. "Maybe your Russian lady was at the funeral. I remember there were a few people there I didn't recognize. Most of them, in fact." Her smile faded. "Perhaps you should talk to Martin."

"Where is your brother? You said the country."

"Igelsfors. It's a little place the other side of Katrineholm. Although he lives outside the village."

It had to be at least seventy miles, probably eighty on country roads.

"Do you have his telephone number?"

Klara sighed. "He doesn't have a phone. He won't pay for a line. He keeps saying he'll get one of those mobiles, but . . ." She shrugged hopelessly. "He takes after our mother in some ways. No good with money."

Elliot considered the prospect of a day on the road with nothing to show for it but some recollections of a funeral that Zoia may or may not have attended. There was a blank here, and he couldn't think how to fill it. Monica Fisk was dead and her children were strangers. But Zoia had left them pictures anyway. Maybe it didn't matter. Maybe the list itself was what counted. But still it felt like he was doing something wrong. The thought of losing the thread now, of reaching the end, made him panicky. If it ended here, it was all for nothing.

He stood up and thanked Klara for her time.

"Won't you stay for some coffee?"

Her daughter appeared in the kitchen door, holding a pair of mugs. She had done something to her hair, combed it back. And there was pale blue makeup on her eyelids.

"Thank you, but I really have to go."

Klara got up to show him out. "Well, it was very interesting hearing about your work. I'll be sure to visit the exhibition."

Elliot stopped dead. There in the tiny hallway a painting was hanging. He hadn't seen it on the way in. About sixteen inches by twelve, a little wooden house on a lake, with a forest of dark pines lining the shore. Oil and gold leaf on a wood panel.

The lake was a rippling field of gold.

"This picture," he said. "What can you tell me about it?"

Klara came and stood beside him. "Oh that. That's where my brother lives now. The place I was telling you about."

"Igelsfors?"

"It used to be my grandfather's summer house. My mother's father. I told you, they had money once. It was sold eventually. I suppose my mother sold it. Anyway, it fell into disuse. But a few years ago my brother bought it back. He had happy memories of the place, you see. He's *supposed* to be doing it up."

"So when was the picture painted?"

Klara shrugged. "I couldn't say. It was in my grandfather's house when I was growing up. So it must have been before the war."

She ran her finger along the bottom of the rough wooden frame. It came up dirty.

36

He found her initials on the back of the picture, in the bottom left-hand corner, partially hidden by the frame. She had written them in a single, twisting brushstroke—*ZKK*—so that, at first glance, it looked like nothing more than a fissure in the grain of the wood. But under the magnifying glass the hand was unmistakably hers.

It wasn't the first time. Several of Zoia's pictures from the 1930s had been signed in this way. It wasn't clear why. One possibility was that Zoia was following iconographic tradition. Iconographers did not sign their work. The point of a sacred icon was to focus people's minds on the divine. The worldliness, the egotism inherent in a visible signature was not considered appropriate. Savva Leskov had enunciated this idea in his *Figaro* essay. It was only when Zoia had found her feet as a secular artist, he said, that she overcame her inhibitions. He thought she had then gone back and signed her early works on gold, at least the ones she had managed to keep track of. Elliot was not so sure. To him these were experimental works, works that were never intended for exhibition or sale. It wasn't that they were palpably unsuccessful, or incomplete. Rather, they were private, pictures by an artist who wasn't yet ready for an audience.

Klara Palmgren listened to Elliot openmouthed. She'd had a vague idea that the picture might have been painted by her grandfather, she said. That was why she'd kept it. She'd had no idea it might be valuable, or even that the gold was real. She seemed thrilled that she was going to be a part of the big show, excitedly calling her daughter over and having Elliot explain everything again.

"I can't say what this painting would fetch," he said. "Things are still very fluid at the moment. But interest is growing. Would you want to sell it?"

One look at their faces told him it was a stupid question.

"Listen, why don't you let me take it to Bukowskis? See what they make of it. If they give it a prominent place in the catalog, that might make all the difference."

Klara had agreed at once and would have let him go without even taking his details, if he hadn't insisted in writing them all down for her. And now he was driving back to Stockholm with an early Zoia strapped into the backseat, wrapped up in a sheet of old newspaper and a length of nylon string. Just like the old days.

A smile crept across his face. At last he had something tangible to show for his researches, something even Cornelius Wallander couldn't ignore. He pictured the double-page spread in the catalog, the painting reproduced on one side, an excerpt from one of Monica Fisk's letters on the other. He would go up to Igelsfors the next morning, maybe take a few pictures of the summer house, dig out some more details about Zoia's visits. Maybe there were even more pictures up there, waiting to be discovered.

It would buy him time. Bukowskis couldn't complain if he was finding them new pictures to sell. Even Kerstin Östlund couldn't complain. At least this way Monica Fisk's children got something.

He left the Volvo in the staff car park, and strode into Bukowskis with the picture under his arm. The girl behind the reception desk was different this time: short mousy hair, plump face, glasses with no-nonsense rectangular frames. She looked up with a professional smile.

"Is Cornelius available? It's Marcus Elliot."

The smile faded as she took in the marks on his face. "I think he has someone with him, Mr. Elliot. Just a moment."

The girl pressed a button on her keyboard, exchanged words with Cornelius's secretary. A pair of security guards were staring at him from the entrance to the main auction room. Beyond another set of doors, a sale was in progress, the auctioneer's mellifluous voice just audible above the gush of air-conditioning.

"I'm afraid Mr. Wallander isn't in his office. He's showing someone around. Do you want to wait?"

"Where is he? Is he downstairs?"

She didn't answer him. "If you'd just take a seat for a moment. Someone will come down."

Reluctantly, Elliot did as he was asked. The last time he was there, he had been given more-or-less free run of the place. Now he had to wait in Reception for someone to *come down*.

He sat for five minutes, watching the clock on the wall while the guards watched him. He was about to complain when the doors to the auction room swung open, and a small crowd of people came hurrying out, pulling on coats and scarves, their business concluded. Most headed for the street, others crowded around the front desk, wanting information. Elliot took his chance, crossing swiftly toward the elevators. A few moments later, he was down in the sub-basement, making his way along the dark, empty corridors, breathing in the building-site smell of damp plaster.

Just as he'd expected, there were lights on in the viewing room. The doors were ajar. He stopped outside and listened, wanting some clue as to the identity of Cornelius's guest. But there was nothing.

He stepped inside. The pictures were all still there. A few more had been added to the walls to left and right. A big aluminum stepladder stood in the middle of the aisle.

"Cornelius?"

A man stepped out from behind the *Orchids in a Red Vase*. "Taking a phone call, I'm afraid. Back presently."

The stranger was middle-aged, soberly dressed in a three-piece suit, with a wine-red bow tie. He had a long, sloping nose, and thin gray hair, which was slicked back, displaying a prominent forehead. In his hand he held an unlit pipe, the smell of which mingled with a faint aroma of Eau Sauvage.

"Savva Leskov. How do you do?"

For a moment Elliot thought it was a joke. He had always pictured Leskov as a youngish man, energetic, opinionated. He had thick frizzy hair and pebble glasses—a passing resemblance, Elliot had always thought, to the young Gustav Mahler. But then, the *Figaro* essay had been eleven years ago, and he hadn't seen a photograph of the man since.

Elliot gave his name and shook hands, mumbled something about working for Cornelius Wallander. He didn't know what else to say.

Perhaps Leskov sensed his awkwardness. He stuck the pipe in his mouth and pointed at the package under Elliot's arm.

"What's this, a late addition?"

His English was flawless, with no more than the ghost of an accent between Slavic and French.

"Yes. Yes, that's right." Elliot took off the paper and held up the picture. "This is a place near Katrineholm. It belonged to a friend of Zoia's. Or her father. Dates from the mid-1930s."

Leskov looked at it, arms folded. "Interesting. Very interesting."

He leaned forward, licked the tip of his finger, and before Elliot could protest, ran it over the gold. The gesture was casual, almost proprietorial.

"Water gilding," he said, as if it went without saying that his verdict was expected. "But poorly executed. See, the gilt's starting to flake here. A problem with the gesso, I expect. Or possibly her choice of wood. The wrong kind of wood'll warp in this climate."

"It was done before Italy," Elliot said. "She was still experimenting with the technique back then."

Leskov nodded. "Quite so." He stepped back, put his head on one side. "Still, it is striking. That golden water. It makes the house, even the trees there, seem fragile. Suspended. Don't you think? As if they're preserved in amber."

Elliot propped up the picture on a table. Until now, he hadn't had time to look at it very closely.

"That's the salient point about this medium," Leskov went on. He was like a man cracking a problem, trying to work out what to say. Perhaps there was another one of his essays in prospect. "That's the draw, if you ask me. The immortality of gold. The way it goes on forever, unchanged, untarnished. Like the sun. In the wrong hands, it's almost *too* perfect. Too much."

"You mean, gaudy?"

"Well, some people think it *is* gaudy." Leskov gestured toward the rest of the room. "All of it."

"What about you?"

Leskov sucked on his empty pipe, eyebrows raised at the directness of the question. Then he chuckled, as if at some private joke. "I admire the audacity. Russia was running red with blood. But she painted it in gold, the color of eternal life. You could call it naive, or you could call it defiant."

Here it was again, the patriotic line. Leskov's view hadn't changed in eleven years. And, hearing it from his own lips, Elliot was surprised at how persuasive it was—if all you had to go on were the pictures themselves.

"But this isn't Russia. It's a place in Sweden."

"Yes. But then again, wasn't everything she painted Russia? At least, the world through Russian eyes. Russia marked her, as it marks us all who are born there."

Out of nowhere, Elliot got a picture of Hildur Backlin, sitting hunched in her wheelchair, waving a gnarled finger. *Her Russia was a dream. A beautiful dream. The real Russia she* hated.

Leskov rattled the pipe against his teeth. "Sometimes I find it troubling though, I must say. Seeing these pictures again after so long. The technique seems so . . . demanding." He gestured toward the big picture of Stockholm harbor. "So practiced. You know, it renders the images almost . . . I don't know how to put it—*mute.* Does that make any sense?"

He seemed genuinely puzzled. But Elliot had always known the answer to that.

"You only get one shot with gold leaf. Every brushstroke is permanent. You can't hide your mistakes. That's bound to make an artist very careful. Very deliberate."

"Ah yes, the mistakes. The pentimenti—isn't that the word? The repentances?"

"Yes."

"Still." The lines deepened on Leskov's forehead. "In another sense, your mistakes are very *well* hidden, aren't they? Very well hidden indeed."

"What do you mean?"

"Well, if you X-ray an ordinary picture, oil on canvas or whatever, you can see what's underneath, can't you? The false starts, the parts that have been painted over, and over and over. You can pretty much reconstruct the process. The artist at work, bungles and all."

"I suppose so."

"But not with these, because of the gold. Gold is impenetrable to X-rays, like lead. And it lasts a lot longer than paint. A permanent, impenetrable skin. Like on the sarcophagus of a Pharaoh, like Tutankhamen's."

The mention of the Pharaoh brought Elliot's head up. It was as if Leskov had been shadowing his work.

A facile grin lit up the critic's smile, "So, as analysts, we're blind. All we have to go on is the surface. Not that Zoia would have been worrying about all that in 1935, of course." Leskov shrugged. "No, I expect you're right. I expect it's the decorative nature of the medium that seems brittle."

Brittle. Elliot had a sense that Leskov was on to something, but it wasn't a development he welcomed. The critic wasn't entitled to insights. He was on the outside. He was guessing, like everyone else, laying down whatever plausible line suited the occasion.

"I take it you won't be buying then," Elliot said.

"Buying? Oh dear me, no. I'm just here to write the catalog. Bit of a rushed job, as they say. But I shall manage."

It took a moment to sink in.

"Excuse me, the catalog? Is that what you said?"

There were voices outside. Cornelius was returning with another visitor. In that moment, Elliot knew it was true. He had been replaced. No heart-to-heart. No final warning. Out.

He should have called Cornelius back. He'd meant to, some time. But when he'd finally got around to it, he'd found the battery in his mobile phone was dead. And there was no way to recharge it at the house.

The other visitor was Leo Demichev. Of course. Demichev had brought Savva Leskov in. They were probably buddies from their Moscow days.

At the sight of Elliot, Cornelius flushed. It was almost comic, the speed with which he changed color, as if someone had pulled a chain in his head.

"Marcus. Well, this is a surprise."

"What's going on, Cornelius? I'm out of touch for a couple of days, and you replace me?"

Hastily Demichev took Professor Leskov by the arm and led him toward the other end of the room, covering the moment with a flood of words.

"A couple of days? Marcus, I've been trying to reach you for a week."

"A week? What are you talking about?"

But suddenly he wasn't sure. How long had it been since the dinner at Cornelius's? He tried to count the days. But the truth was, he had lost track of time. At Zoia's house his routines had followed the rhythm of his investigations, the need to eat and rest, the need to gather fuel for the stoves. In retrospect, even sleeping and waking were hard to tell apart. He had seen the letters in his dreams, and the people who had written them. And in his waking hours he had imagined them, as he stood by the big picture window, watching the sea and the ever-changing sky. They had filled up his world, companions and guides. He couldn't say for how long.

"I told you, Marcus. I needed that briefing. For the Foreign Ministry. I had to do it myself in the end. Frederik was extremely unhappy."

"I forgot. I was working, Cornelius. All the time, I was working. I even unearthed a new picture for you. Over there. Circa 1935, oil and gold leaf on oak. The subject is a summer house near a village called Igelsfors. Although you won't find that information on the back."

Staring at the picture, Cornelius went an even deeper shade of red.

"I'm sure we can come to some arrangement concerning the commission. A finder's fee or something."

He was trying to edge Elliot toward the door. Elliot didn't budge.

"You can't do this. We had an agreement."

"I'm sorry, Marcus, but you gave me no choice. I ask for work and you don't deliver. I ask for evidence of progress, and I get nothing. And then you vanish altogether. You don't seem to understand what's—"

"Understand? You think *he* understands?"

He was pointing down the room. Leskov was standing before the *Actress,* deep in conversation.

"Professor Leskov is the closest thing to an authority there is in this field. We were very lucky to get him."

"An authority? Are you kidding? If he's such an authority, why don't you ask him who he's looking at? Go on, ask him. Who's in the picture?"

"For God's sake, Marcus, what difference does it make?"

"Her name is Hildur Backlin. She lives in a retirement home in Södertälje. I've *met* her."

"Marcus, that's all very impressive, but it's not what we needed." Cornelius's expression briefly softened into one of pity. "Marcus, this is not Picasso we're talking about. This is not Rembrandt. This is a *minor artist.* And she will always *be* a minor artist. Interesting, collectable. Maybe even fashionable, if everything goes according to plan. But that's it. That's all there is." He reached out, put a hand on Elliot's shoulder. "For God's sake, what made you think she was worth all this ... effort? What's in it for you?"

Cornelius's hand was a cold deadweight. Elliot could feel it pushing him down, lowering him into the dark, hopeless depths with all the force of inevitability. Zoia had escaped them somehow, that morning in La Marsa. She had found a way, and it was there in her art. That was what he'd thought. But now he wasn't so sure. The art was brittle, Professor Leskov said. Maybe that was true.

What was in it for him? Maybe nothing. Maybe nothing, after all.

Leskov was coming closer again, talking as he went. But Demichev wasn't listening. He was more concerned with what Elliot was up to.

Cornelius had him by the arm now, and was steering him toward the door.

"Listen, just hand over your work so far, and we'll come to some arrangement. I'll see that you're compensated for your time. I can't say fairer than that, can I?"

At the threshold Elliot turned, took in once again the strange, secret tunnel of gold. Pictures only he had the means to understand.

They wanted him to surrender his work. But that was never going to happen.

"By the way, Cornelius," he said. "The actress. I'm surprised you don't remember her."

"The actress?"

"In the picture. Hildur Backlin."

Cornelius smiled nervously. "A little before my time, I think."

"No, Cornelius. Very much in *our* time. Seeing as how she owns the damned picture."

Cornelius laughed. "What?"

"Don't you remember? Or weren't you shown the original will? I mean, the *genuine* will."

"What are you talking about?" Cornelius was still laughing, but his face had gone deathly pale.

"You should be careful what you sign, Cornelius. You should be careful who you sign up *with*. Keeping bad company never pays in the end. Ask Leo over there."

Suddenly Cornelius's face was up close, close enough for Elliot to smell the sweat on him. Elliot braced himself for the blow.

"I know who you've been talking to. That Östlund girl." Cornelius was shaking with rage. "The one who *calls* herself a reporter. The one we had to fire because she was always drunk."

"Drunk?"

"Drunk, stoned. I don't know what she was on, but I know one thing: she's even more insane than you are. I mean, she's *delusional*."

The others were staring now, Leskov openmouthed, Demichev with a look of cold contempt.

"I'm surprised you weren't able to spot it, Marcus. What with all your recent experience."

Elliot walked away, but Cornelius wasn't finished. His footsteps followed him down the passage.

"I wish I knew what this was about, Marcus. Do you really *want* to destroy yourself?"

His voice was different now. The anger was gone, or at least hidden.

"If you really cared about your daughter, if you *really* wanted her back, you wouldn't do this. You couldn't."

Elliot wanted to answer him, to say something, anything, that would wipe the look of pity off his smug, shiny face. But his heart was pounding so hard he found he didn't have the breath to speak.

37

Lightning marked the skyline in silhouette. Thunder echoed and reechoed. Elliot was halfway across the harbor when the storm broke. He watched a wall of rain slowly engulf the city—spires, office blocks, streetlights—rolling eastward. It swept over the bridge, hammering down on the roof of the car, overwhelming the wipers, bringing the traffic to a standstill, until all he could see were the taillights of the cars in front.

Somewhere in Södermalm he missed the turning. He found himself on an unfamiliar street, stuck in a queue, no longer sure if he was even heading in the right direction. There had been an accident up ahead. Banks of hazard lights flickered in the saturated air.

One of the drivers behind him came running down the road with his coat pulled over his head. Elliot wound down the window.

"Will this take me to the 228? The road out east?"

The driver shook his head. "This goes to the E4. The autobahn. South."

It was only then Elliot realized that south was where he had to go, where he had actually been going. The place that came next. South to Katrineholm, south to the house near Igelsfors where Zoia had worked in the years after Tunis. He had been heading there as if nothing had happened, as if he were still working for Bukowskis, helping to prepare for the big retrospective. Except that he had never been doing that, not really. From the day he had walked into Cornelius's vault, and seen that golden avenue stretched out before him, he had been on a different trajectory. They were bound to have parted company sooner or later. It was just a question of when and how.

He had planned on making the trip to Igelsfors in a day or two, once Mrs. Palmgren had been able to contact her brother. But things had changed. He could no longer afford to wait. At Bukowskis he had allowed his purpose to become confused. And in his anger he had stirred things up more than was wise, making unspecified threats about the authenticity of the will, the will that was, in fact, the foundation stone for the whole Zoia project. He had a bad feeling Cornelius wasn't going to leave it at that. And then there was Leo Demichev. Beneath the urbanity, the man was a gangster, a gangster with connections. That was why he liked the art world. It got him into the drawing rooms of some very powerful people.

It took another half hour to reach the motorway. Sitting in slow-moving traffic, he felt vulnerable. In Russia they were fond of killing people in their cars. In a car you were an easy target for an assassin on the back of a motorcycle. They would ride up alongside, rap on the window as if they wanted directions, and be gone before anyone had even noticed that you were dead at the wheel. Several of Leo Demichev's one-time associates had been killed that way. He bragged about it, another aspect of his personal mythology. He wasn't admitting to complicity, or even hinting at it. But the message was clear: he had lived in that world, survived in it, and that made him stronger than anyone who hadn't.

On the motorway Elliot kept an eye on the mirror. Thirty miles out of the city he turned onto a smaller highway, heading inland. The temperature was dropping fast. The rain had eased, but soon flurries of wet snow were catching on the wipers. The traffic thinned little by little until there was nothing on the road but a silver Mercedes a hundred yards behind him, the beam of its blue-white headlamps drifting in and out of view. Elliot slowed down, wanting to see if it would catch up with him and overtake. But as he slowed, it slowed. He watched it in the mirror for twenty minutes, heart pounding. But when he pulled over at a service station, the car that went on past was a Lexus. Somewhere along the way the Mercedes had disappeared.

He went into the empty diner and ordered coffee. He sat, watching the service station, aware of how crazy it was, thinking he was being followed. As if Leo had the KGB at his beck and call. As if the KGB still existed.

Then he was thinking about Kerstin Östlund. She *had* followed him. At least, she had staked out Bukowskis and then his hotel, which was almost the same thing. What if she really was crazy, like Cornelius said? Delusional. What if her stories about the will, and all the rest of it, were just that—stories, inventions, extrapolations she could no longer distinguish from fact?

A wave of nausea went through him. He pushed back from the table.

He didn't want it to be true. He didn't want her to be insane. He could see her now, sitting opposite him in the Ibis Majestic. He could see that strange-looking depression in her forehead, that scar running up into her hair.

What if she had made the whole story up? He watched the last flakes of snow drifting by the floodlights and tried to imagine how that might be. Zoia had been kind to her, Kerstin had said, at a difficult time. Surely that much was fact. But maybe she couldn't bear for it to be over. Zoia had touched her life, and this was her way of prolonging the experience, of staying somehow *involved*. Maybe Cornelius and his crowd were interlopers in her eyes. They were taking Zoia away from her all over again.

Or maybe it went even deeper than that. Maybe she had never met Zoia at all.

He studied the road map. It was another forty miles to Katrineholm, another fifteen to the Igelsfors turning, another twenty-five on minor roads to the village itself. From there he would have to ask for directions, although it was already nine o'clock. Soon it would be too late to go knocking on doors. He pressed on into the night, wanting to get as close as possible to his destination, preferring to drive than to think. He drove until his body ached and his eyes were smarting.

He reached an old stone-built hotel on a hillside, by a village called Regna, its lights burning incongruously bright in the middle of an empty landscape. He got himself a room and turned in, praying for dreamless sleep.

The next morning he found a voicemail message on the mobile. Cornelius Wallander had left it the night before, about an hour after their last encounter. He sounded conciliatory, though guarded. He understood that Elliot had been surprised at the turn of events, he said. It was bound to have come as a shock. Securing the services of Professor Leskov was a genuine coup, and it was too late to go back to previous arrangements, but obviously Elliot should be fully compensated for his efforts. Obviously. All he had to do was sit down with Professor Leskov and set out what he had found so far. That way nothing would be wasted. He was sure the professor would wish to see that he was credited for his help, so there need be no hard feelings.

It felt to Elliot like a message for someone else. A great distance had opened up between them, a distance that came with understanding. Cornelius, Bukowskis, Leo Demichev, their connection to him had been a hindrance. Now he was free. He could pursue the truth as it should be pursued, without thought of compromise. No nip and tuck to charm the cash from onlookers' pockets. There were no onlookers now. There was only Zoia and him. And it didn't matter if the encounter was private. Maybe it was always meant to be private. Maybe that was the only way some kinds of knowledge were ever won, in solitude.

Cornelius's message rambled on. He wanted Elliot to call him back as soon as possible. He was sorry if he'd said anything offensive. He didn't want Elliot leaving the country until they'd had a chance to meet again. It was important, he said, very important.

Elliot hung up before the message finished.

38

Martin Palmgren sounded like some kind of hermit. He lived in the wilds, in a house without a telephone. According to his sister, he was a sculptor whose work didn't sell. Mostly he earned his money making animal figurines for sale in tourist shops. Elliot wondered how it might go, him arriving out of the blue, unannounced, but it turned out he was expected.

"Klara called my neighbor, Agda. Agda's my lifeline to the world."

Elliot had stopped to ask directions, thinking he was still some distance from the house. But the man shoveling snow inside the gateway turned out to be Martin Palmgren.

"Klara said you'd be here any day. She said you were interested in some family history."

He was a tall man with a short, scrappy beard several different shades of gray. A bulky puffer jacket hung loosely on a thin body.

"I hope this isn't a bad time," Elliot said.

"It's a very *good* time. Like the first day of spring." Palmgren reached out to the sky with stiff, arthritic arms. "Everything's ready for you in the house. Come, come."

And he waved Elliot up the drive.

The house was tall like a barn, flanked by pine trees and silver birches. The clapboard of the walls was laid out vertically, and painted rust-red, the window frames picked out in white. Something about it reminded Elliot of his childhood, of Nordic fairy tales of spells and wolves and children lost in the woods. Repair work was going on. The roof was partly covered with plastic sheeting, and bags of cement and steel guttering stood stacked up in an open shed next to an ancient mud-spattered Land Rover. Elliot got out of the car and stood looking at the house, trying to match it to the one in the picture. The color was different: Zoia's house had been darker, a red like dried blood. But the shape and the setting suggested a match.

Inside, there was more evidence of restoration. The floorboards were up in the hallway, and many of the interior walls were sections of unpainted plasterboard, naked wires protruding from nonexistent fittings. There was a smell of sawdust and stale tobacco.

"How long have you had the place?"

Palmgren was leading him through the ground floor, showing him around. He had taken off his jacket to reveal a patterned gray sweater with holes at the elbows.

"About three years. Another two and it'll be finished." They passed a dirty-looking kitchen. Tins of food, some open, stood on the counters. "You should have seen the state of the place when I got it, though."

Palmgren was doing everything himself, paying for materials bit by bit when he could afford them. It was a labor of love, and he seemed pleased at the opportunity to show it off.

"You must have been very happy here," Elliot said, as they headed up the stairs. "To go to all this trouble."

"My boyhood memories are hazy, to tell the truth. But I remember there were always people here. Guests. My grandfather knew a lot of artists, you know. They came in the summer to work. For refuge, he used to say."

"For refuge?"

"That's what he used to say. He didn't much care for the city."

"But Monica, your mother, she sold the place, didn't she?"

They were on the landing now. Palmgren didn't look back.

"Yes. She did." He walked over to a set of double doors and threw them open. "Now this is what you have to see. This is what I love about this house."

Once it would have been a sitting room or a master bedroom. It occupied half the first floor, a room with a high ceiling and tall windows on two sides. Martin Palmgren had made it his studio. Standing in the middle of the floor were a pair of lifesize figures carved in wood, primitive human forms that seemed to be dragging themselves up out of the earth. Splinters and shavings lay everywhere. His tools—chisels, mallets, saws— were scattered across an old door propped up on trestles. The corners were full of books and old furniture.

Something about the windows was familiar, the proportions of the cross that divided the four panels of glass.

"Take a look at the view," Palmgren said.

The lake was there below them, about a mile of water, ringed with trees. In the distance was a faint blue ribbon of hills.

"In the summer the sun goes down over there. The reflections light up the whole room."

Elliot pictured rippling sunlight playing on the walls and the ceiling. He imagined Zoia, standing where he was standing, brush in hand. Still he couldn't see into her mind, but he was closer now, closer than he had ever been.

He took in the sculptures again. They had been executed with care, worked and worked, but they were not beautiful. Their primitivism was self-conscious, forced. They were the kind of pieces you needed luck and a carefully cultivated image to sell. And it was clear Martin Palmgren hadn't had the benefit of either.

"What do you think?" he said, hopefully. "Of course, they're not finished yet."

Over coffee they talked about the art business. Palmgren seemed to think this was a heaven-sent opportunity to get some professional advice, and catch up on current trends. Elliot tried to sound like he was still in the swim of things. He gave Palmgren the name of some dealers, and offered to take them photographs of his work. Palmgren said he had a whole stack ready.

The pictures were in a small study on the second floor. It was the one place in the house where islands of organization and tidiness were visible among the piles of junk, building materials, and old books. Elliot saw numbered box files along a shelf, and a pair of gray steel filing cabinets.

The pictures were surprisingly good. In black and white, the sculptures had more contrast, edge, credibility.

On a broad oak desk lay a stack of old photograph albums.

"Now, these are all my mother's things," Palmgren said. "Most of them I rescued after she passed away. There isn't much. Some letters, some photographs. She was very lazy about labeling, so it's been a challenge putting it all together."

"You mean, chronologically?"

Palmgren nodded. "There are a lot of gaps, too, I'm afraid. She moved around, you see. Husbands, divorces. I think she must have lost a lot of stuff along the way."

He picked up one of the albums, peeled back a page of wrinkled greaseproof paper. Faces peered out through the white frames, squinting as if surprised by the light.

Elliot stooped to get a better look. A man was leaning against the corner of a clapboard building. Two small girls were holding bicycles.

"So what are you actually looking for?" Palmgren said.

"Everything. Anything."

"Klara said you were writing a catalog."

"It's more of a monograph. Except that there are gaps here too, vital gaps. I'm trying to make sense of it."

"The painter? Or her work?"

Elliot turned over a page. "Both. You see, the research just hasn't been done."

In one photograph a crowd was gathered around a table, eating lunch on a veranda, smiling for the camera, forks and glasses poised. A pause for posterity. But some of the heads weren't turned. A woman with dark hair could have been Zoia.

"I think this is 1929 or 1930," Palmgren said. "About when my parents met."

Elliot studied the smiles, the bright expectant faces. They betrayed no trace of understanding that one day this would be all that remained of them, perhaps the only evidence that they had existed at all, standing where the living stand, lying where the living lie. They smiled at him out of an inescapable void, and the smiles said: *you'll be with us soon.*

The woman with her back to him wore a string of pearls.

"You've never come across Zoia's name?" Elliot asked.

Palmgren was watching him uncertainly, his fingers stroking the underside of his chin.

"I can't say I remember it. But she's the kind of person my mother *would* have known. She worshipped artists of all kinds: painters, filmmakers, theater people. They were really the only kinds of people she was interested in, at least when she was young. I think she married my father because of his interest in film."

"He was a filmmaker?"

Palmgren smiled. "Literally, yes. He ended up working for a company that made film. Film stock. You see, he was really interested in the science of it, the technical aspects. Mostly he shot film just to see what could be shot. He wasn't really so interested in the . . ." He shrugged, as if sharing his mother's disappointment. "The *narrative* possibilities."

"I see."

Elliot turned over another page of the album. Palmgren pointed to a picture of a young couple leaning out of a window, smiling broadly. The woman had pretty, delicate features and abundant blonde curls. The man had a beard and a bookish look.

"This is one of the few pictures she kept," Palmgren said. "Of the two of them, I mean."

"These are your parents?"

Palmgren nodded. "In either 1932 or 1933. Just after they were married. It was taken right here. I can show you the spot."

Monica Palmgren looked relaxed and happy. Her husband's smile was less natural, less assured. But suddenly Elliot knew where he had seen it before.

"You said your father made films."

"Well, home movies. Mainly on holidays. Why?"

Elliot tried to sound like it didn't really matter either way. "You don't still have them, do you?"

There was a dusty attic space at the top of the house, lit only by a small round window the size of a dinner plate. That was where the father's old stuff had gone. Among the boxes stood an array of ancient photographic equipment: an old condenser enlarger, glass measuring cylinders packed in straw, an editing bench partially hidden beneath a waxy yellow dust-cover.

Elliot crouched down and lifted the cover off a projector, a bulky machine in gun-metal gray, with the trade name "Bauer" riveted to the casing.

"That's the sixteen millimeter," Palmgren said. "His pride and joy. But that's a postwar machine. You see, he got this new Bolex in the fifties."

"Bolex? That's a movie camera?"

"Yes. Before that he shot everything on nine point five millimeter. But they stopped making that type of film. Here." He slid out a varnished wooden box and opened the lid. "This is his old camera, the Bolex H9. A collector's item, as they say, although in Sweden there aren't so many collectors, unfortunately." He eased it out of the casing. It was black, with white metal flashing at the corners, and three lenses on the front. "Dad got it in 1935. The receipt's still in here."

Elliot remembered the photograph, the one he had found in Zoia's desk: Zoia in front of an easel, a man with a cine camera standing beside her. *Kristoffer and Zoia at work.* Kristoffer was Martin Palmgren's father, the husband Monica Fisk had ultimately abandoned for a lover in Paris. In happier days she and her husband had walked in on Zoia. She couldn't send them away. She was a guest at the house, borrowing the same studio Martin used today. Nineteen thirty-five. Another one of the unproductive years, before the painting on gold began in earnest. Supposedly.

Elliot stood up. "Where's the film he shot with that, Martin?" he said. "Where's all the nine point five millimeter?"

39

Kerstin hated the days when nothing came in. Sometimes she would sit on a feature she was editing, leave it up there on the screen with one last subhead to write, rather than send it over and watch the screen go blank. The best times were when a late story broke as they were going to press, and they had to make space for it. Then they would give her whole sections to reedit, and for an hour or two she would be lost in the business of rephrasing, cutting, condensing.

The worst days were days like this.

There had been one development: an e-mail from a lawyer in the public prosecutor's office. She had written asking for advice on Zoia's will. His reply was terse. They did not have the resources to investigate allegations based on hearsay or conjecture. As for a civil action, a district court would be unlikely to hear a challenge unless it came from a *prima facie* interested party. Even if they did, no legal aid would be made available. Worse still, the costs of both sides would very likely fall on any unsuccessful plaintiff. In the absence of concrete evidence, he advised her to let the matter drop.

Kerstin had thought of asking the paper to finance an action, but she knew that was never going to happen. She'd written to the galleries, even though she risked losing the story that way, but so far none of them had even answered her. She knew why: Zoia's pictures might be worth celebrating, but her wishes, the woman herself, didn't matter a damn. Zoia was just a name now, nothing more.

She printed out the e-mail and put it in the file. She took the file and placed it in her attaché case, then sat there, listening to the murmur of phone conversations and the rumble of traffic from the street. On her computer the screensaver kicked in.

It happened like this sometimes, a sense she got that she was on the outside of everything, disconnected, lost. It frightened her, the thought of trying to function in a world with so many rules, but no right and wrong;

only the words themselves, behind which lay stranger, bleaker calculations. Calculations she did not know how to perform.

The deputy editor's head appeared over the top of her cubicle. Nicklas Renberg was twenty-eight, a man on the company fast-track. He had center-parted brown hair and fingernails chewed to the point of deformity.

"Kerstin, hi." His face wore an ingratiating smile. "Are you very busy right now?" His gaze drifted over to the cartoon aeroplane doing loop-the-loops across her computer screen.

"No. No, I'm not. I'm—"

"Excellent. Then you won't mind if I put someone in here for the afternoon, will you?" One of the graduate trainees, a lanky, ginger-haired boy, appeared at his shoulder. "A couple of the PCs have gone down."

"No, no. That's fine."

Kerstin got up, still clutching the attaché case. The contents spilled out across the floor.

Renberg clapped the trainee on the shoulder. "Okay, Mats? Go to it." He looked at Kerstin and frowned. "You know, you should take the rest of the day off or something. You look tired."

And he walked away, making a big show of not treading on her papers.

She set off home on foot, took a bus after half an hour, then walked some more. She kept up a brisk pace, letting the wind drag tears from her eyes. Somehow it felt better being on the move, heading somewhere.

Her apartment was in Solna, a few miles north of the city center, at the top of an apartment block overlooking the railway line. She was a few hundred yards away, could see up ahead the dark, slanting roof with its nest of TV aerials, when she stopped dead. She couldn't go back there. It was as clear as if someone had said it to her. She couldn't be there alone. Not now, not yet. For a moment, she thought she was going to faint.

Something knocked against her elbow. A man carrying a shopping bag dodged around her, cursing. She had an image of Nicklas Renberg telling her she should get some rest. But lately she couldn't rest. She had to be physically exhausted before sleep would come. And even then, her dreams would always wake her.

A couple of women were huddled in a bus shelter, trying not to stare at her. Behind them was a poster for the National Museum. Silvia said they had dug out their Korvin-Krukovskys from storage, and had put them back on display. Negotiations were underway with Bukowskis about a possible loan.

Kerstin turned around and headed back the way she had come. Her neighborhood pharmacy was on the corner. She went in, giving her best smile to the pharmacist behind the prescriptions counter.

He grinned back at her, cheeks turning pink. He was in his fifties, and wore a hairpiece that would have been convincing had it been gray instead of chestnut brown. He asked what he could do for her.

"Can't sleep," she said, with a sigh. "The usual."

The pharmacist nodded sympathetically and took a small packet of Amytal from a drawer. "You know, strictly speaking, you should get a new . . ." But then he simply shrugged and handed over the pills.

"Actually," Kerstin said, "while I'm here, can I get two boxes of these?"

40

Palmgren kept his mother's things in the study, carefully boxed up. His father's possessions had been left to gather dust in the attic. But his hands were unsteady as he threaded the film, as if this was something bad he was doing, messing with things that didn't belong to him, as if the old man was going to come back and catch him.

He caught the look on Elliot's face. "This is nitrate film. It's highly inflammable."

They had set up the Pathé Lux in the studio, a boxy metal projector with one spool above the lens and one below. To Elliot it looked like a cross between a sewing machine and a meat grinder, but Palmgren's father had looked after it lovingly, using it to screen his old movies long after the world had moved on to different formats. He had changed the flex and added a transformer. He had even kept a stash of spare bulbs, which he bought when they were in danger of going out of production.

They found the films in a trunk they'd had to force open with a hammer claw. There were maybe sixty in total, all black and white, four-minute spools in slim cardboard boxes. Now at last they were sitting in the twilight, watching blurred shapes drift across the cracked white walls. Focus was a problem. Palmgren thought the film had shrunk over time, and the mechanism was having trouble keeping it in place. He was worried it would get stuck and burst into flames.

They were on the third reel now. Nothing of Zoia so far, nothing of Monica either. Elliot was starting to wonder if there had been any actual filming that day in the studio. Maybe Martin's dad had just been posing with the new camera, shooting nothing. Maybe he didn't have anything to shoot with.

Outside, the trees dipped and swayed. It was getting windy again.

The film made a loud fluttering sound, the sound of a butterfly trapped behind a blind. Then Elliot was looking at a silhouette: a woman's head against a window. The picture shook a little, tilted. The light flared suddenly brighter.

Palmgren peered into the machine. "I don't like that sound."

Elliot could see the woman's face now. It was Monica. Her hair was shorter than he had seen it elsewhere. It made her look more fragile, more vulnerable. She was wearing a jacket and skirt, smart casual for a day in town. She said something, laughed, then walked toward the camera with an exaggerated swagger, a coy finger pressed to the side of her mouth.

"That's your mother, isn't it?"

Palmgren looked up, swallowed. "That's her."

A white flash and she was gone. The wall was just a wall again, flecked with white grains.

"Is that it?"

The grains collected, coalesced. Three pale circles, light reflecting off glass. Lenses. A man in a suit, standing in shadows, his head obscured. Then Elliot realized: the man was filming himself in a full-length mirror, holding the camera to his eye.

"That's my father," Palmgren said. "Around the time my sister was born."

The film was fluttering again.

"I think we'd better let the projector cool down, or we could have a problem."

"Just wait a second."

The image slid from view. The mirror was inside a wardrobe door. Monica stood on the other side, only this time she was holding a camera as well.

Images of the image-maker. Medium as message. All very avant-garde for its day.

It confirmed what he thought: Monica had taken the photograph in the studio. Her friend the artist, her husband the cinematographer. *The only kinds of people she was interested in.* She might have been pregnant. It was hard to tell.

Jump cut: a slow pan of a lake, trees swaying in a noiseless breeze.

"That's right here," Palmgren said, excitedly. "That's the view from the bedroom."

Poplar leaves rippled in the sunshine.

"He's trying out the camera. Putting it through its paces."

Jump cut. Blackness. Then Monica up close to the camera. She pulled back, grinning, a brass key pressed to her lips. The camera jolted upward, followed her across a landing. Shafts of sunlight spilled from adjacent rooms.

She got to a doorway, put the key in the lock, eased the door open.

"That's the studio," Palmgren said. "Where we are right now."

Monica was talking to someone inside, a hand held up to the camera as if to say: wait there.

The image shuddered. The projector motor made a brief straining sound.

"We should turn this off for a minute," Palmgren said. "It's getting too hot."

"Just a few more seconds."

Jump cut. A blur of motion. Burn-out from sunlit windows. A face?

"Hang on. Was that—?"

Zoia.

She was standing at the far end of the room, moving from easel to tabletop, a panel in her hands. Moving, alive, young. Elliot held his breath.

The dark, fathomless eyes.

Monica walked into the shot. The picture wobbled, grew suddenly brighter. Zoia seemed to freeze. Slowly she put the panel back on the easel, smiling at Monica, holding up her hands to keep her back. There wasn't anything to see yet, she was saying. She hadn't even started.

Palmgren squinted. "What's that all over her hands? Is it paint?"

The camera was moving in closer, jarring slightly with each step.

"I'm not sure. It might be some kind of preparation."

"It looks like blood."

Monica wanted a look at the panel. She said something to her husband, laughed, playfully nudged Zoia aside, walked around the easel. Stopped dead.

The picture fluttered. It separated, overlapped: Monica staring at the panel, Zoia staring at her. The camera was still closing in, Kristoffer wanting to see it now, wanting a record on film of a work in progress.

Then Monica was talking, pointing at the panel. Her smile had vanished.

"What's the matter with her?" Palmgren said. "What's she seen?"

They were arguing. Zoia was shaking her head vehemently. The camera went around behind her. She had forgotten it was there. Suddenly she reached for the panel, pulled it off the easel, pulled it into shot.

Swirling shadows. Streaks of something darker. Were there faces in there? Or just patterns?

The cameraman was ducking down, trying to get a better look as the panel dropped to the floor.

Elliot was on his feet.

"Did you see that? What *was* that?"

Up on the wall the image froze, blurred, blistered. There was a hissing sound. A loud crack.

"No!"

A white flame leapt from the projector. Elliot launched himself at the film.

"Marcus, don't touch it!"

He snatched up the reel. It was trailing fire. Flames flashed up his arm, igniting his sweater like it was soaked in petrol. He stood for a moment, watching in disbelief as his arm became a blazing torch.

He opened his mouth to scream.

Then something lurched into him, something hard and heavy. He fell backward, hit the floor with a wrenching thud. The film was dashed from his hand. He saw it go rolling like a Catherine wheel across the boards. Palmgren was on top of him, smothering him, twisting his arm behind him. For an instant he thought it was going to break.

"Roll, Marcus, roll over!"

He rolled, buried his arm in his jacket. The flames died. And then he was lying there, his breath coming in shuddering pulls, listening to the take-up spool on the projector whipping around double-time. Smoke made swirling patterns in the beam.

Then Palmgren was trying to get him up. "Outside now. Into the snow. Come on!"

Elliot held his hand up to the light, saw raw, red flesh, scraps of it burnt black.

Then came the pain.

At the clinic in Katrineholm they told him he was lucky. Packing the hand in snow on the way over had likely saved him from needing a skin graft. They bandaged him up and gave him some painkillers he hadn't come across before. The nurse said they were strong enough to knock a horse out.

Riding back to Igelsfors in Martin Palmgren's Land Rover, he had plenty of time to think about what had happened. Over and over he ran the film through in his mind, trying to fix in his memory the last few seconds. He was certain they were now destroyed, if not the whole reel. His stupid fault. And the only compensation was that Martin didn't seem to care. If anything, he seemed perked up by the whole adventure, like a child who had just got away with some delicious misdemeanor. All the way back he chattered on about his father, and his precious home movies, and all the rules that went with them. Elliot didn't have to do anything but nod.

Something in the film wasn't right: the paint on Zoia's hands and arms. She was using a wooden panel, not a canvas, which meant she was painting on gold. But painting on gold was a precise, exacting business. Mistakes were hard to correct. You didn't get paint all over your hands. And even if you mixed it that way, with your fingers, you would clean them off before letting them near the leaf. There was the clay bole, of course, the last layer of preparation before gilding. But Monica Palmgren had seen a picture, a picture that upset her. And pictures meant paint.

Was it possible that what he had glimpsed was a different kind of painting, a kind since lost, or hidden? Was this one of the Crimea pictures, the pictures Hildur Backlin had said stayed out of sight?

Out of sight, but not destroyed.

But then, who had them? Why hadn't they come forward? What possible motive held them back? Did they not understand what it was they had?

The questions circled his mind under their own momentum, enervating, compelling, at the center something Hildur Backlin had said about artists, something he knew instinctively was true, at least in Zoia's case: *their work is flesh and blood to them. It's who they are.*

The Crimea pictures were the real self-portraits. It was clearer now than ever: if he never found them, he would never find her.

The next morning they viewed the other reels, at least the ones shot pre-war. There was nothing more of Zoia. As for the reel that had burned,

Palmgren said he would splice together whatever was still viable. Maybe they could use some stills for the book, along with some pictures of the house. By mid-day, Elliot was back in the car driving north again, knowing where he was heading but feeling lost all the same. Every time he found a piece of the picture, the picture got bigger, and cost him more. And still the heart of it eluded him.

He was back on the road to Saltsjöbaden when the mobile rang. It was lying on the passenger seat, Harriet Shaw's name back-lit on the screen. He had to pull over to pick it up.

"Marcus, how are you?"

It was a call she didn't want to make. Reluctance bore down on her every word.

"Apart from a little mishap with some cellulose nitrate, I'm all right," he said, trying to counter the mood. "You?"

"I'm . . . well, to tell the truth, uncomfortable."

Uncomfortable. A lawyer's euphemism of some kind, but at that moment stark, brutal.

He swallowed. "Why, what's up?"

A white van went past, flashing its lights.

"Harriet?"

"Things aren't . . . I think we need to review our situation."

"Review. I thought—"

"The ground seems to have shifted somewhat. Miles Hanson, I had a call from him this morning. He was . . . Actually he's being pretty decent about it."

It was the first time Harriet hadn't made sense since the day they met.

"Harriet, what are you talking about?"

"If what he says is true, then our line of attack, our whole approach with respect to your daughter . . . it isn't going to work."

The line of attack had always been simple, and ruthless: attack Teresa's mother. Show the court she was a violent, promiscuous drunk who consorted with illegal aliens and criminals, a woman not fit to raise a child.

Elliot brought the bandaged hand to his forehead. "Why's that, Harriet?"

"Because whatever we can come up with, he can trump. It seems some new sources have come forward."

"Sources?"

"One-time associates of yours. In Russia. Apparently they're prepared to sign affidavits about your . . . *affairs.* Affidavits alleging that you were complicit in criminal activity."

"Harriet, you know as well as I do, all this was investigated. And no charges were brought. Can't you see? This is just a bluff. Miles Hanson's making it up."

"He wouldn't do that, Marcus."

"Why? Because he's a damned lawyer?"

"*Because* he could be disbarred. Deception of that kind, it's just not on."

He heard the professional pride in her voice, wounded pride. Now he was up against both of them: the two honorable professionals against the grubby, mendacious client.

"Then *they're* lying, these Russians, whoever they are."

"Of course that's possible. Miles Hanson knows that's possible. He's not interested in sending you to prison. That's why he called."

"Prison? What are you talking about?"

"Marcus, don't you understand what's at stake here? If Miles is obliged to produce these affidavits, and they stand up to any kind of scrutiny, then Customs and Excise may reopen your case. You could be charged."

Suddenly all Elliot could see was Cornelius, standing beneath the red safety lights. *If you really cared about your daughter, if you really wanted her back, you wouldn't do this.* It had been a warning, and he had ignored it.

A truck went by, hauling timber, loose chains slamming against the sides.

"These sources, what were their names?"

"Miles didn't tell me."

"Did he tell you why they were prepared to help him?"

"I don't think he knew. He said they contacted him. He had the impression . . . he thought they had some kind of ax to grind."

"Meaning they hold a grudge. Meaning their testimony is suspect, right?"

"Perhaps. But do you really want to risk it? What if they can back it up?"

It was clear what she thought about the icon business: that he was in it up to his neck. He had taken a calculated gamble, and lost. And she was right, of course. He had always known what he was shipping, and what it was worth, but he had used mostly black money to buy it, and that money could not be traced. The bank statements said he had paid twenty thousand pounds for a lot he confidently expected to sell for half a million. The VAT office simply hadn't been able to prove it. Demichev had told him the icons were rotting in a flood-prone government warehouse. It turned out they had mysteriously vanished from a museum in Tambov. That was the only part Elliot hadn't known.

It was a crime, a scam, lapse that had been unworthy of him. But he had been punished enough.

"Let them say what they like. I say we deal with that problem when we come to it."

"Marcus, my advice is we start negotiating for access. The sooner the better. The more money your wife has to spend on legal advice, the less flexible she's likely to be."

"Flexible? How about upright? That would make a pleasant change."

"I'm sorry, Marcus. I really am."

"We still have a chance. We can't give up just like that. Just because Miles Hanson tells us to."

Harriet sighed. Light rain began falling on the windscreen. These days defeat always felt inevitable. If only he could reach into the past and haul himself back to the time before everything went wrong. If only he knew when that time was.

"Marcus, I'm afraid there's another issue here. The fact is, the other partners are concerned about the hours I've spent on this. Frankly, they're concerned about payment."

Elliot closed his eyes. "I'll find a way to pay you, Harriet. I've just been tied up here."

"I realize that, Marcus. But I'm not a sole practitioner. I have responsibilities to the firm. I can't commit to spending much more time, certainly not to a hearing, without something on the table. I hope you understand."

Then another call came in, one she had to take. She asked him to think it over and get back to her, and a moment later she was gone.

41

It was Leo Demichev's way of working: indirect, insinuating, deniable—
with a touch of the theatrical thrown in. It left you wondering who you
were dealing with, and how far their influence extended. You felt suddenly
exposed. There was no direction to which you could safely turn your back.

He wooed you the same way. Good things started happening unexpectedly. Obstacles disappeared. You started to believe fate was on your
side, the days of struggle and obscurity behind you. You were seduced by
your own desire to perpetuate that state of being, and corralled by the
dread of upsetting it. Each step up brought a measure of happiness, but
the same step down brought twice as much pain.

In the Bukowksi vaults the plan had been hatched, Cornelius in a
panic about the bogus will, terrified Elliot had found something that
might expose it. He had confided in Demichev, or maybe Demichev had
known about the scam all along. Between them they knew enough to find
out who Nadia Elliot's lawyer was. The only surprising thing was that Leo
had gone to so much trouble. His interest in the Zoia project was about
more than short-term financial gain. Profounder issues of influence and
reputation were involved. Later, Cornelius had been pricked by con-
science and called him. He wanted Elliot to knuckle under while there
was still time. But he had been too frightened to call off the dogs, even
assuming he had the power.

Now they were expecting him to come crawling. To hand over everything, take whatever Bukowskis felt like giving him, and disappear. Or
anything might happen. He was supposed to be frightened. Maybe worse
was to follow if he didn't comply. He remembered the silver Mercedes on
the road to Katrineholm, and wondered if it hadn't been following him
after all.

They could destroy him in any of a dozen ways. He could denounce
them, but who would listen? He was powerless, voiceless. Like Zoia.

He squeezed down on the accelerator, heard the engine growl. Answer threats with threats. Call Demichev and tell him he had gone too far, that he didn't know who he was dealing with. He got as far as searching for the number, but what was the point? Demichev would laugh. He would make some cryptic remark about Russian ways. Or he wouldn't take the call at all. The truth was, he knew Marcus Elliot only too well.

He reached the coast mid-afternoon. On the lawns and verges the snow was thinner, the surfaces pockmarked by rain. The rooftops were dark and wet.

Hints of spring.

On the road outside Zoia's house, he slammed on the brakes. The gate was wide open. A double set of tire tracks ran deep and muddy along the driveway. The verges had been flattened where they rounded the orchard. The tracks turned white again as they reached the house, then disappeared around the side.

He drove in a little way, cut the engine, listened. There was nothing but the buffeting of the wind. The intruders, whoever they were, had come and gone. People were always forgetting to close gates.

Then a voice. Two voices. Men at work. In the background the tinny twang of a radio. Some kind of maintenance going on, perhaps: water, power. Maybe the phone hadn't been cut off deliberately.

He got out of the Volvo, walked toward the back of the house, digging in his pocket for the keys. He could see the back of a white truck now, the rear doors open, steel steps reaching down to the ground. They had parked opposite the front door.

Thieves. He stopped. They could have read about Zoia in the newspaper, and come looking for her house. The spot was lonely enough. They could take their time searching the place.

He looked around for a weapon, remembered there were knives in the kitchen. He went quickly to the door and eased his counterfeit key into the lock.

The draft almost sucked the handle from his grasp. He hurried inside, shouldered the door shut again and stood staring into the gloom.

Everything was different. The table and chairs had disappeared. All the cupboards and drawers were open, the contents—plates, pots and pans, cutlery, even the tins of food—gone. Instead, all over the room, there were boxes. Packing cases. Stacked against the stove were flat packs, ready for use, the name of the removal company printed in red on each.

They were taking everything.

The door to the hall stood open. Men in overalls were maneuvering the dining-room table through the front entrance. Dr. Lindqvist had sent them, or his sister had—taking charge perhaps while her brother was in hospital recovering from pneumonia. She wanted to clear the decks. She wanted Zoia's papers removed, if she hadn't taken them already.

The men were outside now. Elliot crossed the hall and ran up the stairs. Maybe Lindqvist had recovered from his pneumonia. Maybe he had been at the house, gone up to the studio, and found everything: papers, computer, bedding.

He went into the sitting room. The furniture was gone. Zoia's desk was gone. Dust sheets were strewn across the floor.

Too late.

Then he saw the box files. They were stacked up next to the stove. He knelt down, flipped open the one on top. The letters were still inside.

He went up to the studio. The spiral of papers was still there on the floor, although it had been disturbed. Pages had flipped over, or blown across the room. Some of the photographs had fallen down. But the laptop was on the table where he'd left it.

Remove the evidence. He snatched up the letters from the floor, ripped down the other photographs and stuffed them back in the files. His shadow played across the gilded surface of the panel, fleeting, furtive, like the first imaginings of the artist as she reached for the sketchbook.

Gold is a noble metal. It illuminates everything and betrays nothing.

He stopped. What would happen to the papers after the removal men had taken them? Where would they end up?

The myth of Zoia was pliable, profitable. Reputations had been staked on it. The truth was awkward, paradoxical, rife with potential embarrassment. He got a flash of the wood chipper in Dr. Lindqvist's garden, the doctor and his sister impassive as they dropped in the bundles of letters and photographs, one by one.

He went to the window. Down below the men were having trouble with the dining table, trying to work out how to dismantle the leaves. From where they stood they couldn't see the Volvo.

He knew what he had to do.

It took four trips to get everything back into the sitting room. A window gave out on to the back. He took the sturdiest-looking box file and threw it out into the snow. It landed with a gentle thump and rolled over, spilling half its contents. Four more boxes followed. The flimsiest few he rolled in a dust sheet and threw out all together.

He headed down the stairs again, laptop over his shoulder, three more box files under his arm. The men were loading the dining-room chairs, the radio blaring from the cab of the truck.

He drove the Volvo up to the house, threw the files into the back. Papers were still scattered across the ground. He bent down, began snatching them up. With his bandaged hand, he couldn't grip them properly. He stuffed them into his pockets and down the front of his coat. He had to get them all.

"Hey!"

He looked up. One of the men was standing by the kitchen door.

He clutched the last of the letters to his chest, backed away toward the car.

"I was a friend," he said. "Of hers."

The man looked back at the house. He was young, tall. Blonde hair and a beard.

"I'll come back another time."

The man just stood there, looking like he didn't know what to do.

Elliot got back in the car, reversed up the drive, wheels fishtailing through the slush. The other man came out of the house, talking on a mobile phone. As the Volvo slewed out on to the road, he started to run.

42

To the charge sheet is added theft.

Driving back to the highway, struggling to keep his speed down, it doesn't seem like a big step. It feels, if anything, appropriate, in keeping with a nature he's kept in check most of his life, but only out of fear: Marcus the appropriator, Marcus the thief. There's something liberating about it, something thrilling.

Demichev knew it from the first second they met: here was someone he could do business with, a man at home in the shadows. Others have sensed it too, and instinctively kept their distance.

He watches the mirror until he's well beyond the town. The car is full of paper, letters and photographs strewn across the seats and the muddy floor. They're there in his lap and screwed up beneath the pedals. But at least they're safe for the time being. Zoia is safe. Half an hour later, and it would have been too late.

He seized upon the same excuse with the Novgorod icons, the ones he smuggled out of Russia. He was preserving treasures, perspectives that might otherwise be lost, things the world didn't care about. Only this time it's true.

They're going to know soon enough—Lindqvist, Cornelius, Demichev. They'll find out he's taken the papers, and assume the worst: that they contain something important, something that can be used against them. Less clear is what they'll do about it. Most likely, they'll get an arrest warrant. The police will be waiting for him at the airport. They may even be watching the hotel registers, to see where he checks in. Cornelius and his crowd could swing it. They have contacts at the Foreign Ministry. They are plumbed into affairs of state.

He's running, but where to? Where can he possibly go?

On the outskirts of the city, he pulls over. The evening traffic is building. Headlights go by in a ceaseless procession, blinding him as they sweep down the hill. People heading home. Destinations determined, fixed. Not like him. His life plays out to a different rhythm, subject to different forces. He was marked as solitary from birth.

The letters on the passenger seat are crumpled and smeared. He catches sight of a date: *July 1933*. Smeared black words he cannot read. He looks over his shoulder at the boxes heaped on the backseat. He has to hide them. He has to find a safe place, and the sooner the better. The car hire company will give his registration number to the police. If he's pulled over, Lindqvist will get the papers back.

There's only one place he can think of.

At the offices of *Expressen* things are still busy. Through the hardened glass wall Elliot sees banks of desks, all manned, everyone working away in the run-up to the evening deadline. People in shirtsleeves come and go, pausing beneath TV monitors tuned to Reuters or BBC World, before moving on again. He searches for Kerstin Östlund, but there's no sign of her.

The receptionist buzzes her extension. Someone picks up, but it isn't Kerstin.

"She's not in." The receptionist is in her forties, wears a lot of makeup and a home perm. "Do you want to leave a message?"

"Do you know where to find her? It's urgent."

The receptionist relays the message. A biker deposits a package and heads back to the elevator. Incoming calls light up the switchboard.

"Have you tried her mobile number?"

Something in her voice is artificially soft, as if she's speaking about a sick person.

"Yes. It doesn't answer."

The receptionist puts a finger to her earpiece. "Just a second. He's coming out."

"He?"

"Mats. Graduate trainee."

Mats appears conscientiously, summoned by the talk of urgency. He has short ginger hair, and wears a dark two-piece suit that's too big for him.

"You're looking for Kerstin Östlund?"

He takes in the scratched face and the bandaged hand.

"That's right. I've information, regarding an important story she's doing." At the word *important*, the trainee's eyebrows lift perceptibly. "Doesn't anyone know where she is?"

Mats clears his throat.

"Um. Well, not really."

Between routing calls, the receptionist watches them intently.

"Not really? She does work here, doesn't she?"

Mats hunches his shoulders. "Not *really*. I mean, sometimes. She comes in to sub a bit."

A squirm of panic in his guts. "But I thought she was a reporter . . . She was on a story. She said . . ."

The receptionist smiles sympathetically and leans closer. Elliot can see the eagerness in her eyes, her delight at demonstrating knowledge. Most people in the building aren't even sure of her name, probably, but the ignorance isn't mutual. She has dossiers in her head about every one of them.

"She *used* to work here when she was a student. In the summer. Now it's just . . ." She glances at Mats helplessly. "After what happened, you know, people wanted to help her out, but . . ."

"But what?"

She shrugs, as if the rest is obvious. "Well, she's not on the *staff*. Not really in any state to be."

Elliot feels hot, giddy. He steadies himself against the front desk.

"Are you all right?"

"What did happen?"

Mats folds his arms, shielding himself from the discomfort of the moment.

"It's not a secret," the receptionist says. "She lost her child. And there's nothing worse than that, is there? Nothing in the world."

Spoken like one who read about it once in a magazine.

"Can you give me her details? Her home number, her address?"

The receptionist shakes her head. "I'm sorry. We're not allowed to give out information on staff."

"You just said she *wasn't* staff. Listen to me: I really *have* to find her. It's important."

The receptionist looks uncertain. Mats fingers the stubble on his chin, a little curious now, perhaps even wondering if there isn't an opportunity here, a journalistic coup that'll get his career off to a flyer—or, equally, a chance to screw something up.

"I've important information," Elliot adds, looking him in the eye.

The trainee swallows. "This story she was working on," he says. "What was it about again?"

A stone-clad apartment block on the north side of Stockholm. Early twentieth century, lofty but ill proportioned, just old enough to qualify as heritage and, as such, to have escaped the wrecking ball. But that's as far as the preservation goes. Graffiti sprawls across the soot-caked walls. The original doorway has been replaced with frosted glass panels in an aluminum frame. The floor of the hallway, which once boasted a mosaic, has been partially cemented over, and now acts as a parking area for a tangle of bicycles.

At *Expressen* they weren't even sure she still lived there.

The pigeonholes are on the other side, painted in bright red gloss, drip marks hanging from the corners. He rifles through the box marked *M-N-O*, finds flyers for rock bands and fast-food restaurants, a postcard from Morocco addressed to someone called Hedberg, junk mail with postmarks six months old. One of the items of junk mail is addressed to Kerstin Östlund in apartment 5B. On the envelope is written: *DEBT CONSOLIDATION AT UNBEATABLE RATES.*

The lift is out of order. He takes the stairs, feet pounding on worn stone, his way lit by low-wattage bulbs in filthy glass fittings. With every step the sense of foreboding is stronger.

Kerstin Östlund, another living link to Zoia, another life gone off the rails. She's unbalanced, they say. Cornelius says she's delusional. Part of him screams: *Stay away.* But there's nowhere else to go, nowhere else to hide the letters. For all they say about her, she's the only one who can be trusted.

Mats, the trainee, said she hadn't been seen since yesterday. They were expecting her to come in that morning for a couple of hours' work, but she didn't show up. He said that was unusual.

Out of breath, Elliot reaches the fourth floor. The door on one side is boarded up and secured with a padlock. The door opposite is blue, *5B* drawn in felt pen above the lock.

He knocks, gets no answer, knocks again. Somewhere inside, water is running.

Leave a note. It's all he can do. Like being back at college.

He rummages through his pockets, finds a ballpoint and an old envelope. He leans up against the door to write.

Dear Kerstin—

The door rides back, just an inch or two. The bottom is snagged on the fringe of a rug, enough to stop the latch from snapping shut.

Through the narrow gap he glimpses an expanse of Turkish kilim, beyond it scuffed stripped pine flooring. The sound of running water is louder.

"Hello?"

He pushes back the door a few more inches, using his foot to flatten down the rug. A train clatters by outside, blue sparks lighting up the ceiling. He sees a pair of dirty trainers, a fax machine, an unmade bed, condensation running down a window. A cone of electric light falls on a cluttered bedside table: a paperback book lies open flat. There are packets of what looks like medicine, empty foil packaging spilling out.

A bathroom echo. The tap is running at half pressure, somewhere between on and off, air rasping in the pipe.

He steps into the room, goes to the table, reads the name on the boxes: *Amytal.* The trade name for amobarbital, aka blue heaven. His pharmacist didn't recommend them. Among sleeping pills, barbiturates are old technology. He recommended benzodiazepines—more expensive but more targeted, safer. Less risk of overdose, he said.

The foil packets hold twelve capsules each. They're both empty.

"Jesus Christ."

A paneled door. Light underneath. A faint curl of steam.

He runs. The door swings back without resistance, and then he's looking at a claw-foot bath, full to the brim, water spilling over on to gray linoleum.

He can't move, can't bring himself to take the last few steps.

Go and tell your mother her program's starting.

He knows what comes next. He knows.

Walk. Look. *Do it.*

He puts a foot forward, then another. Looks.

She's lying there under the cloudy water, naked, hands at her sides.

Her dark hair drifts about her face, like blackbird wings, covering her cheeks. Just like the last time. Tears cloud his sight. He reaches down, puts a hand behind her head to lift her out.

Her eyes flash open. They're dark and flat, as if painted on paper.

He jumps as she surges up out of the water. Back from the dead.

Water cascades onto the floor. "Get away! Get away from me!"

He collides with the door. "I thought you were . . . The pills. I thought you were . . ."

She's huddled up in the bath, coughing, blinking. "*Elliot?*"

"I thought you'd taken an overdose."

She pushes the wet hair off her forehead, blinks some more. "What?"

"I saw the empty packets. The Amytal."

She clears her throat. "It took me months to get through those." She closes her hands around her breasts. "Now get out! Or I'll scream till someone hears."

"Okay, okay. I'm sorry."

He backs out of the bathroom, pulls the door shut. He's almost back on the landing when he hears her voice again.

"Marcus?" He stops, listens. "What the hell do you want?"

43

———•———

"I don't believe it. You took *everything?*"

She had come out of the bathroom to find box files and papers covering most of the floor. Elliot had spent the last ten minutes going up and down to the car. His heart was beating so hard he could feel it in his throat.

"Could I have a drink? Anything."

Kerstin frowned, rubbing at her wet hair with a towel.

"There wasn't time to be selective. It was everything or nothing."

She went to the sink and poured him a glass of water.

"What happened to your hand?"

"I burnt it. It's not serious."

She frowned and knelt down by the nearest stack of papers, picking up a letter in Russian. Elliot knew the handwriting, the paper: correspondence from Zoia's first husband, Yuri, 1923–27. By now he could identify most of the correspondents without having to see their names, or even read their words. There was individuality in the handwriting, just as in the stroke of a paintbrush. There was self-expression and self-depiction.

"I still don't understand," Kerstin said. "You had the list of recipients. Why did you want all the rest of it?"

"They were going to destroy it. They were going to put it through a shredder."

She opened one of the box files and took out another letter: a draft, incomplete, Zoia to Alain Azria, spring 1931, stationery from the Hôtel Grand Saint-Georges, Tunis. *With you I would transgress all spheres of love.*

"A shredder? Why would they do that?"

"Because they don't understand it. They're afraid something will upset their plans."

"What makes you so sure?"

"I just know. I know it the way you knew about the will."

His hand was throbbing. He grimaced, reached into his pocket for the painkillers they had given him at the clinic and gulped a couple down. When he looked up again he could see Kerstin was still waiting for him to explain. She still didn't understand why the papers were important enough to steal.

He lowered himself onto the threadbare sofa, picking at the bandage on his hand. "You see . . ." He sighed. "It's difficult to explain. It's hard to put into words."

"Try."

The trouble was, it sounded insane. Words crystallized the insanity, made it harder to ignore. But then Kerstin was supposed to be insane too. Maybe it wouldn't matter to her.

He shrugged. "It's where I found her. That's all I can say."

"Found her?"

"In the letters. Hildur Backlin, she said Zoia was in her pictures. That was the place to look. But I couldn't see her there. I couldn't see anything. When I look at her work it's like I'm looking in a mirror."

He sat looking at the floor, waiting for Kerstin to throw him out. She was quiet for a while, then he heard her get up.

"Have you seen this?"

She was holding out a postcard. It was a reproduction from the National Museum: the Oscar Björck portrait of Zoia.

"They've taken it out of the store room. It's on display in the Modern Swedish section. I went to see it yesterday."

Zoia, beautiful but eerily calm, a Greek goddess, icon-like, immaculate. Björck's portrait was the best, the most honest. He painted a mask because a mask was what he saw.

"I haven't looked at this in a long time. It's better than I remembered."

Kerstin sat down on the bed, put her hands between her knees. In the bathroom she had pulled on jeans and a sweatshirt, but without drying herself properly. Patches of damp showed through the fabric.

She wasn't throwing him out after all.

"So you went to see Hildur Backlin. Did she say she had been promised a picture?"

"It was almost the first thing she said. But that wasn't why I went. It was before I found the list, before you found me."

"Then why did you go?"

"Hildur modeled for Zoia, back in the thirties. They were friends. I was hoping she might know something about Zoia's thinking back then."

"In the thirties."

Elliot nodded.

"The twenties and thirties. Those are the years that matter. That's when the die was cast, you see."

It was the first time he'd talked to anyone about his work. Until now, it wasn't something he thought anyone else could appreciate. But Kerstin was different. Her connections to Zoia were instinctive. They had nothing to do with politics or commerce. He had a sense she was entitled.

"So you're not really interested in Zoia's life past the age of—what?— thirty-seven or something."

"I'm interested, but, like I say, the decisions that defined her whole—"

"And how old are you?"

"Me? I'm thirty-eight. Why?"

Kerstin shook her head. "Never mind. Tell me about Hildur Backlin. Did she help you?"

"Yes, she did. Though she wasn't exactly clear about everything. She's very old, very sick. Some of the things she said . . ." He shrugged. "I haven't been able to work them out." He turned the postcard around in his hands.

"Are you going to tell me?"

"She said something about the Crimea, about Sevastopol. She said those places stayed out of sight, in Zoia's work. At first I thought she meant Zoia had never painted them. But now I think she was talking about pictures Zoia *did* paint, but which she kept hidden. That's why I asked you about them at the hotel."

He drained his glass, watching Kerstin over the rim, wondering if she really knew something, if she was ready to tell him.

Another train went by. She got up and closed the blinds.

"That bandage looks dirty. You should change it. They say you have to keep burns very clean, or they get infected."

She had a good-sized medical kit in the bathroom: lint, cotton wool, antiseptic. The cabinet was full of pill packets and brown plastic bottles. He wondered, as she carefully removed the old dressing, if hypochondria was among her neuroses. He found his gaze seeking out the faint scarlike depression beneath her hairline.

"You want to know how I got that?"

She had been watching him in the mirror.

"No, I'm sorry I—"

"The forceps slipped, when I was born. They said I *really* didn't want to leave the womb. They had to drag me out—how do you say it?"

"Kicking and screaming?"

She laughed. "Kicking and screaming. My head was black and blue, my mother said."

She eased a pad of gauze off the base of his thumb. The flesh underneath was purple and shiny. The sight made him shiver. Even the good skin was dark yellow from the iodine.

"It's not too bad," Kerstin said. "It's starting to heal."

Thumb, first two fingers, the palm of his hand, these were the worst places, but the skin had been thick there, and much of the swelling had gone down. Kerstin dampened some cotton wool.

"That hurts. Take it easy, will you?"

She was holding his hand over the washbasin.

"So tell me about the Paris self-portrait," she said, as if she were just making conversation. "What's the story there?"

He hesitated. "You mean, why is it important?"

"No. I *don't* mean that."

She ran the cotton wool under the cold tap and carried on dabbing at his hand, a little harder now.

"How did you know?" he said.

"I told you. I have a friend at Bukowskis. She gave me the number of the man in London who claims to own the portrait. A Mr. Paul Costa. So I rang him and told him I had a message from you, and he didn't sound at all surprised. He even went to get a pencil."

"That's an old trick. You must have caught him off guard."

"It was rather early in the morning. So, I was right. You are the real owner."

"Yes. It's been in the family for a while. Thirty years, more or less."

"So why the front? Unless it's stolen property."

"It's not."

"Then . . . ?"

She reached up into the cabinet, took out a tube of antiseptic cream. It was strange, seeing her like this, energetic, practical, no-nonsense. Like the laughter, it wasn't what he'd been expecting.

"It's a question of ethics, partly. I can't write in a Bukowskis catalog about a picture I own. They're fussy about that sort of thing. Conflicts of interest."

"And the rest?"

"The rest?"

"You said it was a question of ethics *partly.*"

Elliot watched her slick the cream lightly across his palm. It felt cold.

"I didn't want it counted as one of my assets. I've got divorce proceedings coming up. Anything a court knows about, it can take away."

"I see. You didn't want to share the money with your wife."

"I didn't plan on selling it at all. Then I got mixed up in this residency battle, for my daughter. And then I didn't have any choice. Lawyers are expensive."

Kerstin wiped her forehead with her wrist. "I heard about that. I heard you were trying to keep your daughter."

She put the top back on the tube of cream, put the tube in the box, and the box in the cabinet. She made him sit on the edge of the bath while she got down a fresh dressing. It felt undeserved, all this care and attention. He wished he could say something to make her laugh again.

She sat down beside him, took the dressing from its paper packet.

"Thirty years ago you would have been a little boy," she said.

"Eight. I was eight."

"So who bought the picture? Your father?"

"No. He hated it. He didn't want it in the house."

Kerstin held the dressing taut across the palm of his hand. "So, your mother then?"

Elliot slowly flexed his fingers, nodded. "Yes. She was Swedish. She's dead now."

"I know. I'm sorry."

She began to wind the gauze around his hand. It was as if she were winching up the truth, dragging it up from deep inside him. He wondered how much she already knew. Years ago, on a drunken binge in London, he'd told Cornelius Wallander, in strictest confidence, the story of his mother's death. It was an uncharacteristic lapse, one he regretted almost immediately. Cornelius was not a man who could resist spreading stories.

"She bought the portrait a couple of weeks before she died. She used to come back here on her own sometimes, to see her family."

"Was it very expensive? Was that what annoyed your father?"

"I don't know what it cost. I don't know if it cost anything. There's no record of the sale. She might have been given it."

"By Zoia?"

Elliot shrugged, as if he hadn't already made up his mind on that point.

"It's possible. It's possible they knew each other."

"But you don't know that."

"I've no direct evidence. Nothing that would stand up in court. But they were connected somehow, I'm sure of it. I mean, why *that* painting? Something so important, so . . . irreplaceable."

Kerstin put a hand on his arm. There was a safety pin in her mouth.

"Sit still, will you?"

"The thing is, I don't believe Zoia would give that picture—or sell it, for that matter—to anyone who didn't understand it. Who didn't understand what it meant."

"A kind of initiate?"

Elliot hesitated. Kerstin glanced up at him as she took the pin from her mouth.

"In a way, yes."

"Maybe that was what your father didn't like." She pinched at the gauze and slowly slid the point of the pin between the folds. "An expensive gift, some relationship he couldn't be part of. Where he didn't belong."

For a moment he was sitting on the stairs again, listening to the screaming. That terrible sound. Hot tears streaming down his face.

He closed his eyes.

"He used to call my mother an ice maiden. He used to say she had to keep her distance from everyone else, or she'd melt. He never felt he was good enough for her. Then suddenly she was gone."

He looked up, saw that Kerstin was watching him again, studying him. She looked troubled.

• • •

With his hand freshly bandaged, there was no reason to stay. He said he would make arrangements about the papers, and take them off her hands as soon as possible. Meantime, he would find a guesthouse somewhere where they took cash and didn't bother about forms.

Kerstin thanked him for the list, invited him to have a drink before he left.

"It's a kind of schnapps," she said, taking a long, square-sided bottle from the fridge. "Someone I know makes it in the countryside, for a hobby."

"It's moonshine?"

She smiled as she poured out the shots.

"I happen to believe that getting a little drunk now and then is a fundamental human right, even if our government doesn't. Don't worry, it's safe. Only fifty degrees proof."

It was like swallowing fire, fire with a hint of cherries. Kerstin pulled out a phone directory, and watched from across the tiny kitchen table as Elliot scanned the pages for somewhere to stay. Nothing looked promising. And then there was the question of how he was going to pay for it.

"Tell me about your wife," she said, when they were on to the second glass. "Who is she? How long were you married?" He looked up from the book. "Do you mind me asking these personal things?"

He found he didn't mind. Back in England he did—or would have, if anyone had been tactless enough to try it. But here, now, it was different. He found her curiosity flattering.

He told her everything, from the day he first saw Nadia to the day she finally left. The alcohol made it easier, the warmth of it like a little furnace in the pit of his stomach. The story went differently from the way it had been in his head all these months. For once he was not making a case, for the courts or for anyone else. Nadia's point of view loomed larger. She had been lonely in London, he saw that clearly, at least. Lonely, disorientated, trapped by obligation. And all his strenuous efforts at providing— even to the point of breaking the law—had only made it worse.

Kerstin asked a lot of questions. She wanted to know about Teresa, and what the divorce was doing to her. It struck Elliot that she had been alone since her baby died, disconnected from the world around her, the way people who returned from wars often were. She was struggling to reconnect.

"What I don't understand is . . ." She was reaching for the bottle again, though their glasses weren't empty. "Why you have this lawyer, and all these people you're paying to try and get your daughter back. They can't tell you who she should stay with, can they?"

"That's just the way it is in England. The adversarial system. My people make a case, her people make a case. The court takes its pick."

"That's not what I'm asking. I'm asking about you. What *you* think."

She reached over with the bottle. Elliot covered his glass with his hand.

"If I didn't think Teresa would be happier with me, I wouldn't be fighting for her."

"Is that what you're doing? Fighting?"

"What do you mean?"

Kerstin began to refill her glass.

"I don't know. Only it seems to me if you were really fighting, fighting with all your heart, you'd be there. That's all."

He finished his drink, got up. It was time to go. She told him not to be ridiculous and to take the couch for the night. It was too late and too cold to go looking for somewhere else. He didn't have the strength to refuse.

Half an hour later they were lying in the darkness on opposite sides of the room. That was when he asked her what she knew about the Crimea pictures.

But she was already asleep.

The night passed fitfully, the throbbing in his hand dragging him to consciousness again and again before releasing him into his dreams—dreams of skin grafts and gilded flesh, living tissue incised with dog-tooth blades. He saw Anubis with a woman's body, an image on a tomb wall, flickering. Then he was in the studio, watching it all in a silent movie, with Kerstin this time, anxiously looking over his shoulder, waiting for the film to ignite again, although it never did. Then the home movie became his home movie, and he was watching his childhood in bright, grainy colors: two-year-old Marcus waddling across the lawn in baggy trousers, into his mother's waiting arms, squinting into the camera with the sun in his eyes.

· · ·

When he awoke the next morning, Kerstin had gone. He had no idea where. He pulled back the blinds. There was thick fog outside. A train with its lights on slid slowly into town. Everyone getting on with their busy lives.

In daylight the apartment looked sadder and dingier. The few touches of affordable style—the kilim rug, the contemporary vases and lamps—did little to disguise the underlying shabbiness. The bottle of schnapps stood on the table where they had left it. The pills were still there by the unmade bed. For a few short hours Kerstin's place had felt like a refuge. Now it felt like a sentence.

He searched for his mobile phone, switched it on, expecting a cascade of voicemail: from Harriet, from Cornelius, maybe even from the police. But this time, almost for the first time, there was nothing. *You have zero messages.*

They were all done with him. He was passing out of their lives, a journey that had only been delayed by his escapades in Sweden. Just as the phrase went: he was history.

He made coffee and stood by the window, staring at the trains and the boxes of Zoia's letters. Doubts crowded in. He had wasted his last chance at normality, and he had done it for this, for the promise of knowledge that was only ever that—a promise. He was on the outside, as he had always been. Only this time there was nowhere else to go.

It crossed his mind that it might have been the same for Zoia. But that couldn't be. Zoia was strong, a survivor. When all was lost she had found something new, a light to guide her, a way back to wholeness. And it was there somewhere, just as she was, in the pictures she had made. Only it was written in a language he still could not understand.

He got dressed, looked around for his shoes, found them at the foot of the sofa next to a ring binder with a yellow Post-it note stuck to the front. It wasn't something he'd taken from Zoia's house. On the note was written a message in black felt pen:

Marcus: <u>The Crimea</u>. Here are the letters from Zoia (photocopies) I found among Karl Kilbom's papers. I hope they help. Kerstin.

Sevastopol

44

Kursk Province, Southern Russia, November 1920.

It was the first train from Moscow in a month. Sixteen freight wagons and a soot-caked engine, snaking its way across an empty land, wheels clanking on loose rails. A week on, they were approaching the plains of the Ukraine, three days, four at most, from the Black Sea.

In Sevastopol their lives would begin again, her mother said. No one would know them there. They would close the door on the past—their mistakes, their grief—and keep it shut, forever. Zoia didn't put up much of a fight, though she wept as they finally pulled away from the station. Their lives in Moscow were over. To the Reds they would always be class enemies, to everyone else, provocateurs and informers. Hatred encircled them. Even Andrei had left them for Petrograd, embittered and angry, marrying a girl he said he did not love.

People were crammed into every inch of space, not just inside the wagons but on top of them, between them. They piled their sacks on the buffers and hung on as best they could. Every major station along the way was besieged with people carrying bags. There were thousands of them. The train was in constant danger of being hijacked or raided, despite the contingent of soldiers guarding the mail car. But they had been lucky so far. They had seen none of the armed gangs that had brought most of the railways to a standstill.

Zoia, her mother, her grandmother, dressed like beggars, huddled in a corner, two wagons behind the engine, close enough for the soot to blacken their faces. Around them, sacks of scrap iron, wire, coal, bedsprings, whatever people in the towns had managed to pilfer, and now hoped to trade in the countryside for food. These days everyone in Russia was a black marketeer, everyone except the bureaucrats and party officials, who got special rations. You had to barter for food or slowly

343

starve to death. Factory workers helped themselves to the produce from their factories—engine parts, ingots, bottles—and when the machines wouldn't run anymore, they stripped those down instead. There were no rations for people without state jobs. Members of the "former classes" sold their clothes and their ornaments and burned their books for fuel. And when all that was gone, they sold themselves or their children. Andrei had written to her from Petrograd that the Nevsky Prospekt was now lined with pretty young bourgeois girls, whose price was a lump of coal or a scrap of bread. Winter made things worse. There wasn't a tree left in Moscow. Empty buildings were gutted in a matter of hours, people helping themselves to floorboards, beams, roof tiles, drainpipes. In the hunt for food and heat, Russia's imperial cities—palaces, boulevards, churches—were being torn down by hand, brick by brick.

Most nights the train stopped, sometimes at a station, usually in the middle of nowhere. If there were trees or bushes nearby, people would light fires by the trackside, though not since they left Orel. After Orel they were in bandit country, and fires were forbidden. If the moon came out, the engine would start up again, without warning, feeling its way slowly along the rails, keeping an eye out for barricades. One night, camped out on a slope above the train, they heard the sound of shooting in the distance. Everyone went quiet, even the young drunks who had been brawling. There was another volley of shots, then another, then silence. The next morning, as they rounded a bend, they saw a village in flames.

Stories came out of the southern war—from Kharkov, Voronezh, Tsaritsyn—stories of horror. The Cossacks flayed their prisoners alive, or buried them headfirst, leaving their legs sticking up in the air, taking bets on which would stop kicking last. The Cheka plunged their victims' limbs in boiling water until the skin blew up like a balloon, and could be peeled off in one piece. Parents were forced to watch their children being tortured and killed. Captives were thrown into blast furnaces or rolled around in nail-studded barrels. In the class war, torture was the only worthwhile entertainment. All causes, all argument, had given way to terror. And since the logic was example, not punishment, it didn't really matter who the victims were.

Skin was the torturer's favorite target. Without skin, a man was revealed before his own eyes as just so much raw meat. Living meat and screaming faces. At night, the stories became pictures in her head.

Every mile they traveled took them deeper into the war zone. The places they passed through had changed hands several times. By every village there were makeshift graves, crows digging into the dirt with their beaks, piling in with outstretched wings. In one place they passed, Zoia saw a peasant family lying behind a shed—two old men, a woman, a boy with ragged black hair. They looked like drunks passed out on the street. But when she saw their grinning mouths and the hollows of their eyes, she knew it wasn't sleep that had taken them.

One night Zoia woke from a parched slumber to find the wagon half empty. She left her mother and grandmother, and eased herself down onto the siding. A trickle of people were picking their way back down the line, going carefully, silently. She followed, wanting to know what the attraction was. Three wagons down she caught up with a woman in a long shawl.

"Where are you going?"

But the woman did not seem to hear her.

The procession disappeared into the shadows. There was a path, winding its way up a wooded hillside. It was so dark all Zoia could see were patches of stars overhead, framed by the branches. She stumbled, felt someone grab her by the arm, help her up and move on. She was cold and hungry. She wanted to go back, but up ahead now was a point of light, a flame. It moved through the trees, leading the way. Then there was a second flame, and a third. They seemed to drift among the trees, as if held by invisible hands.

Zoia thought she was dreaming. But it was a stranger, calmer dream than any she had had lately.

In a clearing there was a tiny church. She could make out a wooden dome, crumbling whitewashed walls. By starlight they were almost luminescent. She drew nearer, aware of voices. Chanting. At first it was so faint she had to strain to hear it. Since her secret wedding to Yuri a year ago, she hadn't set foot in a church. Participation in religious rituals was a crime. Even her grandmother, who was superstitious and prayed every day, had stayed away. But something inside her wouldn't let Zoia go back. She tried to stop, tried to think of the child she was carrying, and what would happen to it if she was arrested. But it was no good. Her feet kept walking, following the light and the gentle, swelling, voices.

She stepped through the door. Candlelight danced on the vaulted roof. There was a smell of incense that was sweet and familiar. A woman led the chanting. She was out of sight, up in a gallery somewhere. Her voice was clear, too beautiful to be coming from any of the ragged people down below. Zoia shuffled forward, aware now of the priest's voice, steady, deep—so deep it seemed to be coming up out of the earth.

And then she was at the front. The altar had been burned, and the screen that had framed it. The cross and the altarpieces were missing. Streaks of soot ran up the walls. She counted six bullet holes. But something had been saved. It stood propped up on the charred frame of a table: a picture of the Virgin and Child on a gilded panel.

It was just another icon, a relic of old Russia, the gold dulled with soot, barely glistening in the candlelight. There was nothing special in the Virgin's pitying face, or the blue enfolding robes. Nothing to bring tears to her eyes. If there were tears, they were from exhaustion and hunger, and the sense of dread that never left her. She had a sense the icon had brought her here, to show her something, to offer her something. But that was her delirium too, her very weakness talking. It made her angry to think of it. She wiped the tears from her face. They left pale smears on her filthy hands.

She wasn't going to pray. As children they had all prayed for the czar and his family a million times, but they had been shot just the same. She had prayed for her father and stepfather too. So what was the point of praying for Yuri, locked up in his asylum? What was the point of praying for their child?

Yuri didn't even know yet that he was going to be a father. She had tried to pass him a note on her last visit, but it had been confiscated by the guards. Better that way, her mother had said. Yuri had enough to worry about. She told Zoia to keep the baby a secret, for all their sakes.

Zoia ran out of the church and back to the train. She hid herself among the sour-smelling bags and her grandmother's skirts. She lay down to sleep, wishing dawn would come soon and they could get moving again. But the sound of the chanting was still in her head. When she closed her eyes all she could see was the icon, the mother and child, the flaking gold glimmering like sunlight on spring snow.

It took her where she didn't want to go. The Sparrow Hills above Moscow. The day she saw Yuri for the first time. Young, handsome faces turned toward them as they came running through the woods. Tatiana Argunov with her rosy cheeks, the young Countess Maria in her big fur hat, Raevsky and Count Orlov smiling as they held up the rabbits they'd shot.

—*We thought you'd been abducted.*

Their breath making steamy plumes in the cold air.

—*I was. But I escaped. I'm lucky to be alive.*

And the toast was "eternal friendship."

They were all dead now. Orlov, Countess Maria, even friends who were absent that day but who were counted among their circle. Interrogated, tortured, shot. The countess's family was not allowed to see her body. The things that had been done to her. Then they were arrested too.

Only Yuri remained. He had served the revolution by exposing a White Guards plot. He would soon be released, if he was well enough. He would go back to his wife, and take up the life of a Soviet citizen in the employ of the state. His survival was proof that the plot had been real.

The night their friends were arrested, he told her he had done it all for her. He said it was the only way they could be together.

In the nighttime she saw the young countess and the others standing on the path. She saw their trusting smiles.

The next day they crossed into the Ukraine. Six hours without stopping, eating up the distance, the wagon rocking so violently it left bruises all over their bodies. In the engine they were desperate to cover the miles as quickly as possible. Soldiers leaned out of the cab, hanging on by one arm, scanning the way ahead, rifles slung across their shoulders. Through a crack in the wood, Zoia watched the land slide by. Dust clouds swirled on the horizon, reaching up into a gray sky. She longed for a sight of the sea, for the smell of it. She thought of her and Yuri, steaming out across the blue waters, beyond the reach of Russia and its ghosts. When she saw him in the prison asylum, shuffling past her under guard, he hardly seemed to know who she was.

The wheels locked with a bestial scream. The wagon jolted, hurling her to the ground. Over the hiss of steam there came shouting. Zoia heard her mother telling her to stay down. The train was under attack.

Zoia closed her eyes and hugged the floor of the wagon, waiting for the volleys of gunfire. But there was no gunfire. She heard the guards shouting for everyone to stay on the train.

She crawled back to her spy hole in the side of the wagon. They were on the outskirts of a small town. She couldn't see the name. But there were warehouses, a freight yard. It looked like another train was standing up ahead of them on a parallel track. There was a host of red flags flying from the guard's van.

She heard the sound of hammering. Jeers. It was hard to see clearly with the steam still billowing from the engine.

In the entrance to one of the warehouses stood a group of soldiers with red stars on their caps. They were guarding a stock of grain. Sacks were piled up behind them. Two of them had taken up firing positions, and were training their sights down the line.

Then Zoia saw it, out of the corner of her eye: something heavy being dragged along the ground, around the end of the other train. It wasn't another sack of grain. It was a man, barefoot, ragged, a flap of red flesh trailing behind his head. The soldier that was dragging him carried a pair of rusty-looking hunting rifles over his shoulder.

There *had* been an attack, a raid on the grain store. Partisans maybe, or peasants come to take back what was theirs. But the soldiers had been ready for them.

The wagon jolted again. Steam clouded her view. They were moving again, rolling past the requisition train. Through smarting eyes she glimpsed a man on a freight wagon waving at a crowd of soldiers beneath him, arms stretched out high above his head. There was another man on the next wagon down.

Her mother screamed. She grabbed Zoia by the shoulders, tried to pull her away. A woman by the door crossed herself and buried her head in her hands. And then Zoia understood: it was one prisoner to each wagon, nailed to the sides by the hands, alive.

The soldiers whistled and gave the thumbs-up as the Moscow train rolled by.

45

The White armies had fled, and they were not coming back. One hundred and fifty thousand men had sailed away in Allied ships, bound for Constantinople and Marseilles. The Don Cossacks had retreated to the steppes, leaving a trail of bloody pogroms behind them. In Sevastopol, there was no possibility of deliverance, no possibility of escape, only hunger and the dread of reprisals.

Zoia's mother had a *belle époque* diamond tiara sewn into the hem of her petticoat, and pearls concealed in the heels of her boots. Zoia's bear, Mishka, had been hollowed out and stuffed with lace and silver. To make it last, they had to break up the jewelry, spending one stone at a time. A handful of pearls got them an attic room above a looted furniture shop on Ekaterinoslav Street. A sapphire got them some logs and brushwood for the stove. They took turns sleeping on the narrow iron bed.

For days they hardly ventured out. The streets were full of refugees, wandering aimlessly, looking for anything they could eat or steal. At night there was darkness and silence, broken only by the sound of shooting. When they saw the Cheka raid the building across the street, they packed up and moved on, toward the outskirts of the city. For seven more pearls, an old Armenian woman let them stay on her floor, along with a couple of Jewish families who had fled from the Ukraine. She knew places where you could still get food, if you timed it right. In derelict warehouses and stable blocks, they paid in diamonds for wormy fruit and salted fish full of bones. There wasn't much time to haggle. Everyone was frightened of being arrested or robbed.

The city Zoia remembered, the place of light and affluence, had fallen. In the streets, behind the stately, classical facades, a more primitive state of being had returned: the Russia of barbarian hordes. No law but the law of the tyrant. The station and the squares were full of beggars. On the promenade above the bay, where once Zoia had strolled with her governess under a pink chiffon parasol, there were now only prostitutes. They lined the way on both sides of the street, and every day there were more. Zoia saw soldiers and sailors buying them up half a dozen at a time. In the narrower streets, children were on offer, girls and boys of nine or ten. Zoia thought they were only begging until she looked into their eyes.

Her mother wouldn't talk about what to do next. She seemed to be waiting for something. Zoia was scared. Until now her mother had always had some kind of plan. It was five years since there had been a man in the family, but they had survived because she was always thinking ahead, anticipating dangers, pouncing on any sliver of opportunity. In Moscow she had cultivated contacts in the state bureaucracy, enough to get sporadic work for both of them, typing and filing. She had played the black market skillfully, making the most of their valuables and keeping them well hidden, even from the nosy people they were forced to live with. Yet here in Sevastopol she seemed at a loss. They were doing nothing, drifting into destitution, one jewel at a time.

"The air here is doing your grandmother good," she said one morning, as if she knew what was on Zoia's mind. "Another winter in Moscow would have killed her."

They were bent over the bathtub, trying to wash their sour-smelling clothes, although they had no soap.

"So . . . how long are we going to stay here?"

She wanted to know where her baby would be born.

Her mother wrung the water from a bundle of gray petticoats. Even after three years, she felt the humiliation of manual toil. Zoia could see it in her face—had seen it the first time she came home and found her shoveling snow while the building superintendent looked on and laughed. There was no shred of acceptance there. Anger kept her going, that and the dream of one day taking back what they had lost. To her mother, the greatest sin was weakness. And though she sometimes cried in the night, or woke screaming her dead husband's name, by morning she was always herself again, watchful, practical.

"I don't know how long," she said. "There are people here we have to find first."

"What kind of people?"

"People who can help us."

"You mean, help us escape?"

Her mother looked up sharply. It was the kind of thing you weren't supposed to say out loud, the kind of thing that could get you arrested.

She looked down again at her raw, red hands. Her voice became wistful. "We might still have a chance of that. If we keep our eyes open. Of course, your condition doesn't make things any easier."

Her condition. That was all the baby was now: a state she had thoughtlessly succumbed to. As if she were still a child, not a seventeen-year-old woman with a husband who was still alive. When she first realized she was pregnant, she had taken it as a sign of hope. Whatever Yuri may have done, whatever mistakes they had made, here was a new, blameless life. The child would need a mother and a father. All other considerations should be secondary to that. No one could hate them for wanting to care for their child.

When she first told her mother, she had gone very quiet, barely managing a smile. She wanted to know how it had happened, with Yuri locked up in the asylum. Zoia explained: it was the day she had taken Yuri to the dentist. He had developed an abscess, and for a hefty bribe, one of the asylum officials had given permission for him to be treated outside. They had made love in his parents' flat, a hungry, silent coupling like none before. Yet it was enough. The child would be the new beginning that would heal all wounds.

That was three months ago. Since then they hadn't discussed the baby again, except in passing. Her mother had told her what to expect, about the sickness and the fatigue, but the child itself was hardly mentioned. There had been no talk of names or the future, as if to picture the child would only make it more of a burden. That morning, washing the clothes, was the first time it had been mentioned since they left Moscow.

"I don't understand. What difference does the baby make to our leaving?" Zoia said. "There are still more than four months left."

Her mother didn't answer the question.

"We need someone to help us. A man of influence. There are still men of influence in Russia. And men are men. The things they want are always the same. No one can change that."

"But we don't know anyone down here."

Her mother brushed the hair away from her eyes. "We must find a doctor for you, Zoia. There was one I knew of from the old days. A Dr. Grigoriev. If only I could find where he lives."

•   •   •

That night, for the first time, Zoia felt the child move inside her. The shock of it brought her upright, a hand to her belly. Then it came again, and a third time. Not random spasms—communication. One, two, three. The child was speaking to her, telling her it was alive, growing, wanting to be born.

In the darkness, she smiled.

There were two of them now, mother and child. Like the icon in the church. She knew now what it meant. It meant that there was no going back. Yuri had to be forgiven, and they had to go on, together, whatever people said. Her mother had talked of divorce. Divorces were easy in the new Russia. But that was not going to happen, because they were a family now. One betrayal did not excuse another.

There and then she named the child: Alexander. Tall and blonde, like his father, dark-eyed like her. Already she could see the little boy in his father's arms. She could see him standing tall in his cadet's uniform.

The way he settled down again in her belly told her he liked the name.

Alexander Yurevich.

At Matilda Kshesinskaya's villa he would have cut a dash. The ladies would have watched him from behind their fans during those sultry summer soirées. Their hearts would have skipped a beat when he came near them.

Her son, her pride, her comfort.

She wished she could tell Yuri. She wished she could tell him that everything was going to be all right. She thought of him in his cell, haunted and broken, and wept. She should have found a way to tell him about his son. It would have given him strength. But it didn't matter. She would be like her mother. She would be strong for them all.

She crawled to the window, and got on to her knees for the first time since she was at school. She looked up at the hills and the faint, glimmering stars, and vowed to God and the Virgin that she would never betray this sacred trust. She would bring her child into a world radiant with love.

She fell asleep saying her son's name. In the morning, she went looking for a church, so as to thank God again and make her vow properly. But every church she went to was shut up or guarded by soldiers. She ended up outside St. Vladimir's Cathedral, staring up at its tall white walls and its dome of celestial blue. She remembered it from childhood, being taken there by Mademoiselle Élène, but it seemed even more beautiful now, beautiful and undefilable, like an embassy of heaven.

She knew this was the place for her vow, the perfect place. But every door she found was locked, and though she went around and around, pounding on them one after another, no one heard her. Or if they did hear, they would not come to let her in.

When she got back to the apartment, her mother and grandmother were gone. They came back hours later with some tins of French army rations and a cake of coal tar soap, wrapped up in rags. Her mother wouldn't let the soap out of her sight. No one was allowed to use it until nightfall, and even then she stood guard over the tub as Zoia got busy with a bucket of cold water.

"Nice and clean for the doctor," she said, watching Zoia soap her small round belly.

"The doctor?"

"That's right. I found him. Dr. Grigoriev. He was retired, but now . . . "She shrugged. Russia's troubles fell on the old hardest. "We're going to see him tomorrow. He's very good. Very experienced."

Zoia blanched at the thought of being examined by a man. It had never happened to her before. But she had to go through with it, if it was for the good of her child. She doused herself with water.

"I felt him kick last night," she said, shivering. "And this morning."

"Kick? Who?"

"The baby."

Her mother took the soap from her, and put a cloth in its place. It was too dark for Zoia to see her face clearly, but she didn't seem impressed.

"I've thought of his name. He'll be called—"

"Don't be foolish!" Her mother was suddenly angry. "Now get dry, before you catch a chill." She snatched the cloth and began to rub Zoia down briskly. "Don't you know it's bad luck to say such things? Very bad luck."

Zoia had never known her mother to be superstitious.

"His name is Alexander," she said. "Alexander Yurevich."

Her mother stopped the rubbing. She was still for a moment, as if a great weariness had come over her.

"Why must you do this to me, Zoia? Why must you always do this?"

Then she put the towel down and walked away.

Dr. Grigoriev came to the door wearing carpet slippers and a crumpled linen suit. Even allowing for his being retired, it surprised Zoia how old he was, stooped over, hollow-cheeked, milky pupils fixing on her through a pair of grubby-looking pince-nez. When he smiled, she saw the glint of gold in his teeth.

A pair of earrings: South Sea pearls set in a cluster of small diamonds. They had been a gift from Zoia's stepfather on the occasion of their fifth anniversary. It was a high price for a medical examination.

Grigoriev dropped the earrings into his top pocket.

"Did you bring me soap, like I asked you?"

He wanted soap too.

Zoia's mother produced the bar. Grigoriev unwrapped it, held it up to his nose and sniffed. "This will do nicely. We can't take risks with infection."

A nurse hovered in the background, gray hair, expressionless face. She was not introduced.

"Get the girl ready while I wash."

They were in a hurry. The nurse opened a door and stood back to let Zoia pass.

"Go on," her mother said.

An empty bookshelf along one wall, a window with panes of dirty frosted glass. The sunlight shone through with a brownish tinge. In the middle of the room, a table, higher off the ground than normal, like a butcher's block. Fat leather straps hung down from the sides.

The nurse fluffed up a pillow. She wore a gray dress and a white apron.

"You can undress behind the screen. Everything but the chemise."

She left the room again. Outside, her mother and Dr. Grigoriev were talking. The doctor wasn't happy about something. It was too late for that, he said. But she was insisting. When she insisted, it was always hard to say no.

She heard shouting in the street. Zoia went to the window and peered out through a broken pane. They were in a narrow street behind Nakhimonsky Avenue. Zoia remembered it full of shops, trams clanking up and down, men in straw boaters hanging on at the back. Mademoiselle Élène had bought some white flowers there, and put one in Zoia's hair.

She got undressed.

"Get up on the bench, then."

So that's what it was: a bench. The doctor was arranging things at the far end of the room. Instruments made of metal. Zoia hugged herself. The room was cold.

The nurse came back in, stirring a steaming glass of tea. Zoia's mother followed close behind.

"Drink this," the nurse said. "It'll relax you."

Nettle tea. She had become used to the taste, though this was different. There was a strange, nutty bitterness.

"All of it," the nurse said.

When she was done, they led her to the bench, and told her to lie down. Her mother took a seat by the window. Zoia couldn't see her there, but she could hear her breath coming and going, laboring a little.

The doctor gave the nurse a nod. "If you please."

The nurse drew up the chemise. Zoia felt the heat rise to her face, a pulse so strong it made her feel faint. She had never felt so naked, even with Yuri.

He felt the doctor's fingers on her belly, pushing and probing, dry and leathery. She wasn't cold anymore. Sweat trickled along her hairline.

"Is everything all right?" she asked.

She looked up, saw the doctor bending over her with a stethoscope, holding it near where the baby had kicked. Her ribs and hips were stark and prominent. It made the bulge in her womb more noticeable.

"Everything is normal."

No reassurance in his voice. Only reluctance, verging on irritation. Zoia lay down again. The light in the room was brighter. The ceiling moved above her head, the cracks drifting across her line of vision, crossing over each other. She was going to fall off the bench. She gripped the edge with her fingers.

"The speculum."

The nurse handed something to the doctor, some mechanical device. Zoia didn't want it anywhere near her.

"Don't," she said. It was someone else's voice coming out of her. "Don't, I'm . . ."

What was she?

"I promised."

Insect wings buzzed in her ears. A swarm, a cloud. Whining, mocking. She tried to swipe them away.

Cold metal inside her. She jumped. They had drawn her legs up. She felt straps tighten beneath her knees. She couldn't move.

The metal beak cranked open.

"What is it? What is it?"

Her mother's hand, icy cold against her face. "He has to see, dearest. Lie still."

"I don't like it here, Mama. I want to go." The words came out slurred.

"Be patient now."

"Keep the flies away."

"There are no flies. Lie still now."

They let her legs down. The doctor moved away to the side, shaking his head. He'd said everything was normal, but he had lied.

"Prepare the saline injection then." He looked at Zoia's mother, frowning. This was not his idea. "I've no morphine. You'll have to keep her quiet."

The nurse had something in her hand. Glass and tarnished silver. A four-inch needle.

She tried to move off the bench, but her legs felt heavy. "Wass she . . . *doing*?"

Her mother began to caress her forehead, running her fingers through Zoia's hair. She was humming a song, an old lullaby. Zoia reached up, grabbed her by the wrist.

"I wan . . . go now."

Gently her mother prized the fingers free and rested her arm down on the bench.

"Zoia, you know why we're here. You've known all along. Don't pretend you haven't."

The flies were crowding her sight now, black swirling specks, waiting their chance to feed. She fought to sit up.

Her mother was at her side. There were tears in her eyes.

"You must be strong for us. You're the one chance we have now.

You're beautiful and clever, and men adore you. But not like this, not with . . ."

"*Axander Yuvich.*"

She managed to get her legs off the bench. The doctor stood watching her, the nurse beside him.

Her mother was on her knees, the words streaming from her, like a babbled prayer. Zoia had never seen her that way, not even the day they learned her stepfather had been killed. Zoia had never seen her so afraid.

"They'll come for us. Sooner or later they'll come. They hate us, Zoia. They'll always hate us." She brought her face closer. "If your father were here, it's what he'd tell us to do. He'd say we have to survive."

"No. He woon . . ."

"We have to make a clean start, Zoia, like we said." She was choking back the sobs. The tears were running down her face. "A new beginning. It's what you want, isn't it? Isn't it, my darling?"

Zoia couldn't see properly. She couldn't tell which way was up. The whole room was rotating. She was going to fall. She reached out, felt her mother's grasp. Her head went down onto the bench.

"I promised," she said. "I promised."

But she kept hold of her mother's hand. It was the one thing in the room that was real now, concrete, the one thing she could depend on. Everything else was a dream. And after dreams you woke up.

"You'll forget this," she heard her mother say. "You will. You'll have your whole life to forget."

Zoia closed her eyes.

The contractions brought her around, screaming. It was pain like she had never known. Something went over her mouth, *into* her mouth. A gag. They had tied her down by her wrists. She looked down, saw her knees raised. The doctor and the nurse had masks across their faces. They had blood on their aprons, their arms, their hands.

Her blood.

The pain seemed to expand, convulsing her whole body. She tried to reach for her mother's hand, but her mother was no longer there.

The pain subsided, washing out of her like the tide. That was when she saw what was in the doctor's hands. She saw its face.

• • •

24th July 1933

Dear Karl,

Forgive me for writing to you like this. There are things I have to tell you, even though you may not want to hear them. But I want you to at least know everything that has happened to me.

Almost a month ago—I see the date was 28th June—I wrote you a letter which I never sent. And maybe I wouldn't be writing now if I didn't know that at ten o'clock this morning—it's now eight—I'm going to have to face Mama, who's coming from the country, and say to her things I know I can't say, and somehow find a way to do it. Karlinka, please try to understand me. I have no strength any more for this thing they call "living." Simply no strength. I am fast approaching that state of mind where I will no longer fear the dark, just because it is unknown. I am not there yet, but if only you knew how I have longed for this courage.

Karlinka, as I wrote before, I want to tell you that I have no one to blame for this broken life but myself. But now, at the age of 30, I find myself at a point where I am completely incapable of creating anything of value. It has been the deep desire to make something whole and complete and of real worth that has both haunted and sustained me all my life. You told me that I should be less ambitious in my goals, but with a fervor that scares me I have gone on searching and searching. I have given too much of myself to that search, and the worst is knowing it is all for nothing. That is why there are no new paintings, why there can never be any paintings anymore.

If you look at all that has happened to me, you will understand that I could do nothing else. I cannot live a normal life, and know it will be that way forever. Consciously and unconsciously I have broken that life into pieces, so that it is no use to anyone. I know this, and I no longer ask for anything, but still I cannot escape my dreams. Imagine, it was not until I was sixteen years old that real life began for me. Imagine the madness, the unreality of my life as a child, and then what happened afterward, being raised without a father by women who did not understand the times they were living in—and even less what I needed from life—which was not surprising given the world they came from. And then, there were the children who were taken from me—the first I did not know how to fight for, and the second, which you know I only gave up under the wildest protests. Maybe if that had not happened, everything could have been saved. Or maybe it would have ended up even more of a mess. It pierces my heart to think of it, even now.

I was mixed up when you found me, thanks to all that had happened. That was how I started my married life with you. You, who are the only person who has cared for me, though in a strange way. You have never understood me, or longed for the same things I have longed for. And yet I owe you so much. You, with your intelligence and your steadfastness, you have made something of yourself. You have supported me and have given me the means to work—the opium of my existence after all that has collapsed around me.

It is not your fault that I am too weak to go on fighting, and mend what has been broken.

46

Stockholm, March 2000.

Zoia's mother had been wrong. Zoia never did forget. The first chance she got, she ran away to Moscow, hoping she could put things back the way they had been somehow. But it was impossible. The operation in Sevastopol left her unable to bear children. When she got pregnant again in Stockholm two years later, the doctors told her that carrying the baby to term would kill her. She'd wanted to go ahead anyway. She was ready to trust to God or fate or providence, and was even eager to throw herself on their mercy. But Karl would not allow it. He would not allow his wife of one year to leave him, not that way.

Elliot closed the file. He sat before the window in Kerstin Östlund's apartment, watching the trains go by, yellow eyes moving through the fog.

It was a punishment for destroying Yuri's child. This was Zoia's belief, the burden she carried. The mother's duty was to sacrifice herself for her child. But in her quest for new beginnings, Zoia had let the child be sacrificed for her. The devil had kept his side of the bargain: the deal had delivered everything she and her mother had hoped for. It had proved the key to their rescue, their freedom. It had bought them new lives in the safety of Sweden. Everything Zoia tasted, everything she became, was made possible by that journey to Sevastopol. Her art had been bought with the blood of Yuri's child.

A woman like that was not fit to bring new life into the world.

Hildur Backlin said Zoia didn't like children. She told the story of their trip to the restaurant in Östermalm as proof of the aversion: Zoia throwing down her napkin and storming out because they made too much noise with their playing. Did Hildur know the truth? Did she understand what Zoia really felt? Elliot nodded to himself. Of course she did. It was one last piece of spite, one last splinter of revenge for the friend who had humiliated her.

360

People like that take what doesn't belong to them.

Hildur had been a star of stage and screen. She knew how to handle an interview, how to make it work for her. And she knew about Sevastopol.

There were pictures Zoia did not allow the world to see, dark scenes that haunted her, sleeping and waking. They were part of her history, part of her. Kandinsky's pupils were taught to look at the world through the inner eye, the eye of the self. Hildur Backlin said he would find the artist *in* her art. Zoia had searched for a way of expressing what lay within her, something that encompassed the whole, and some time after her letters to Karl in 1933, she had finally found it. In secret she had made flesh the whole woman. She had found her way in gold.

Illuminates everything, betrays nothing. That was what she told the *Baltic Arts Review* in 1969.

Elliot stared into the fog. There was a line of streetlights above what must have been the far embankment. They burned brighter, then duller, then vanished. Somewhere the sun was up, but if anything it was getting darker.

The paintings on gold were celebrations of a perfect world, a world renewed. In those Depression years, between revolution and war, they had sold well. But there was no clue to inner turmoil, even if the flowers were made of silk, and the faces were masks, and the palaces gleamed with too much innocent splendor. This was a world dreamed up in a children's nursery. The gold was the gold of the sun on water. It betrayed nothing, but it expressed nothing either beyond its own opulence and the echoes of Orthodox religion.

Elliot looked down at his hand. The burns were throbbing, as if, beneath the bandages, a second heart was beating. He edged aside the gauze and got a glimpse of the raw flesh beneath, shiny and tacky to the touch. Gold was the skin of the gods. When the ancient Egyptians gilded their sarcophagi, they expected their work to last for all eternity—and were it not for the tomb robbers, it might have done.

A permanent impenetrable skin.

Even the critic Savva Leskov saw that connection. He had mentioned Tutankhamen when they met at Bukowskis. He'd talked about X-rays, about how gold was impenetrable to them, like lead.

His thoughts snagged on the memory: *X-ray an ordinary picture and you can see what's underneath. The false starts, the parts that have been painted over. But not with these.*

Analysts were blind, Leskov had said. All they had to go on was the surface. No one could see the artist's mistakes, her pentimenti.

Elliot stood up. The file fell from his lap and hit the floor. Photocopied letters spilled across the boards. He brought a hand to his forehead.

The Crimea pictures. He knew where they were. He knew.

He saw Zoia in Kristoffer Palmgren's flickering film, interrupted. He saw the dark smears on her arms.

He saw the knife, the wolf's tooth blade—used for burnishing, the textbooks said.

He saw the look on Monica Palmgren's face when she saw what was there on the panel. It wasn't just clay, as he'd assumed. It wasn't just a preparation prior to gilding.

He braced himself against the window. An express hurtled by.

Zoia to Andrei Burov, February 1928: *all my life, all my traveling, has changed nothing. When I stand before the easel, this dark mood comes upon me and all I want to do is hide.*

And she *had* hidden. She had hidden the truth of herself beneath an image of the life-giving sun, had sealed it there beneath a golden mirror— ever-present, but known only to her. And onto the mirror she had painted visions of innocence. The world through uncorrupted eyes, the eyes of a child who had never been born.

Underneath, the Crimea pictures were there: torturing, excoriating. Her pentimenti. The things she repented of, scratched and scored into the clay with a wolf's tooth.

Anubis, the Keeper of Secrets.

He remembered Hildur Backlin again, watching him out of the corner of her eye as she waxed lyrical about Nikolai Gogol.

. . . he turned to God in the end. Starved himself to death as an . . . act of penance.

Of all the things she could have said about the great Russian playwright.

Zoia's choice of media made special demands. It took an eccentric like Foujita to set her thinking along such unconventional lines. But it was what kept her alive. Gold was what made creation possible, just like

Hildur said. Zoia had honored Kandinsky's exhortations to the extreme. She had put herself into every work, but masked—her confession, her penance not meant for mortal eyes. Behind her public art of shining gold was a private art of grief and shame. The two coexisted in the same space, like ghosts and men.

She was never free. Not for a single day. Sevastopol was her prison for life.

Elliot started across the room. Somewhere between the house on the coast and Kerstin's apartment, his notebook had been mislaid. The boxes were all mixed up, their contents scrambled during the hasty evacuation of Zoia's studio. He emptied them one by one, thinking maybe what he was looking for wasn't in the notebook anyway, but on some other loose scrap of paper. He emptied his suitcase and rummaged through the tangle of dirty clothes. He opened up his computer, found the notebook sandwiched between the screen and the keyboard.

He flicked through the pages and saw the note: *Hildur Backlin— model*. Beneath it was her daughter's name and the number, and that of the care home.

What had Zoia drawn? What exactly? If Hildur knew so much, she might know that too. He had done enough to be let in on the secret. No one had the right to keep him on the outside anymore.

He picked up the phone and dialed. The line rang twice. A cheerful female voice came on the line.

"I'd like to speak to Mrs. Hildur Backlin, please."

"Thank you."

Floaty mood music, strings and piano. It seemed to go on forever.

The voice came back. "Are you immediate family, sir?"

Solicitous now, not cheerful anymore.

"I'm a friend. My name's Elliot."

"I'll put you through."

A buzz. Someone picked up midway through clearing his throat.

"Mrs. Backlin? This is Marcus Elliot again. I came to see you a while ago about—"

"I'm sorry, Mr. Elliot. You're through to Daniel Renberg. I'm one of the counseling staff here."

"Counseling staff?"

"You were a friend of Hildur's, I understand."

The stranger had a heavy accent, and what sounded like a lozenge in his mouth. Elliot heard it clack against his teeth.

"That's right. Can I speak to her? Is there a problem?"

"I'm afraid I have bad news. Hildur Backlin passed away last night. From a stroke. It was her second, as you know. Her family was with her at the end."

A well-practiced speech, like something read from a card. For a moment, Elliot wondered if it could be true.

"We would like to express our sincere condolences. If you wish, we can send you details of the funeral arrangements once they have been settled upon."

Hildur Backlin was dead. Zoia's model was dead. The one person who could have completed the picture. The one person who could have told him he was right.

He got a crazy idea that she had died to frustrate him. She had died to keep Zoia's secrets safe.

"Would you care to leave your details?" Mr. Renberg said, tucking the lozenge into his cheek.

Elliot checked the date on the kitchen calendar. He checked the time on his watch. There was still one more way to find out what Hildur wouldn't tell him, one more place to look. He plugged in his mobile phone, found the number he was looking for, and made the call.

47

The clack of heels on polished floors. Hushed voices receded down a corridor. At the public prosecutor's office Kerstin sat waiting. Even the receptionists kept their voices down. Riding in the lift, she'd caught whispers on the landings. The place survived on crimes and allegations. Forensic evil pumped through its bureaucratic veins. There were CCTV cameras everywhere. She fought with a sense of the absurdity: being here in the name of a dead woman, a woman beyond the reach of human wrongs. She had seen it as the repayment of a debt. But it wasn't just that. It was something she had to do, something she needed for herself.

Behind his desk, the investigator took his time reading over Zoia's list, making brief notes between frowns and sighs. It was obvious he would have preferred to send her away. It was obvious he didn't think he could.

Her thoughts drifted back to Marcus Elliot. She felt his hand on the back of her neck. She saw him standing over her through the blur of soapy water. He'd thought she'd taken an overdose. He'd thought she'd drowned herself. According to the rumors at Bukowskis, that was how his mother had died. He had been the one who found her. *Can you imagine?* people said. And the truthful answer was: *No, you can't.*

Elliot blamed Zoia. A part of him did anyway. Somehow Zoia had lured her mother to her death, lured her away from his father and him.

"How did you come by this?"

She looked up. The investigator wore a mustache, striped shirt, and gold cuff links. Anglophile dressy. Thirty-five going on sixty.

"A friend of mine has been cataloging Madam Zoia's papers. He lent it to me."

She wondered where he was now, if he'd taken off again on his quest, driving through the city or beyond it, chasing another scrap of Zoia's past. He was curiously selective, though. Zoia to her mid-thirties was all that interested him, as if things beyond that were too obscure or insubstantial to be worth investigation. As if he could only measure her life against his own.

She feared for him. She feared where this search was going to end. She knew what it was to lose something that could never be replaced.

The investigator got up. "I'm going to make a photocopy, do you mind?"

"Please, go ahead."

He left the room, leaving the door ajar. They were up on the sixth floor, tall, dirty windows looking out along Klarabergsgatan. Crosstown traffic queued in the fog, silent behind the wide-spaced double-glazing. In the distance, orange sunlight caught a strip of metal on the top of an office block.

For a moment, she felt lost. Being here, making progress at last, it wasn't how she had imagined it. She was on the road to vindication, thanks to Marcus Elliot. Wrongs would be righted. But there was no sense of impending triumph. There was only sorrow and a disquieting sense of distance. Soon this wouldn't be her fight anymore. She had been carrying a burden and would finally lay it down. This was what Zoia would have wanted. And then—it came to her with the shock of unexpected certainty—it would be farewell. Time to let go. Time to worry about the here and now. Fighting for Zoia's wishes, she realized, had kept her close. But it had kept her from living.

She hunched her shoulders. Without Zoia the world was emptier, lonelier. She wished she could see her one last time.

The investigator came back in. He had consulted his colleagues, he said. The list did not constitute proof that Zoia's will was not genuine. It expressed an apparent intention that might easily have been superseded. Such things happened all the time. But, given what he called the unusual circumstances, they felt compelled to investigate. They would examine the alleged will, and the circumstances surrounding it, and if there was evidence of fraud, they would uncover it.

It was done. The will was now the *alleged* will. The investigator kept on talking, explaining how they would go about their investigation, and what they would need to find before the document could be declared invalid. But Kerstin wasn't listening anymore. All she could think of was Marcus Elliot. Her journey had come to an end. But what of his?

The Paris self-portrait, the picture everyone had been looking for, that was where it had all begun for him. It stood like some mythical creature at the gates of the underworld, the place where Hanna Elliot had gone of her own volition, the place where all secrets were revealed.

Perhaps it was true what Marcus believed: that his mother and Zoia had known each other, that the picture had been a present. It was just like Zoia. When she liked somebody, her embrace was swift and unstinting. And Kerstin could see how that might provoke jealousy, especially in a husband unsure of his ground. Then there was the possibility of a sexual dimension. Maybe Zoia recognized in Hanna a woman stifled by the conventions of marriage, a woman whose deeper instincts had been denied at a terrible cost. Certainly Zoia had talked to Kerstin about that, and with an authority that spoke of experience. She had loved women as well as men in her time. A portrait of a woman disguised, her true nature hidden from the world, it was hard not to see meaning in such a choice of gift: identification, blessing, perhaps even a kind of release.

But Marcus had been a boy of eight. To him Zoia's art was a mystery, a dark magic that had come into his life, dissolving all ties. A few days later, his mother had gone, leaving him bewildered and alone, forever.

The child's world view was egocentric. What happened, good or bad, happened for a reason, and the reason lay within. Was Hanna Elliot unworthy of her son? Or was the son unworthy of his mother? Like his anger, the questions had resurfaced with the Paris self-portrait. And little by little, Marcus's world had unraveled again.

Two women living in exile. Two women speaking a secret language, speaking of things he was not allowed to know. Here was a source of fascination. Here was the hunger to understand. But it was a search for which she could see only one possible resolution, and one possible end.

She was out on the street when her phone rang. Elliot sounded different from the night before: calm, determined. It scared her more.

"I want you to see something. I need a witness."

She thought she heard voices in the background.

"Marcus? Where are you?"

"A hardware store. A couple of blocks from your place."

"What are you doing there?"

"I needed some things. I'm going out to the airport now."

"The airport? You're leaving?"

Elliot said something, but a passing truck drowned out the words. Kerstin huddled against the wall.

"Marcus? Are you going back to London? Is that what you said?"

"Not yet. It's the painting, Kerstin. It's here."

As if he had been eavesdropping on her thoughts.

"Your painting? The self-portrait?"

"It's here. I want you to see it. I want you to see all of it."

"I don't understand."

"I want you to meet me there."

"Marcus? What are you—?"

"It'll be in the warehouse by now. That's just outside Märsta. I'll give you directions. I'll tell them to expect you."

It didn't make any sense. Why did they have to go out to some warehouse? Why did they have to go now?

"What are you going to do, Marcus? Aren't you going to sell the portrait? You told me you were going to sell it."

On the road, a van cut in from a side street. Angry horns blared.

"Marcus?"

"I'm going to show you something extraordinary. Something no one but Zoia has ever seen."

"What? Marcus, what are you talking about?"

"It's time to open the tomb."

48

He hasn't gone half a mile when the car dies. He stares with mute incomprehension at the dashboard, tries the ignition, once, twice, then realizes what's happened: he's run out of petrol. On his dash from the coast he was too distracted, too keyed up to notice the yellow warning light below the gauge. Now the tank is bone dry.

He can take a train to the airport, take a taxi to the warehouse from there. He has just enough cash for that, although not enough to get back again.

It doesn't matter.

Paperwork and ID checks keep him at Security for fifteen minutes. Men with ill-fitting uniforms and hair in ponytails. The consignment forms name Paul Costa as the shipper. Even with a fax from him, it takes more phone calls to London before they let him into the holding area.

The packages are stacked head-high in steel cages. The warehouse is as cold as a meat locker, bright white lights suspended from the rafters. Near one corner, water falls in a silvery thread from a hole in the roof, spattering against the cement floor. The walls vibrate with the noise of taxiing aircraft.

They escort him to a cage beside a fork-lift truck. The hazard lights are still going above the cab. No one has thought to search him. They even lend him a Stanley knife to get through the packaging. They unlock the cage, consult their printouts, and pull out the big flat box he's looking for. They secure the cage again and leave him to it with scarcely a sideways glance at his bandaged hand.

He's stared at this picture a thousand times since he found it in his father's house. But this time it'll be different. He'll see it now with different eyes, the eyes of the initiate, the eyes of one who knows.

He props the box up against the floor of the cage, and starts cutting through the thick adhesive tape. Inside the box, the picture is bubble-wrapped to three inches thickness, a cocoon of milky plastic. With only one good hand, it takes forever to get through it. He hacks and tears, breathing hard. He wants to see that face again, the dark eyes, the red lips. He wants to see the picture for what it is.

He throws the last sheet down. And then she's with him once again.

Her expression was always enigmatic: not frowning, not smiling. He stares, beginning to see something he has never seen before: beyond the ethnic disguise, her face is actually a lifeless blank. It's the gold that's alive. It pulses, shimmers. Blood pumps through hidden veins.

He steps closer. Self-portrait in a mask—self as illusion, self as fake. It's an invitation to look beneath the surface, but only to those who know. And most of her life no one did know. It was a portrait of a Chinese princess in Paris, some unnamed acquaintance Zoia met, probably at one of those costume parties they were fond of in Montparnasse. Zoia had kept up the pretense for forty years, until Mrs. Hanna Elliot turned up in the autumn of 1970.

The Stanley knife will score, but will it peel? He needs a flayer's tool, an angled blade that won't dig in too deep. Take off the leaf, but leave what lies beneath: Zoia's Sevastopol, Zoia's *pentimenti*. In the hardware store he bought a pallet knife with a three-inch blade, flexible but bevel-edged, sharp enough to cut through flesh. The man behind the counter told him to use it with caution. It could slice you open if you weren't care-ful, he said.

The frame is lacquered wood. It comes away with a sharp crack. He takes the pallet knife from his inside pocket, brings it up to the panel. The handle is smooth and hard, difficult to grip with his bandaged hand.

Start with the face—no, start with the unpainted gold: top left, bot-tom left. The steel blade moves from point, to point, his silhouette drift-ing like a shade across the glimmering surface. A ghost of the present invades the past, invades Paris, 1929, invades Zoia's house in October 1970, wanting revenge, wanting rest.

No sign of Kerstin. He nods to himself. She isn't coming. But then, why should she? All she wants is to prove a point, and to kick-start a jour-nalistic career. She wants a world where everything's done by the book, a world without equivocators like him.

His hands are shaking. He switches the knife to his left.

He came to Zoia's life with naive expectations. He sees that now. Something in her work made it possible for her to shake off history, to forget what she had lost, and begin her life again. He hoped to find healing in those grafts of immortal skin. But he was fooling himself. Behind Zoia's gold is poison. The spells on the tomb are curses, outpourings of unvoiced rage and grief. Contagious. Lethal. She sealed them there for protection, to protect herself.

Hildur Backlin said the gold was what Zoia loved. *Made it all possible, you see.*

Dr. Lindqvist told him she painted to stay alive, that day they first drove out to the house. Who'd have thought the old man meant it literally?

He presses the knife against his face, draws the cold blade absentmindedly across his unshaven jaw.

One life saved, another taken. The poison found its way out. It took his mother, made him an orphan at eight years old. Despair, cheated of one victim, claimed two more.

Secular icons from an artist rejected by God. Zoia painted churches and monasteries, but only from the outside. She couldn't cross the thresholds in spirit or in body, though she tried.

This broken life.

Tears prick in his eyes. He dashes them away with his sleeve. Let the poison out. It's time. He leans his shoulder against the cage, presses the blade against the field of gold. He has to cut now. Put aside the instinct to honor and preserve. He has to cut and scrape and score until everything's laid bare. There's no alternative, no way back. His whole life has been leading him to this.

"Marcus?"

It's like a voice in his head. A woman's voice. It takes him a moment to realize he's not alone.

"Kerstin." He manages a smile. "Just in time."

"What's this all about? What are you doing?"

Even wrapped up in her long coat she looks cold: shoulders hunched, hands buried deep in her pockets.

"Sevastopol. It's right here. Under the gold. Everything's under the gold."

He steps back so that she can get a better look, thinking she'll understand it all instinctively. As she walks over, reflected gold lights up her face. She's beautiful in this light, deified.

"So this is the self-portrait." She puts her head on one side, frowns. "I thought it would look like her. But it doesn't really, does it?"

Even now she plays with him.

"That's the point. That's the message. You have to look beneath the surface. Don't you see?"

Her gaze fixes on the pallet knife.

"Marcus? What are you doing? You're not . . . You're not going to *damage* it?"

"X-rays won't work. They can't pass through gold."

She stares at him, still struggling to comprehend. As if preservation is what matters here. As if this is somehow sacrilege. He would have thought the same until a few weeks ago.

"Christ, Marcus, you must be joking. You *can't*." She steps in front of the picture. "This is a valuable work of art."

She doesn't understand. He shakes his head, angry now.

"Fuck art."

He pushes her aside, but then she's back, holding on to his arm, shaking him as if she wants to wake him from a dream.

"Marcus, wait. This is crazy. This is *insane*."

Words without meaning.

"I want to see. That's all this is. I want to see."

"You've no right to destroy this picture. You *need* this picture."

He wishes she could understand. He wishes he could explain. But he sees now he's come too far to share. Some things must be experienced to be understood.

"I've got work to do, Kerstin. Please, get out of the way."

She steps aside, just one step. She watches him raise the knife, watches as he digs it into the edge of the panel. He wishes she wouldn't watch him with those dark eyes. Her pity touches him.

A plane comes in, engines screaming.

Their work is like flesh and blood to them. It's who they are.

Hildur Backlin, Zoia's friend and enemy, still keeping the secret days from death.

The blade shudders against the wood, like a razor hitting bone. He has to go in finer, find the gap between gesso and gold. He yanks out the blade. Part of him just wants to destroy.

Kerstin reaches up, puts her hand on his.

"What if there's nothing there? Marcus? What happens then?"

"There's something. If you knew what I know . . ."

"What *do* you know? Marcus, you never even met her."

Kerstin's in his way again. He pushes her back, but she holds on to him. Like Zoia and Alain on the beach at La Marsa. The day she wanted to go bathing in front of everyone. Sensuality as opium.

Kerstin wants him to look at her. "It's just like you told me. Last night, remember? You said when you looked at Zoia's pictures, it was like you were looking in a mirror. That's exactly how it is. That's what's happening. *Think.*"

He shakes his head. The idea is so bizarre he wants to laugh.

"I've heard you. Everything you say about her, everything you . . . *envisage:* It's you. *You.* This story in your head, whatever it is, it's yours, not hers."

He's short of breath. He grabs hold of the cage, looks down at his feet. The cement floor is slick and sliding. There's too much going on in his head. Overload. He's going to vomit. He shuts his eyes, sees only the living gold.

"You're wrong. I know what I know."

"The Zoia *I* knew was at peace. She couldn't have helped me otherwise."

"At peace. I don't think so. Resigned maybe."

"Marcus, listen—"

"*NO!*" She steps back, stunned. He breathes deep. "You should go now. It was a mistake to drag you out here. I'm sorry. You should go back now to . . . whatever it is you do."

It comes out sneeringly, an insult. He can feel it hit home in the single pulse of silence.

"You've no right. You've no right to pry. That's what you're doing, you know. You know that. You're *prying* into what doesn't concern you."

"I want you to leave now."

"This won't help you understand anything. It won't."

He straightens up. "Just. Leave. Me. *Alone.*"

He knows that voice, that cold anger. His father's.

Slowly Kerstin's hands go back in her pockets. He knows how this looks to her: worse than Lindqvist's stealing, worse than Cornelius's lies. This is Zoia's legacy. This is destruction that can never be undone. Why does she care about those things?

He wants to say something to make it better, but no words come. Too late anyway. Thirty years too late. He doesn't know how to reach for her. Never has. That part of him died when he was eight years old.

He hears her turn and walk away.

What if there's nothing there? What happens then?

Her footsteps grow faint.

The truth is behind the gold. That's what matters. Secrets hidden for eternity. Zoia's communion with the unknowable God. Answers.

He grips the knife with both hands, casts one last look over his shoulder.

Kerstin is still standing there, watching him. In spite of everything, he finds he's glad.

"There's another way you can look, if you must look. I think I can arrange it, if that's what you really want."

Elliot remembers infra-red reflectography from his dealing days, but the few images he saw back then were unimpressive. The basic technique has been around since the early 1990s. You shine strong infra-red light onto a picture and record the image onto infra-red sensitive film, or look at it through a TV camera adapted to receive infra-red radiation. Infra-red is better at penetrating paint layers than visible light and is especially good at revealing carbon black underdrawing. The TV method is supposed to be more sensitive, and can see deeper, revealing evidence of alteration, hidden signatures, as well as drawings the artist never meant the world to see.

What Elliot recalls are blurry black and white images, carbon lines so faint they could be mistaken for shadows.

Kerstin says the techniques have improved. Some optical engineers at the university have built a prototype infra-red scanner. Specially designed computer software combines images gathered from different angles to build up high-resolution pictures. The experts at Bukowskis go down there a lot, especially when authenticity is an issue. The drawing behind a fake is usually very different from the drawing behind an original.

Kerstin says the scanner will see through the skin of gold. She's sure of it. He can test his ideas with the dispassionate instruments of science, if he's so sure of them.

They drive back to town in silence, the picture back in its box, strapped into the backseat of Kerstin's car. The sun is a bright copper disk in a misty sky. He loses track of the direction as they pass through unfamiliar suburbs. Streets and buildings give way to woodland, then reappear again. Outside a red-brick church, Kerstin stops to consult a street map, then does a U-turn and takes them back half a mile the way they've come.

Maybe it's true. Somewhere along the line, he lost all objectivity. But when? It's impossible to pinpoint the moment. In any case, it's the very subjectivity that feels most like truth. How can you profess knowledge of pain you can't feel, or beauty you can't see?

The engineering faculty is a low 1960s block obscured by screens of silver birch. Flaking white paint clings to cement walls. Elliot climbs out of the car. Crows call from woodland invisible in the mist.

Kerstin makes a call on her mobile while Elliot unloads the picture.

"You're in luck," she says, hanging up. "They're all ready. They haven't tried anything gilded before. They're quite excited. You want the Applied Optics Department, second floor. Ask for Dr. Lars Halvorsen."

"You're not coming with me?"

"I've things to do. Besides, I don't want to see, remember?" She restarts the engine, showing him a sad, faltering smile. "Good luck, Marcus. I'll see you around."

He walks alongside as she reverses out. "You really don't think I should do this, do you? Why?"

She stops, looks out over the hood of the car. "Tell me something: do you think they're beautiful?"

"Beautiful?"

"Her paintings. Zoia's paintings."

It isn't something he's thought about for a long time. It isn't a question he's ever needed to ask.

"Yes. Yes, I suppose I do."

"So why isn't that enough?"

He frowns. "Enough? I don't understand."

She watches him for a moment, then puts the car in gear and drives away.

The scanner is mounted on a metal frame, three foot by five. The lens and the infra-red lantern are bolted to a platform that slides up and down a tall mechanical arm. The arm itself travels laterally along the forward edge of the frame. Cables trail over the top, connected to motors, transformers, computers, and a large high-resolution monitor.

Dr. Lars Halvorsen has gray hair and a cool, surgeon's manner. He and the other technicians encourage Elliot to keep his distance. It is essential to avoid vibration during the scan, they say. Even tiny movements can render the data useless. He sits alone at the back of the darkened room, trying to glimpse the picture building up, line by line, on the screen. Zoia's self-portrait lies on its side, held in the jaws of a sturdy metal easel. They prefer it that way. They get the best results, they explain, when they minimize the vertical distance the scanning eye has to travel. In any case, the picture will display the right way up.

Kerstin was right: they're excited at the prospect of testing the system on a specimen like this. A few minutes into the setup, it's clear to Elliot they've forgotten he's even there.

The infra-red lantern casts visible light too. Under its reddish beam, the gold glimmers like the embers of a dying fire. Elliot sees a little iron stove in a two-room attic, high above the Rue Cézanne, sees Alain Azria, sneaking around the studio, burning to know Foujita's secrets, hungry for the rush of initiation. The best guess on the Paris self-portrait is that it dates from the year he and Zoia met. Elliot feels Alain's hunger. Initiation implies exclusivity. It's one better than acceptance. Congenital flaws are superseded, erased. How many Tunisian Jews are awarded the Légion d'honneur?

Across the top of the screen there is now a single bright ribbon. The scanning system boasts a possible four thousand shades of gray, a vast improvement on previous capabilities. But so far there's nothing to see but a faint swirl of shadow. One of the technicians says something about traces of carbon. Dr. Halvorsen tells him to reconfigure the contrast.

He doesn't only understand Alain's hunger: he feels it. He feels the force of childhood loss as well, the eternal sense of something missing, a part of you that was left out somewhere, and can never be found. He knows Karl Kilbom's need to be the rescuer, the way he hoped to build love and faithfulness on a bedrock of gratitude. As if that could ever work.

Most of all, he knows what it is to be unworthy of a child. To know her future will be brighter without you, however much you wish it wasn't so.

Zoia's life is a mirror, fashioned for him. He sees himself in it, frozen in the moment, as in a portrait: captured, essential. Understood.

Kerstin is right: he came for Zoia's secrets, but it isn't hers he has found.

The scanner completes another vertical sweep. The technicians are gathered around the monitor. Dr. Halvorsen points something out, making circular motions with his finger. He wears a wedding ring. There are issues of definition, questions about whether the gold is deflecting back too much light. The scanner pans across Zoia's painted eyes.

It was there in the studio all along, gilded and ready, waiting for him: a portrait of Marcus Elliot. Zoia's last work. A special commission, not for auction or resale. A work destined for the most private of all collections. To the living from the dead, a gift of gold.

He walks with Zoia through the rooms of the gallery: Sergei Shchukin's Matisses and Picassos, Ivan Morozov's Gauguins and Van Goghs. He pauses before Zoia's favorite, *Memory of the Garden at Etten*. He follows the dappled road as it winds out of sight. With each step he feels the warmth of the sun on his back. He sees beauty in the flowering garden.

The scanner passes over Zoia's red mouth.

Dr. Halvorsen leans into the screen. "You see this here? What is that?"

The technicians are agitated about something.

"That's carbon of some kind. No doubt about that."

Halvorsen looks back over his shoulder. "Mr. Elliot? Do you want to take a look at this?"

He stands at the gallery doors, the ones Andrei Burov held open for Zoia in the spring of 1918. He can come back anytime, lose himself for a while. The pictures will always be here. In the meantime, he can walk out into the light.

"Lars."

A technician grabs Dr. Halvorsen by the sleeve. From the base of the scanning arm comes a straining, grinding sound.

"Shut it down."

Someone flicks a switch. The scanner shudders to a halt. The technicians straighten up, groaning. This has obviously happened before.

Dr. Halvorsen shakes his head despairingly. "I'm sorry, Mr. Elliot. The simplest piece of technology in the whole setup, and it keeps going wrong. We'll have to replace one of the motors." He looks at his watch. "It could take a while. Maybe you could come back tomorrow."

The lantern still burns, making a circle of pink light on the golden surface. It looks like a setting sun.

It's as if he can feel its warmth inside him, giving him strength. He gets to his feet.

"You know, that's okay. Your machine could see, couldn't it? Through the gold."

Dr. Halvorsen folds his arms. "Oh sure. Metal that thin is actually translucent. It's just a question of adjusting the wavelength."

"Then you won't mind if I take the picture now."

The technicians look at each other. "But we've only just started the scan. I thought you wanted us to look for some kind of underdrawing."

"That's all right. I think . . ." Elliot nods to himself. He wants to be sure about this, finds he is. "I think I've already seen what I needed to see."

He wraps up the picture and carries it outside. The mist has mostly burned off in the afternoon sun. The unfamiliar landscape crowds in, a mass of sharp detail.

How far is it to the nearest bus stop? How far is it back to his car with its empty tank?

A horn sounds. Kerstin's Volkswagen is standing by the gate. She has decided to wait for him, after all.

He walks over. It's a struggle not to run.

"Are you stalking me again? Is this what this is?"

She squints up at him, not quite knowing what to make of the humor. "You're insane. Do you know that?"

He shrugs. "Temporary insanity. Will you settle for that?"

She studies his face. "You didn't do it, did you? You changed your mind."

"I didn't have to. Zoia zapped the equipment. There was smoke coming out of it and everything." Kerstin starts laughing. "I thought I'd better get out before things got any worse. I just hope I can still start the car."

Kerstin shakes her head and turns on her engine. "So I suppose you want a lift then?"

"No thanks. It's turning into a nice evening. I thought I'd walk."

"You *are* insane. Get in."

She leans over and opens the passenger door. And it comes to him this is really the beginning of something, of friendship or more. He won't have to fight to make it happen. He won't have to shore it up with proofs of indispensability. The two of them are past that already, for better or worse. Zoia gave them that too.

The street map is lying open on the passenger seat.

"Oh I see," he says, as he climbs in. "You need someone to map-read for you. That's what this is. You need someone to get you home."

49

Stockholm, July 2000.

The Stockholm public prosecutor's office was unable to establish whether or not the signature on Zoia's will was genuine, and for a while it looked as if Kerstin's efforts had been in vain. But then came an unexpected breakthrough. An examination of the computer on which the will had been drawn up, a computer belonging to Peter Lindqvist's lawyer, Thomas Röstman, revealed that the document had been prepared after the date on which it was purportedly signed and witnessed. In fact it postdated Zoia's official time of death by seventeen hours.

Many people felt the impact of the ensuing scandal. Lindqvist, Röstman, and Cornelius Wallander were arrested, charged with various counts of fraud and posted bail, pending trial. All were said to have confessed to their involvement, although Wallander continued to insist that he had merely been helping out an old friend. He had been led to believe that the fraudulent will had been drawn up according to Zoia's wishes, even if she had not been able to sign it. He resigned from Bukowskis immediately.

Kerstin broke the story with an exclusive in *Expressen*. This was followed by feature articles that explored every aspect of the case, including the campaign to drum up international interest. The articles cited Marcus Elliot as the man principally responsible for unearthing the truth. Two weeks after the first story appeared, Elliot received a check from Bukowskis: payment in full for his work on the catalog he had never written, together with a bonus "for expenses" and a note from the CEO, Frederik Wahl. The note thanked him for the "special diligence" with which he had carried out his researches, and for helping to head off "a most serious turn of events." Kerstin was offered a position on the staff of *Expressen*, but turned it down in favor of a junior reporting job on a rival paper.

Bukowskis canceled the Zoia retrospective. With the ownership of so many pictures now in doubt, they had the perfect excuse. In truth, the revered auction house was anxious to distance itself from the whole affair as quickly as possible. A smaller exhibition was organized for later that summer at a gallery in the Katarinavägen district of Stockholm, where Zoia had lived and worked during much of her lifetime. The Paris self-portrait was one of the pictures secured for this event. A number of works owned by Leo Demichev were also placed there, although some of the most significant ones were reportedly sold privately in Russia. The size of the sums involved was never made public.

For reasons of their own, the Swedish authorities moved swiftly to redistribute Zoia's estate, according to her known wishes. The Palmgren and Backlin families were among those receiving pictures, all of which were subsequently sold. The remainder of the estate, including the house in Saltsjöbaden, was divided among a number of Swedish charities, as per Zoia's instructions. Finally, after lengthy consultation, Zoia's papers were donated to the national archive at the Swedish National Museum.

Elliot returned to England at the beginning of April, two weeks before the date set for the residency hearing that would determine Teresa's future. By this time, Harriet Shaw was feeling more optimistic about taking on Miles Hanson in court. Hanson's mysterious Russian sources, who had been threatening to expose her client as a criminal, had suddenly vanished. Hanson had been forced to admit that he was now quite unable to trace them. Harriet began to entertain the idea that they had indeed been nothing but an invention, and was even considering a complaint to the Law Society. "It only goes to show how desperate they are," was her upbeat assessment.

But the hearing never took place.

Marcus Elliot and Nadia met by arrangement at the cafeteria in Holland Park. It was a place they both knew, but not one that held any special significance in the history of their years together. Elliot preferred it that way. He was determined to avoid appeals to nostalgia, however tempting. What he wanted to talk about was Teresa, and her future.

It was hard at first. He queued up for coffee while Nadia sat alone outside, crossing and uncrossing her legs, occasionally shooing away an opportunistic pigeon. She looked pale and fragile and was wearing more perfume than the occasion required, but there was a wariness, a stiffness about her that did not augur well. She had come, though, that was the main thing. Elliot suspected she had ignored her lawyer's advice in the process.

They went through an uncomfortable five minutes of chitchat. He told her something of his work in Sweden, and his plans to write a book on twentieth-century Russian art, for which he was close to landing a commission. She told him about a part-time job she had found at a music shop. It was the first time they'd talked to each other the way acquaintances talk, and it felt unbearably artificial. When they moved on to the subject of their daughter, even uncontroversial areas, such as her play group and her antics at home, he could feel Nadia tense up, as if in anticipation of attack.

"Where is she now, by the way?"

"With Maggie Williams."

He frowned. "Maggie . . . ?"

"They live across the road. Maggie and Tom. They have a three-year-old. Josh?"

"Oh yes. Of course. Josh." He had a vague memory of a smoky barbecue and a garden full of people he didn't know. "I'd really like to see her."

Nadia nodded silently for a moment. "Okay. When?"

"How about today? We could go back together, surprise her. Just for a while."

"Right now?"

"It was just a thought." Nadia looked at him, no doubt wondering if there was a catch, if she shouldn't call her lawyer first to be sure this wasn't some kind of trap. "I want her to see us together, that's all. It's been a while."

He kept his gaze on the football game underway in the South Field. Out of the corner of his eye he saw her swallow.

"Okay." She tried to laugh. "She keeps asking about you anyway. I'm tired of trying to explain why you aren't there."

"Well. Maybe you should let me try. Then she'd know what to expect."

Nadia was very still for a moment. They were way off limits already, and heading for a *sub judice* minefield.

"I don't understand. You're saying—?"

"I'm saying, suppose Teresa goes on living with you," Elliot said, looking into his empty cup. "How would that work?"

From then on everything was easier. Nadia said she had no plans to return to Prague. She had decided, despite all the disadvantages, that it would be better for Teresa to remain in England, in London. And she had already decided that she should see as much of her father as the circumstances permitted. It was important she didn't grow up thinking her parents were enemies. She said she had only fought as hard as she had because her lawyers had told her she had no choice. Elliot had planned to freeze her out completely, they said, to have her declared unfit and to take Teresa away forever. Of course, the lawyers had been right.

They worked out an arrangement on the spot. Elliot knew it was as generous as most courts would have awarded him. All that was required was an exchange of letters, and it would be done. Elliot even raised the matter of Nadia's drinking. She told him she had successfully quit, thanks to the help of a musician friend called James. He had stayed up all night with her on a couple of occasions, when it looked like she wasn't going to be strong enough to hold out. But she had it beaten now. These days, she said, there wasn't a drop of alcohol in the house.

There was more they could have talked about. Elliot had thought a lot about the two of them, about where it had all gone wrong, about what had been wrong from the start. But in the end it was actions that mattered more than words. And in their agreement to put aside rancor, and play full parts in their daughter's upbringing, there was a tacit admission that there had been fault on both sides. The mistakes could not be unmade, but that didn't mean they had to be relived every day.

Before Sweden he had planned, at some time in the future, to establish once and for all if Teresa really was his child. He had even gone so far as to find out what a DNA test would cost, which turned out to be more than he could afford under prevailing circumstances. But in England he found that resolution melting away. His marriage to Nadia was over; but his feelings for Teresa would endure. Driving away through twilight streets, waiting at a red light as the evening traffic streamed by, he nodded to himself: this was knowledge that could not change what he felt in his heart. And if that was true, it was knowledge he did not need.

The exhibition in Katarinavägen went well. There was not the level of international interest that the Bukowskis event would have generated, but most of the pictures sold. Monica Fisk's children, Klara and Martin Palmgren, earned useful sums. A show was planned in Gothenburg that same autumn. One of the works that did not sell was the Paris self-portrait. Even with a new frame and an explanatory note regarding Zoia's oriental appearance, it seemed to puzzle most buyers. And then there were the lingering doubts about attribution.

The morning after the exhibition closed, Elliot and Kerstin dropped by the gallery to pick up the picture again.

"So what are you going to do with it now?" she said, as they loaded it into the back of the car. It was a sunny day in August, and everywhere people were walking about in shorts and shirtsleeves, as if still on holiday.

"I've made arrangements," Elliot said. "I'm going to drop it off right now."

"But I thought we were going to the coast today."

Elliot held open the passenger door for her. "We are."

They had talked about going to Saltsjöbaden one last time. Kerstin wanted him to see the house as she remembered it, in summer. It was a very different place this time of year, she said. Besides, since his last visit to Sweden the house had been sold, along with the remaining furniture, and she was curious to get a look at the new owners.

"Sofia and Nicklas Lindström," Elliot said. "They seem like a nice couple."

"You've spoken to them?"

"They came to the gallery one evening. They're really pleased to have the picture."

"Wait a minute. You're *giving* it to them?"

"More of a permanent loan. At least until I think of something better. The condition is, it stays at the house. I think they plan to put it back in the sitting room, opposite the balcony."

Kerstin watched the green country flash by. A small sailing boat went past on the back of a trailer.

"That's a good place. She'll be able to see the sea from there."

The Lindströms had been in their new home just a few days. Most of their possessions were in packing cases, and their furniture was still swathed in plastic wrapping. Nevertheless, they insisted on giving their visitors lunch, which they ate outdoors around a picnic table, shielded from the sun by a brand-new green sunshade. Nicklas Lindström turned out to be an architect; Sofia, a speech therapist. They still had a small flat in Stockholm, but planned to live in their new house year-round, if possible. They had two children, the younger of whom had just started at school.

After the meal, Elliot and Kerstin walked along the bay. The pine woods were heavy with the scent of resin, and the shadows were cloudy with insect wings. It felt very different from the way it had in winter: more alive, more anchored in the here and now. A mile away the town was still busy with holidaymakers, though the peak of the season had passed.

"This is where I first found her," Kerstin said. They had reached a shady spot beneath one of the big umbrella pines. The swaying branches framed the wide sweep of the shore. "It was a day just like this. She was sketching with this big floppy hat on."

They stood watching the breeze push feathery breakers up the beach. To Elliot it was still a lonely place, lonely but beautiful, the two qualities as inseparable as the water and the light. The gulls were now tiny white dots circling over the farthest point of land, marshaling, it seemed, before heading out to sea, eastward across the Baltic, perhaps as far as Russia and the islands of St. Petersburg. Elliot watched them disappear one by one, until, a few minutes later, they were gone.

He took Kerstin's hand. "We should get going. The Lindströms have still got a lot of unpacking to do."

They walked back through the orchard and across the unkempt lawn. A dark blue Volvo estate was now parked in the drive. There was a multicolored beach ball in the back, and a mess of sweet wrappers across the seats. All over the house the windows were wide open.

The Lindströms appeared in the kitchen doorway. Sofia had a smudge of dirt across her forehead.

"We've hung the picture. It looks wonderful. Come and see."

Elliot and Kerstin looked at each other.

"Thank you, but I think we really have to be on our way. Maybe another time."

They said good-bye and walked to the car. The Lindström children had just returned from a boating trip. They and their friends were inside now, playing hide-and-seek, chasing each other up and down their new house. Elliot got behind the wheel and wound down the window. He could hear the children laughing. He could hear their footsteps on the stairs.

Author's Note

———◆———

The letters quoted in this book were all found among Zoia's private papers, and I have reproduced them faithfully, although not always at full length. The events of Zoia's early life in Russia and elsewhere are drawn from accounts she herself gave subsequently, from her correspondence, and from other historical sources. The principal characters appearing in these parts of the book are likewise factual, although in some cases, such as that of Alain Azria, the names have been changed.

By contrast, the character of Marcus Elliot and all other characters appearing in the modern-day part of the story—Cornelius Wallander, Peter Lindqvist, and Leo Demichev included—are entirely fictional, and any resemblance to actual persons, living or dead, is coincidental.

Acknowledgments

In the last year of her life Zoia entrusted her private papers to a young Austrian filmmaker by the name of Angelika Davenport (née Brozler). Angelika not only allowed me free access to this extraordinary archive, but also, together with her great friend Camilla Bourghardt, set about translating, cataloging, and collating the thousands of items it contains, a colossal task which is still in progress. I would like to thank them for their generosity, encouragement, and trust, without which this book would not have been possible.

Thanks are also due to barristers Samantha Knights and Louise McCullock for guiding me through the tortuous byways of English family law; Michel Marie of the Angladon Museum in Avignon for all the detail on the two Foujitas in that remarkable collection; Dr. Natasha Chibireva of the Moscow Institute of Architecture for help with the research on Andrei Burov; Dr. Richard Williams of the National Gallery and Birkbeck College, London, for his pointers on gilding techniques over the centuries; Vessel Ruhtenberg in the U.S.A. for sharing information on his grandfather, the Bauhaus architect and Zoia confidant, Jan Ruhtenberg, and to Neal Carpenter for further details on the same; Bruce Lindsay of art dealers Harris Lindsay for help with the import/export issues; and to Peter Sington for his input on various points of physics and chemistry. In addition, I'd also like to express my gratitude to first-draft readers Claudia Geithner and Patrycja Stepinska for their comments; to Atlantic editors Clara Farmer and Bonnie Chiang and Alexis Gargagliano at Scribner in New York; to literary agent Peter Straus and his assistant Rowan Routh for shepherding the enterprise, and to publisher Toby Mundy for his enduring enthusiasm. I should also like to offer special thanks to Christopher Zach, analytical psychotherapist, author, and poet, for his many invaluable ideas, insights, and suggestions over the past two years.

Finally I should like to thank Uta Bergner for encouraging me to write this book in the first place, and for putting up with me while I did.

PHILIP SINGTON read History at Trinity College, Cambridge, and worked as journalist and magazine editor for nine years. He is the coauthor of six thrillers, which have been translated into twelve foreign languages and have sold over a million copies worldwide; he has also written for the professional stage, large and small screen.